D0406466

By the same author

DREAMS
of the
KALAHARI

CAROLYN SLAUGHTER

A FIRESIDE BOOK
PUBLISHED BY SIMON & SCHUSTER INC.
NEW YORK   LONDON   TORONTO
SYDNEY   TOKYO

Copyright © 1981 by Carolyn Slaughter
All rights reserved
including the right of reproduction
in whole or in part in any form
First Fireside Edition, 1988
Published by Simon & Schuster Inc.
Simon & Schuster Building
Rockefeller Center
1230 Avenue of the Americas
New York, New York 10020

Published by arrangement with Macmillan Publishing Co., Inc.
First published in Great Britain by Granada Publishing Limited
FIRESIDE and colophon are registered trademarks
of Simon & Schuster Inc.

Manufactured in the United States of America

1   3   5   7   9   10   8   6   4   2 Pbk.

Library of Congress Cataloging in Publication Data

Slaughter, Carolyn.
Dreams of the Kalahari/Carolyn Slaughter.—1st Fireside ed.
p. cm.
"A Fireside Book."
ISBN 0-671-65905-7 (Pbk.)
I. Title.
PR6069.L37D7   1988
823'.914—dc19
88-1946
CIP

For my mother and father,
who took me to Africa

PART ONE

Some beautiful, sacred memory,
preserved since childhood, is perhaps the
best education of all. If a man carries many
such memories into life with him, he is saved
for the rest of his days.
DOSTOEVSKY

T HE SMALL GIRL SAT ON THE SAND UNDER A THORN TREE. With a small stick she stirred a dimple in the sand, stirred and hummed. She looked up listlessly, shading her eyes from the sun as the trees in the distance began to wobble and as splashes of illusive water rippled the sand. Her face, when she looked down again, was tense, hostile with concentration. It was an oval face, the eyes green, large, and cold. The nose was small and straight, but she felt that it was badly marred by freckles, as were her cheeks. Her mouth was full and pale; it looked sour. She began to stir again, grimly, chanting a song that the boy had taught her. The beetle was not to be coaxed up out of the dimple, so Emily tossed the stick away, then picked it up again and, very deliberately, shoved it down deep into the beetle's home.

The gray Kalahari sand spread itself wearily toward the pink line of the horizon; Emily thought of this as a mouth that swallowed the sun at the day's end. She did not want to see it happen, so got up slowly, tugging at her blue skirt and stuffing both hands into the square pockets, one of which was almost torn off. She made tracks with her bare, flat feet; the soles were as tough as an African's and no longer felt the scald of the sand, nor thorns, nor broken glass.

"I will walk on diamonds," she whispered, and smiled, pushing the sole of her foot down hard on a thick black thorn.

The bush gave way to green as she walked back toward the village. Mopani and acacia trees grew close together, surrounded by banks of tended grass, geraniums, and nasturtiums. The air lost its smell of dust. A small congregation of purple-gray doves cooed and strutted in the shade. Emily leaned against a tree, wanting to keep the quiet of the veld with her, not wanting to go home.

When, into this silence was dropped, as from a great height, a scream.

It seemed to rise, higher and more shrill, in arches of pain. Then stopped. Emily, who had started violently, waited, sniffing the air. The cry repeated. She began to shake, then to run at great speed toward the river, toward the sound that still struck, higher and louder. There was a pitiful moan as it ended.

The wind pushing against her face was warm; the sweat on her forehead beaded and ran as she sped down the scuffed grass slope toward the monkey-trees that straddled the river.

"Em-il-ee."

She ignored the shout, ran faster, breathing regularly. The voice called out again; this time the last syllable of her name ended impatiently. Emily came to a halt; she pushed the sweat back into her brown hair and turned to watch the African girl running heavily toward her.

"Come, missy, you come back now. The madam she says you're not to go to the river."

"Why not?"

"Trouble, big trouble."

"What trouble?"

"I don't know." The African woman rubbed her hand across her eyes and down to her mouth. She was young, but her big body did not like to run. She smiled again, and her cheeks seemed full of gobstoppers.

"You come now, missy, you come."

"No." It was said quietly, matter-of-fact.

"Please now." And suddenly the shiny brown face showed fear; her head jerked as she began pulling at Emily's arm.

"I want to see, Violet. You go back."

"You get me big, big trouble."

"Just say you couldn't find me."

"It's no good. They know. The madam she knows when I lie."

"Rubbish, you just think she does. Go now, hurry."

Emily pushed her, then turned and walked slowly down toward a low wailing thread of sound. She saw a small group of people by the river's edge. It was the schoolteacher, Mrs. Coetzee, and around her were some Africans, talking nervously among themselves. Slightly apart stood a young, striking-looking African woman with slow eyes and a high, tapering forehead. Her eyes were bright and tearless and barely blinked; her nose quivered. She held a white apron to her mouth; she was moaning softly into it and rocking her body sideways. The blond Afrikaner woman snapped at her to shut up or move away. The African woman did not move, did not seem capable of movement, but lowered her eyes. Mrs. Coetzee ordered two of the African men to go down into the water. They backed away, muttering, the whites of their eyes prominent and shiny. She shouted rudely—one seemed to rear like a horse and shook his head violently. Looking behind her in irritation, Mrs. Coetzee saw two young gardeners from the District Commissioner's house and called out to them.

"Tom, Jeremiah, come here—quick now, man."

They ran, their ragged pullovers flapping against their arms. One was wearing handed-down khaki shorts that were so large that the boy looked in danger of losing them at any moment.

Emily was standing a little apart, quite still, watching a pale body lying facedown in a little clearing among the reeds. The body rocked gently; it looked peaceful, the arms reaching out above the head, the pale hair combed by the water. The top half of the body was naked and the skin was pearly; the legs seemed blown up in dark gray bags. Two small ducks threaded in and out of the reed, ducked, were gone.

The two boys entered the water reluctantly and began to pull the body toward the bank, through the reed, and onto dry land. The Africans retreated; Mrs. Coetzee moved forward purposefully. Julian, who always knew the right moment to appear, said right next to Emily's ear, "Don't look." She turned her face away as the man's body was dragged slowly up the bank. His head flopped forward and banged once on the ground. He was held and hauled by his shoulders, so that his legs and arms scraped the ground; water poured from the gray trousers as they deflated. There was a foul stench and Mrs. Coetzee put her hand to her mouth.

"Turn him on his back. Quick now," she snapped.

Emily knew that Julian would be watching every detail closely and would tell her about it later. As the body turned, the Africans called "Ai, Ai" in a hushed chorus and then began to whisper to one another.

Mrs. Coetzee reeled, then straightened her Afrikaner back. The man's hair was slicked down into a point in the center of a smooth gray forehead. His stomach was eaten away, it was clean and dark inside with pieces of flesh hanging in ribbons. One of his ribs was cleanly picked. His guts were missing; his eyes and nose were missing; his mouth was perfect, parted, slightly blue.

"Turn him back again," Mrs. Coetzee whispered.

Then she told Tom to stay while she dismissed everyone else. She saw Emily looking down at the ground, rubbing the side of one foot against the other. The child was very pale.

"My God, what are you hanging about here for?" She put an arm around Emily's shoulder and felt the cold movement away. Emily did not know why she had moved away.

"Go on, up to the house now. I'm going to get the doctor—or someone. . . ." she added almost plaintively.

Mrs. Coetzee left, taking big strides up and away over the grass to the houses beyond. She turned and called out, "Hurry now; go home."

Emily looked straight ahead. The crickets' chorus began to subside in the bushes; an African woman was gliding in the distance with a jar of water balanced on her head. Only the crying woman remained. She had dropped to a crouching position a little way off, her hands and face buried beneath her apron. She made no sound now. Emily bent her knees and placed her elbows on them, lifting her hands to cover her face, to be more in harmony with her. The two crouched, rocking a little. Brown ducks with tattoos of white across their backs rose from the water with a whir of wings. The sun was gone, suddenly.

Someone was coming. Emily did not look up. The servant girl stood patiently until Emily lowered her hands.

"What is it, Violet?" Her voice was wan.

Violet whispered, "Now there is trouble. The house is hot with voices. The master has come back."

Emily shrugged, then butted her head in the direction of the woman.

Violet went over and spoke to her, her voice a little aggressive. The woman began to talk excitedly, almost babbling, hitting her forehead with the palm of her hand. She pointed to the water, to the man.

"What's she saying?" Emily asked.

"She says that there is a spell on the morena; he should have been eaten by the crocodiles; he has been in the water more than a day."

"Yes," the child said, dreamily, looking at the body.

"She says that evil spirits have touched him."

"Is that why she's afraid?" Emily asked, getting up.

The woman looked at Violet, then at Emily. The question frightened her. She began to back away. When she reached the first line of mimosa trees she began to run wildly in the direction of the kraal.

"She's lying," Emily said flatly. "Go back now, Violet. I'm coming."

Violet left and Emily watched as her big behind moved like a stone under the dark blue uniform with the starched white apron ties at her waist.

Emily lifted the wire hoop of the gate and pushed it open, jumping across the cattle grid. The flat brick house, with its green roof and surrounding veranda, looked less raw in the dusk. The green water tank to one side of the house was sprouting bougainvillea; tubs of untidy geraniums were lined up beside the front door. She strolled around to the back. Opening the wire-netted door, and walking into the house—she was struck in the face. She staggered against the doorframe, seeing a color like licorice in her head as it spun, while the pain spread across her cheekbones and into her eyes. And he stood there, her father, in his khaki shirt and shorts, his face more red than usual, his mustache emphasizing the thinness of his lips and the width of his jaw.

"Why won't you ever bloody well do as you're told?"

She looked at him coldly as he continued to yell; then she bolted swiftly into a private well of thought that excluded his clamor. Her face was tearless, dignified, refusing to be humiliated. But her silence and composure seemed to enrage him.

Her mother came and stood silently beside her father. Emily looked at her arms, folded tightly across her breasts, which were small and flat. Her hair was red and gold, short and curly, with a soft bang across her wide forehead. Her eyes were blue and watery; her skin the color of a glass of milk. Her mouth, with its scarlet wrapping, began reproving.

"You should not have gone to the river. What a disgusting thing to see!"

"I didn't see anything."

"Don't you bloody well lie," her father yelled. "Mrs. Coetzee said she saw you there."

Emily remembered the pale back, the hair spread on its pillow of water. What was he shouting about? There was no blood. The killing of the chickens and pigs in the backyard was different. The dead man looked all right.

"I didn't see when they turned him over; only Julian saw"— sullen, wishing she had not said it now.

"I swear to you, if you mention that name again, I'll skin you, d'you hear? I never want to hear it again—understand?"

Her shoulders were wrenched in his hands; he shook her like a rag. And she, wild with impotence, thinking, I'd like to spit in his face, scrape out his eyes with a tin can.

"Bernard!" Emily's mother whispered, moving as close as she dared to a reproach. The look on her child's face of stifled pain and isolation cut her, but she sealed it, thinking how difficult Emily always seemed to be. Catching her mother's thoughts, Emily was reduced by them.

"Go and wash your hands for supper," Lilian said.

Safe in the bathroom, Emily felt a small sense of relief that at least she had not, this time, been accused of her worst sin. This was one she could not deny; she was accused of it most often, and it was the one thing that provoked the anger of her parents to an extraordinary degree. It was the sin of imagination: she had too much of it, it should be got rid of.

She looked hard into the spotted mirror in front of her and saw her cropped brown hair grow long and lustrous, the eyes turn blue and soft, the mouth lift and smile. And wearing this new, amiable face, she was able to approach the dining room calmly.

She stopped outside for a moment to hear what her father was saying. "Stupid bastard, he's only been out here a few months, and look what a mess he's made of it."

"Yes, I know, but Moira said that he had a girl in England who'd jilted him."

"So what? He came out here to do a report, not to muck about with native women."

Emily opened the door to hear him mumble impatiently, "Anyone who gets up to that kind of thing won't last two minutes here. Bloody fool."

Emily sat down and unfolded her starched napkin; the folds were stuck together and ripped apart like paper. Her plate was piled high with roast mutton, sweet potatoes, and carrots. Her stomach rose to see the gravy circling the dark meat.

"Hurry up, it's getting cold."

Lilian had lost interest in her food; she put down her knife and fork and looked listlessly at the ceiling until she noticed Emily watching her and said impatiently, "Eat your food, Emily, don't push it around the plate."

Emily watched her mother use her knife to push the fat on her plate to one side. Then she let snippets of mutton fat slide into her fingers, and from there fall to the floor, where a puppy, a spaniel called Caspar, lay at her feet.

"That bloody dog shouldn't be in here. Don't feed it, it's disgusting," Emily's father said, loading his mouth at great speed. His wife stiffened but obeyed, asking Violet to take the dog from the room. Emily loathed her for this submission and loathed her father even more for the way he tormented the dog to get at his wife. Then the thought of Caspar, cradled in her mother's arms, made the knife in Emily's hand plunge down into her meat, leaving a gash.

Her mother did not notice. She was smiling a little, her spoon elegantly scooping up the golden pudding that went to and fro from her mouth. The puppy came sneaking in again and settled himself on his mistress's feet. The husband and father got wearily to his feet, throwing his napkin down into his half-finished pudding. He left the room, while Emily's mother carried on calmly scooping, never lifting her eyes. Emily took up the pudding in front of her and relaxed, watching the soft curve of her mother's neck above the blue linen dress. But the pudding would not go down Emily's throat, it seemed to stick there and coagulate. Emily's eyes fixed desperately on her mother's averted face with the old passion of her babyhood: What shall I do to make her notice me? She watched as Caspar was picked up tenderly.

"I bet you wish it was a baby." The words had tumbled sarcastically out before Emily could catch them.

Her mother turned. She looked a little puzzled. "But I hate babies," she said.

Emily went to the drawing room and sat down in one of the deep chairs that had come with them from England. On the wall above her head was a wooden mask with the eyes and mouth cut out in deep slits; the other wall was decorated by a vast pair of kudu horns set on a wooden slab. The polished parquet floor was softened by skins—one, the skin of a lion with its head sticking up and its mouth open, showing great snarling fangs. Around the bullet holes the fur had rubbed away. On the walls there were dull prints of flowers and scenes of Dorset. The tables were small and round— they had been bought from Peter Jones; stacked on top of these were out-of-date London magazines. English lamps and shades gave a dim light to the room and obscured the dust that settled endlessly on every surface. In spite of the African ornaments, it was an English room. It passed a small tribute, a platitude, to Africa; for the rest it brimmed with an unhealthy nostalgia, a view of England, of home, which no longer existed except in the little dreamworld of exiles.

Emily heard her mother walk slowly down the corridor, past the ferocious elephant gun and the .375 magnum express hanging high on the rack. When she had passed, Emily got out of her chair and sat on the floor near the door that led to the stoep with its red polished tiles and gauze wire-netting. Her father's study was next door, there was no sound from in there, though that was where he was.

A brisk tap on the stoep door, and then a voice with a faint Scottish twang called out loudly, "Mr. Jones?" Emily heard her father's swivel chair creak and she scuttled out of sight.

"Oh, it's you, Dick," Bernard Jones said curtly, opening the door to a tall, tanned man in gray flannel trousers and an open-neck Aertex shirt. Dick Thompson, the district veterinary officer, sat down in one of the cane chairs. He had not been asked to sit down, but he stretched out his legs and folded his arms behind his head all the same.

"Stifling night, hey?" There was a little silence in which Emily, who had moved closer to the door, felt embarrassed that her father was not going to offer Dick a drink. She remembered with shame the little remarks she had overheard about his stinginess.

"A bad business, then, down at the river?"

"Christ almighty, the people they send us—haven't a clew." Bernard's voice had taken on an impatience; he went and slammed the door; it whanged back, then flew open again. He kicked it; it kept its place.

Dick Thompson was looking sympathetic, thinking about the suicide. "Well, the poor bugger," he began mildly. "They get lonely—they're not used to the life." He was not the marrying kind himself, but could understand these things. Bernard Jones was made more impatient by his colleague's tolerance.

"Then they've no business here," he snapped, "wasting everyone's time. Now someone else will have to be sent out." There was a little more to it than this: Bernard Jones had been irritated that the Government had sent someone out in the first place; he felt he knew everything there was to know about sleeping sickness and did not see why he had not been asked to write the report himself. Now some other oaf from a laboratory would be sent to get under his feet.

"And I'll tell you something else, these chaps think they know the lot. The last one had the nerve to tell me quite categorically that only one tsetse fly in a thousand is infected with sleeping sickness. That's tripe."

"Why d'you say that?" Dick was a little embarrassed.

"Because I've bloody well been there; I've lived in the swamps, spent months there."

In spite of himself, Dick felt he was becoming infected by the other man's mood. Although he understood the peculiar slant of their barren life, and why nothing was ever taken calmly or kept in perspective, he still found it difficult to quite avoid doing this himself. He was just as starved of stimulation, just as desperate for some form of provocation. He changed the subject.

"Hey, Bernard, do you remember old Tshekedi?" (He was the chief who had ordered that a white man, who had persistently been mucking about with black women, should be flogged.)

Bernard did not care for this kind of anecdote. "Before my time," he said, looking at his watch.

Dick quite enjoyed getting on Jones's nerves; he continued. "Well, there was quite an uproar—the bleeding Navy was even called in to depose Tshekedi." He chuckled to himself, remembering how the tribesmen had calmly handed their chief over to British justice and then, just as calmly, welcomed him back a month later.

"Well, the natives don't like it any more than we do," Bernard stated stiffly. He wished Dick would go. He was tired suddenly. Not of life exactly, though it sometimes felt like that—but of his own life. Of the diabolical climate, the stinking natives, his sick, tired wife with her pallid smile, his odd, infuriating child. But most of all he was sick of himself, who had not fulfilled any of his dreams. Frayed dreams now, of long ago. These had hatched in a dreary, tightfisted England that had viewed him with disdain, even though he had fought for her. So he had turned to Africa because it seemed open and willing; turned to it with enthusiasm, because there was no other way to look at it. He had once had a fantasy: himself striding up and down in a helmet with a polished cane tucked under his left arm, viewing his subordinates with scorn, treating them with stiff, sharp discipline. How had things turned out so discrepant? In this godforsaken hole he was being buried alive. He was set apart from it, too, separate from the others, who at least came to life when the sun went down. They dared to eat and drink excessively; they gave vent to passions and fantasies which they could not have indulged elsewhere. But, even here, he was trapped by his inner inadequacies, fears that made him adhere to a stringent life, finding relief only in sudden cracks of anger and endless, useless malice. And there was no fine edge to his malice; it was not sharp and stunning as the slice of a knife through a finger. It was petty.

Emily walked down the corridor to her room at the end. Opposite her room was the spare room with its private bathroom, where, occasionally, important visitors from overseas stayed. Her room was the last room of the house, apart from another veranda. Here there were tin trunks, battered by journeys on ships, now covered with flower-printed material. In one of these was her mother's wedding dress, which had aged like a complexion and smelled bitterly of moth balls. Through the netting she could see the blank expanse of the garden, with the lemon, pomegranate, and fig trees obliterated and the moonlight faintly catching on the leaves of the grapevine.

Emily checked the outside door, then reassured herself that the bathroom window was closed. Once, a snake had got in through it and lay coiled in the cool of the bath. She went to her room, snapped on the light, and quickly looked about her. She sighed with relief: no bats, but there was the strange, dark smell of them. She opened the cupboard door, looked under the bed, then felt safe.

She put on the night-light beside her bed, without which it was impossible to contemplate the night, and got into bed. The electricity generator was pounding quietly in the darkness of the garden; its rhythm was infinitely comforting. Beyond and above this sound was the far echo of drums sobbing, of a kaffir dog howling at the moon.

It is morning. A steamy wind whips up the sand and small thorn wreaths are tossed up in the air where they spin and fall before being dragged off into corners. Violet comes in with a cup of milky tea, which Emily takes and begins to drink in bed.

"So, no school today, missy," Violet says with a chuckle, going to the cupboard to take out a cotton skirt and blouse. Emily's face brightens as she remembers it is November, the beginning of the long, summer holidays.

In the kitchen, Emily sat at the long wooden table eating her brown porridge with lots of white sugar and milk. At the other end of the table, her mother was counting out the servant's rations: brown sugar (they never had white), meal, bread, and a little meat. Mpande, the cook boy, a sturdy, black-skinned man from Nyasaland, watched her carefully, and when he was given his share, he put his hands together gratefully, ducked his head and smiled. Emily was wondering why the natives had so little meat when they loved it best of all. Johanna, the kitchen woman, had something to say about this, which was that once, long moons ago, before her tribe had been pushed out of the good land by the Zulus, they had had green grazing lands and cattle with oiled coats. That was the time of feasting and pride. "Then," she used to say very low, very troubled, "then we were ourselves."

Emily's mother said, locking the stores away in a cupboard in the pantry, "Your father has gone for a few days—tsetse fly clearing." Emily watched her mother carefully for any sign of good humor and detected it finally in the absence of that thin, vacant smile that tugged listlessly at her lips. Mrs. Jones turned to Mpande and Violet and said they could leave at five today, as she would cook for herself that night. Their faces grew round and they thanked her many times. Then the cook boy got out the china bowl and began to pour in the flour for the bread making.

Emily looked at her mother and smiled conspiratorially, but, to break the moment, her mother said, "You're forbidden to go to the river today, and don't go near the kraal either—stay around the yard. Mrs. Brink is doing my hair today." And she pulled one of the tight curls disconsolately before leaving the kitchen.

Emily walked slowly around the garden, picking nasturtiums, sucking their nectar from the slim, pointed spouts; kicking the whitewashed boulders laid out in lines marking off the gravel drive. Sweat prickled between her thighs and under her arms. In the distance she could hear the piccanins laughing by the river, the birds screaming, the wind whooping between the trees. Being separated from this was to her a deprivation as strong as hunger. She didn't know how she would spend the day until she could escape the garden.

Her mother took to her bed. A little later, Emily crept into her mother's room, close to the mosquito net that danced lightly to the rhythm of the fan in the ceiling. Peering through the floating net, a strange look passed over her face, something that never revealed itself except in secret. She was quite unaware of it: that creased need around her eyes and mouth as she watched her mother sleep. The woman did not stir, deep and safe as she was in her dream of home—of that portrait of herself: How perfect it was, that past, that concocted happiness, that yesterday which, unlike tomorrow, could never be spoiled. Her daughter tugged at the net restlessly, wondering if she should cough or drop something, but knew that her mother would be angry if woken, and then it could be days before the starched look left her face. Emily released the net and kicked at it with her foot, moving toward the door with the hard look clamped back on her features. But as she reached the door, she knew that her mother was awake now but would lie with her eyes closed and wait for her daughter to go.

Emily ran down the garden, jumped the grid, and listened to her feet thumping on the dusty track leading down to the river. Just before reaching it, her body swerved and stopped. She looked: the river was like a long green evening dress with sequins down the center, it glittered glamorously, unruffled by the sun's glare. She walked on, then took a small track away from the village, toward the bush, where the kraal lay. She walked now with a quick, stiff energy. Her hands, gripped at her sides, spoke of a rage, a suppressed passion beyond the normal bounds of an eleven-year-old girl. The face was arrogant, the lines sharp and knowing, and but for the neat grip pulling her hair back from a side parting, she could be any age.

A few African women were walking toward the large circle of huts surrounded by mud walls decorated with red stripes and dark brown half-moons. The wind billowed around their skirts and flapped the doeks on their heads. They talked incessantly to one another. Emily watched the babies jogging on their mothers' backs, strapped close with a strip of cloth or a red blanket. Vaguely she remembered being carried like that herself, by Johanna, when her mother had been too ill to look after her. It had been the most reassuring part of her childhood, all day long to be carried close and warm, taken down only to be fed. Her mother, when she left her bed to come grudgingly back to reality, seemed to lose her head at the sight of her child carried this way. So Emily was unbound and brought down to earth. Johanna passed Mrs. Jones her child, but she would not receive Emily back into her arms, as though she thought the contact might dirty her also.

Johanna did not live in the servants' quarters at the bottom of the garden; she went back to the kraal in the afternoon, unless she was wanted at the house for a particular reason. Now she was squatting in front of a large iron pot with three clawed feet that sat on a small fire. Into this pot she poured some mealie meal, and did not look up when Emily walked up to her, in case she spilled it. When she had finished, she began to stir, adding a little more water to the pot from a tin. She exchanged a look with Emily that deftly conveyed her amusement that Emily should continue to visit the kraal after being forbidden. The child squatted down in the sand and looked around her. Other women were getting their fires going or adding extra fuel to those already burning. Their voices, high and elastic, called out cheerfully to one another. Beautiful black babies, with flies at their eyes like currants and strings of blue beads around their fat bellies, banged tin cans together and clapped their hands. A little boy of about four kept charging around Johanna's fire, swiping at the air with an imaginary spear and uttering blood-chilling yells, until she sent him off with a "Get out of here, Sorry; go and play somewhere else."

"Why's he called Sorry?" Emily asked.

"Because his mother already had too many and didn't want another."

As the mealie pap bubbled and popped in the pot and Johanna sang a song that the women sang in the mealie field, Emily slipped into a dream. A dream that had incubated in the stifling classroom as Mrs. Coetzee droned on about Shaka the Terrible, warrior of a million spear thrusts and ten thousand deaths. Johanna, with her passion for violence, had filled in additional details, so now the myth lay, bright and cruel as a jewel in Emily's head. Shaka had become the man, or the myth, by which she judged everyone, including herself. The man she married would be like him.

Turning to Johanna again, Emily said, a little sad, "Where are the warriors now?"

Johanna stared at the question, and stirred the slush in the pot more quickly. She, too, looked sad, as the heart of the desert is sad. The place where the two of them sat was haunted, as they were, by the dead—all the starving who once took shelter there, away from the plunder of warriors who swept through the land, leaving only weak tatters of tribes behind them.

Johanna shrugged but she was angry. She said nothing. In a little while, she smiled; then she laughed and said, "If you could only come in a few nights' time, there is a famous drummer coming, and we are to make a feast for him. Then you will see the warriors. They will not fight, but they will do the next best thing— they will dance until they drop. Ah, if only you could see this thing, missy."

Emily's eyes grew large and brilliant with excitement. She had learned from those around her that the tedium of life demanded constant and dangerous distractions. Here again was one: an adventure that would need to be planned with the utmost caution.

She had never gone to the kraal after dark, had known of the feasts only by the wild singing in the night and the volley of the drums. The servants the following morning always looked dazed, with heavy lids and a sick, melancholic gaze on complexions faintly gray. Europeans could then be heard complaining about kaffir beer and dagga and the effect these produced on idle, useless servants.

Emily's mother was sitting on the stoep, in the dark corner where the bougainvillea kept out the worst of the day's glare. Her legs were crossed elegantly—she was one of those women who made an art of this movement. She was wearing a smart black dress with scalloped edges at neck, sleeves, and hem, and her black shoes were pierced with little diamanté stars. Emily coveted these shoes, but not to wear, simply to possess.

"Why are you all dressed up?"

"Oh, I'm not, not really." She smoothed her hair absently and flicked a fly away. The soft scent of talcum reached Emily's nostrils, and she could see the powder clotting in the little hollow between her mother's breasts.

"God, it's so hot still, and I've spent the day under a dryer." Mrs. Jones picked up a fan and swished it a few times. "You ought to have a bath, dear," she said, aware of a sour smell on the child. As Emily walked off, she said lightly, "Um, someone's coming in for a drink. Violet left you something to eat in the kitchen." Emily walked on, the polished stone floor cool on her clammy feet. Her mother's voice, a trifle nervous, stopped her again. "Oh, and by the way, don't mention that Uncle Tor came, will you? Your father doesn't like him, you know."

Emily turned her face full on her mother and smiled a mocking but indulgent smile.

Her mother was trying to ignore this look, but finally said, "Why do you have to look like that? It's so unpleasant in a child."

"I won't say anything," Emily said, desperate to please, looking down at the floor.

Her mother gave her approval by saying, "Do come in and say hello, won't you, dear, Uncle Tor's so fond of you."

And you wish he wasn't, Emily thought, as she opened the creaky door and crossed the lion's skin, stepping hard on its head.

Uncle Tor was no uncle. He was one of the many Scandinavians who were attracted to Bechuanaland; and his tanned, enlightened face, with its smooth, buttery head of hair, added something exotic to any gathering. He spoke Setswana like a native, and was a fine hunter; he also had an obsessive interest in the Bushman. He had recently come up to the north to continue his study of native customs and could be seen squatting in the sand with little groups of Africans at their kraals—provoking them, making them laugh, gleaning their myths and magic. He would give reasons, when asked, for this strange interest, which went beyond the bounds of his university course. But these were incomprehensible to the colonials about him. His information about the early civilizations of Africa, their culture and skill, their work in gold, wood, and stone, was dismissed. It needed to be.

Now, Tor sat on the stoep with Lilian Jones, drinking a large gin and tonic, his long legs flung out in front of him, his pale boots crossed, his expression pensive. Emily approached, bearing peanuts. He touched her lightly on the arm and said, "So, what have you been up to, then?"

She shrugged and smiled at him. "You tell me what you've been doing, it's far more interesting."

"Well, I was up in the Makgabana hills yesterday, and an old man told me some wonderful stories. You'd like to hear about it, Em, wouldn't you?" He said it as though Emily's mother would not be interested, and Emily was glad of her exclusion. She nodded gravely, but did not sit down when Tor motioned to the chair. Regretting her moment of generosity, Lilian got up, saying there were things that needed seeing to in the kitchen. Tor watched her go.

"Well?" Emily said impatiently, "what happened?"

"Hm? Yes, well, I was told this by a really ancient fellow—he was not sure of his age, but I worked out that he must be at least a hundred and eleven years old. He was wrinkled as a prune and his eyes had lost all their color; they were like a very pale blue marble; but he could still see quite well. I asked him to try and remember what he'd been told as a boy about the white man's coming."

Emily did not move, all her attention centered on Tor's lips and occasionally moved to his hands, which he used little in conversation, so that any gesture he did make had great force.

"One day, far off by the sea, white men came in ships with wide, white wings; they shone like spears in the morning sun. These men had skins of sickness and eyes like sandstones. They had weapons which exploded and spat out fire. First they brought groundnuts and beads and took what they wanted. Later they brought plagues and death and took what they wanted. Later still, they taught the people things that were best kept hidden—then they went their way. . . ."

Emily shook herself a little as Tor's voice slowed. Lilian had returned to hear the last half. She looked bored. Emily wanted to kick her. Tor continued quietly, "Imagine how dreadful we must have looked to them—with our gray, blotched skin and terrible pale eyes; our bodies covered up, our heads helmeted—children ran screaming into the bush at the sight!"

Lilian Jones gave Tor a sideways frown and said, "Oughtn't you be off to bed now, Emily?"

Emily did not try to stay longer. Nor did she kiss her mother good-night. She had once done so, but her mother's slight movement backward upset her—she wasn't going to throw herself at anyone. She said good-night in a distracted way.

"You shouldn't tell her things like that, Tor; she's at a funny age. She's so strange, anyway, her head's full of rubbish as it is."

"She's not so strange, but she's got an original mind. It's not influenced by people or books; she thinks for herself."

Emily's mother looked puzzled. "Well, if you mean she's odd, she's certainly that."

"Nothing wrong with that. But no, it's much more than that. She has a way of looking very deep and direct into the center of one's eyes, not shifting her gaze. I've seen victims squirming a little beneath the intensity of her scrutiny. People studied in this way can't but reveal what they'd most like to hide. That's why she's thought of as creepy; it's the closest one can get to it."

"She *is* creepy; she gives me the creeps anyway—always pretending she knows everything that's going on."

"She probably does." He laughed and got up to walk to the table and pour more tonic water into his glass. He was almost talking to himself when he said, "She also has a strong sense of threat, a need to defend her inner world."

Mrs. Jones did not understand this, so it aggravated her. "She likes to make trouble; she seems to want people to get the wrong impression. I don't understand it."

"Oh, I shouldn't worry about it," he said lightly. "She just needs to be secret, even to be misunderstood. However—" and his voice deepened—"I'm not sure that this life is good for her."

"She makes things up all the time; it's infuriating. She doesn't see what I see. She has a terrible imagination."

"Imagination is never terrible." He smiled, seeing the inadequacy of this woman, the slowness of her intellect. "But she needs outlets for it." He thought of the stiff father, so terrified of imagining anything that he settled always for the most obvious solution. He feared for Emily, wished that she could relate to other children, remembered with consternation that she treasured no toys, read no books, and forced herself instead to an utterly draining creativity in all she saw around her. Like all solitary children, secret children, she was an acute observer. But this child somehow, he thought, was more, was a splitter, a vivisector of emotion, but not in a way that could enhance her existence.

Emily walked out of the back door and leaned quietly against it, looking up at the stars: what would they smell of? Mushrooms? Heather or pine, sea water or polished silver? The stars were planted in thick rows, on velvet, and they seemed to hum. Here was a path to peace, sitting alone listening to the stars. Here she ceased to be an unruly child and let the stars do their magic. She whispered to the hunter in the sky, "They have mown you down, Lobengula, son of the mighty Mzilikazi, like grass under a scythe.

They have snapped your assegais and darkened the pastures with blood where once the young warriors danced in a crescent moon and tossed the enemy up on the horns of their triumph. No women run out to meet you, to stroke your cheeks, to clap their hands at your magnificence." And she began to weep. The intensity of her despair ran down her cheeks, soaking her nightdress. She had not learned to feel, or to cry, with moderation.

Neither her mother, nor Tor, saw her face watching them through a crack in the curtains. Emily's feet were planted firmly on some vile-colored zinnia plants; she could see, without stretching, the two people eating at a table—a table beautifully laid with a fine white tablecloth and two sun-bruised roses in a cut-glass vase. Emily's mother looked happy; her cheeks were flushed and her whole body seemed unusually animated, soft, and pliable. Tor was wearing another face, a fiercer, harder face than the one he'd worn for Emily. She felt a little frightened, a little exhilarated by it. Emily watched him with great tenderness, the long, broad hand around the glass, the body that leaned casually to one side in the chair. She put herself in her mother's chair so that his gaze could be directed at her instead.

His hand reached out and took her mother's, stroking the long, red fingernails; she smiled back at him, lifting her eyes. Emily's ribs, pressed against the cold, hard cement of the windowsill began to pain her, and the pain insidiously crept through her rib cage to her guts. She pressed harder. Tor reached over, and with one hand in Emily's mother's curls, pulled her toward him and kissed her. Emily gave a little gasp in tune to her mother's; her heart began to vibrate; she could feel the wet pressure of his lips on her own, the hard bones of his jaw; her legs crossed and clamped together.

Tor pushed back his chair; he was smiling a smile Emily could not fathom. She could not tell what he was thinking, and she had no inkling of what he felt. He dropped to the floor and easily, quickly, ducked beneath the white lawn tablecloth and was hidden from view. Emily saw her mother's eyes widen, her mouth fall slowly open, and her arms, resting on the table, seemed to shudder as her shoulders straightened and went rigid. Then the innocent, almost schoolgirlish face of her mother stiffened, grew quite violent with fear. Emily trampled over the orange and yellow zinnias and scrambled away—startled and frightened, adrift in a world of ignorance, because this had nothing to do with the farmyard, nothing at all with the simplistics of school-yard whisperings.

Safe in bed, with the little light making the shadows swirl and the curtains dissolve into apparitions, she began to think, almost with desperation, of the others—the imagined lovers of her mother; those lumped shapes she felt she saw beneath the mosquito net when her father was away. She had heard laughter and whispers; she had heard the glasses clink and kiss.

A jackal barked; the generator made a soft putt-putt noise, then spluttered into silence. Emily, with her hands between her knees, began to smile. She had transformed Tor again, this time into a father. She thought of him with affection, as a man full of stories; a man who did not shout and bellow, nor kick the servants, nor spend his anger on weaker things. Tor could mend things, make animals out of paper and wood; he was a person you could talk to about anything; sit beside watching a sunset. Most of all he was a hunter, a man of real courage, to admire and respect. Perhaps even someone to run out and embrace at the end of the day.

But, if a man is going to hunt, Emily remembered with relief, he must keep away from a woman, or she would suck away his strength and bring him bad omens. On this comforting note, the child closed her eyes and decided that she would never bleed. It was the devil's mark that he had entered. She would, thanks to Johanna, always be able to recognize the devil: he had a sour, hot stench, and one's flesh went hot and then cold if he was near. She would recognize him. She slept.

It was the boy, the ugly boy with freckles like splashed mud on his cheeks and the foul red hair. She wanted to go on his slide: the steel wire that ran from the topmost branch of the sycamore tree to the trunk of another a hundred yards or so away. Emily looked up and up into the green petticoats of the tree, and there he was, André, his copper head butting wildly with the force of his exertions on the steel wire. He flung up his legs and then swung them right back behind him, all the while plummeting down to earth. He did not see her; his face was tipped to heaven.

He landed with a soft thud and yelled, "Hey, Em, you gonna have a go, or is it too slippery for you now that I've greased it?" She felt herself harden with the challenge. He had gone up the tree again and stood a moment on the platform before flying down again.

"Come on, come on, Em. It's fantastic today."

She was afraid. He had even greased the iron pulley that circled the cord. The slide was now lethal. She stood and watched as he shinned up the tree trunk yet again, as he braced himself on the wooden platform, spat on his hands, and reaching out, tightened his hands around the wooden handles of the pulley. He flew like an eagle, yelling, and dropped lightly to the ground before reaching the far tree trunk. Julian, with his low, brave voice, said quietly, "Come on, Em, do I see a white mouth?" She looked André straight in the eye, walked up, and said, "Of course I'll do it."

"Go on, then."

She turns briskly to the tree and begins climbing like a cat, hands reaching for that knot in the trunk, the fork that cradles the foot, the branch that will swing her to the topmost branch. She sways a little on the platform, looking down: his head is like the sun below me. I am melting with heat and fear. How far away his grin. Julian, damn you, why must I always be proving? She rocks, swaying a little with the wind—hot, but less dusty among the layers of leaves. Slowly she pulls the string that returns the pulley to the top. How slowly it climbs! She holds it, feeling the warmth of André's hands. She runs her damp palms on her skirt, then spits on them, once, twice. Must not look down. God, how greasy this cord is, like the foal's to its mother. She takes a deep breath, squeezes her eyes shut and throws herself forward. She flies: so this is how it feels, to jump the cliff, to soar above water, to die. The pulley races her downhill. She forgets to let go at the right moment—now, now. The tree trunk rushes toward her; she crashes straight into it with a dull, deep thud. But no cry. André turns, screaming.

. . .

Violet is wearing a beautiful clean apron; the bloody one is soaking in the sink and the water is a little pink. She tries not to look at the left side of Emily's face. Emily is painting a still life, her paper and paints spread out on the kitchen table. She asks Violet, "How do I paint white on white? Do I just make an outline?" Violet is baffled that she should be asked such a sophisticated question. "How do I know, missy?" She is even a little cross that she was asked, because it makes the extent of her ignorance apparent to her. Violet looks down at the painting of the grenadilla flower, with its purple ferny center and the long stamens, and says, "It's so good, looks as though you could pick it up." Emily's face is turned toward Violet, gentle, grateful. The black woman cringes, twisting her hands together, to see the blue, battered flesh and the eye sunk in a mess of puffed red tissue.

"Oh, missy, why do you do these things. Why?"

"Because I must."

Violet went back to the sink and rubbed as she'd been taught to rub: how best to wash the madam's clothes without wasting the soap. Her hard knuckles rubbed and pulled at the persistent bloodstains; if it was not immaculately white, she would have to wash it again, and again. The madam liked plenty of white, plenty of starch; that meant plenty of washing. She wondered as she worked why the child was not liked; she heard the things they said about her. She turned back to watch Emily painting, one hand resting in her lap. Where was the badness in her? She just had a need to suffer. She was a woman in that already.

The side of Emily's face was almost healed by the time her father returned. The bruising was still there, but the colors were muted—lilac and a pale daisy-yellow. She heard the black Chevrolet spinning the stones on the driveway, the grate as it skidded outside the front door. She crept around the corner of the house and kept out of sight behind the water tank. She did not want to see her father but suddenly longed to talk to his driver, Peter. Her father walked into the house and Peter stood beside the car. Emily walked over to him. He leaned back against the car and watched her, saying nothing. He was a tall, pale African, with the clearest brown eyes and clean, regular features. His nose was not flat or spread, his mouth not particularly large or heavy; the undersides of his hands were as pink as a white man's. Emily remembered with a little flush the first time she had seen him, outside the Government offices. He was standing much as he stood today—the fingers of one hand spread out on the rump above the headlight of the car. And she had felt weak, with a coldness down her spine, and had wanted to stand close beside him. His English was a mission boy's: his voice careful, polite, but strangely caressing. He was turned out in policeman's khaki, starched and buttoned, his brown boots glossy, with no speck of dust. It did not occur to her that there might be something immoral and shameful about what she felt for him; her response to him was instant and devastating—it was blind to his disability.

Peter was mildly amused by the passionate gaze of the small girl who looked up at him so openly; but his amusement was not willful or unkind; it was reminiscent, tender.

"Was there any trouble, Peter?"

"No, no trouble, miss, the men were working well; there was no illness, only one man was stung by a scorpion, but he is well again now."

"Did you see any Bushmen?" He jerked his head back, a characteristic gesture of his, then leaned forward, making the space between their heads smaller.

"No one sees the Bushmen now! Sometimes you think you see a little pointed chin among the reeds, or his broad shoulders shaking the grass. But his eyes will see you long, long before you ever see him—and if you tried to catch him, you'd make a fool of yourself. He runs with his mind, as though he were an eland bull hunted by crafty warriors. Once, years ago, a German military man found a Bushman and chased him for sport as though he were a beast. It was a shocking day."

"Oh, Peter, not like that—tell me properly."

Peter looked at the door of the house.

"He won't come back yet," Emily said quickly. "Go on. . . ."

"Well, it was long ago. A Bushman came here at night. He did not come to the kraal, of course, there'd be no welcome there, and he would not stoop—he is overproud of his ugly yellow skin, thinks it is better than brown!" He laughed with real humor. "Anyway, he crept here for a reason no one could decipher and was caught by a policeman who said he was stealing chickens. This could only be true. He spent the night in the lockup, and the next morning this military man, I will not slip his name, decided that the Bushman would be hunted by men on horses."

"But that's not fair, he could not possibly get away!"

"Ah, he could run, that he could definitely do. They gave him a start. He knew he was the quarry, he probably knew that he must die, but he ran without pausing for thirty miles. Then, as they grew closer, he sprinted ahead again at full speed, with long strides, his shoulders gleaming above the grass. His little neck and head never turned, the sand flew up behind him, and he ran as if to victory, as if his poison spear was about to strike the biggest, fattest buck; as if something out there called to his spirit, cheered him on."

"So they did not get him?" Emily gasped.

"Ah, yes, miss, they got him, because this small military man got angry; he was infuriated by the Bushman's strength and courage, and he saw that the afternoon was growing dark. He thought that they would lose their quarry—so he shot him. Not to kill, so he said, but he shot for the back, just as the man was heading into a dense patch of bush. And the Bushman fell. Oh, slowly, slowly, he fell. Like the greatest of beasts: turning in the wind, his arms raised to the sinking sun. As he died, he covered his face with his hands, so that none could see his agony. So he died."

The girl was crushed. She looked down at the ground and suddenly kicked at it savagely, so that the little stones flew up and hit the belly of the car. Filled with an intolerable rage, she yelled at Peter, "But why, *why*?"

And he shrugged. "Because they can."

Like a high wind hitting a wall, her anger collapsed. Watching her, Peter wondered: she had seemed to him to become, for that brief spell, a Bushman herself. He felt nothing very intense for the Bushmen, having his own people's indignities to wrestle with.

Without another word Emily walked away to the back of the house, leaving Peter leaning against the car, watching her, smiling.

In the back garden, she tried to get to the lemon trees without being seen when she heard her father's voice calling out loud and cheerful, "Hey, Emily, I'm back."

Her feet dragged; she tried to speed them up. She wondered if he had caught sleeping sickness.

"Your mother told me about your face; doesn't look too bad," he said, prodding the fading bruises. She stepped back. He laughed, making his little joke, "D'you deserve a walloping for anything, then? Ha-ha-ha." It was a flat laugh, just skirting away from a sneer, a strangely colonial laugh.

Emily's mother was holding a carved wooden elephant. She did not look at it. Bernard Jones said, "Show her what I bought, then." Emily was handed the elephant to examine. It was dark red iron-wood, delicately carved, smooth as a sea pebble and polished so that it seemed almost on fire. Two chiseled pieces of white wood, matchsticks probably, had been used for the tusks; the trunk was raised high and proud. She thought it was beautiful but did not say so. Beauty was an emotion you did not share.

"Not bad, eh?" he said, with enthusiasm. "The silly bugger said he'd been carving it for weeks and wanted two and six for it. Quite stubborn he was, too, but I beat him down." And now Emily could see that his pleasure was overflowing, for he was a man who took no joy in a thing for its own sake, because it was lovely or straight or strong, but only if he had succeeded in getting it for less than its real worth.

"How much do you think I paid for it?"

Emily did not reply, shrugged a little.

"Go on, guess!" he ordered, slightly irritated that no one was participating in his triumph as they ought.

"I really don't know," Emily said, very coolly, and he found her maddening.

"Well, guess, then, can't you even bloody well guess?" he snapped, and it was like the mental arithmetic he would suddenly force her to do on car journeys, when her mind was far absent, beyond the thorn trees, the long cinnamon washes of sand.

"One and sixpence?" she said vaguely.

"No, sixpence!" he yelled, like a man winning the Derby.

Emily looked down at the elephant lying on its side in her palm. It was a work of love. An unpleasant sensation seemed to be coming off the wood. She handed the elephant back to her mother and moved away, holding her head very still, concentrating on this movement. As she left, she heard her father say to his wife, "But you like it, don't you? It's nicely enough made, it's good work." He was desperate for approval, but his wife's voice said, "I'll put it on the mantelpiece." She was thinking, and she did not know why, of her own father, a sergeant with a vicious temper and a cane that he used to rock on his knees before slashing out with it at the air. She looked remote, and the odd little smile fastened itself to her lips again. "I'll go and lie down, I think. I feel a migraine coming on."

Bernard Jones was left standing alone, his jolly homecoming in tatters. He could not understand it; he had even brought a present.

Lilian Jones remembered something and she turned, frowning, a little sullen. "You must have a word with Mpande," she said. "He's difficult again, grumpy, lazy. . . ."

"He's always grumpy."

"This is more than usual. He keeps saying he wants to go home, hasn't seen his family for years. He's impossible."

"But I've just given him a pair of my old trousers!" Mr. Jones was a bit shocked.

"I know. It hasn't helped."

"Look, I'll sort it out later, when I get back. I've got a lot of office work to catch up on. There's bound to have been a mess-up while I was away. I'll deal with him later."

His wife looked a little anxious; she clutched her white handkerchief in her hand. "Well, don't . . . it's not so serious really. . . ."

"Perhaps we should just get rid of him," he said, tired of the endless problems with servants. Why couldn't she sort them out? It was not his province.

"No," she said firmly, "cook boys are too difficult to get. And

I'm not teaching someone else all over again, either. It took me long enough with him, and still I have to watch him all the time."

"Stupid bastards," he said angrily, beginning to feel them responsible for all his problems. "Takes forever to get anything into their thick skulls." And suddenly he did not know what the hell he was working for, anyway—for what? For whom? No one seemed to appreciate him at all.

Emily was running as fast as she could toward the bush. The heat was deep and dense. These are the dead hours: between noon and three, when nothing stirs, when all things are in a dream of death. Johanna said this was the hour when ghosts moved about and spirits stirred.

This bush is so hot; there is no shade, no place to hide. The sun beetles are quivering with a high insistent lament. The air has no movement, the animals sleep. Only a horde of white ants move regimentally up and around an anthill. Emily heads for a little hollow where once, in the early spring, there was a thin pool of water. It is dry now, but a scruffy flat thorn tree makes a patch, not of shade exactly, but of sunlight deprived of glare. She picks up a stick and begins chopping at the sand, then squints, looking far out into the drought-stricken veld. The sand throws up reflections, and walking on these, like a man caught in a motion he must repeat eternally without progressing, she sees the ghost of Mathiba, chief of the Bamangwato, who still wanders this wilderness, his mind crazed by malaria, his eyes plagued by flies. He walks in one place, sometimes wailing, sometimes howling out in agony. However hard he tries, he cannot pull out the spear that he plunged into his heart.

In her bedroom, Mrs. Jones sat on her bed, clutching the little spaniel, Caspar, to her. She was worried about the dog; he had started life so bouncily and yet in the past few months had declined to the stage where he now looked limp and forlorn. He whined and shivered and spent most of his life under her bed. Lilian Jones felt utterly miserable as the scraggy body quivered in her arms: his character had been corrupted, and she, with some little instinct for animals, knew that they could only be corrupted by humans.

She put the dog down and swung her legs slowly up onto the bed. With a sigh she lay still, waiting. And it came: the migraine tore into her temples and filled her head with pain, and a sheer dancing light flared behind her eyes. She began to shake and the shaking grew into sobbing. She felt cheated by life; no one had ever told her she would feel like this; it was too much. She wondered again if she was ill, but she was just lonely, that was all, just lonely. And there she stopped, at the loneliness, for even this she could not really understand. She lay in baffled pain, pushing her fingers into her head, feeling utter alienation.

The sobbing had at least helped her to relax, though the pain in her temples was excruciating. But here she was safe; here she could stay. From a little drawer beside her bed she drew out a black chiffon scarf that she folded into a narrow strip and placed across her eyes. She lay down again, one arm flung above her head. She thought about nothing.

Her migraines had slowly, in a state of starvation, become real nourishment. They could be made to last and last, day after dull day and deep into the cool nights when her husband could not bully her for a fragment of her solitary pleasure. And sleeping is so good for me, she thought. I shall rest a lot and then look my best at the party. And you will come, won't you, you will come? Nervously her fingers felt her throat and jaw, and she was tempted to rush to her mirror to reassure herself that she had not let herself go. It was the constant fear in her life, as she now saw her neighbors with their English peaches-and-cream complexions drying and curdling; or the tough Afrikaner women with faces stained and stretched by the sun. Their hair, like everyone's in those parts, was coarse and dull, and the women's often colored with cheap colorants. She loathed these friendly women with their home permanents; their borrowed cups of tea or sugar as an excuse for a conversation. She treated them with disdain and spoke condescendingly, especially to the Afrikaners, studying her painted fingernails so that she would not need to raise her eyes.

She liked best to remember herself as she had been: a young girl, blond, fair-skinned, pretty. She would then invent a childhood worthy of her: a growing-up on a Cornish farm with a rich, fond father and constant mother. But as she grew older, these consolations began to dim; she found it harder to conjure them up: her mind was closing, narrowing.

Flirtation had been her only accomplishment; she had learned early to trail her eyes, to laugh exposing her throat. She knew how to control men with the least hint of sex; she would let this peek, like lace on a petticoat, and then, just as quickly, withdraw it. If the art was shallow and short-lived, she did not know it. She could show no tenderness, having never known it. Her mother had died when she was small; her father was always away in the Army; an aunt had brought her up with her three cousins, but she had never felt one of the family. From her eldest cousin, she had picked up her small handful of teasing tricks; she never added to her repertoire.

She had married Bernard, quite simply, because he seemed strong; her impression of him was based entirely upon his impression of himself. She had been deeply disappointed in him. She soon saw that he was neither strong nor sure, merely a shouter, like a boy at school who bluffed and bullied. The glossy future he had promised for both of them had materialized into an administrative job in a colonial desert. The first time she set eyes on that dry, motionless bush with its windless heaven and calm, terrible heat, she burst into tears. It was the only time. In public, it was the only time.

As for Bernard, if he was disappointed in his marriage and rigid with frustration, he nevertheless had his work, which he churned up into a kind of importance. He improved his position. But there was not enough for him to do. He began constantly setting himself tasks and composing reports to impress his superiors, which frequently put their backs up. In the Protectorate there was little call for such industry; it was, moreover, a little ridiculous. The days flowed sluggish as the river: there were a few tribal councils to be attended, court cases, an occasional murder or marriage, areas to be checked up on, a fair amount of paperwork.

The throb of freedom gathering in the hills seemed a long way off, another world away. Bernard and his colleagues took no notice. They were there to do a good job, to keep things ticking over gently, to avoid any trouble—because Bechuanaland and the British prided themselves on its long drift of peacefulness, its stretch of slow, sleepy progress.

At first Lilian had headaches, then fits that resembled convulsions; these the doctor referred to as nerves—common enough in his experience of those parts. Bernard did not look closer into these manifestations, putting them down to the fact that she was delicate and highly strung. She could still become gay at parties; she organized the servants almost adequately, though she could sometimes be overbearing. She was friendly in a distant way to Bernard's superiors and their wives, but stood apart from the rest. Only in her illnesses could be traced the presence of stifled hysteria, but no one was looking for it.

And Emily grew and became more strange. Lilian could find no comfort in her, though the girl was desperate to console and support her mother. Finding no response, Emily grew increasingly obsessed by her mother's private life, her life behind the mosquito net. She suspected her mother always, as a matter of principle, and watched her closely at all times. But Lilian did not watch Emily. Lilian was becoming very good at seeing nothing, doing nothing, feeling nothing.

At the beginning of the summer, Emily went with her mother to call on Theresa Joubert, the wife of a man at the Public Works Department. Mrs. Jones rather sneered at these duties but knew it would look bad if she did not visit.

Mrs. Joubert was breast-feeding her new baby. Lilian was put out by the scene and was about to leave the room, but Theresa motioned to a couple of chairs and told the servant girl to please fetch some tea. Her mother told Emily to go and play outside. On the other side of the door, Emily stopped to hear Theresa's soft Afrikaans voice say, "How long did you breast-feed yours, Mrs. Jones?"

Mrs. Jones, a little startled, replied, "Oh, for as short a time as possible," and then, after the laugh, with a little start of revulsion,

"I never liked that kind of thing." Theresa Joubert's eyes rose high and wide with incomprehension. Emily found herself tracking down her mother's thoughts—"Just like the natives, this dreadful place, these dreadful people . . ." And suddenly she hated her mother deeply, with the same feeling of lack she had when she watched the African mothers talking quietly and carefully to their children.

After the tea, Theresa Joubert, her baby drugged and smiling, turned to the stiff, slim woman who was visiting her. And, as a kindness, wanting to help Lilian, who seemed to her unhappy, with that pale stretched mouth she had begun to recognize in the British in Africa, said, "Mrs. Jones, I wonder, would you be interested in helping us at the clinic? I've just begun there myself. A lot of the little black kids around here have eyes almost blinded by infection. They walk miles with their parents for a little medicine; we really can't keep up with them, and could really do with a bit more help."

Mrs. Jones, feeling herself irritated by the round Afrikaans slur to the woman's pronunciation of the letter R, shook her head, "I don't think I'd be too good at that, really."

"Oh, I'm sure you would. No experience is needed—there's Dr. Ramsden for that, but we give out pills and penicillin—hundreds of aspirin. It does all help."

"Well, you see," Lilian said, rising, "I wasn't really brought up to think of working, that's the problem." She smiled in a superior way and thanked Theresa for the tea—wishing that the visit had turned out differently, but she did not know how. Her mouth was pulled flat as she walked to the door. Outside, a blast of hot air hit her; she looked at the square of garden with its horrible new house plonked just behind a patch of green grass. She went home, feeling exhausted.

Emily was swinging on the gate at the bottom of the garden; it squeaked as it swung swiftly to and fro. She was a small child, who grew slowly physically because she did not want to grow. To her, being an adult was an impediment. Once you were an adult you were not quite right. She was smiling. She jumped off the gate, walked away a little, then looked back at the gate.

"There is no question, Julian, that I can't jump it."

"Do it, then." How quietly Julian speaks, right beside my ear, almost inside it.

"Watch me closely, then, I might not be able to do it twice." She breathed in, wriggled her toes in the sand, then took off and hurled her body high, high into the air, over the wind and down the other side.

"There." Puffing, grinning, wanting to beat her chest like Tarzan.

"Yes," he said, a little surly, "but your foot caught a bit." He forced himself to be gracious, as boys must sometimes. "It was a good jump."

She was walking past the servants' quarters: three little rooms, all identical—an iron bedstead, a hard, stained coir mattress covered by two blankets, no sheets; a chair no longer wanted in the house because it was old and broken; a few tin cans as cups, a rag of carpet. Violet's room boasted a large, cracked mirror, a jar of Pond's Vanishing Cream, and a small paper bag of sweets from her boyfriend, the kind that had "Sweetheart," "Valentine," or "I love you" printed in pink upon circular or heart-shaped sugary surfaces. One of her used starched caps lay crumpled on the bed, next to an old candlewick dressing gown. The madam had given it to her when it had lost its color.

Mpande's room was more cluttered; he had been with the family much longer. There was an old painted cupboard with a deep crack in the door; inside hung his one handed-down suit (given as a bonsella when he had rescued Emily very bravely from a snake when she was a small child), the trousers he had recently been given, and an old battered black hat with the crown missing. His bed was neatly made: red blankets with vertical brown stripes at each end and brown hemming in the rough wool. There was a Bible on his table, which was an orange box covered with newspaper, and beside the Bible, his most treasured possession—his mouth organ. On the wall was a photograph torn from a magazine, of Elizabeth, the young queen, wearing white satin and jewels— the one person he put before his chief and loved with the deepest loyalty.

The last servant's room was empty at present; there was no garden boy because a gang of prisoners came every day to work the garden.

Emily was toying with a branch of Christ's-thorn. Sometimes they were put in vases inside the house, the little red flowers gave small pinpricks of pain and color. She snapped off pieces and let them fall, deciding as she did so that she would not go to where the bird was buried. It was Julian's bird, of course. It was dead. Julian had this disgusting way of digging up the buried bird each day; he had first buried it a week ago. He was interested in decomposition. She had no such interest and would not go, at least not today.

She was under the lemon trees, picking the thick, plasticky leaves, crushing them for their scent. The shade here was like entering water. She bit straight through the peel and began sucking at the pale flesh of the lemon; she had trained herself long ago not to wince at the first slash at her tongue.

She realized with a shock that it must be lunchtime: that was her father's voice at the kitchen door. She began to stalk, becoming one with the shade, head thrust up, nose forward. The insects in the trees kept up a high, insistent chittering. Emily's father was shouting; his words unnaturally rapid but monotonous at the same time, like the volley from a machine gun. An image of his face made her stop in her tracks; at her feet the soft sand wore his face like a shroud: hair slightly coiling at his brow, eyes flaring, then narrowing, his mustache twitching. She took two long strides until she could actually see him. She watched, taking in each minute detail of this incident, which, like all the others, would become an integral part of her thoughts—not merely seen and recorded, but branded on her personality.

She saw Mpande standing there, surly with patience, gray with concealment. He began to talk; he had immaculate manners, to be polite was as natural to him as breathing. He was explaining why his work was bad; why he could not be as lively as the madam would like; why the young girl, Violet, was a torment to him. He hoped it would pass; he hoped the master and madam would be patient with him—it was the bad time of year for him: the summer filled him with sorrow, made him feel the keen edge of solitude. Emily's father seemed about to explode; he was standing on the stone step and suddenly smashed the side of his fist against the doorframe. Mpande had become a stone. Then he took a step backward, so that it appeared for a moment that he was actually about to walk away. Mr. Jones leaped the step, flew at the African, and dealt him a wild, unaimed kick, which landed on the top part of the shin. Mpande lost his balance, fell backward into the dust. A chicken squawked and fled; there was a long silence. Emily felt tears falling down her cheeks; she did not touch them, but her nails made deep half-moons of blood on the undersides of her hands. She shook herself and, quietly, with a complete purity of motive, decided to kill her father.

Mpande did not move; his whole body was a rod of rage, which he could, at any moment, have used to destroy in seconds that weak dog, that petty tyrant. His hand reached out and cupped itself around the sand; he clenched it fast as though a knobkerrie, a slender assegai, lay there. But knowing, oh, knowing too, too well that there was not even interest on his side, he pulled himself up deliberately, so that his pent-up strength seemed the more ominous. His face turned slowly to the thick beige socks followed by pink knees; the long khaki shorts, the shirt with its flare of red neck, the thin mouth, and, above that, the screwed-down eyes of a coward. The black man, the "cook boy," stared up, resting on one elbow with a look so like a jeer that the white man wanted to aim a rifle at this cheeky animal and fire. But he turned on his heel instead, slamming the kitchen door behind him.

Emily instinctively moved to go to Mpande, but checked herself. He wiped the dust off his trousers, straightened the rope that served as a belt and ran the back of his hand under his nose. Then he gave a soft demonic laugh: it was the laugh of a people biding their time. He walked down to the servants' quarters, the bottoms of his trouser legs flapping in the heat and dust that surrounded him. A long way off and he was transformed by the sheen of the midday sun; he seemed to be swaying, walking on air, and yet not moving at all.

She went in to lunch. Her mother was sitting unnaturally

straight, her father was speechless. No one dared to utter, afraid of the consequences if the quivering pool of his rage was rippled by a word—any word, however carefully culled. The knives clinked at one another; the chewing sounded uncomfortably loud. A cream-colored fan turned in the ceiling, stirring the pulpy smell of chicken and potatoes. Bernard Jones was eating his potatoes. He had always eaten potatoes twice a day—boiled, preferably— and he saw no reason to stop now. To change meant to question and consider, best to stick to what one knew.

Emily watched him shovel the food efficiently into his mouth and dispose of it with barely a movement of his jaw.

"Dog's sick, is he?" he asked sharply of his wife.

"Not sick, exactly." Mrs. Jones's voice slipped into her napkin and hid there.

"Hm? What did you say?"

"Well, he's all right, just seems to shiver a lot."

Mr. Jones's temper had been assimilated a little by the food and was dispersing; he could now be jocular. "He just needs a good run—or a kick up the backside—ha-ha."

The mother and daughter's knives and forks came to rest with scarcely a whisper; the glasses of cold water were lifted, tasted, and replaced. Emily was thinking of the two-bore shotgun used for game but decided the elephant gun would be better. How shall I kill him? How? Shall it be short but violent, with blood on the walls and guts on the carpet? Or still and savage: a long knife, beautifully chiseled, with a point of perfection?

"Pud?" he asked loudly, passing down the steamed pudding pierced with currants, lying in a trench of slick custard. Lilian Jones shook her head wearily and replaced the starched napkin in the silver-plated ring, then twirled and twirled it.

"Well, I'm off," he said. Bernard Jones left the table; the room grew cooler. Violet came in and, seeing Emily squashing the pudding into the sides of the plate, swiftly snatched it up on her tray before Mrs. Jones could see and order it to be returned at the next meal. Emily smiled and winked; Violet winked; Mrs. Jones thought she heard Caspar cry and left the room.

Outside again, the sun had such force it seemed to be resounding like a drum, and Emily, squinting up into its face, reeled a little. She wanted to go to the river, to the little shallow pool where the green boat lay. There she could reach out across the water and pull up water lilies, pale blue and pink and white, with long, long stems and green floating leaves that could bear the weight of trotter birds and small stones. She could send a leaf off with a twig and sail, to voyage out there beyond the reeds and rushes in the still, silver center.

But then she remembered Mpande and went instead to find him. He was sitting on the step of his room, eating a mound of solid mealie pap with gravy and a few chunks of meat. He would have the same for his dinner, without the meat. She sat beside him. He ignored her, breaking off a lump of the porridge and rolling it into a ball before slopping it in the gravy.

"I'm eating my dinner," he said.

"I know, but I wanted to ask you to help me fix my puncture."

"You can do it. I've showed you many times."

"But I like you to do it with me."

Silence.

"Please, I'll bring the water and the kit and everything. When you're finished."

"Okay, but it's needless." His voice was lighter. She ran to the garage to fetch the bicycle and tools and poured water into the bucket from the tap, under which a bush of parsley grew, thriving on the drips. She took her time so that he could finish in peace.

"Here," she said, digging down into her pocket and producing a squashed cigarette.

"He counts the cigarettes in the box."

"I know that. You think I'm stupid? I got it out of the big tin."

He laughed and took the cigarette with pleasure, "I thank you, missy, for your kindness."

"Well, I'm glad you didn't accuse me of stealing." She laughed.

He said, looking keenly at her, "For us, to steal from a European is no sin; to steal from one's own people, that is a sin."

She understood what he was saying and changed the subject. "Why're you always so darn polite?" she asked gently, because his control was a wonder to her.

He sucked at the cigarette and sighed with a quiver of pleasure. "I was taught by my mother always to be polite, to speak to people with decency." She leaned forward, wanting him to go on, and he did. "We were taught throughout the years to walk in the ways of our forefathers, to avoid the temptation of wealth, to share our goods with our neighbors and live in gentleness with our own. If a man rose to be a tyrant, he was restrained. We grew together like a tree, slowly, and no one branch could rise and rush up to find a new patch of sunlight. Only the chiefs and kings found their own sunlight—because this was wanted, this was chosen by all. Now it is different, now these things have become as sand and hold no water."

Emily, feeling him slip into melancholy, knew the process and wanted to arrest it. There were days when sadness awoke when she did; it stayed on when the dream had ended, and all through the day it hovered. She turned to a known comfort and handed it to him.

"Do you remember, Mpande?"

It always worked: it transported him to a place—past—that rid him of present sensation. He seemed to jolt himself; he looked up eagerly. "What, missy?"

"Do you remember how, when I was little, we used to have such odd conversations?"

"Oh, yes, indeed I do."

So they went through the routine again: the same questions, the same answers; wearing straight faces, like a ritual, to banish the nasty episode of earlier. And while they spoke Mpande was skillfully shelling the tube of its tire.

"I used to say, didn't I, 'Why do you smell so awful, Mpande?' "

"I, missy?" His eyes shot up to heaven. "I don't smell awful, it's you."

"*Me?*"

"All white people smell."

"But that's what we say about you!"

"I know, missy"— very serious now—"but it's not true."

They laughed. Mpande, having extracted the tube, was pumping it up, resting the pump on his knee.

She hit him loudly on the arm, still laughing, "Okay, then, what do we smell like? You all smell of sweaty armpits, never washed."

"Well, missy, white people do not smell like people." He was grinning broadly, and Emily was cutting out a patch while he dried the area of the tube where the puncture was.

"I always liked that," she said. "Go on, then, what do white people smell like?"

"Like things, missy, like things. You know that Mrs. Verster that comes to the house sometimes, well, she smells just like the table when Violet's polished it. And some smell like a rose that someone has squashed under the foot."

"And I, Mpande? What do I smell like, you old bugger? I haven't asked you that before."

"Now, that's not decent talk for a young girl. You stop that, you hear?"

She shrugged. "Okay, so what do I smell like?"

He thought, pressing the patch down onto the glued surface of tube and holding it there. "Well, you smell like the washing, when it's hung and drying. But when you're angry, when you shout and bang your head, then you smell bad. Like the river when it's swollen and heavy with mud. A smell as though it carries dead things in its waters."

Emily wrinkled her nose thoughtfully and began to put all the bits and pieces back into the tin. Mpande, as he slowly began to tuck the tube into the tire, began to think of his wife and how beautiful she used to smell first thing in the morning, at five o'clock when he woke her to make the fire. Or at night, as she crouched by the fire and stirred the pap and looked up at him with eyes not black, but deep nut-brown with little flickers of blue—full of softness, shiny with love. It was a hard thing, thinking of her, her whom he had not been able to see for nearly five years, nor his children. They were almost grown now, the eldest thirteen, and the Lord only knew when he could get the fare together again to visit them and his village in Nyasaland.

He shook himself. "Well, missy, it's now ready for the next thorn," he said, aiming for a little joke, because he liked her; she was daughterly to him. She got him to do things for her, but he did not mind that, though he pretended to.

"I must go up to the house now, missy, there's a multitude of work for the madam's party."

"I'll come and help you later," she said; then she grinned, jumped on her bike, wobbled a little, pushed off, and rode swiftly down to the river.

Bernard Jones was worried about the party. He did not trust parties, particularly his own. They had a way of making people behave alarmingly, particularly the women, and then he could not control things. There was something indefinable about women that terrified him, although he would have been stunned had anyone told him so. Any strong woman brought to mind his mother, with her sharp, small eyes and her cutting tongue.

As he counted out the bottles of gin and whiskey, he remembered that there had been a time when he had liked being with his wife at a party. Her bright laugh had helped reduce his uneasiness; she had stayed close to his side, as though she wanted him to protect her from the glances of the men present. But, unaccountably, when they had come abroad, parties seemed to bring out something else in her; her jolly laugh that he had loved had gone shrill and false. She no longer clung to his arm or looked at him before answering a question. She had begun to flaunt herself, and her flaunting seemed an attack on him, rather than something she did for her own benefit. He missed her, but he could not begin to admit it.

In the kitchen, Mpande was stabbing, with little wooden stakes, small chunks of cheese and onion, or a prune wrapped in bacon. The sausage rolls were flaked and golden, the cheese straws plaited as neat as a pigtail. Later, there would be wild duck, which must be roasted long and slowly, for they could be tough, and some bream for the missionary and his wife, who would not eat meat. Mpande watched Violet, broad and happy, folding the white napkins into shapes that bore themselves like crowns. Emily was helping her,

but did it more slowly. Mpande and the girl, Violet, fought endlessly over their duties, their food, their hours. She was of the
Bamangwato tribe; she thought herself superior; he was from a far
place that she had never heard of. Ah, but she walked so quietly on
her large, flat feet, and the spread of her hips was homely and
encouraging, as women's hips should be. And if she would but
smile at him and show her tongue, he could be young and lusty like
that brute, her boyfriend, who beat her.

The napkins were all done; the ducks dressed; the potatoes
peeled and sliced. There were vats of fruit salad and homemade ice
cream and two huge green watermelons.

"Go and have a rest now," Emily ordered. "The madam is out
and won't need you for a bit."

She wanted the house empty so that she could explore. She was
certain that there were things that the house still had not divulged;
secrets hiding in drawers she had not yet got to. She had found the
thin box of love letters from her father to her mother, but they
were boring. There was, however, one drawer in her mother's chest
of drawers that was always locked. Emily had recently found a key
in a silver-topped scent bottle; she was going to try it.

The drawer opened. It was full of papers: a marriage certificate
with a black ribbon around it, a few cuttings from old newspapers,
a lace hankie, and then, a photograph. A photograph of Lilian as a
younger woman, with the tall blur of her husband behind her. On
her knee sat a child in a sailor suit and Lilian was smiling at the
child gently, her hand cupped softly around the curly hair. Emily
flushed with pleasure at this demonstration of an early love for her,
but Julian said, "Turn it over, turn the photograph over." He was
wiser always, knowing corruption was endless. She turned the
photograph over, and there, in her mother's hand: "John Martin,
two years old."

Julian was silent now, knowing the sickness in Emily's heart:
what other secrets were hiding from her? In the locked wooden
desk there might be a poem somewhere, addressed "To my son,"
a lock of golden hair, a little boot in tissue paper.

Julian said, with the sweetness he always produced on such

occasions, "You can be a warrior queen, and everyone knows that warrior queens are the fiercest of all." But she could not be consoled. She wanted to know whom to blame for snatching this big brother from her, this blond to her brutish brown. This boy who could have taught her things that she had had to learn alone; who might have been the requited warmth that she ached for.

The sun was beginning to lower itself to the red horizon. A male mamba shook with grief in the wild poplar tree by the District Commissioner's gate: his mate had been clubbed to death by the convicts clearing out the old well. Emily was walking down to the river; she stopped when a giant heron rose up with a serene rush of wings, its elegant legs stretched back, thin as a reed. It was so beautiful that she suffered a small shock.

She was sitting close to the reeds, looking out across the water; a golden bream burst through with an open, pouting mouth, then sank again. Her thoughts were gentle and unhurried, because all the sights, smells, and colors around her had nothing to do with man and his frightening ways. She became one with the silence and was made free by it. It was here by the river that all turmoil left her; it was here that she spoke to Julian hour by hour, about how things would be when they were older; when they had freedom. Not that she intended to leave, ever. The desert around this loop of water was a reflection of her own soul.

She ran on to the kraal and found Johanna cutting chickens up into small pieces and smearing them with an amber-colored paste made from wild berries. Johanna smiled at her and announced, "See there, the drummer, he has arrived." Emily looked across and saw a middle-aged African, very black, very tall, with a big nose and wide nostrils. His head was down low, though he occasionally jerked it upward and squinted at the sun. His long fingers strummed against an ox-hide drum. He kept stopping, as though some connection he was searching for was missing. The warbling voice of a young mother plucked at the cooling air; her voice rose higher and higher until it became painful to listen to.

"She is singing," Johanna said before being asked, "about how we dream, how we will always dream, about fat cattle and our own green grass. But now, with the young men gone and our young girls wanton, we dream of blood again. She is woebegone because her man went away to make money for them and was beaten to death by a gang in a location in Vryburg."

"Why do the young men always go?"

"Always for money. For the bright lights of Joburg, for the deep mines that cough up gold forever."

"But they come back, don't they?"

"Ai, they come back, perhaps, but if they do they are not the same ones that went. They become tsotsis and have forgotten the old ways. They work for the mines and reap a different harvest—a jacket perhaps, a knife, a cheap scent for their girl. And a different kind of swagger, one that shows too clear the hole in their pride."

"But the chiefs will deal with them and make them stop."

She laughed, a hoarse laugh that ended in a cough, "No, the chiefs were broken before you even remember; humiliated in front of their people and forced to shameful promises. Their land was taken; there is no power without land."

"But you could be sacked for talking like this," Emily whispered.

"Oh, yes, I'm a cheeky kaffir all right." She giggled like a young woman and poked Emily in the ribs with her finger. "Hey, you know, there is a witch doctor coming tonight, missy."

"Why is he needed?" Emily asked, feeling light wisps of fear at her neck.

"It is the elders; they are talking bloody rubbish: they have agreed to a new tax that all are too poor to pay. We want to go back to the Government and tell them no. The elders should do this, but they are afraid. They need to be given courage. The Government has a small mouth; it cannot eat us all."

"Can I see the witch doctor?"

Johanna hesitated, but her generosity overcame her caution. "Yes, you come. But come after dark and keep out of eyesight, here behind the wall. They won't want you to see it."

"I'll come. I've got to go now, Johanna." Johanna went on turning the chicken in the thick paste so that all the surfaces were coated. She covered it with a clean white cloth when she had finished.

Emily ran back to the house; the shadows were making long spear shapes on the ground; crickets were low in the bushes and a night plover let out its sweet, high wail. She made her way carefully from the bush to the darkening trees, watchful for snakes, her ears stretched for any unfamiliar sound; but the danger decreased as she passed through the grass banks of the village and up toward the house.

This was the best time, when her mother emerged from the bath smelling of Goya talcum powder, her hair bound carefully into a silk scarf, to keep out the damp, which might flatten her curls. She was sitting in front of her dressing table, drinking a long glass of gin to calm her down. Emily walked in to see the long, pink slope of her back in its frame of black taffeta. The dress was high in the front with little scooped quarter sleeves, a nipped waist, and full, billowing skirt, sibilant and gleaming. Emily's emotions were complex as she looked into the mirror and saw her mother's face—not beautiful, but striking, with the high, tinted cheekbones, the neat red mouth, the halo of golden hair with its soft high bang that gave her face a childish, wistful quality. There was a haunted expression on her mother's face tonight—it was often there—and it touched and frightened the child. But Emily was quick enough to recognize the vanity, the emptiness, and the resentment there also, and this angered her. For what she needed was unqualified pride.

"You may powder my back, dear," the woman said, proud, becoming generous because of it. "And the pearls could do with a polish. In the box, there, do that first." And the air seemed to fold them closer together.

As she was polishing the pearls with a blue cloth her father came in. Lilian Jones looked up and said, "Oh! . . ." and looked down again. Emily moved closer to her. Bernard looked flustered and hot; his khaki clothing was dusty and crumpled. He sat on the bed and began to take off his boots. He began: "That bloody Dick again . . . upset about the shooting . . . can't keep calm, that man . . ." He grunted, yanking at the boots, letting them fall loudly.

Lilian started, then said with a scraping of interest, "What shooting?" Her mouth moved into an inverted arc as she squinted to apply mascara from a square brush. He was irritated that she never remembered what he was doing.

"The cattle, in the foot-and-mouth area. Of course it's a bloody business, but what can you do about it? Getting upset never helps anything."

"Hm, that's on Brink's farm, isn't it?"

"And the surrounding land; some natives have to give up their stock, too."

Lilian spat delicately on the block of mascara and rubbed the brush hard into it.

"That's a lot of money down the drain." She sighed.

"Brink can bloody afford it," Bernard said resentfully, looking for a clean shirt in the cupboard.

"Dick should be used to it by now," Lilian said, hoping that this tacit agreement with her husband's point of view would close the subject.

Bernard noticed the pearls being polished. It warmed him; nothing gave him more pleasure than the sight of a gift he had bestowed. "Ah, wearing those, I see." And, turning to Emily, "I got those for your mother in Bond Street, before you were born." Emily thought of the baby boy and found her fingers growing rigid as she tried to fold the blue polishing cloth.

"Here, I'll put them on," he offered extravagantly, "darn good pearls . . ."

Emily was certain that she saw a small spasm at her mother's throat, a nerve flushing with blood. Quickly she moved the pearls. "I have to do the powder first, or it'll go all over the pearls."

He was hurt. He lost interest and headed for the bathroom. Emily picked up the big, pink powder puff with its satin band and began to dunk it into the round vat of musk rose; a fine mist settled on the table. Emily powdered the flawless back, moving carefully down its slope, not touching the black taffeta.

"That'll do." Impatient. "Now just dust my shoes a little, will you?" Another layer of scarlet was applied to her mouth; then she picked up a tissue and clamped her mouth over it, leaving two perfect red lips, complete with creases, on its surface. Her mouth came away with a loud smacking sound. Then she rose, waiting for approval.

"Oh, you do look lovely!" The child was transported, and this was important because, for all her vanity, Lilian had no confidence in her beauty.

"The dress is lovely; it suits you perfectly," Emily said, imitating something she had once heard someone say. She smoothed a crushed fold. Lilian turned in front of the long mirror: was it her? Was it really her face that brimmed above the austere black with such radiance?

"Yes, it is nice, isn't it? I ordered it from Bulawayo. Surprising you can get such a nice frock in such a dump." Her brow furrowed a second; then she laughed. "Your father hasn't seen the bill yet!" She was more concerned about this than she cared to think: once he had bellowed and bawled for a whole night when she'd bought an expensive pair of shoes without consulting him. Her mind veered in another direction: she found it so hard not to be distracted. "I wonder," she said, almost to herself, "if Tor has come back from Palapye?" And her face took on its blankness as she sank down into that desolate place where there was nothing to alleviate her ennui. Her daughter grew restless but half wanted to stay, though the atmosphere had now lost its intimacy.

In the kitchen, Mpande was rushing up and down in a white, starched apron, his face aglow with pride as he pulled the ducks about in their brown juices and oiled their backs with his spoon. A mountain of freshly baked white rolls, dusty with flour, were being transferred from racks to white-napkined baskets by Violet. She was splendid in her best frilled apron and starched cap. Her face was unusually pale, as she'd been lavish with the Pond's cream, and a pungent smell of lily of the valley rose from her ears and wrists. Mpande and Violet worked smilingly together; he, tense with awareness that her scent made him covet her frantically; she, cool and composed, but dipping her eyes shyly.

"Hey, missy, you get out from under my feet; we're working busily here," Mpande said, on the edge of irritation.

Emily moved to the other end of the table and began eating peanuts, before being rebuffed again.

It was beginning to grow dark; there was a slight breeze. Emily decided that there was just enough time to run down to the kraal before the guests started arriving, and she would be expected to hand around the nuts. Down the garden, over the gate, down the dust track and out across the strip of veld she ran, and in ten minutes could see a big roaring fire splashing light across the walls of the mud huts. There was very little noise; she had expected singing and thought they might even have started eating. The hush was ominous, so she slowed down and began to approach Johanna's hut from the rear, keeping in the shadows. Once there, she waited. A bat dropped through the sky, plunged wildly upward, then disappeared behind a pile of boulders. A woman led in a cow for milking. The last rays of the sun slumped quickly behind the black hump of the koppie.

The Africans are sitting quietly around the fire. An emaciated kaffir dog creeps slowly toward the fire, its body curved round with fear. "Voetsak!" a man shouts and it flees.

An old man is crouching in the sand close to the fire; he is mumbling, rocking. Everyone is hushed. Suddenly, he topples from his haunches and lies quivering beside the fire. Then his head jerks wildly, as though pulled by a wire, and he begins to scream out, high and ecstatic. All faces watch him intently, their heads nodding a little. The glow from the fire makes streaks of silver across his cheekbones, lighting up his mouth each time it tears open and shrieks. He leaps into the air with the agility and force of a young man and begins to pound his feet on the earth rhythmically, again and again. What he is conveying is instantly understood by everyone except Emily; she tries desperately to remember the things Johanna has told her. She sees from his movements that he has become a warrior. But then, without warning, his movements change; he falls to the earth, then gently rises up, weaving his body gracefully in and out of the firelight, his head pushing forward, his mouth opening and closing noiselessly.

Then his arms rise high, and he seems transported by giant strides that carry him up into the air, where he seems miraculously to hover. He makes no sound. He collapses. A man steps forward and covers him with a brown-and-black blanket. There is silence; then Johanna begins a low, soothing chant, almost a lullaby. Emily is calmed. The circle of bodies around the fire relax but do not speak.

He wakes quickly and easily, demanding drink. He speaks quietly now, his face heavy with exhaustion. He says the spirits are ashamed of the men with women's courage. The gourd is handed from fist to fist—the kaffir beer with its stink of yeast, with its sour, thick taste, slops down their throats. Their laughter bubbles up, becoming wilder, freer. One man backs away from the circle, because their talk makes him frightened. He is mocked and hooted at by Johanna. She clicks her tongue in rebuke; he slinks off into the huts.

At the other end of the kraal, the drum begins to throb with a low, insistent beat. People emerge from their huts; they gather round the drum, clapping their hands and stamping their feet on the ground. The drum picks up their enthusiasm: the beat quickens, tightens, becoming louder and louder—proud now, like a call to spears, like thunder in the night when war clouds are gathering; like the feet of the impis as they dance across the veld.

Emily started to back away, afraid of their laughter, envious of their courage. She remembered Johanna's warning: "If you let us into your hearts, it might be a danger; you might also let in our evil spirits. The spirits that have always protected us could find no home in your heart; they would devour you."

Her feet pounded home. The house was lit up; she could see Mpande's head moving to and fro through the kitchen window. She walked around to the front, where the trees in the garden were decked out with green and red lights. Laughter issued forth from the wide stoep. She went around to the back again and entered through the kitchen door. She made her way toward the noise.

And there they all are: cigarettes at their mouths, drinks at the ready. Their faces, though they shine with spirits, are anxious. The missionary and his wife stand to one side with little glasses of tomato juice; they are thin and spiky, odd and out of place in this gathering. The missionary, Arthur, wishes he could slip away before dinner and get back to the exercise books that need correcting. Gladys, his wife, had looked forward to coming, to talking to her own kind away from the awful corrugated-roof house, but once here, she feels out of it. She has grown so used to silence that conversation now buzzes in her ear with the mindless intensity of a fly behind a windowpane. Then she sees Emily and approaches her with relief.

"How are we, then, Emily?" she asks kindly.

Emily is put off by the dreary little black dress that Gladys wears. She does not know where to look—at the parched skin of the throat, with its brave velvet ribbon, or the sere blue skin around Gladys's eyes.

"Oh, I'm fine, thank you." There is a silence as both look around the room, both disguising their dismay at what they see.

Gladys tries again, "Did you get those little booklets I sent you?"

"What booklets?" Emily is aware that her voice is ungracious, but is unable to make the effort of changing it.

"About Jesus."

"Oh, those, yes, thank you," she says quickly, moving away.

Emily's mother was winding her way through the packed bodies in the drawing room. Emily watched her coming. She was walking in an affected way; her head unnaturally poised, her arms held away from her sides, as though she were preparing for a ballet step. Lilian was making for her daughter and, upon reaching her, snapped, "Where've you been?"

Emily's face grew sullen. "In the garden for a bit."

"Well, hand round the snacks, then, and do something to help, for a change," she said crossly.

Emily, with the sausage rolls, which she jabbed quickly at one person after another, saw the vet, Dick, sitting tired and depressed in an armchair. She dumped the tray of sausage rolls on a little table and set up position as close to him as she could get. An

Afrikaner with greasy blond hair—the farmer Brink—was sitting next to Dick. He felt more at ease with Dick; this was not his crowd: they'd asked him out of pity. He and Dick had spent the day shooting his cattle and then supervising their burial in a deep ditch that the boys had then sprayed with lime. The experience had left him hotly resentful: it was the bleddy munts, careless, stupid; you had to watch the buggers the whole time. They'd nearly fouled up the whole operation this afternoon by trying to avoid handing over their diseased cattle. Dick said nothing; he twirled the stem of his Sherry glass and listened.

Emily, absorbed by this conversation, felt sorry for poor Dick, who looked deeper and deeper into his glass, as though some solution lay there. He understood people like Brink, but he did not like them. He reminded himself that they were cruel because they were bored, and afraid. They were all exiles and had found refuge here: refuge from what they were, what they might have been in their own place. He was the same: he had come out here because he could not have achieved a great deal in Scotland; he was better away from stiff competition. But, God! this harsh place offered no shelter. It was merely a place to hide. Perhaps they had all, once, sought enrichment by what was strange and wild, but had found that the land rejected them—utterly and eternally it was indifferent.

"Oh, God!" Emily groaned, seeing her mother look yet again toward the door, her face puckered by anxiety. The door did not swing open to reveal Tor, by whom the whole night would be redeemed. Lilian's laughter, tinny, hysterical, floated above the conversation and the clinking of glasses.

Her father was standing guard by the drink table, his eyes trained on the bottle of Gordon's gin, which was being splashed lavishly by George Baker into a tumbler. He gave it to Moira Lucas, who had already had far too much. Little pearls of perspiration sparkled on her forehead below the mane of fine red hair. She swayed happily toward George; they both knew the routine.

"When's dinner?" she demanded, tossing her head at Bernard.

Emily, her eyes darting from the glistening faces that surrounded her to the flintlike faces of her mother and father, felt absolutely certain that she had not been created by those two people. There was nothing flamboyant or exuberant about either the pinched, mustached man with his obsession for switching off lights or the sad woman flattened by resentment. Emily's face became occluded and then slowly parted to reveal her most bitter fear. Each thought, as she heard her mother's high laugh reach its crescendo, condemned and destroyed her: am I like her? God, could I ever be like that? She turned away in humiliation and shame, seeing the bright scarlet mouth open, the head thrown back in the coquette's pose, the small finger crooked foolishly as it tipped the glass: I could kill her, I could kill her.

There was not much time: soon the dancing would begin, and her mother would come and tell her to go to bed. Emily decided to move in on the colonel. She went over to where he lounged against the doorframe with a cool grace quite lacking in the others, looking out into the night. His trousers held their creases like a fan: his navy-blue jacket scorned all dust; his silk cravat was softly tied. He had a fluffy mustache the color of rust, which limped around his small mouth.

He was toying with the idea that people could become primitives, could revert, surrounded as they all were by such barbaric forces. The strange thing to the colonel was that not one of the people present would accept that for a moment, nor even consider it. They believed that they imposed their culture, their emotions, on Africa when they came to live in it. Whereas he knew that things happened here—accidents, deaths; they happened so easily precisely because of the raw forces exerted by the country on its inhabitants. Having played with this idea, he discarded it like a tough piece of meat and looked out to where the trees were swaying under high waves of moonlight.

Emily stood close to him. He was thinking how beautiful the country was. To him it was unmarked, with a purity that you sometimes saw in very young men. It was formless too, except very early in the morning, when the little koppies filled up with blue, and in the evening, when the light gave the distance some shape, something you would like to touch, but warily. He did not see Emily watching him, her eyes misty with admiration. She knew what it felt like to be him.

Then her mother's voice called out, "Dinner's ready," in a blithe voice. Emily set off for the kraal, running through the mealie field at a gallop. The Africans drank on. One drank from a Coca-Cola bottle and one from a plastic baby's beaker, but mostly the gourds were passed from hand to hand—kaffir beer, a drink that burned in thirst, that blotted out hunger. The women were swathed in bright cotton, wound tight across the tops of their breasts and reaching down below their knees—bold blues, strong oranges, with brown and black patterns, with the tough texture of newness and the smell of the store. Large earrings weighed down their ears. The men, in assorted tatters, sat with their knees up, discussing and pondering. The women's conversation fluttered between one another, but if their voices grew too loud or shrill, they would stop and subside, beginning again in a respectful lower key.

Emily sat with her back to Johanna's hut and drew her knees up in contentment. She lifted her face and began to pick out the stars as easily as if they were old and familiar toys. But something was stirring by the camp fire. It was the women, the women who moved their legs and began lightly to shake their hips. The men watched and waited. The drummer moved to the biggest drum and began to muster a slow, penetrating volley. Then the women rose and stretched out their arms and the drummer went wild. It was like hail on a roof, like the tumult of a waterfall hitting rock, like a storm in the treetops. The men grew restless; they wanted to be out there with the women. But they must wait. Then, in one voice, the women's lips pulled back, showing their teeth and their tongues as they called out a harsh, husky howl. The men sprang up, and they became as one rhythm, one song under the stars. Emily watched in awe, a pulse in her blood straining to be with them, to be them— simple, stupid, passionate—living inside the earth, not on its crust.

But now it was changing. Bodies roll toward one another as if in a swoon, then back, then forth. The women—arms wide, hips butting—rise and swirl, heat rising from their flanks. The men begin to pound the earth, humming as they swoop, fastening their hands around the women's waists. They crush them against their bodies, then release them, only to crush them again. A high, wailing crescendo slices the air.

Emily, who had shuddered with excitement and disgust, now felt a cold trickle of fear and began to retreat. Someone saw her. A man, tall, with the firelight behind him, rises. He roars out an insult in his own tongue. They all rise. They stamp their feet; they chant and jeer. She slips and falls—they scream with laughter. She gets up again and runs, her breath carving into her stomach. And the dream returns: there are thousands and thousands of naked feet, looming out of the hills like a black cloud of locusts. They have come to strip the earth. Savages, spiked and speared, with shaved heads and bodies clotted with stain and dung, screaming—blood, blood, blood.

At her garden gate, she stopped. Her heartbeat was painful, her lungs seemed tied up with ropes. She forced her body to go slack and gulped in the air noisily. And, after a little while, walked slowly up the path. This time she did not go around to the front but entered the kitchen quietly, when no one was there.

In the drawing room, the lights had been switched off, all but one small lamp in the corner. The carpet had been rolled away, the chairs pressed back to the walls. The music on the gramophone had changed from loud jazz to sloppy tunes. Couples dragged each other around in circles; sweaty hands left grease marks on taffeta and silk. The women's curls drooped and their noses shone. The men had discarded their jackets and ties, and a mild stench of sweat and booze wafted with them as they pushed their partners across the parquet floor. One woman slept in a chair, like an overtired baby, in her dress of soft pink ruffles tipped with lace. Her mouth was wide with contentment; the skirt she had ironed herself (not trusting the girl with the delicate georgette) was scrunched up behind her back; her shoe dangled, suspended by one painted toe.

Men and women not related to each other in marriage could be seen making for the garden. Mr. Jones surveyed the scene with rage: he had tried to tell people to leave—it was after one o'clock —but had been ignored. Now he walked around, frantically emptying ashtrays out of windows into flower beds; sneaking out with unopened bottles. It was all too late: he realized that things had happened in spite of himself, yet again. He had not intended to have one of those wild parties, gossiped about in hotel bars all over the Protectorate—yet here it was, all going on under his roof, and he could do nothing, nothing. He stormed out of the room, making for his bedroom, wondering how much the bloody thing was going to cost him.

Lilian, perched on a high stool, her elegant legs crossed to reveal much of her thigh, watched him go. She was pretending to listen to the new man at the Public Works Department; but she was apprehensive, kept looking toward the doorway: still Tor did not come, and the night grew more slippery as her laughter thinned and trembled, ending in something like a sob.

When Bernard reached his bedroom, he found that his bed was occupied. He gained the first satisfaction of the evening ripping the sheets off Phyllis and the husband of the sleeping lady in pink. They yelled with laughter and wrecked the bed trying to cover themselves. His face purple, Bernard pushed and punched them out of the door, and then collapsed in fierce misery onto his bed—his own bloody bed, dammit all.

After a moment, there was a soft knock on the door. He went to open it. There stood Phyllis, still covered by the sheet, looking contrite.

"Well?" he snapped.

With a whoop of merriment, she whipped open the sheet to reveal her naked, shiny body. Bernard thought he was going to choke.

In the garden, Emily and Julian were tracking down a fat woman on her own, Sybil White. She was drinking brandy from a bottle, her head tilted back, a fine gold trickle mixing in with the sweat on her neck. She tossed her hair up and leaned against a tree. On the veranda, perfectly visible from the darkness, a man watched, with no expression on his face, his wife disappear into the garden with another man.

"Quick," Julian said, "get going, or we'll miss them." They

followed at a distance, until the couple stopped at a willow tree in the middle of the grass.

"Look," Julian hissed, as the man's hand slipped expertly into the envelope of the woman's blouse. The willow leaves parted, then swished together again and there was a stillness, until an arm, wearing a gold bracelet, was flung out from below the willow branches. It lay limp on the grass. Emily watched as the hand began to stroke the grass softly, until it began pulling it out like hair by the roots.

Dick, slamming the door behind him, walked out into the garden, to see Sybil coughing, her face lit up, a ghastly blue-green color, by the fairy lights. He did not want to speak to her; he was going home, but felt he must be decent. He offered to take her home and suggested gently that she see a doctor about that cough. She laughed in a disenchanted way, "What the hell for?" Emily, close enough to hear, was struck suddenly with a dread of things to come. Why did women, like her mother, like Sybil, have this yawning void inside them that they did not even try to fill? The throbbing in her body went still; she decided to go to bed.

The kitchen was in darkness; Emily went through to the corridor beyond. Here she saw the colonel, the head of the police, known by the natives as the Tail of the Monkey, because he never stopped working. He was talking to the District Commissioner; they enjoyed each other's company and would have found the evening intolerable without it. The colonel was saying that his nephews would be coming to spend a fortnight of their holidays with him; he was looking forward to it—would take them shooting, do a spot of riding, have a good time. Emily stood quite still in the darkness of the corridor, all her attention riveted by his words. Now she smiled to herself; now she knew how her days would be spent.

Three days later Emily was preparing herself for an event she could not specify but knew was approaching. Since the party, she had kept away from the kraal and met Johanna's shaded looks with apologetic smiles. She felt to blame in some way for their behavior toward her. Her mother had barely left her bed; she was now suffering from insomnia and acute dizziness. Her father had begun obsessively taking the braking system of the Chevrolet apart, insisting that someone had been tampering with it. She kept away from him entirely. And spent a lot of time discussing with Julian the implications of the visit of the colonel's nephews; it was a year since they had been there.

Emily first saw the boys with their uncle at the house of one of the pilots. It was six o'clock and still warm; a few women were swimming in the pool, and the children were running about, untwisting little blue bags of salt to shake into their crisp packets. Coke and whiskey flowed; the servants came in with plates and napkins and, finally, a table, with thick bloody steaks and fat lengths of boerewors. A big African man, with a starched chef's hat on his head, was attending to the fire. The steaks were slapped down onto the grill and a spitting and sizzling erupted; the sausages leaped and burst, in a hurry to shed their skins. Everyone was happy. Including the chef, who knew from experience that very few people would be able to finish their steaks, so there would be leftovers for his family, for many families, in the kraal. His madam was generous about such things; many madams insisted that leftover meat go to the dogs.

The colonel's two nephews were sitting apart, as they always did, close to each other on a white painted bench near the swimming pool. They did not speak, but both watched the colonel constantly. The eldest boy, Gerard, had a striking face: strong, sharp bones and a tight, well-formed mouth; his chin was round and smooth; there was a slight shadow above his upper lip, which he was cultivating with a razor. His nose seemed a little big for his face and his eyes were a pale brown, almost golden in color. His very fair, soft hair flopped down over one eye and he had a nervous, appealing gesture of brushing it back from his brow. He was thirteen, but there was little of childhood left in him. His brother, Timmy, was nine; he seemed to perch beside Gerard like a nestling to its mother. He looked up at his brother's face as if seeking instructions on how to feel or behave. Timmy's face was plump and pretty still, with large blue eyes and delicate straight eyebrows. He was slim, neat-hipped, with long legs that gleamed a golden tan beneath his shorts. His tennis shoe had a hole in it that he had clearly cultivated, as the shoes were brand new. The two of them sat, sipping Coca-Cola self-consciously, their eyes trained on their uncle.

The colonel himself was deeply occupied in a conversation with the District Commissioner, George Hampton. They were sitting apart from everyone else on wicker chairs. Gerard and Timmy moved over to them, and Timmy was hoisted onto his uncle's knee and rested back against his chest. Gerard, for some reason, seemed upset. Emily watched him closely, seeing the boy's eyes stretch as if he was preventing himself from crying. He was standing next to his uncle's chair, but his uncle took no notice of him. All the colonel's attention was taken up by the little green grasshopper that Timmy was showing him. Their heads were close together; their hair looked beautiful placed side by side: one gold and glossy, the other muted and mat. The colonel's manicured fingernail stroked the wings of the grasshopper as it sat in Timmy's cupped palm.

"Mrs. Thompson says it's time to eat," Gerard said loudly, and his voice seemed to take rapid slices at the air.

"There's no need to snarl," said the colonel lightly, flicking a piece of dry grass from his nephew's shirt. Gerard moved back sharply, his face quivering. The colonel looked at him, then said soothingly, but not without a smear of sarcasm, "Ah, the shame of it! How you've grown up, and now, no doubt, you're tormented like all boys of your age. Only Timmy here is free, is innocent. You have no dreams of round girls, do you, Timmy?" and he stroked the fluffy hair and tipped the boy off his knee.

"Nor do I," snarled Gerard, then turned, cunning, "And how could I, dear Uncle, how could I?"

The colonel pulled himself up straight and neatened the turned-back cuff of his sleeve. He was a man who missed a uniform. He drew the pained smile on his lips into the resemblance of a grin and walked with his nephews to the braai, Gerard striding out in front. The colonel, seeing how tall Gerard had grown, how taut the shorts stretched across his buttocks, how angrily his arms soldiered by his side, felt sadness, a sense of loss, of growing old.

He remembered how sweet Gerard had been at Timmy's age, what games they had had.

Watching them, Emily remembered how she had sometimes crept into the colonel's house. The colonel's bedroom smelled of incense; she recognized it from the Catholic church she'd been to once. The walls were lined with books, big books mainly; the bed was low on the floor; it was covered with a tapestry that ended in fringes. Once she had turned back the cover and pressed her nose into the pillow; on a second visit she had got into the bed and stretched out between its smooth sheets, breathing in a strange musty aroma, a dead odor like decaying roses. So strong was the colonel's atmosphere in the room that Emily felt certain if she fell asleep there she would dream his dreams. Beside the bed was a picture of Gerard as he'd been at about eight, inscribed, "To my dearly, dearly unc. from his loving neph."

Soon after the braaivleis, Emily went back to the colonel's house. He was away for the day, in the bush, and his nephews, strangely, had decided to stay behind. Emily walked casually up the back garden and made her way to the swimming pool. It was a very deep, long pool, with clear blue water, and on the bottom of the pool there were strange fish paintings. The colonel had done them himself: mythical creatures with long spiraling tails, fixed eyes, and sealed mouths. Their bodies were entangled, so that it was not clear which tail belonged to which body, nor indeed where one stopped and the other started. The fish, painted in purples and greens, gave Emily a distinctly uneasy feeling, as if she were looking down into a pit of snakes. The pool was surrounded by thick bougainvillea bushes, cropped to a height of seven feet, so that the pool was entirely private, being entered by a wooden gate that could be locked.

It was here, on the grass surrounding the border of dark blue tiles, that the brothers sat, Gerard reading on his stomach and Timmy floating on a lilo in the water, his arms trailing, his hair slicked down, his eyes closed.

"Put on a shirt or you'll burn," Gerard said, not taking his eyes off his book. Emily stood back from the crack between the fence and the gate as Timmy quickly pulled himself up out of the pool and reached for a white T-shirt, which he put on before slipping silently back into the water.

"No, come out here," Gerard ordered.

Again Timmy clambered out, his T-shirt gummed to his chest and stomach.

"Sit down." Timmy sat in the shade of a dark blue parasol stuck into the soil by a spike. He was looking down at Gerard's back with fixed fascination.

"Well, Timmy?" Gerard said, running one finger slowly down his brother's leg.

"Do you want me to?" Timmy asked meekly.

"Don't *you* want to?"

"Well, yes, if you want me to . . ."

"Shut the gate, then, properly. Lock it."

Timmy did not move, his eyes and mouth were awash.

"Aren't you going to do it?" Gerard asked impatiently, indicating the gate, pushing his book away.

"I don't know," Timmy almost wailed.

"Forget it, then," his brother snapped. "Go on, piss off and don't bother me."

He retrieved his book.

Emily breathed more easily; she had been wondering what she would do if the gate was closed.

Timmy, his cheeks very red in the hot sunlight, went and sat very close to his brother, who moved away, tossing his head as though flicking off a fly.

Timmy said gently, putting a hand on Gerard's arm, "I will, Gerard, I will now."

"No, forget it."

"But I will." And his two soft hands lifted from their attitude of supplication, separated, and then found each other again between his brother's thighs. Emily felt that her stomach would explode when the hot stick of Gerard's groin sprang up, and his brother's hands moved and pummeled—while the small flushed face, weeping, averted, sank. Gerard fell back onto his towel. Emily fled the garden, smashing at the poinsettias, trampling the sunflowers panting up at the sun.

But a day or two later she was back in the colonel's garden. She was relieved to see Gerard and his brother playing like two puppies at the shallow end of the pool: Timmy was cuffing the water, to try to prevent his brother's lunging and ducking. They were laughing, spitting water, holding their noses and throwing their heads backward, so that their hair was scraped back from their foreheads, giving them an oiled 1930s look. Gerard, being careless and overexcited and, moreover, very strong for his age, suddenly hit Timmy a blow in his right eye. Timmy howled, and then pulled himself out of the pool, to crouch on the tiles with his arms around his knees, gulping and sniffing. Gerard took him into his arms, comforting him, apologizing, peering anxiously at the eye.

It was not long after that Emily heard the slapping sound of sandals on the paved path leading to the pool. It was not the walk of a servant. Emily decided that the noise must be coming from the Chinese slippers that the colonel kept beside his bed. She vanished behind the bushes. And waited. It was the colonel.

As he entered the enclosure, Timmy's voice sang out hello in a sweet, clear soprano.

Gerard snapped, "Shut up, Timothy," grinding his hip into his brother's side.

"Oh, not Timothy," the colonel's voice insisted, buttery, most mild in his censure. "Timos, perhaps, or Timo; Timothy sounds so mothy." He laughed alone. "Timmy is better, suits him so well, wouldn't you say so, Gerard?"

"Obviously I wouldn't. He's too old for that name now, in any case."

"Ah, so that's it! Well, I shall continue to call him Timmy, mayn't I, dear boy?" The colonel turned his long, narrow eyes, his delicate mouth with its rusty mustache, on Timmy.

Timmy shrugged, "It's okay. Mummy calls me that."

"Well, there we are," the colonel crooned, then stopped as his expression became troubled. He moved over to Timmy, took his face in both hands and peered at the eye, which had shrunk, the tissue around it flushed and swollen. "What's this, what happened here?"

Gerard blanched, but continued to look fierce.

"You, was it?" the colonel almost whispered, soft as a caress.

"No, no," protested Timmy, frightened his brother would be punished, reading only menace in the colonel's question. "It was a mistake, when we were roughing about . . ."

"Of course, dear boy, naturally. We'd better go back to the house all the same. I'll put something on it."

They trooped silently up to the house, the colonel's long fingers curled over Timmy's shoulder. Timmy was shivering now. He felt a terrible soppy desire to cry, but did not dare, and did not really understand why he should want to anyway. He was not in pain; it was just that a little shoot of panic was growing inside him. He wanted to go home, to see his mother smile at him with a grin that pushed up her cheekbones. Gerard walked on the other side of him, looking sideways at the eye, to see if it was worsening. Timmy wanted to move closer to him, but did not, just kept on walking dumbly, like a person trying to make his feet move properly.

Cold presses smelling of witch hazel smothered Timmy's eye. He lay back on the chaise, his arm hanging off it. His brother sat beside him like a sentry; the colonel sipped a glass of whiskey and felt angry with Gerard for being so surly. What had got into the boy, anyway? He looked positively satanic these days. Where did children's love go at a certain age? He had only loved the boy, after all. Never hurt him. Yet now he behaved as though he had been ill-used, damaged even.

"What's the matter, Gerard? We were always so close, like friends, like brothers."

"Not quite like that."

"Oh, I think so." The colonel began to rub his finger around the rim of the glass, until it sang, until it squeaked.

"Oh, stop that noise!" Gerard yelled, getting up in agitation.

"Heavens, and aren't we touchy." The colonel smiled with determination. The flesh of his cheeks was less taut, but there were attractive creases at the corners of his eyes.

The old fart! Gerard said to himself. He actually believes he did something to change me, to make me the way I am. But I've always been this way, before I knew him, before I even remember. I just recognized him as being the same as me.

Gerard looked tenderly at Timmy, whose mouth was buried beneath the cotton wool. Timmy was not the same, he thought protectively; Timmy could be marked, but he, Gerard, would see that it did not happen, would prevent it, whatever the cost.

"Come on, Timmy," he said, "I'll take you to bed."

The two brothers left and the colonel's eyes narrowed as he drank down his whiskey.

Emily noticed one evening, watching her father get out of his car and walk to the house, that he was becoming a little hunched. He entered the house like a man expecting nothing. Like a man entering an empty house that no woman's hand has warmed, no child's disorder made homely. No one came to greet him at the door; he would have to go to his wife's room, maybe even wake her, before he would be noticed. Emily went to the kitchen. Here Mpande was polishing brass buttons; he huffed on them, his wide mouth dark inside, the inside of his lips pink. He applied his cloth, making the raised insignia wink and gleam.

"Good evening, master," Mpande said quietly, as Bernard Jones entered. He stood up and pushed the newpaper with the buttons onto one side, as if he did not want his master sullied by seeing the dirty work done on his behalf.

"Where's the madam?" Bernard asked.

Emily answered. "She's in her room, she's got a headache." It was flatly, inscrutably spoken.

"I want a word with you." She followed him into the drawing room. Through the window she could see the evening dipping dramatically into darkness; insects clattered in the trees; bats were swooping and diving, and the air was glittery.

"Your mother, as you know, is not well. She needs a rest. I'm taking her for a week to the Victoria Falls. You'll be going to stay with some friends of ours near Lobatse for a couple of weeks, some people called the le Roux. They have a big farm, lots of land. They're the ones with the daughters who go to the convent near

Bulawayo—where we thought you could go soon, probably next term, if I can arrange it. So that's fixed, then. I'll take you to Francistown and you can go by train. You're big enough to go alone; they'll meet you at Lobatse. You'll leave in a few days and so will we. Try to make yourself agreeable when you're there, will you? I've got some work to do now."

Emily walked out without a word. He was puzzled that she had not been pleased, had not even expressed what she might feel about it. As it happened, Emily felt nothing about it at all; she vaguely remembered meeting Mr. le Roux once, he had spent a long time talking to her father about meat; he was a cattle farmer and exported a lot of beef to the Transvaal. In the meantime, there were more important things: there was only a little time left for the colonel now. She decided that she would spend most of the next day hanging around his house, and try to get Julian to come. If she could. Lately, Julian had seemed unreachable.

The next morning she woke early. She walked out into the false calm of the morning; clouds were being pushed up into great banks. Beside the river, speckled starlings and weaverbirds were landing on the rushes, and, out of sight, a thrush shook notes delicately from his throat. In the bush, the guinea fowl would be feeding; bush flies and wild bees would be hunting. And soon the sun would blot out all the morning's soft transparency, reduce all things to a deadening glare that would burden and overpower everyone.

When Emily reached the colonel's house, the cook boy told her that they had all gone out before dawn, shooting, in the direction of the Bushman Pits, and would not be returning until much later. Emily was consumed by jealousy, imagining them out there, watching the sun rise, driving the Jeep deep into the bush to find buffalo and springbok, who would all be making their way toward the river with some urgency, now that the summer was at its height.

In the early evening she made her way back to the colonel's house, as though some magnet drew her there. This time she was rewarded to hear sounds of splashing and laughter coming from the swimming pool. It was still hot, the morning breeze had quite gone, and she felt sticky and dusty as she walked cautiously through the trees to the pool. Once in position at the gap between bushes and gate, she peered in. The colonel was swimming with his nephews, and the oppressive atmosphere of the last occasion had completely disappeared. Emily could see the colonel's brown shoulders and arms ploughing through the water; he was a strong swimmer for a slightly built man. Timmy was swimming underwater, his hair was spread out, and the water was so choppy that all the sea fishes were dissolved into a swirling mess of colors.

Gerard was floating on his back looking relaxed; he had shot a buck, and the colonel had relied upon his experience and maturity throughout the day's shooting. Timmy did not mind the shooting itself, but he hated having to ride with the corpse of an animal lying at the back of the Jeep close to his feet. Now, they all talked together about the events of the day: the giraffes gliding with their eyes in the sky; how dry it was, how low the streams and lily-laden creeks, and what a shock it had been to see the wildebeest suddenly charge out between the blackthorn trees, heads down, feet swathed in dust.

The colonel pulled himself up and out of the pool. His shoulders bunched; he rose elegantly. Emily saw his neat, low waist, the slopes of his hipbones, the pale flesh of his buttocks—before realizing that he was naked. Once out of the pool, he lay on a black length of towel, flat on his back, his arm curled under his head. He was not as relaxed as he seemed, but he got up lightly and filled a glass with whiskey from a bottle beneath the parasol. He drank from the glass heavily, then refilled it, replacing the bottle in a bucket of ice.

It was obvious that they had been there for some time; there were the remains of tea, sponge cake, and biscuits, a white teapot and paper-thin china cups with curly handles. Presently, Gerard got out of the water. He, too, was naked, his body long and lean, beautifully proportioned, with strong muscular shoulders and arms. He rubbed himself vigorously with a towel and sat down fairly close to the colonel, his knees drawn up to his chin, his face now becoming rigid.

Emily, watching them, felt in a trance, a removed state, as though she looked down on these things from a height. She had

never seen a naked man. The beauty of Gerard's body was a profound shock. She had seen the little piccanins of course, but, as they
grew older, they donned small skin loincloths that tied at the back
above naked buttocks. But they were different somehow, another
species. What she had seen filled her with awe and alarm. She felt
hot and restless and then, in sudden rage, wanted something to happen, something to disturb the close camaraderie of the other sex,
who seemed to be locking her out. If she had been made differently,
she thought bitterly, if she had one of those things, those red-hot
pokers, she could just saunter in there and join them. But she was
quick to discipline herself. That, after all, was not her purpose
here. She had a purpose; it might appear to be that of a simple
observer, a voyeur even, but it was far, far more. She was an insti-
gator, a stirrer of magic; someone who could will things to happen;
who could peer into the crevices of people and delve among their
desires, and pluck out the one thing, the vital thing, that only
needed to be drawn out into the light for it to properly exist.

The colonel was asleep. Gerard looked down at him. He smiled
nastily. Emily realized that she was not close enough. The air was
beginning to whir, to crackle with some electric power. She worked
her way carefully around the side of the fence and dug out a little
peephole that allowed a view of all that was happening. Timmy
now climbed out of the water and began eating some sponge cake,
his face still wet, so that water dripped onto the cake. Gerard was
reclining on one hip, still surveying the colonel closely, who
seemed vulnerable under the youth's scrutiny. Their nakedness had
become immaterial now; something far deeper and darker was at
work. Gerard looked hectic with plotting. Emily realized with a
shock, which immediately ceased to be shock, that he had been
putting on an act earlier, that his friendliness and ease with his
uncle had been a sham.

Gerard went up to Timmy and slapped the cake out of his hand.
Timmy's mouth flew open; the cake fell onto the grass sodden with
water and jam. Gerard whispered something with a fierce, intense
gesture, piercing his brother's arm with his nails. The boy backed
away, his left eye huge and almost rolling, the hurt one shrunk
purple in its socket. Timmy was trying to make himself run away;

he looked behind him and turned toward the gate. Gerard tightened his grip; then, with a visible effort of will, he pulled his face into a different expression: he began to laugh softly as though explaining a joke. Timmy relaxed, bent and reached for another piece of cake. Gerard led him gently by the arm over to the colonel. Very gently the two of them, one lifting, one tying, bound the colonel's ankles and then his wrists firmly but not tightly with a silk dressing gown cord cut into two pieces. They used Boy Scout knots. The colonel, who had been breathing heavily, almost with difficulty, woke up and laughed to find himself a captive. Timmy sat on his stomach and began to tickle him under his armpits. The colonel began to wiggle and giggle; his face took on a fatuous, totally undignified expression quite appalling to Emily, who had always seen him as the essence of manliness and decorum. Now he was like a kid or, rather, worse, like a soppy adult trying to suck up to kids.

It was getting dark and a little cold. The moon made a shy, solemn appearance. Gerard seemed to grow impatient; his eyes looked stark; his cheekbones darkened and lengthened. With a swift, violent movement, he dragged the colonel by his arms off his towel across the slippery tiles, so that he balanced on the edge of the pool. Between clenched teeth, but forcing a totally unnatural laugh, Gerard ordered Timmy to help him push the colonel into the water. Timmy knew now that something was dreadfully wrong, but he was unable to resist; he bent with the automatic obedience instilled in him all his life by his devotion, his fear, his shared guilt with his brother, and took the colonel's legs.

The colonel said angrily, "Pack it in, Gerard; if this is your idea of a joke, I don't think it's funny."

Gerard tipped him into the water. He landed on his face sharply, as though he fell on glass. Gerard was in after him and pressed his ducking head back under the water, back and back, methodically, his hands over the colonel's mouth. The water churned, the colonel's body bobbed, powerless, clumsy. His eyes were wild with terror beneath the water, his mouth opened wide as it escaped Gerard's gagging hand, his teeth snapped, trying to enter Gerard's flesh. The colonel fought like a devil, thrashing his body about, his feet unable to touch the bottom of the pool. Gerard was very carefully wearing him down, preventing him from snatching more than the tiniest gulp of air as he surfaced, before being relentlessly pushed under again. Once, the colonel managed to butt his head into Gerard's stomach, winding the cool, ruthless intensity of his maneuvers. In a spasm of terror, Gerard smashed his uncle's head against the concrete side of the pool. The mythical painted snakes stared on and up from the bottom of the pool, unconcerned, as a red lily sprouted on the surface of the water beside the colonel's blow. Timmy whimpered and collapsed in a heap. Barely glancing at his brother, Gerard now began to exert all his strength—his eyes bulged and reddened, his bottom lip jutted forward, as he held his uncle's head down, down, down. His hair clung to his forehead, his muscles looked as though they must crack the skin of his shoulders. A minute passed. And then another. Eternity. The water gurgled gently with laughter. The submerged body became a soft, yielding thing; little round bubbles popped up. The body rose, the arms lifted as if in a gesture of tired abandon; the gray-gold hair was thick and languid.

The boy, beside himself, dragged his own slack and spent body out of the pool. He began wildly to dance and stamp his feet, raising his arms to some primitive god up beyond the moon's solitary fang. A slow hissing sound came from his mouth, his head rocked back and forward like a snake. Then he whooped, he howled, his feet thumped, his back arched, he beat his hands upon his chest. He began to swirl; around and around he went, spinning on his own laughter, tears pouring down his cheeks. He stopped, he put his hands up and out, looking up at the sky as if presenting a gift. He was at peace now: innocent, tribal, triumphant. He collapsed in exhaustion and lay quite still.

The growing cold woke him, quickened him to where he was, what he had done. A European again, he grew purposeful, cunning, the coverer of tracks. He lowered himself into the water, as Timmy rose up with dead eyes and a lolling head. Little guttural sounds were emanating from his throat. "Dress," Gerard ordered, and the boy moved, picked up his clothes and began to cover his body with them, slowly, in confusion. He did not shiver; he did not speak.

Gerard unwound the cords, making sure no marks showed. The

blow on the head had been a good thing after all. He walked over to the whiskey bottle and, carefully measuring his steps, dropped it onto the tiles. The golden liquid ran into the water. Gerard returned to his uncle's body; he pulled the head above the water; the blood still seeped. He scooped some blood into his hand and let the head fall back; then he spattered the blood on the side of the pool, near the whiskey and broken glass.

"I'm a genius," the boy whispered; then, feeling that he was about to be sick, he climbed out of the pool and began to dress.

PART TWO

And how can there ever be any real
beginning without forgiveness?
LAURENS VAN DER POST

T HE TRAIN CHUGGED ALONG DESOLATE WASHES OF SANDY terrain, sprinkled with thorn trees and the odd riveled carcass of a buck or hare. The air shimmered with the pure stillness of drought before rain. Black tussocks of smoke blew back through the window, lining Emily's nose and ears with grime. She sat looking out of the window, smiling, cradling the sun in her lap.

Her father had handed her her suitcase and an orange and thought all was well. Her mother, when Emily had gone in to say good-bye, barely lifted her head from the rumpled pillow. She stared at her daughter with a certain vindictiveness that Emily did not question. The expression was so often there: it was general, not particular. Once, long ago, its withering beam had set the child puzzling for hours upon what she might have done to occasion such blame—for it was blame that she read there. Now she shrugged it off, would not be burdened by it. For she had changed.

After the party she had tried to comfort her mother. She had wanted to sit by her bed and pass a tumbler of iced water, an aspirin, an orange cut into eight. On one occasion, she had waited beside the bed as her mother slept and not moved for hours. During this vigil she had been gathering all her courage to ask her mother a question.

Lilian woke; she took the glass of water and drank from it, a little sip, as though the water hurt her, then pushed the glass away. Lilian looked at Emily, who knew that this was her chance and she must take it. Her mouth watered with dread; her hands went damp and chilly, but she was brave. She expelled it quietly—"Do you love me?"

Lilian panicked. Her mind began milling about like an insect above an electric light, trying to find a place to settle in safety. She pulled the pillow about, reached for another sip of water.

"Don't be silly," she mumbled.

It was impossible for the child, whose heart had emptied, quite drained away.

On the train, Emily forced herself to chew on these thoughts. Then she began to look with total absorption out of the window as the train shunted into another little siding just like the last: a strip of cement plonked down on another little outpost of civilization, this time, Gaberones. A flat building with a bench in front of it, a few newly planted trees and hordes of small piccanins jumping up at the train windows with thin outstretched arms, "Give me bonsella, give me penny." The guard shouting "Voetsak" as they swirled in their own dust and regrouped farther down the line, presenting small carved animals and skin bags for sale. Emily threw out her father's orange. She intended it for a sickly girl who stood quietly at the back. As the orange hit and split in the sand, all the brown bodies doubled down in a flash, as hands began scrabbling and punching for the orange. Which eventually was borne off in triumph by the biggest boy there, who, by the luck of the biggest, had also snatched up a half-smoked cigarette. Finding no other gratuities, they began to shuffle cheerfully in the sand, waiting for the train to pull out.

Emily settled back in her seat as the train pulled out again, as the leaping piccanins became smaller and smaller, until their waving hands were gone. The train roared on, faster and faster toward Lobatse.

She was shuffling and stacking things in her mind, slowly, tidily, so that she could see what they represented. Some evil had gone out of her. She felt certain of it. But it confused her, because surely she must be the epitome of all evil: she had witnessed a murder; she could, just by calling out, have prevented it. Yet she had not, she had participated by watching, by provocation. It had been her murder, too. That was the crux of it, that was it. It had been her murder, too. The evil in her had been earthed and neutralized by the colonel's murder. He had been the victim; he had stood in for the murder she wished in her heart.

And now she wondered, was it true? Was it real? Had it been dream or sleep? Where had it happened—in her heart or out there by the pool? Now all she was left with was not the memory of the deed but its effect. It had left her clean, light, grown—and because she was altered, she was free, extraordinarily, wonderfully free.

The train jerked into Lobatse. The steward asked if she would be taking lunch. No, she said, as adults mouth words, with conviction, "No, I get off here." She began to gather her things together, ran a hand through her hair and squinted at her face in the mirror. With a suitcase in one hand and wearing her brave new face, she marched down the corridor to the end and out of the door onto the platform.

Two figures were coming toward her, smiling warmly. She turned and glanced behind her, but the smiles were aimed at her. She saw a short, square man; as he walked his arms parried the air and reminded her of a boxer. The woman was taller than he was, dark haired, with olive skin. Her arms and legs were slender, as was her waist, but her hips were large and she walked with a rolling amble. When they came closer, Emily could see that the man's face was as squarely shaped as his body; he had fierce amber eyes, a mop of wiry golden hair and a dimple in his chin. The woman's face was longer, with the large brown eyes of a meek animal. She had a wide, gentle mouth and her cheeks were flushed. She was wearing a red dress with little yellow bees flying all over the cotton.

"Emily?" they both asked together. She nodded shyly.

The man grabbed and hugged her so that the air thumped out of her mouth.

"You're strangling her, Henri." The woman laughed, then kissed Emily on both cheeks and began to lead her away by the arm. The girl was overwhelmed.

"I'm Rena, this is Henri, the girls are in the truck." Henri picked up the suitcase as though it were a basket of eggs and followed them. Emily walked lightly, no longer conscious of her ugly white shoes, which were too big for her. There was a blue truck in the road outside the station; standing up in the back were two girls, one a little older than Emily and one of about sixteen. They jumped down off the truck to say hello. They both had long, very gold hair; it was scraped back from their foreheads and plaited all the way down their backs. Emily touched her stubby brown hair with shame. But her suitcase was tossed into the back; the two girls put one foot on the running board, one on the wheel hump, and hoisted themselves into the back. Emily did the same. The truck revved up, the wheels snarked in the sand, made a turn, and then roared out of the little dorp.

The wind plugged their mouths and sent the pigtails flying straight out behind them, as the two girls, who'd been introduced as Joy and Jean, yelled at Emily to hold tight as they sped through empty bush on a dead-straight road that only once boasted another traveler: an African, walking with a battered suitcase and his coat draped over the back of his head. The truck screeched to a halt and Henri spoke to the native in Setswana for a moment, then motioned to the back of the truck. The man clambered up gracefully and sat down in the corner farthest from the girls, his knees drawn up tight, nodding and grinning at them, amazed by his good fortune.

"Jesus, what a pong!" Joy, the eldest, said.

After an hour's drive, they reached two white arched walls with a long grid stretched between them, and a sign that said Bonnington. Here Henri stopped and the African climbed down, thanked Henri profusely and continued on a long journey that would take him two more days' walking before it was completed. The truck bumped over the cattle grid and up a long drive with a flat L-shaped house at the end of it. It was surrounded by lush green grass, a low white wall with creeping bougainvillea and, beyond that, mulberry, quince, and fig trees, and a tennis court.

"We're home," Henri said proudly. "We built the house in the shape of an L, for le Roux and for luck and, by God, we've been lucky!"

"Not really," Rena said gently, remembering the droughts, the disasters with cattle. "You've worked hard, that's all."

"Well, I'm lucky to be able to, then," he said brightly, and prodding Joy in the side, he said, "Go on, then, show Emily around the place before lunch."

A veranda lapped the whole length of the grass in front of the house like a moat—behind it, a long line of rooms. The drawing room was dark and cool, with family photographs on polished surfaces. Beyond this, the kitchen: a huge, homely room with a wooden table and chairs, gauzed windows and doors, and a big old-fashioned stove that pelted out heat like a train. Long lines of biltong hung in the pantry. Some strangely dressed African women were busy heaping the table with dishes of food.

Emily was then taken to the girls' room and she stood back in surprise to enter a room as large as a dormitory, containing eight neat beds, four on either side.

Jean laughed and said, "There are eight of us, eight girls and one boy. Two of my sisters are married, two are nurses, and the other two are on holiday in Cape Town. Do you want to sleep here, or on your own?"

Emily thought hard. "I'll sleep here," she said firmly, and they chose her a bed.

A servant came in and put down her suitcase. He was introduced as Nature, and he kept ducking his head and grinning, saying ,"Nice to meet your acquaintance, missy."

They went to lunch, the first of a fortnight's gorgeous lunches, when the whole family sat together in the kitchen and feasted on cold venison or beef, with big soup plates full of salads and hot homemade bread and butter.

In the kitchen Emily stared at the African women. She had never seen such lovely black women. They were tall and slim, with long foreheads and gently sloping eyes and soft, fine skin. The one adjective that seemed to suit them best was noble. They stood very straight, wearing long, Victorian-style cotton dresses and high, beautifully folded turbans. One looked at Emily closely and quietly pronounced, "She should be called the goat." Rena smiled and assured Emily that it was a compliment: one who was hardy, determined, surefooted.

Henri looked up from carving thick slabs of cold beef and asked, "You've not seen Damara women before?"

"No."

Henri smiled and turned to them respectfully, "Well, they're not women, they're ladies." The elegant women smiled coyly at one another and carried on with their work, while Henri slapped the meat down on plates and explained, "They came originally from Southwest Africa; they rose up against the Germans there, who in turn destroyed their tribe. Those who survived fled over here. The women looked down; their faces did not flicker. They laid the plates down; they spoke and offered food with exquisite courtesy and then retired.

"It's a funny thing," Henri continued, "they've never been depraved by their misfortune, never forgot their customs—they're loyal and courageous people. When you think how those stinking Hottentots were completely ruined by a little tobacco and whiskey. It just goes to show that you can't make generalizations about the natives."

Emily was later to see a completely different side to this man, this farmer of Huguenot stock, who refused to respect anyone not deserving of it and who could be quite ruthless if any laborer was lazy or impudent. His theory, which he explained to Emily, was that the native, generally, had to be treated like a dog. When he came to you, unbroken, undisciplined, you had to fight him, physically sometimes, to make him know you were the boss. He did it with his workers. And in return, they thought him a god; they worshiped his autocratic savagery and worked harder for him than they would for anyone else. He had built a school for the African children with his own money. Education being to them better than gold, he felt he deserved their devotion forever. Mostly he got it. Their wives brought little presents to Rena, and their small boys begged to work in her garden. It was Rena they loved with pure adoration, unsullied by fear; they called her the dove, and it was a legend among her servants that she had never been known to shout at anyone.

Emily was happy. For the first few days she explored the farm. The two girls often went off with their father to the other lands in the truck. Emily stayed behind; she was not ready to hazard her happiness by sharing it with other people. There was a dam with an island of trees in the center, where wild birds roosted. The piccanins used to bang into the water off the rocks, clutching their knees and yelling. She watched them walking around the dam throwing stones in the water. The country here was far drier than where she had come from. There was no river to encourage trees and flowers; water was stored in large reservoirs and dams. This was the bush: every morning the sun shot into the sky and hung there threateningly. The thorn trees creaked; the insects shuffled and sang incessantly; the sands stretched on forever.

Emily began to spend her time with Rena in the store. This was a little way from the house, facing the main road. In the shady stoep in front of the store, Africans crouched, their feet cracked open by the heat and dust, wiping the sweat from their faces and lifting the heavy cloth bundles from their heads. The occasional truck rumbled in, but mostly the store was for Africans. Inside, Rena sat in one corner, firmly behind the till. Henri insisted on this —"You can't trust any bleddy native, they all steal," he used to snap, as if this was a disease peculiar to Africans behind tills. So Rena had to be there all day long, though she sometimes crept away for short spells, when she thought she had found a boy she could trust. But Henri was right; they all stole, and she could not get too angry because she knew why, even if he didn't. She did not admit it, but she resented a little having to spend her days trapped in the strange, musty odor of the store, knitting, always in white, for her grandchildren. To keep the wool clean, she frequently dusted her fingers with Johnson's Baby Powder and kept the ball of wool in a soft muslin bag; and it was as if these things kept at bay the flies, the dust gathering on bottle tops, the noise and the smell, the stifling dreariness of each day.

Emily would watch Rena's fingers dart over the clicking needles:

she would suck the boiled sweets and gobstoppers constantly offered—but mostly, she would just stare at Rena's bent head, at her high, round cheeks and dusky skin, at the mouth always curved and free of tension. Once she blurted out, "I wish you were my mother," and felt guilty.

Rena said quietly, "But you've got such a pretty little mother, she's so dainty and smart. I'm just a big lump beside her."

Emily had to be calmed down: she thought Rena perfect. She was one of those women whose clothes seem determined to get as close to the flesh as possible. Whatever she wore seemed to accentuate her roundness. Emily thought it was wonderful, how a woman should be. Rena hated it.

The two of them would sit swatting flies as Africans came in and out. They spent hours in the store, looking, feeling, comparing, discussing—and then beginning all over again. There were fat rolls of crisp, rough cottons in splashy colors; these were kept up on high shelves and had to be handed down for inspection. The roof of the store was hung with bicycle tires and wheels, blankets, saucepans and kettles, paraffin tins, and spades. Most of the floor space was taken up by large sacks of grain, mealie meal, sugar, dried milk, and groundnuts. The front displays showed great jars of sweets. There were pots of Pond's Vanishing Cream, Vaseline, disinfectants, tins of condensed milk, and salt, and beads of all shapes and colors. The small children were always given a milk lolly or a handful of sweets after their mothers had unknotted their handkerchiefs of coins and made their purchases.

The days passed too quickly. Once or twice Emily went with Henri and his daughters to the mealie lands on his other farms. He used to wake at five, eat a hearty breakfast of three eggs and a large piece of steak. He was jolly in the early morning, with that pride in the ownership of land, in watching things grow, however slowly or inadequately. It was fresh and cool, and clouds, like giant swans, burrowed in the blue. The piccanins were out trailing sticks in the sand; the women were at work in the kitchen. By six o'clock the whole farm was humming, and by this time Henri's truck was well on its way to check up on the laborers who worked the fields some distance from the farmhouse. They, when they heard the truck approaching, leaped to attention, leaving their mealie pap, and made a great show of industry. Henri would scowl convincingly, and sometimes, if he was pitched into a temper, he would get out his sjambok and pursue them into the bushes, where they would peer out like buck until he had settled down. The boss boy would be the first to come out, smiling, obsequious, "My baas, it was not as it seemed. The boys had just that very moment sat down in the shade; we have been working our idle backs off since early morning." Henri would call him a bloody liar and cuff him loudly on the head; the rest of the men would come out, knowing the danger had passed.

Emily watched the cattle being branded and sprayed; the young bulls injected and castrated under an omnipotent sun that pounded down on their heads. Large circles of sweat pooled under Henri's armpits and in a triangular shape at the back of his shirt; his face glistened; his felt hat was pushed back. He said that he worked harder than any black, and the hardest work was making the blacks work. They worked his land with the enthusiasm of all serfs: lazy, limited, uninvolved. Once it had been their land, they could not remember when.

Emily found it invigorating to be with him; he had a brute force with an undercurrent of sensuality. He and his daughters always swam naked in one of the round reservoirs before going home. The first time this happened in Emily's presence, she was shaken to her back teeth and would not take part. Looking up at the circular cement tank, which rose about eight to ten feet from the ground, she could hear them laughing and splashing as they swam about and cooled off. She longed to be there with them, but could not, her rigors were too well formed. She waited—itchy and prickled with heat—livid with the world. Afterward, Henri would ruffle her hair with a cool hand, and she wanted to reach up and hold it there.

After lunch they would all sit on the cool veranda and eat mulberries and thick cream out of glass bowls. The sugar scraping at the bottom was the only sound that accompanied the insects in the grass. Henri sat close to Rena, with his thigh pressed close to hers as they drank strong coffee with rusks. At this time of day, all things were flattened and dreary. Jean and Joy would disappear to their room; Rena lay down for half an hour and then trudged down the track to the store. Henri went off to his cattle, and Emily went out to the veld.

She walked very slowly out beyond the sheds and the barns, beyond the deserted dam with its limp willows, and on to the end of the fences. Here there was nothing. The heat flared up from the ground. She strained her eyes at the horizon, then threw her arms wide into the air, letting out a pure whoop of joy. She stripped off her white shirt, blue shorts, white pants and stood there stark naked, bleached by the light, her arms held tautly above her head. She turned, slowly, majestically, like one receiving the honor of her subjects. She felt the sole possessor of the veld. All the menace of the thorn trees had become submissive; the denuded sand, with its crusting of jewels where the sun caught their fire, was hers, hers entirely. A vast emptiness bore down on the lone girl and intoxicated her, so that she began to leap and dance, seeing the giant strides of her shadow. She chased it up and down, yelling, laughing, wild with life, on the brink of it and so greedy for it that she wanted to possess it all.

She heard laughter. She knew it was him. She stamped her feet lightly as a soft summons and called out, "Shaka, Shaka," in a low, husky voice. The sun hypnotized her: she saw him, sleek and smooth and black as blood, dancing naked on lilies in an icy dawn, his plumes trembling as he clapped. He moved forward, smiling, frightful as a snake.

She was faint; her head whirled one way, her stomach the other. She knelt in the sand and dropped her head down onto her knees and stayed there, aware suddenly of her thirst, of the harsh smarting of her skin. The smell of her sweat came to her. She got dressed and went home, blistered but exultant. In the kitchen, she put her head under the cold tap and let the water roll over her; she opened her mouth and drank.

For the next two days she lay in the dark with sunstroke. But in her own mind she had undergone some sort of initiation, and nothing that had gone before would have the same power to hurt or warp.

Every evening on the farm, a long trestle table was laid out on the grass beyond the veranda. The family gathered, Henri said grace, then settled himself to carving the venison: great slabs of dark meat served with rice and potatoes, pumpkin and beans, and a thick brown gravy. Then family or farm matters would be discussed, and as they ate, the sky became cluttered with stars and it grew colder. This was the one time of day that Emily could study the male offspring, the long-awaited son and heir. Rena had told Emily that she had always wanted a son with red hair and freckles. Finally, the ninth time around, there he was, colored in as though by a magic wish. Now, at eight, the boy was pale-skinned and shy, with his mother's gentle disposition and little of his father's toughness.

Danny Boy seemed to know that his father was disappointed in him, and it crushed him. Henri felt that the boy had been unmanned by the adoration of his mother and sisters, and he meant to make good the deficiency. But Danny Boy could not be interested in guns, in cattle, and riding and chasing the kaffir dogs. He was the most placid child Emily had ever seen, yet underneath, she began to see, he was terrified: of his father, whose manliness was too strong a challenge; of the demands made on a character not yet robust enough to support them. And he was livid, too, for not being allowed to go his own way. Emily watched him and it hurt her to see him suffer, because now, for the first time, she had begun to study other people with compassion.

But after dinner, Henri would settle himself on the swing and ask Danny Boy to fetch his ukulele. Then, as the Damara women cleared the table, he would begin to strum. Emily was impressed by the way Rena thanked the women—as one would thank a friend, with proper gratitude. They knew the difference and would do anything for her because of it. Henri's rich voice would boom out "Sarie Marais," "Sally," and "My Old Man Says Follow the Band," and the swing creaking and the clattering ukulele filled Emily with a wide sense of freedom.

On other nights, things were different. The eating was disposed of as a mere necessity, and then they would dress in warm clothes, coats even, and all climb up on the back of the blue lorry, with guns and rugs and a flask of brandy. Rena did not come shooting; she would wait up till everyone came home and then make hot coffee. The truck rumbled off to the lands. Joy sat in the front with her father; Jean, Danny Boy, and Emily stood up on the back and took turns to jump off and open and close gates on the way. When they arrived at the big lands, someone on the back of the truck, Danny Boy usually, held a large flashlight, which he trained on the far fields looking for the bright night eyes of the buck. The truck bumped slowly along the track.

Two silver sparks are caught and held in the beam of the flash-light. Emily bangs on the roof of the cab, it stops quietly, as though the machine itself were part of the conspiracy. Danny Boy holds the flashlight absolutely still; the springbuck is hypnotized, stunned into a quivering stillness, his eyes like tiny beacons in the sur-rounding blackness. The gun is aimed and fired. The night cracks open; two blue neons are put out, there is a little faraway thud.

"You got him," Joy says with casual approval and leaps out of the truck. Danny Boy, his flashlight still faithfully gazing at the empty place, begins to shiver and cough.

"Come and get him with me, boy," Henri calls gaily, offering his son this trophy. But the boy holds back, then reluctantly, as though he has no option, clambers off the truck and makes his way across the field, but does not attempt to catch up with his father, who is already some way ahead.

"Get the sacks ready to lie him on," Joy ordered, taking a swig from the brandy flask.

"Hey, don't do that," Jean said, grabbing the flask from her sister's mouth, so that it spilled down her front.

"Now look what you've done; he wouldn't have noticed other-wise, damn you!"

"Well, now he will," Jean said tenderly. "You get away with too much around here."

"Ag, he wouldn't care," Joy said, and she tipped it again, then looked out across the moonlit fields with her hands on her hips. Emily was impressed.

Soon Henri and Danny Boy returned, dragging the buck. Danny Boy was breathing heavily. His father was worried about him and this made him impatient. "Go on, leave it. I can manage."

Danny Boy dropped the buck's hoof and seemed to wipe his hands against his khakis, nervously, repeatedly. Joy, with her father, hoisted it up onto the back of the truck.

"Well, that'll do for meat; we'll just knock off a few of those blasted springhares." And Henri stood back in satisfaction: the hunter who has filled the pot.

"Do you eat the hares?" Emily asked.

"God, no, the dogs do. But the hares are a pest; they root up the plants and make their burrows among my best crops. Here, you have a shot at one. I'll hold the gun a bit."

The first shot was like a kick in the shoulder; Emily reeled back and Henri laughed—she'd missed the hare by bleddy miles, he said. She had one more try and nearly got one. This made her decide to practice daily on the target. There was a strange exhilaration in a gun, a sense of belonging to a long line of hunters, warriors—a brave order of men. They drove back to the farm singing. Henri drove like a madman; they held onto the grille at the back for dear life, banging into one another and shrieking with laughter. Emily's face was radiant, ringing with happiness.

In the store the following day, a child came begging for some old clothes. She was wearing a tattered rag, the discarded dress of a European child, which both her sisters had worn before her. As she spoke, barely a whisper, her eyes flared in humiliation, then dropped. Her belly was swollen with hunger, and her knees were grotesquely large on the twiglike limbs. Rena opened the big drawer at the bottom of her desk and pulled out some of her children's old clothes. She handed some to the child, who ducked her knee; and then handed her a lump of bread and a handful of sweets. The child opened out her hands for the sweets, and for Emily, watching, a familiar shock returned: those pale pink palms, like ours, like ours; pink tongues and gums—just the same. She could not understand why she so often felt frightened. She remembered how when the Chief and his wife had come one evening for a drink—an extraordinary thing which happened rarely —her mother had put out the oldest glasses. Emily had watched her wash out these glasses again after they had been washed by the servants.

"But we're the same," Emily began in confusion. Before Rena could reply, the boss boy at the store had gone up to the child and taken some of the clothes from her. He addressed Rena gravely, "Missus, this is a wrong idea; the child will show these to others who will want as many. Just give her one, then no more will come."

"But they always come, Michael."

"I know, missus, and you always give too much. It's a bad encouragement."

"Oh, let her have them," Rena said wearily. "Please, just this time."

He handed the pile back ungraciously. "Madam, you do not understand these people," he said, offended. "To give is only to make others want." And so it was, Rena thought; nothing you could do was enough, or the right thing. But to do nothing was unthinkable. She watched the child leave the store, looking back at Michael, holding her clothes proudly, fiercely, as if she had paid heavily for them.

Outside, three o'clock, with the sun high in the sky, the afternoon sprawled like a fat, lazy woman. An old Land Rover pulled up outside with a squeak of brakes, and Rena, without lifting her head from her knitting, said quietly, "That will be Willie Swart." She pronounced the *W* as a *V*.

Emily looked up as a thickset, obviously Afrikaans man walked in. You could tell by the shape of his head: squat at the top and moving down to a narrow jutted jaw. His hair was cut almost in a crew cut. His face was lean for his body; the skin dark and stretched by the sun; his eyes, from squinting, seemed narrow, burrowing in among the creases.

"How are you, Willie?" Rena asked, and Emily thought it a

feigned politeness. He did not bother to answer her. He began to speak in a gruff, dissatisfied way about the fact that there had been no rain; he had damn all left to feed his cattle on.

"You should build a silo perhaps," Rena said gently. They themselves had a number of these huge, high storage tanks for fodder.

"What with, man?" He slid his hand angrily under his nose. "We're not all bleddy loaded with it. You want to be a poor Afrikaner, man, and see how you like it."

He was off again. Rena prepared herself to hear him out. "We've never recovered from it, from those bleddy British. I'm telling you, they'd rather give it to the kaffirs than to us. You don't know how it was for my folks—hell, man, hell, I'm telling you."

"But that was long ago, Willie," and her hand rose to smooth the black curls of her forehead, where a blue vein throbbed.

"You think it's different now, hey? To be an Afrikaner around here is still to be pig shit. It may be different in the Free State or the Transvaal, not here, you better believe it."

"Oh, I know you've had bad luck, Willie. Did your boys come back, by the way?"

"Which boys?"

Rena looked at him, puzzled, then recalled that he had a way of forgetting things; sometimes even accusing people of making up stories about him.

"You know, the ones who ran off, went back to the bush."

"Oh, those. Well, some of them came back with their tails between their legs: I might not be able to pay them regularly like the rich, but at least I can pay them once in a while." He laughed savagely.

"Perhaps, Willie, if you weren't so hard on them, were a little less free with the sjambok, they'd work better, stay, even if you couldn't always pay them on time?"

"Ag, you're too soft, man. Kaffirs hate weakness; they don't respect you unless you slap them down. They like it; they like to be kicked about, it's what they understand."

Emily wondered why he should be saying this, when he obviously thought he'd been kicked around and he clearly didn't like it.

"Everyone responds to kindness, Willie," Rena said evenly.

"Not kaffirs," he said firmly. "Look, man, God made black and white, He separated night and day, we must just carry on what he started. . . ."

Rena backed and changed direction. "How's Lottie? I've been meaning to go along and see her. I'll go later today if she's there."

"She's always there."

"How is she?" Emily noticed, with surprise, a little clipped chord in the tone of the question.

"The same." Then, angrily, "I don't know, how should I know . . . but there's a weakness there, I'm telling you, there must be some blood that's not Afrikaans in Lottie. She was never what she should have been."

Rena did not raise her voice, but her eyes were flashing with indignation. "She's had a very bad time, Willie; how can you talk like that? I'll go around this afternoon with Emily," Rena said briskly, and turned to smile at the girl. "Emily's staying with us for a bit. Now, was there anything you wanted from the store?"

"Yes, I wanted a sack of sugar and a roll of barbed wire. You'll put it on the slate?"

"Willie, you know Henri goes crazy when you don't pay cash."

"Look, man, I'll pay you at the end of the week, I promise you, I'm getting rid of a few of my cows."

Rena looked at him with pity, with shame. Willie's deficiencies had to be covered, had to be hidden, or else what disorder might descend and threaten them all.

Rena said sharply to the black man listening, "Go and put Mr. Swart's things in the back of his Jeep."

The native smiled mockingly and very slowly went about his business.

When it was a little cooler, Rena drove the old van down a pot-holed rough track. Stones clonked against the underbelly and thorn bushes scraped at the paint. Finally, she pulled up at a rusty gate. Just before Emily jumped out to open it, she laid her hand protectively on the girl's arm and said, "This is a sad place, Em, and I don't want it to upset you."

Emily unhooked the gate, climbed on the first rung and gave herself a big push with one foot that sent her swinging right to the other side of a very rough track. They drove down it carefully; it was covered by weeds and blackjacks, and previous rains had made deep ruts on its surface.

At the end of the track was a solitary farm, raising mealies and a small herd of cattle. The cattle were nearly all gone. Willie Swart was a drinker and as he ran out of booze, so he ran out of cattle. As they drove up they could see on either side the weeds taking over and strangling the mealies; they were scraggy and brown; some had not bothered to grow at all. Chickens that had not yet been stolen squawked and ran in all directions. Two mangy kaffir dogs lay panting in the shade from the roof to the stoep, spit dripping from their jaws. A dead creeper was hanging in brown rags across the windows. Rena stopped the van, and they got out and began to walk toward a dilapidated, one-story house with a gauzed stoep in the front. The windows had once been painted green, but only small slithers of that color remained.

As they approached, the thin, plaintive melody of a Brahms lullaby rose from the center of the house. Emily, standing quite still, with her head tilted back, jerked slightly at the sawing sound of a wrong note. She hesitated. Rena took her arm and said, "She plays that piano all day long, though some notes are missing and some are stuck, and once Willie smashed a broken bottle across the top."

"What do we do?" Emily whispered.

"We'll go in and wait till she's finished playing; she sometimes gets upset if you interrupt her at the wrong moment."

Emily stared at the woman playing the piano. She wore a black dress oiled by age. He small back bent forward over the keys; she swayed a little, her head tilted to one side, her eyes closed. Once she had played at the church and at children's parties, but after it happened, she could not; she could not see people.

Now, she played to stay a little alive, as the bush crept closer, as the mealies toppled into the sand and the track to her house became obliterated by thorn bushes. Sometimes, her back would slump, her head would fall forward onto the piano. She would remain like that for hours, not knowing or caring where she was, confused when the old houseboy came to lead her gently to her room. And, Lord, what she saw in his face: the black man pitied her; he despised her! His smile could have turned milk as he led her, a victim, a slave, to her room and laid her down. When he had left, she would snatch up the striped cloth of the counterpane and stuff it into her mouth—disgusted that he should be so intimate as to touch her, to put her down and now to leave her so. He would have to go. Ah, but who would send him, who would tell him?

What she wanted was a son. But there was only the surly boy, David, Willie's nephew. He was eleven or twelve. He lived with her, having just arrived half-grown one day. He had come because he had been thrown out of the boarding school that had housed him since his mother's death. His father, Willie's brother, had deserted him. The school said David was unteachable. So he had come to help Willie on the farm; but Willie did not live there anymore and never came near the place. He had forgotten them both. He lived in a hut with a native woman. He might as well have been dead, it would have been the same. Better.

Lottie turned, and her face spun up at them like a plate thrown across the room. Rena moved forward quickly, "It's all right, Lottie, we've just come to see you for a little, don't worry."

Lottie did not seem to hear. Her skin was freckled, so were her eyes; they were a pale moss-green with flecks of brown; her mouth was long and very white. On her cheekbones two small patches of color were forming.

"Is there anything you need? Anything we can bring you?" Rena asked, desperately.

Lottie shook her head, lifting a face that reflected defeat of the quietest, most terrible kind. She turned back to the piano. Then her hands descended slowly, touched the keys. She said, "This is Bach."

Emily left the room as an animal bolts in the presence of danger. She wandered through the house, ending up in an empty kitchen. It was filthy. She stood by the window and looked out over a dusty backyard adorned with a few fig trees and a dented petrol drum. In an old tire, painted white and filled with soil, a few geraniums were growing.

Suddenly, Emily felt quite certain that someone was standing behind her. She turned quickly and let her arms fall at the same time: she caught him off his guard by the speed of her action. He had backed away from the doorway in an instant; had she taken one more step he would have disappeared. She stood quite still and waited. He moved slowly into a position where he could see her, but his body was out of sight behind the doorframe. She did not insult him with a smile. He was wearing a dirty, torn white shirt stuffed into old gray trousers that were too large for him; but it was not the disrepair of his clothing that affected her: it was the crawling red rash that covered his arms and hands, heavily scored by his nails.

She began to walk quietly toward him like a cat, fixing him where he was with her eyes. He wanted to run. His face was quivering. She stood in front of him, not too close. He turned and fled. She ran after him, through the corridor, out onto the stoep, through the door and out into the sunlight. He disappeared behind boulders and thorn trees. She chased him, running as fast as she could. She stopped and stood in an open place between boulders, confused, when again she sensed him, not behind her, but ahead of her. She waited, panting, sweating with heat and tension. He ducked out from behind a boulder and stood there, directly in front of her, blocking her way. She retreated a little. He said nothing and she knew that he could not. He was beyond speech; had discarded it because it was inadequate for his despair.

She told him her name, like someone offering a cup that held water. He took no interest. "You must get away," the words flashed out of her, straight to his center. "You have to leave, get away, get better. . . ."

His eyes opened, blinked, then emptied.

Emily knew then that he had to be rescued. She stumbled on, "Rena will do it; I'll tell her, she'll take you away. . . ." She said clearly, "Rena, the woman who came here with me, she'll come and take you from here. I promise, I promise she will help you."

When Emily reached the driveway, she saw that Rena was waiting in the van. Emily climbed in and smiled at her, but, seeing her preoccupation, said nothing. Rena started the van.

Driving back down dusty tracks, they passed the kraal that housed Willie Swart's laborers and their families. Dogs barked, and some Africans lifted their faces and watched the van pass with expressionless stares. A little band of piccanins began to run after the van, shouting and waving their hands. Emily noticed, with a shock, one and then two pale-colored children running among the coal-black piccanins. One of these, a boy of about eight, stopped suddenly. His face shook with a spasm of hatred. He picked up a rock, ran, then hurled it savagely at the van. It struck Emily's side with a hollow explosion. Rena drove on at the same speed, but her jaw and mouth stiffened, as did Emily's. Neither said a word. They drove back home past another kraal nestling into a peaceful evening ritual—profoundly aware of the forbidding calm of the evening, of the vulnerable peace of the country.

There were only a few days before she was to go home. It was early evening; the air remained clogged with heat after the sun had gone down; there was no tug of wind.

He drove up in a Jeep. He roared up the drive so fast that Rena, sitting on the veranda, swatting the air with her fan, looked up and clucked with disapproval. Emily was picking mulberries and putting them carefully into a large china bowl; they were too ripe and squashed on her fingers. Her lips were black from the juice. The face of a man looked out at her from the open window of the Jeep; he was grinning. She felt faintly dizzy.

She stopped picking and walked up to the house. She saw him leap out of the Jeep and walk, almost run, up to Rena. Her feet began to drag, she was reluctant, even her curiosity was dwarfed by this strange new shyness. It was her body that was shy. The ticking impatience mounting in her over the past month seemed now to be forming into a shape. She was at the stage when girls bite their lips with frustration, seethe and sigh and don't know why; find undecipherable messages in a catch of music, a phrase in a book, a beautiful sunset. When sadness is something almost delicious; when traps in the mind spring back to reveal a wide emptiness, an expanse waiting to be filled—with what? What? And in the night, tossing in bed, she would want to shout: When will my life begin? Something happen; something change? Oh, when is it ever going to *start*?

"This is Emily," Rena said, with an approval that made the girl want to fling herself at Rena.

"This is Emily," the man repeated as a tease, "and her mouth is black."

Emily's face flushed and her eyes burned, but he noticed and said, "But in a good cause." His hand reached toward her, dipped into the bowl and took two plump mulberries to his mouth. Her eyes gripped the hand—broad and brown, with square, cropped nails. He lounged sideways in his chair; his eyes touched her briefly and she shivered. Odd-eyed kid, he thought carelessly, before turning back to Rena.

He was telling her about a witch doctor on the farm where he worked, who had forecast rain within the next few days. Rena listened carefully and did not scoff, as her husband would have done. Emily had put down roots where she stood watching him. She saw a wide brow, heavy eyebrows, skin taut and tanned across the cheeks and chin, wide eyes like golden, glinting beads. He was laughing and his mouth seemed to insist: I'm charming, see how my teeth with their perfect white slopes catch the light, sparkle when I smile! Her nerves contracted; she saw him again: his face was lean and chiseled; there was a deep line down one cheek; his hair was thick and dark and his eyes were cold. He had a beautifully cruel face; she felt if he snarled, he would look like an executioner.

"You will stay to dinner, Patrick, won't you?" Rena asked, and he accepted. Emily noticed, now, a soft slur in his voice, which placed it outside the flattened sounds and dead vowels of the South African accent. He did not sound foreign, but on the other hand, he did not sound English.

As they sat around the table at dinner, Emily could observe his effect on everyone. Danny Boy no longer sat next to his father; Patrick did. Emily sat on the other side of Henri and shifted her chair so she could see him more clearly. The electric light from the stoep was too far away to light his face, and it seemed to her that he moved in his chair until the light fell on him. Joy was making no secret of the fact that she was not impressed. Emily saw with irritation that this caused Patrick to become, at one time, cool and confident and, in the next instance, hesitant and insecure. When these ploys failed, he tried to impress her with some story about hunting, or a long hazardous journey into the heart of Namaqualand. Joy would always steer the conversation closer to home, but her boredom was too deliberate. Jean was shy, almost speechless. Rena was relaxed and obviously took pleasure in hearing him speak; she encouraged him to dominate the conversation. Henri chewed on in his usual way, taking everything in, glad of the company of another male.

At twenty-five, Patrick was a tough, seasoned human being. He had come out from Ireland at the age of nineteen; there had been a bit of a mess with a young girl before he left. His father had a cramped little farm in Kerry; Patrick was the second son; the first had tripped off to England at fifteen. Patrick had resented any scrap of work done on his father's behalf and could not wait to get out. His mother's silent fury about the girl from the village precipitated his departure. Patrick stole his aunt's savings and fled.

By this time Patrick Gallway had traveled all over South Africa and Rhodesia. He had wanted to see everything before choosing a piece of land to settle on. He had very little money of his own, only what he had earned at various jobs—as a lorry driver or a salesman. Not having any capital meant that he had to join a farmer as a trainee, work with him for some years to test his abilities, and after that try to buy a piece of land and build his own farm. What he wanted was land that he could break, impose his will on; he was bored by the submissiveness that he inspired. He had finally found what he wanted among the hills in the Lobatse area of the Protectorate: a small farm near the Notwana river, owned by a Welshman, Trevor Owen, who had two daughters, neither in any way submissive.

At the table, Emily studied Patrick. She could imagine perfectly being married to him—living on a farm that was theirs, with cattle and horses, chickens and ducks. She knew how it would be. But not children, never children.

The table had emptied; only Rena, Patrick, and Emily remained. Emily, who had barely seen the girls go, had needed reminding to say good-night to Henri when he retired to bed at his usual hour. Patrick was talking softly. His elbow rested on the table; his right hand ploughed through his hair, then came to rest under his chin. Rena said something and Emily started into life.

"So, you'll be thinking of marrying soon, then?"

Emily's breathing stopped, as if she were a woman in a room alone with a man and another woman stepped beside him and said, "Hello, darling."

But he laughed. "Oh, no, not yet," and he turned to Emily in the same teasing way. "When she's old enough, perhaps." It was the first direct remark he had made to her all evening. It was so light, so airy, that it blew right above the two adult heads and vanished in an instant.

To Emily it had all the certainty of a written pronouncement.

She watched him pull back slowly from the table, stretch, and rise. "I'll be up so early in the morning, you won't see me," he said to Rena, "but I'll be back soon. A beautiful dinner, thank you, wish I ate so well at Owen's." Emily thought he made everything seem so easy.

They began to walk across the grass to the dimly lit veranda, where the light bulb was festooned with insects.

Emily could not bear it, could not bear to see him go, so quickly across the dark, cold grass. Turn, turn, she willed fiercely. And he turned. He saw a very young girl, wearing a full green skirt, white blouse, dull brown hair. She regarded him mournfully, her heart at his feet. He reached in his pocket, smiling; came toward her and held out a tiny silver coin.

"Here, take this tickey, and when you're sixteen, ring me. Don't forget now," and his hand touched her shoulder. He laughed, a beautiful, cold, tumbling sound.

Rena smiled gently, "Hurry to bed, Em, dear." And the door clapped to behind them. She was so cold she could not move for a while, and the thought that stoked her mind was: He's not very old; when he stood beside me, there was hardly any age in his face. Not so old, not more than twenty, and soon I'll be twelve.

The cock crowed in the blue dawn; the sun had begun to surface. She had not slept all night and had huddled by her window, looking out across the grass to the towers of the silos; to the far humps of the bluegum trees. Now the dawn had come and she would watch him go. From her window she could see the front half of his jeep. Now the door of the sitting room opened from the inside; it closed quietly. A dark, fast-moving figure walked down the length of the veranda and disappeared around the side of the Jeep. Her breath was stuck at the base of her stomach. The engine turned over. Her eyes, wide and green and fixed, opened, then clenched shut.

Two days later there was the first sign of a storm. People began to watch the sky for clouds; threw back their heads and sniffed. The splintered thorn trees, the cracked earth torn open by hooves went still, waiting. The witch doctor huddled over his bones and fur, clenched his temples, doubled up in the sand, and pressed his tongue into the dust.

The air becomes sodden, heavy with electricity; clouds pile up, then slip away. The wind rises, then sinks. Chickens climb on their perches and dogs whimper. Tiny flickers of lightning cut into a vibrating, bloody sky. It splits open as the lightning strikes, as the thunder explodes. Sand and bushes are whirled up by a ferocious wind, then discarded. A cold unearthly gloom spreads across a sky gone purple; the thorn trees are fragile, gaunt as burnt sticks.

Then it descends. The lightning is uninterrupted; jagged spikes of silver dart across a black sky, detonating every second. The rain falls, smashing at the caked earth, scraping up the soil and flinging it away in pale torrents. It rains, it rains.

At the farm, faces watch at the kitchen window, awestruck, watching the trees. Henri, recently back, having felt the signs in his knees as always, paces up and down, cursing the rain for not falling with a little temerity; for flattening his crops and rushing all the precious topsoil away. Then he laughs, and takes a little swirl with Emily, saying, "Think how the dams and reservoirs are filling. Think how the ducks are loving it! And the kaffirs happy as hell doing nothing!"

In the kraal, the Africans who had been singing and dancing with a frenzied urgency are now huddled happily inside their huts. The witch doctor smiles and demands a drink; when he gets it, he feels he can ask for another and another. Children peer around the corners of the huts, then fling themselves under their blankets as the spirits boom down in unison. The women hum and oil their bodies; the men nod and smile and make barriers from old planks against the open doorways. They will sing all night.

The rain that whisked the koppies away in a torrent of silver light, stopped. The wind tearing up and down the treetops settled down like a tired, unruly child at bedtime. Water jumps off rocks, then begins a slow trickle. The sun comes up. The day is as clean, as sharp, as a whistle.

Emily walked out with Rena and Jean to the rough veld beyond the dam. This was a pilgrimage that Rena and her daughter had made together many times before, but Emily felt resentful of Jean's presence, wanting the experience this time to be hers exclusively. When they reached the long stretch of sand, she stopped, they all stopped, filled with wonder. Small wild iris and primulas had thrust straight up out of the sand; among the rocks, red, purple, and mauve clusters of tiny windflowers had blown into life. Emily bent, pressed her nose close and snuffed in a delicate scent of honey, which disappeared immediately, as though it offered one inhalation only. The bush seemed to sing below a sky deep blue and generous; thorn trees had broken into bud; rough bushes were dusted with blossom and the rocks put on green. The birds were thick in the trees. Animals wooed one another, and in the distance, a herd of springbuck came prancing, leaping six feet up into the air. Way beyond, Africans were out collecting wild carrots, cucumbers, little gold melons, and magic herbs. Emily knew that at home, by the river, white lilies would have appeared near the rushes and the weaverbirds and speckled starlings would be competing noisily for territory. She was suddenly overcome by longing for what she knew best, what she loved with the passion of familiarity.

And, in that moment, knew also, with a shock sharp as a cut, that Julian had gone, gone forever.

It was 4:00 A.M. and black on the platform. Emily stood with her father, a small white suitcase clutched in her hand; a large square black trunk beside her. She turned to look at the railway hut with its white bench and then at the separate shack with a corrugated roof, which was for Africans. The train would thunder in on its way to Rhodesia, stop for a few minutes, then roar out again. She was nervous and excited. Her father said nothing. Then the train came in, filling her nostrils with a spicy smell of smoke. It shunted; it stopped.

Emily's father was hurriedly running down the length of the train, looking at the labels in the windows. "Here, this is it," he called, and she picked up her suitcase and waited for him to come back, so they could both carry the trunk and get it onto the train. He was bad-tempered, worried that the train would pull out again, leaving either the trunk or the child behind. He snapped at her and she stiffened against him again, though the idea of going away had a moment before almost saddened her. He began to curse the railways, said there should be a guard, someone to bloody well help—and couldn't she hurry up, for God's sake. She was startled again by the promiscuity of his hatred. He banged his ankle on the corner of the trunk and swore again. They managed to drag it up the stairs and push it into a corner. Emily noticed the name "le Roux" on the window of the compartment and felt relieved that at least she was not alone; Joy and Jean would be asleep, but they'd be there in the morning.

She stood by the window of the train; her father stood on the platform, looking about him. The train jerked. He stretched up, kissed Emily quickly—told her to behave herself, told her to pull up the window. She looked at him through the glass as the train shuddered out, waved once, saw him turn to go.

She felt cold and rubbed her arms with her hands. The dark countryside began to race by; faster and faster it went, while the rhythm of the train was as comforting as far drums. Still holding onto the white suitcase, she slid back the door and entered a compartment which breathed in, out, in, out. One of the lower berths was empty; it had a little package on the pillow marked with her name. She sat down and carefully peeled off the paper. In a box inside was a thin gold bracelet, and on a link hung a gold cow with a pinprick of green stone for her eye. A white card with Rena's writing on it said, "All best wishes and lots of love for your first term at Santa Maria's, Rena and Henri." Tucked down the side of the box was another small piece of paper, which read, "I thought you'd like to know that I took Lottie back to stay with her sister in Kroonstad. David is living with us for a bit and Danny Boy has actually managed to get him to talk—only a few words, but it's a start."

Emily turned out the light above her head. She felt her eyes filling with tears and marveled at the kindness of life.

She woke with the sun tickling her face. She felt as though she'd been shaken and stirred all night, and the train was still at it. The bunk was hard and the sheet had come away, exposing a slippery surface to which one of her legs had stuck.

"Oh, so you've arrived," Jean said, sitting up, her eyes narrow from lack of sleep; her hair tied back in a coiling bush, now that the plait was unbound.

"Hm," Emily said, watching the girl's hair crinkle in the sunlight. "Thanks for your mother's present; it really cheered me up."

"That's okay. You nervous about starting school?"

"Hell, no."

"You will be when you get there," Joy said grimly, letting down a long pair of tanned legs from the top bunk. "Bloody dump it is; the nuns are foul; not a bit of freedom now for three long months. Jesus, I'll go mad." She jumped down lightly and went to the small round table by the window; she lifted the metal cover and it became a basin.

"At least you've only got one more year," Jean observed placidly.

"If that bitch, Immaculata, doesn't kick me out first."

"She won't. She thinks she's done worse by resigning from the unequal struggle for your soul. You're lucky: she's given you up."

Jean turned to Emily and said with a frown, "Hey, Em, you'd better know, she won't take kindly to you, not being a Catholic, I mean . . ."

"You're damned, kiddo, eternal flames—that's what she means." Joy grinned, tipping her body forward to shake her large breasts into her white cotton bra.

"Shut up," Jean said. "It's just that she's, they're, all the nuns, I mean, are a bit bitchy to the girls who aren't Catholics—not directly, of course, but in an underhanded way—like making them attend all the services without giving them any of the perks."

"What perks?" Joy scoffed.

"Well, what I mean is," Jean continued patiently, "like the lily that is put on everyone's plate at Easter, except for the non-Catholics; like the fact that they never get a new missal or veil, but some tatty old thing. . . ."

"Of course, if you'd consider being converted to the true, the only faith, well, that would be another matter," Joy said.

"I'm not really religious at all, in any way," Emily said. "But I went to the Sunday school a few times when I was little," she added hopefully.

Joy laughed. "Hell, how odd, no religion!"

"If you've never had a religion, you just might like it," Jean said dreamily, remembering the pleasure she had once found in the Lent rituals.

"Once we had a Jewish girl at school," Joy remarked, now completely dressed, but stuffing her feet into a pair of grimy tennis shoes. "She had to come; there was no other school for her to go to. But the first Easter she was there, some of the girls got over-excited, stirred up by inflammatory remarks made by the angelic penguins, of course—about evil Jews, murderers, etc. etc. Some girls hung her up by the wrists from a beam in the gym. They left her there all night with a black hood over her head. The next day she was asked to leave the school. The nuns said that she was a bad influence on the character of the girls."

When the train pulled in at the station, they were all dressed in their purple-and-white-checked dresses, with purple blazers and straw hats. Joy had scraped almost all the lipstick off her mouth, but she left a little as a mark of defiance, as a link with the outside world.

When Emily climbed off the train, she saw a tall, thin nun walking evenly toward the group of jabbering girls. A guard flung their trunks carelessly onto the platform, knowing the nun would not tip him. The piccanins scattered in the direction of a well-dressed woman escorting her daughter, also wearing the convent purple, to the exit. Emily stared at the nun, who walked in such a singular way: it was as deliberate as a march, not a hurry, not a glide, but something in between; something ordered and obedient. As though, long ago, her legs had forgotten their will to gallop or pirouette or glide. She clapped her hands briskly when she saw them, once, twice.

"Now, girls, remember you are wearing your uniforms; you are a reflection of the school and of the Blessed Virgin."

The girls went still as though plugs at their backs had been pulled. The nun continued, smiling a cool, patient smile, which showed small teeth set in a lot of gum.

"I hope you've all enjoyed your holidays and are now pleased to be back." Though the girls scowled, most of them were secretly relieved to be back to the neat, nipped existence.

Emily's eyes were trained on the wimple framing the nun's face and moved to the round black crown: did she have a shaved head, or hacked-off hair? What would happen if she, Emily, just reached up and yanked that off? The nun said, "So this is Emily?" with a pitying tone. The girl felt her back stiffen and her eyes flew to the crucifix on the nun's breast.

"Answer me, answer me, child," she insisted.

Emily's voice rasped out, "Yes," too loud.

"Yes, Sister."

"Yes, Sister," the girl demurred, moving her eyes up to the nun's, which did not flicker, but seemed to mock.

They walked two by two out of the station, leaving the trunks to be collected later.

"That's Sister Emmanuel," Jean whispered. "She's vicious and

Immaculata adores her; they're inseparable, so don't cross her."
The black robes of the nun slapped against the red earth outside
the station; there was a rim of white all around the hem. Her back
was very straight, but her head had a bowed and humble aspect,
as if she were secretly reciting, "I shall walk with my eyes averted;
I shall feast my thoughts on heaven."

The nun drove the school bus almost recklessly down the road,
out of the little village, lined with fig trees, and out to an isolated
stretch of veld. The bus then hurled itself down a hill, past some
fields of mealies and on to the gates of the convent. These were
opened by a postulant, wearing a coarse white blouse and a heavy
gray skirt; she pushed the heavy iron gates with both hands, her
whole body bent under the strain. Slowly the gates began to creak
and shift.

"Shall I help her?" Emily asked impulsively, rising from her
seat.

"Sit," Sister Emmanuel whispered, "sit. She has chosen to do
gates as a penance. Suffering, you will find, my child, is the only
way to humility, and humility the only way to Our Lord." The
atmosphere in the bus tipped at her words; it descended on the
heads of all the girls present, pushing them down. Joy's face now
wore a cold, expressionless mask; Jean sat very straight, smiling
gently, like a woman doing a task that she understood so to perfection that it left her mind free for other things. A new girl was
crying in a corner.

The grounds of the convent were laid out with beautiful old
trees, pines, cypresses, elms, and poplars. There were no young
trees, and from the cropped stretches of grass to the rockeries and
rose gardens, there was an air of things never changing, year in,
year out. You could almost imagine that the seasons would not
touch them, either. Beyond the gardens were the playing fields,
the vegetable gardens, and the swimming pool. The nuns belonged
to an Oxford order, and there was no shortage of money, which
was not reflected in the fees.

The girls, at the beginning of term, went in one by one to make,
or renew, acquaintance with Sister Immaculata. A line of girls
were queueing up outside her door. Emily stood next to Jean, who

whispered, "Always be very polite to her, curtsy when you go in and—"

"How?"

"How what?"

"How curtsy?"

"Like this, twit, just quickly bend your knee, bob. You have to do that when you go in and out of chapel, too. Just look and copy."

This was unfamiliar to Emily, who had always done things her own way. She scowled.

"Look, Em, in this place you have to *obey* in everything, absolutely everything. There are hundreds of rules, and we live by bells. You'll pick it all up quickly, but don't start off by thinking you can change anything."

"Okay." Emily grinned because Jean's earnest face was so puckered and her dark freckles seemed to be fading in the cool white corridor. Emily looked about her: there was a big, square room to her right. It had brilliantly polished red tiles on the floor, high white walls, and a ceiling decorated around the edges like a wedding cake. On the walls were two holy pictures, one of St. Christopher and one of St. Francis, carrying a lamb. In one corner was a large statue of Our Lady wearing her favorite colors: blue, white, and silver.

Joy, who was standing in line just behind Emily and Jean, came forward and, pointing to the statue of Mary and the Infant, who looked like a minute man, whispered, "There, for your information, Em, is the pure and spotless Virgin, who makes anyone wanting a proper husband feel dirty—and there He is—the miracle boy who never cried or crapped and never made that patient, soppy look leave His mother's face."

"You think you're so darn smart," Jean hissed, offended as always by her sister's mockery.

Emily laughed as Joy drew a circle like a halo above her sister's head when her back was turned. A nun swanned by and frowned hard at Joy, but it was only Sister Hilary, and she was all right.

When her turn came to enter, Emily was nervous, but would rather have been torn limb from limb than show it. The head mistress had her head down, writing, as Emily closed the door behind her and slowly approached the big oak desk. She went on writing as Emily stood there, then, without lifting her head, said, "You forgot to curtsy, my child."

Emily ducked, almost banging her knee against the front of the desk. The nun lifted her face. And stared. The girl stared back. It became a contest. Without dropping her eyes, the nun said, "I see we have here a proud child, a child with a will flexed and unbroken." Her face had grown pale at the impudence of the child's staring, at the steel tendons she sensed in Emily's spine and wanted to snap. "But"—and how could anything so conciliatory sound so accusing—"you are not one of us; you are not of our church," she said quietly. "But you will have to follow our rules here, Emily, bend to our ways, or it will be very hard for you. Will you try to do that?" Emily thought she detected a tone less frigid that she could respond to a little by nodding. But pride had still to be humbled and the head mistress began the task.

"Here, it is customary to lower the eyes when spoken to," she said mildly. Emily's eyes hit the ground, then rose again. "It is not proper to pit one's small will against those put in authority over us by Our Lord Himself." Emily found that her eyes, far from falling to the depths required, had in fact flown to the oil painting that hung above Sister Immaculata's head. Her mouth dropped open. A sad-faced man with long curly brown hair looked down on her. His forehead was torn and bleeding, with thorns embedded in the flesh; his chest was gashed open to reveal his heart, also circled by thorns; his hands, spiked, were folded together; they bled, the bone showed where the nail had been hammered through. The girl was overcome by horror and fascination. The nun spoke on, but Emily did not hear her. In an excruciating moment she knew that this convent, this strange otherworld, was the right place for her. She moved closer to the picture. The nun was forced to raise and sharpen her voice.

"Emily, I am speaking to you."

Then, and only then, the girl relinquished the painting of Jesus and turned her face full on the nun.

She saw a large square face that was flushed with anger; there was a brown mole below her left eye. The nun had a narrow nose with delicate nostrils; a flat, compressed mouth and brown eyes beneath heavy black eyebrows. A little vein was pulsing in her cheek.

"Emily, I'm afraid we've made a very bad beginning here. I am prepared to offer you a little leniency due to the nature of your upbringing, but I do expect from you total cooperation. Is that clear?"

Each of her words, though reasonably spoken, had the quality of pebbles hitting a rock.

Emily said, "Yes, Sister," and at last lowered her head.

The papers on the desk were flicked and turned. "I have seen your old reports; you will have to do better here. Your father tells me you have scant interest in mathematics; we will have to see what we can do about that." Emily shuffled her feet preparatory to departure, mentally bending her knee into a curtsy. But Sister Immaculata had not finished.

"You will realize that we do not really like to take non-Catholics here, particularly at your late age—it is so difficult then to mold them to our ways, so much slack to gather in. Your father pressed, though, that your mother felt the strain of your presence. You are a difficult child, I believe?" Emily gasped, tasting for the first time the cold, sweet cruelty of nuns; the shapely edge of their sarcasm; their ability to drop the knife right between the bone.

"That will be all for now, Emily. Send in the next girl, please." Her hand took up the pen again and began to make notes in beautifully curved italics, like the arches of a Gothic church.

Dumb with humiliation, Emily ducked and walked quickly to the door. Jean was waiting. "God, you look as though you've seen a ghost! Was she awful?"

Emily nodded, said nothing, feeling that in the room with its paintings and holy books, its statue of St. Theresa with its red light burning, she had encountered the presence of pure evil.

There was a short service in the chapel—some prayers, some hymns, a benediction—and out they trooped. Emily felt bewildered by the atmosphere; the high vases of iris and carnations, the wistful scent of incense, and the low drone of the organ. Kneeling on the hard floor—kneelers were not permitted—she looked around her at the lowered, veiled heads of her contemporaries; at the sweet, peaceful expressions on their faces as they lifted them to make the responses. They were not like girls, but like flowers. The veils softened their flesh, darkened their eyes, and gave them an unearthly serenity. She felt then that they possessed a secret, something from which she was excluded. The priest raised his hand, carved the air with the sign of the cross. Two hundred hands were raised and flitted across bent faces as in the culmination of some magic rite.

Supper in the refectory was a humble affair: brown bread thinly sliced, the butter scraped off rather than spread; a limp soup with traces of vegetables. The nuns were not present; prefects presided at the tureens and each girl received exactly two ladles of soup. Nothing could be left. After grace, noise seemed to rise like bubbles in a kettle, and it did not subside until the chairs were scraped back and a volley of voices rattled, "Bless us, O Lord, and these Thy gifts, through Christ Our Lord, Amen."

Then the head girl told everyone to wait, as there was to be a short address from Sister Immaculata. The atmosphere drew in, was held, then resettled. Sister Immaculata walked in through the gap between the rows of tables on either side of the refectory, toward a little platform at the front. The walls of the room were lined with pictures of martyrs; on one side of the platform was a painting of Mary. Emily noticed that throughout the school Mary had prominence over her son. The nun, tall, well-built, with a magnificent carriage, as though her rightful place was at the head of an infantry battalion, rode on a cloud of hushed breath. The swish of her skirts, the click-click of the keys at her waist, the little squeal of her sturdy, rubber-soled shoes were the only sounds in the room. She ascended the platform and indicated that everyone resume their seats.

Sister Immaculata bestowed on them all a smile of pure graciousness.

"Girls, new and old, I'd like to welcome you all to Santa Maria's for the new term. I trust you're all well rested and are now ready for the ardors and discipline of school life. This, as old girls will know, is the term when most is expected of us: we will be preparing for Easter and entering the rigorous time of Lent, when Our Lord will be testing each one of us to see how much we are prepared to sacrifice and endure. We will be planting our bulbs as usual. Now, it has come to my attention that some of you feel this little performance to be pointless, some say severe, even, but the point of the exercise is for you to understand the effect of the mind and spirit upon a living thing—just like yourselves. And that if you nourish and protect your bulbs with a spiritual devotion, they must surely blossom for you. Those of you fearful of the result must be doubtful of the sincerity of your labors. It has been a long custom of our order to follow this little practice, and after some consideration, I believe it to be right to continue."

Among the girls Emily felt a hostility rise, but the nun quickly brushed it aside and continued, smiling, "That will be all for now, except to wish you all a good and peaceful night." She swept out regally between the rows of chairs.

Once the door had shut after her, pandemonium broke out, with sighs of irritation and a general chorus of disapproval. All the girls filed out. Emily was searching for Jean and found her on the stairs going up to the dormitory.

"What was all that about bulbs?"

The girl who was walking up the stairs with Jean sneered and said, "It's a medieval practice that Immaculata takes pleasure in. At the beginning of the Lent term, we are all given little pots with bulbs planted in them. Depending on your piety during Lent, the thing is supposed to either flourish or wither. It's like trial by fire or water. If your bulb doesn't do well, you're guilty of bad thoughts and your bulb is displayed publicly as proof of your failure to make a good Lent. If it is considered to be a fine specimen by the bitch, then it is given an honorary place outside the chapel and you're saved."

"It's curious," Jean said quietly, "how predictable the results are."

"She bloody well fixes them! Who do you think plants the ruddy bulbs in the first place—who gives them out?"

Jean, normally protective of anyone under attack, was silent.

Emily, marveling at the competence of the nun, felt strangely excited by the fact that here she was surrounded by remote, extraordinary beings, people who were not people—creatures set apart to live hushed, intoxicated lives. Here was a place to sit tight and watch things transpire.

Soon the world of the convent became familiar; she no longer noticed the crucifix over each door, with a dried palm leaf tucked behind it; her fingers dipped as casually as anyone's into the bowls of holy water shaped like shells. Jean had given her a rosary, which she treasured, though she cared little for its uses. At Mass and during most of the other services she would escape easily into another world.

She transported herself back to a beautiful barren place, wide open, uninhabited, vast as her mind. The dust billowed through the windows and settled on the flowers and candles; the incense rose and blurred the senses; the small, earnest priest provided a background hum as mesmerizing as bees. When she prayed, and she prayed with fervor, her prayers were addressed to Patrick. He was real; she had seen and heard him; she could put her future in his hands. In the chapel, with her face hidden behind her hands, she could see him as if in sunlight. She repeated his words like a psalm.

During lessons, she would sit up very straight, her spine not touching the chair back, as was required of her, as she required of herself for Patrick. She folded her hands together and listened as the nuns tried to encourage learning by their sarcasm and delicate malice. She could do what was needed with half her mind, then dispense with it quickly and slip back to dreaming: of a little house by the river's lap, a garden deep in grass, carpets as voluptuous as the colonel's, sheets as sleek as Rena's, and slithery black nights that never ended.

Emily had always regarded schoolwork as repetitive drudgery; it was obvious stuff and mind-slackening. It turned one away from what was sharp and real and immediately experienced. She understood the importance of basic skills; these she learned quickly; the rest were peripheral. It seemed that all that was expected of her was to do things in an identical fashion to her schoolmates; that she was being asked to streamline her achievements according to a low and predictable standard, which was judged by sour women. The girls who excelled in the classroom seemed to her to be merely the ones with the most retentive memories.

Sister Immaculata, however, had a surgeon's skill in slicing through any reverie. She then went in with a knife and drew forth the offending thing for public inspection. Emily troubled the nun like a stone in the shoe; she could not quite see how she could bring the girl under her will. But she was confident.

At the beginning of Lent, Emily walked out of the chapel into the evening light and smiled at Sister Christiana, the new lay nun from England. She was beautiful and shockingly young, with a soft round face and two deep dimples in her cheeks. She had pale eyebrows and greeny-blue eyes, and it was rumored that she had red hair. Everyone used to wonder how she could bear not to look at herself ever again: no mirrors were permitted in the school, and the nuns were not allowed to polish their shoes in case they might catch their reflections in the shine.

It soon became obvious to the whole school that Sister Immaculata was disturbed by the untidy state of the lay nun's soul. Sister Christiana had been used to a kinder, more patient discipline in her community in Oxford. She had come out to Rhodesia before taking her final vows to find that Sister Immaculata had extended, according to her own inclinations, the rules whereby nuns should live. One of the Sister Superior's first duties toward her new sister had been to break her of her attachment to worldly goods. It was done with stunning simplicity.

After prayers, Emily, who had not lost her habit of spying, watched the sisters all walk into a small meeting room. She took up a position by an open window. The nuns all stood quietly with their hands tucked into their black sleeves, their feet together, and their heads lowered. Sister Immaculata did not tell them to sit, but she did ask Sister Christiana to step forward. When the lay nun stood before her, her face honest and open as a daffodil's, her superior began to speak in a voice hushed and mournful, delivering her speech with all the expertise of an actress reaching for an Oscar.

"Sisters, as you are aware, we have taken a vow to give up our lives for Our Lord. Our little sister here has not felt the final knot of that vow, but she has agreed already to renounce her past, to begin a new life in the service not of self, but of Christ. We must be kind to her, for she has clearly not understood the full implications of her promise."

Sister Christiana's face had lost its glow. She darted back through all her activities of the day and could not actually feel that she had done wrong. But the standards in this remote convent were so utterly unlike those of the convent that had hatched her.

Her superior continued in the same even, patient tone. "Sister, it grieved me just now to see that you possess a rosary of a most unusual kind. . . ." The lay nun started, then quickly produced the rosary and held it out openly in the palm of her hand like a child proving her innocence. Sister Immaculata took a fleeting look at the milky amber beads and then threw her eyes sideways at the other nuns as though the sight was offensive.

"And where, Sister, did you acquire a rosary of this sort?"

"I have had it since my childhood, Sister. We were not required to give up religious objects when I joined the community."

Sister Immaculata was shocked. "Not required to give up religious objects! This, surely, Sister, is far more than that, is it not? It is a symbol, a remaining link with a world you have vowed to forgo, with memories and people for whom you have no earthly use now. How can it not be given up? How could you not have willingly tossed it aside? Joyfully, like a bauble a child has outgrown, like a dress that no longer fits."

The young nun seemed to clench her hand harder around the rosary, her face red with indecision and shame.

"Well, Sister, we are awaiting your opinion?"

When she spoke, her voice was a low, sad thing. "I did not realize . . . yes, I suppose it must be so. . . ." Yet her fingers held faster and she bit her lip, letting her head fall forward.

Sister Immaculata's voice grew rich and warm. She held out

her hand and the nun put into it the golden beads; they lay there for a moment, full of luster, round as butterdrops. Then the hand closed. It was as though light went out in a darkened building. Sister Christiana lifted her head; her entire body seemed to swell; her face quivered with a remote radiance. In that moment she looked as though no human emotion could touch her; no sacrifice be voluptuous enough to shake her state of grace.

Sister Immaculata turned and walked a little and elegantly tossed the rosary into the wastepaper basket. It was as if a blow had been struck at the lay nun's flesh, at her easy childhood, her obedient girlhood, when, rapt in a chapel in Oxford, she had heard the wind warble in the trees and knew it as His voice. Sister Christiana's face, when she pulled it upward from where it had sunk on her breast, was pinched. Her rosy cheeks had gone, the dimples flattened, the plump mouth thinned and twisted.

"When you have recovered yourself, Sister," Sister Immaculata said caressingly, as one speaks to a child one has injured necessarily, "please come to my study, and I will give you a rosary that is like ours. You will find the black beads just as agreeable to prayer."

Emily stood rigidly against the wall outside; she was filled with hatred for Immaculata and an almost suffocating pity for the lay nun. After the incident with the rosary she began to pay particular attention to Sister Christiana. She already had some following among the more romantic girls, who imagined her the victim of a broken romance. Emily, however, was more concerned with her present and, in particular, her relationship with the Sister Superior.

It was said that Immaculata set Sister Christiana all the most gruesome tasks: the ones normally reserved for servants and those taking punishment. Such duties were scrubbing the chapel floors and removing every scrap of wax from the candlesticks.

Pretending to pray, Emily would watch Sister Christiana. She was like a child at play, completely absorbed in keeping house for a lord and master who would never materialize at the end of the day. She seemed to be nearing a perfect pitch of being in the chapel, when each action was a prayer, each drudgery a devotion. The girl, watching her with mounting fascination and envy, could not find what she was seeking, could not understand the reason for such love, for love it was: the nun was besotted by Christ.

Something in Emily's experience told her that there was a connection between this life and her past, this nun and herself. She was not satisfied until it began to filter through: the nun was as isolated and obsessed as she herself. Though she could not rationalize it, the life of the convent was so mindless that, in fact, it became pure mind. It reduced everyone to an elementary state. It confined them in a tunnel that narrowed as it traveled forward to nothing but the next chime of bell. But the environment molded character in a particular way, left it aching for something more, something shiftless, unidentified.

Something had to be made of the tedium, the apathy—and only one emotion would do—passion. It was a passion that grew and blossomed in convents, in deserts—where life achieved an unbearable intensity by its very barrenness.

Once, as a joke, Emily, with the aid of a nightdress and dark towels, dressed up as a nun. The girls in the dormitory shrieked with laughter. Emily looked in the little hand mirror that the lovely Bronwen hid in her drawer, and was amazed. For the face that gazed serenely back at her was quite striking; her cheekbones were sharp and high, her eyes a glittering green; her chin, pinched in with the white towel, no longer seemed hard, and her mouth was not sullen. She was not pretty, but she fancied someone might consider her good-looking. She thought of Patrick and yearned painfully to be sixteen. Cut off in her own world, she did not notice that the room had gone silent. She spun around. It was Sister Hilary, who looked mild and sad.

"I'm sorry, Emily," she said, "but I'll have to report you to Sister Immaculata."

The news of Emily's masquerade spread like a bush fire through the convent. Emily, who had not before drawn attention to herself, found herself now the center of attraction: a heroine in an hour. And she enjoyed it.

"So, Emily, I believe you have something to tell me?" Immaculata said softly, raking the girl's face with her eyes.

Emily managed to reply clearly. "Sister, in the dormitory, I dressed up as a nun."

With beautiful severity and directness, the nun said, "Why?"

Emily had no answer. The idea that crossed her mind was that she had wanted to be like Sister Christiana, but she could not say so. Sister Immaculata, never one to waste a moment, bent her head to her writing. Emily did not know whether the interview was over or not, so stood there, twisting her feet, as the nun, with a deadly composure, finally said, "And how is your bulb doing, Emily?"

Now here was a question she could answer easily. "Very well, Sister, thank you, the —"

She was cut short by the blast of fury that sprang out of Immaculata's face. "That, my child, I cannot believe," she snapped, almost breathless.

Emily stood to attention, looking down, expecting the worst.

Instead, the nun's voice turned milky. "Emily, I'm afraid that now you've forced me to make you understand that you cannot set yourself up in mockery of a sister of God. I must ask you to be the only girl in the school without a bulb this Lent. You must sacrifice it, together with your willfulness." Looking at Emily's blank face, the nun went on sweetly, "Emily, I do not do this to be cruel, only so that you may come to understand that humility is the only way to salvation; that strength in overcoming suffering is the highest virtue."

She continued, "I am considering writing to your parents about this matter, Emily." And there she knew she had struck home. The nun rose from her desk and walked to the window. "In the meantime, I shall announce to the school that you will be placed in solitary confinement for the entire weekend and no girl may communicate with you in any way. I would also like from you an essay on a great man, and I would like your work free of that unfortunate tendency to precocious thought that so often creeps into your English and Scripture essays. You may go. I shall pray for you, my child."

. . .

Emily was quite unable to submit to Sister Immaculata, or to God. She saw them both as ultimate and angry authority, whose purpose was to humiliate. They wanted to destroy her will and her freedom. Jesus, she felt, was romantic, but he had been damaged beyond recognition by the church. And He was gone. All that remained was the idea of God; and God, like all gods, was cruel.

But in spite of her initial revolt against the hermetic quality of the convent, she had come to feel the attraction of a life that ran true and straight. Sister Immaculata's insistence that all girls were there to develop character, to be strong, so that no pettiness in the outside world could corrupt or distract them, had its appeal. The insistence on endurance, on forcing the soul to triumph over pain and humiliation—these things she had begun in herself years ago, alone and in secret. Now she thought that life would be shiftless without such restraints.

During her solitary weekend, Emily wrote an impeccable essay for the Sister Superior. She chose Immaculata's favorite saint, St. Augustine. In her essay, Emily made a point of dwelling on the sinful life of St. Augustine before God claimed him. Having begun *The Confessions* with boredom, she soon found that she was swept away by the almost physical passion of the man for his God. His love came as a shock to her senses: how could anyone feel like that, have such an abundance of love for a presence in the mind? And the man was not a fool. She wrote and wrote about him, and dared to slip in the comment that it was perhaps Augustine's mother who really had the final victory, having cajoled and wept throughout for her son's conversion to her faith. This book was to color forever her idea of religion, and during the coming Lent she reread many of its passages with a strange exultation, as if here was something wonderfully powerful, and human, which made God almost tangible by the sheer force of one man's imagination.

Sister Immaculata scratched across the essay, in writing particularly ill-formed for her, "This is sheer insolence and mockery. You will write it, again and again, until you get it right." Emily did what she was told, but Immaculata never felt satisfied with the results, even though there was finally nothing that she could actually point to as being offensive. She now felt, however, actively undermined by the girl, as though Emily's existence in the school directly threatened her authority.

It was Holy Week. Suddenly all the months of chapel night and morning, confession on Saturday afternoon, two Masses on Sunday and evening prayers, seemed petty in comparison to what was to follow. For six weeks the nuns had given themselves to fasting and penance; and the school, to a lesser extent, had done so also. There was no meat on Wednesdays or Fridays. Those nuns in need of particular mortification ate no meat at all for the entire Lent. After Palm Sunday, the statues were swathed with purple veiling and the altar coverings were dark and dismal. Sister Christiana's touch could have made something profound of these mysteries, but she was no longer allowed to spend time alone in the chapel. Her sprightly walk had sagged into the dreary penitential pace of the others; her face had a haunted expression that matched the thin and altered shape of her body. She no longer let slip her quick inadvertent smiles, and Emily felt a lowering in herself; the starkness of all things was increased by the loss of the lay nun's company.

Emily had made a pronounced attempt to lead a calm life during Lent; not to ruffle Sister Immaculata; to be polite and considerate at all times to all the nuns. She noticed, though, that Immaculata's tongue had not lost its aptness, nor her face its peevish expression. In fact, there was something vaguely tormented about her as she flogged everyone to greater efforts, to quicker knitting for the mission children; to greater attention to their devotions.

During Lent every girl was expected to give up things—sweets, books, unkindness, impatience, loudness, and other such vices. What most of them actually tried to give up was swearing, or sweets, if their figures would benefit accordingly. Deep inside each girl, however, lay a serious commitment to the season, and this had become magnified to extreme proportions by Ash Wednesday. Then, each forehead bore its gray stigma and each face a deep solemnity. Emily felt deprived because she was not confirmed and could not go up with the others to take Communion.

On Good Friday, the retreat began with the rising bell. From that moment on, every girl dedicated all her energy to keeping her silence. Breakfast was missed that day, and the entire morning was spent in the chapel. The altar was stripped bare. The Gospel of the Passion was mournfully, endlessly sung. A few of the less hardy girls fainted and had to be propped up with their heads between their knees. The minutes and hours trailed by; there was a dense, breathless atmosphere.

After lunch, consisting of bread and water, and no sound but the scrape of chairs and the tinkle of cutlery, they had an hour to read a religious book upstairs on their beds. Then they were herded down to chapel when the Angelus pealed out three o'clock. There they watched and prayed with Christ for three solemn hours, during which a procession moved sadly around the walls, stopping to chant beneath each picture depicting a different Station of the Cross.

At this point, Emily felt that she had lost her grip on the world: the walls of the chapel were reeling; she had lost her sense of sight and smell. Her mind was on fire with images: of the whip pulling out pieces of Christ's flesh, of the cap of thorns delving deep beneath His skin. She was shivering, on the point of collapse, when the girl beside her quickly pulled her from her knees onto the wooden pew and pushed down her head. The world from this upside-down position slowly recovered its rightful position.

Exhausted by emotion, everyone left the chapel. There was then a short recreation until the supper bell. Emily walked far out to the end of the hockey pitch and sat down in the grass under an oak tree. She had a hideous desire to shout out loud or laugh shrilly. She was frightened because she felt so strange, so changed, as if she had lost her balance. She had been moved and horrified by the long stretches of time when she was left in the pit of her own silence. Nothing before had affected her so strongly or so painfully: had she not in fact felt His presence, tasted of His passion? He was there, He was there. They were all certain. She sensed it, but was afraid to trust it. For it would mean a new order of things; a death of the old Emily she knew and relied upon as her one guide in an otherwise threatening world.

The bell rang out loud and clear on the morning of Easter Saturday; it seemed like the first day of the world. Breakfast was simple, and everyone talked as though they had been silent far longer than twenty-four hours. The girls wore white linen dresses with short sleeves and blue and lilac veils. There was a service in the chapel that began with prayers and benedictions—and then, in a ceremony of sweeping power and beauty, the veils were flung back from the statues, and loud, ecstatic music broke out from the organ. The priest, in his white robes, brought in the Paschal candle and lit it. The nuns walked in, bearing tall vases of lilies and iris, white daisies, and basins of roses and placed them upon the altar. The whole chapel shook with alleluias.

Emily waited, sunk into the atmosphere like a bee in honey, dazzled by the exuberance and joy as one is dazzled by the sheer silver breadth of the sea. She was waiting for one stunning moment of revelation, for a sign in her own heart that would say, "I believe, I believe; this I can give myself to utterly, with all my heart and soul." The moment was whirled away from her as the organ pealed out its melody, as the nun's feet treading the pedals danced a jig as she pumped out the opening bars of the hymn and the chapel seemed to rise and cheer.

Outside, the lined-up bulbs greeted her like a reproach, and a first pang of misery hit her as she appreciated the superb strategy of the head mistress. Some of the bulbs were stunted, others were in full bloom; the majority had petals sleekly folded together like hands at prayer. Each girl picked up the bulb bearing her name and took it proudly or with a shamed face into the hall. Emily felt humiliated and pained like a child denied a kiss. Her emotions, which had soared in the chapel, now descended too fast for her to control the tears that rushed to her eyes.

Inside the hall, with its raised platform where the Sisters and prefects sat, everyone lined up. Each girl then had to walk up and present her bulb to Sister Immaculata. The girls would then fall into two categories: those who had made a good Lent and those who had not. It seemed incredible to Emily that the pupils should abide by this arbitrary choice of goodness, but submit they did. And it must have been because there was felt to be some justice in the way the ax fell. For, sure enough, there on the left stood a score of girls with reputations for rudeness, idleness, or weakness all standing together. On the right, the smiling holies stood, again a most predictable collection. And standing completely alone and exposed in the middle of the hall—stood Emily.

Immaculata turned her attention to Emily, "You will all observe a new girl to this school who has achieved some kind of record in her short spell with us. She is the first girl I have ever felt bound to deprive of her bulb. The reason is known to you all; but what I think is probably not known is the sheer willfulness of her character. You all see her there before you. Is she humble, is she meek? Has she directed any attention to the faults so carefully pointed out to her?"

Emily stood her ground like a Trojan, her face white and damp.

"There are some girls who begin by being detrimental to themselves and end up polluting the entire atmosphere. . . ."

By then, when Emily felt that the screws were tightening beyond endurance, something extraordinary happened. One lone pair of feet began to stamp loudly on the wooden floor. Sister Immaculata's eyes scourged the collection of girls on the right-hand side, where the sound had come from. The stamping did not stop, and within seconds another pair of feet had taken it up, and another and another, until the whole floor was echoing with defiant thuds. Louder and louder they stamped. The Sister Superior was gray with rage; she could not speak; finally she was expelled from the hall by the sheer futility of her presence.

Then, and only then, did the head girl jump onto the table on the platform, wave her arms magnificently only once and, as the din subsided, she yelled, "Pack it in," with the energy of a train entering a tunnel at full speed. There was silence. "Okay," she said firmly. "Now all get back to what you're supposed to be doing. I suggest that everyone now behaves perfectly till the end of term. Anyone trying to muck about after this will have me to deal with. Now, scram." And she leaped off the table, the maroon head girl's belt emphasizing her neat waist and straight, strong hips. The hall was empty in seconds.

Sister Immaculata never referred to the incident.

It was nearly the end of term. Emily was carefully stacking into a pile the Easter cards she had been given; she was glad that she had received so many. She looked out of the dormitory window; a small figure in a gray coat walked slowly out and stood in front of Sister Immaculata. It was Sister Christiana. Immaculata's hands were, as usual, hidden in her sleeves, so that all that could be seen was her large blunt face, which was very composed. She spoke for a few minutes. The lay nun ducked her head, picked up a traveling bag, and walked forlornly toward the driveway. A black car drove up, came to a halt, and she stood dumbly by the door, unable to open it.

Emily flew down the stairs, descending them two at a time, and out into the open. Sister Immaculata stood by the rhododendrons, watching the car pull away, her hand raised in farewell. Emily shrieked at her back, "Where is she going? Where? Tell me." The nun spun. Her face, once so neat and orderly, turned thin and appalled.

"Be silent." She almost screamed.

"Where has she gone?" Emily repeated sullenly.

Sister Immaculata ordered her features to obedience. "Sister Christiana—not that it is any of your concern—is returning to England, for her health. That is all." She moved away, trying to separate herself from this loud, contorted child.

"It's you, you. It's vicious, it's evil; it's nothing to do with Him, with your precious Christ. It's all you. She was good." Emily's face was made jagged by rage.

The nun backed away, a feeling of strangulation at her throat. "Good?" she repeated vacantly. She could have been afraid. "What would you know of goodness, my child? What can you under-stand? You are not even of the faith." She was shaking again, her supports were leaning—she must get away.

Emily turned and walked away.

Over the next five years spent in the school Emily was to pine for the bush. There was a limit to the amount of time she could bearably spend away from it. Soon after she started attending the convent, her parents moved from the place by the river to a dustier, more desolate little dorp farther south. Life was utterly changed without that glittering hoop of water leading to deep swamps; without the large, extravagant birds; the pink and white water lilies, the bream, the barbel, the wild ducks skidding across a watered sky. A place without water was a place without hope; it merely survived because it had to. In the same way, Emily learned to survive without the river, without the life and beauty it be-stowed, missing it, but overcoming the loss.

Coming back to school, she had also to recover from the pain her mother's presence always inflicted. Lilian's life had now settled into a more severe form of drought; her voice seemed to have been thinned by the heat; her famous laugh had evaporated into thin air. Only the maladies remained.

And Emily began merely to observe her mother; she tried to make it an observation exclusive of need, and as she grew older, she forced herself to forget her mother, even as she herself was being forgotten.

As for her father, a dry crust as thick and brown as suet had formed over his heart. He could not bear to feel. The only emo-tions that still functioned were those of anger and irritation; these piled up in him in great banks of rage and frustration. He had forgotten about love. The use of the word was liable to make him sneer.

Life at Santa Maria's had completely altered, too. When everyone returned after the Lent holidays, there was no longer a Sister Immaculata. She had been returned to England "for her health." There was a new Sister Superior, Sister Benedict, a small, neat nun with a dreary little face and teeth that stuck out. She spoke briskly and firmly, and under her rule the school quickly acquired an atmosphere of less restraint, of calmer discipline. She had clearly been chosen for the job because of her common sense. The nuns were seen to be lighter in their ways, less stringent in their attitudes, and no longer feared risking a good laugh if the occasion demanded it. Though the atmosphere of the convent was less hysterical, it was also duller as a result.

Emily watched to see whether a gap would open in her soul, through which she might see, as she had during Lent, a glimpse of God. But the need was not great enough, and it required too stern a sacrifice. Religion had to be taken to the extreme for it to ease any real hunger. Either she could believe it to the complete conclusion: the taking of a veil—or not at all. There were still to be moments of rapture in the chapel, moments when her whole adolescent soul craved to be consumed. But only at Lent; Christmas was paltry and without dramatics, a fairy tale for children.

She was thirteen, and the life of the body began to dominate. She had changed from a bony, straight shape to something rounder. She was small. Her hair straight and thick. Her eyes still a chilling green. Religion had given her a brief sip of heaven. Now it would ease into a convenient outer acquiescence, while inwardly she would start to pull down, stone by stone, the great pillars of belief upon which the Catholic dogma is based. Because it had come to her one day as a vast release, to know that it was, after all, possible to be moral, to be good—without the necessity of a religious belief.

And so, all in a day, in a moment, like a conversion, she transferred her need for devotion and dedication, her pent-up passion, back to humanity. To one person, one gentle deity: Virginia.

Virginia was a girl of seventeen. She had very white skin, crystal-blue eyes, and a crown of curly gold-and-brown hair. She was just a girl, shy, a little stooped—because her tallness was a trial to her; because her hair was willful rather than beautiful. Her eyes were too small; her mouth was fragile and sometimes pinched by the pain she too readily absorbed around her. That she was solemn and intense as an icon, or the sixteenth-century religious paintings of women, caused her to be beautiful and remote to Emily, who, as yet, only watched her adoringly from afar.

Emily did not dare speak to the older girl. She watched, she placed herself at points in the corridors, on the grass around the swimming pool, where Virginia might pass. And if she did, Emily would press herself up into a straight line, and words would form behind her tongue, words she had practiced in secret, words ungainly as boulders, such as, "Virginia," "Hello," and "Can I carry that?" But they never reached the tip of her tongue.

Virginia could dive like no other girl, and when Emily watched her diving off the top board, she metamorphosed into a river bird. In her black satin swimming suit, she would run on long, palely tanned legs down the board, then leap up at the end, fling her arms high with her fingers pointed—then jackknife so that her hands touched her toes in midair. She would straighten and plunge like a streak into the depths of the water. When her head rose in its white bathing cap, Emily was breathless with admiration.

When Virginia was dressed again, Emily watched her walk away to the common room where the prefects had tea. She was rosy as an apple, with the sun sliding off her tight damp curls. And then one day she turned her strange shifting gaze and saw Emily staring at her in a way she recognized. She smiled at the girl who she admired for her stand against Immaculata.

After that, Emily had the courage to do what other girls who had crushes on the seniors did—she took a little bar of chocolate wrapped in paper and left it on Virginia's bed. She made sure that some of the girls in the dormitory saw her put it there: she didn't want her generosity to be anonymous. The next day there was a note pinned to the messages board with her name on it. It said:

Dear Emily,
Thank you for the chocolate, but you shouldn't have. I'm sure you need it more yourself. But thank you, Nestlés is my favorite and I ate it all myself.

Love, Virginia.

Emily read it so many times that the folds in it became threadbare. She used to carry it around in her breast pocket like a talisman.

Dear Emily,
What a beautiful little hankie, which you embroidered with your own fingers. It's *too* sweet. When shall I use it? When my heart is broken? On my wedding day? I shall of course invite you to my wedding. Who taught you to sew so well? It quite makes me ashamed of my own ragged little stitches.

Dear Virginia,
No, I wasn't too miz. in chapel last night. I was just a bit worried about getting another order mark and getting hell from Sister Hil. But you did cheer me up when you smiled and I felt better instantly. How can you be so good and sweet and still exist in a rotten dump like this?

Dear Emily,
I'm so glad Shirley has given you such a nice white-and-gold box to put my letters in. I'm not sure my letters deserve such glory. But Shirley does need your continuing kindness, poor little orphan, so do be sweet to her. She clearly adores you. I hope that you're working hard and not got any more order marks.

Dearest Virginia,
I saw you sitting outside after hair washing and your hair was like pale licks of fire. Who put all the curls in like that? My hair is straight and boring as grass. You are *not* to be worried about the Diving Gala, of course you will win the cup. And if by some extraordinary trick you don't, I shall steal it for you.

Dearest Emily,
Yes, I did have a nice half-term. We went to the drive-in and to a braaivleis with some friends and then had a party, and there were some fairly nice blokes there. Did you have a nice time with Helen? I hear her parents are a bit odd and won't have servants! Just wait till you start going to parties:

your eyes are like two green hills, and someday men will break their necks on them. Hope you sleep very well tonight and dream of me!

Dearest Virginia,
I was only sad because I keep thinking that this is your last year here and then you'll be gone, and how shall I get on without you? How shall I even breathe without you? I don't want to go home for the holidays. I want the term to last forever. I have been so happy and I don't want it to end. I want you to have more time to talk to me without having to go off when the ruddy bells ring. And now I feel more miserable than ever and I will think about it all night and perhaps howl a bit. Please, please can I have a photograph of you, and one of your hankies?

Dearest Emily,
Here is your hankie at last! It looks a bit creased, but I tell you, my girl, that bit of cloth has come all the way from Paris, so now when you have a terrible cold you'll be able to use a REAL Parisian hankie—aren't you lucky? Did you have a nice day? I haven't seen you properly tonight, and I hear that you were upset this morning about the photo Penny took of me for you. Don't be silly! The photo would have been awful if it had come out. It's late; you must sleep, so au revoir (French, so ask someone who knows French).

Dearest Virginia,
On the hockey pitch today, everyone in the form was talking about the form party we are going to try and have at Lesley's house for next half-term. And I got so worried, because I don't know any boys and I've never been to a party, except when I was tiny, with jelly and stuff . . . perhaps I'll just not go. My hair is horrible and I look so small, and people have always said I've got an odd face. Have you had a fight with Vonnie, because she looks so sad?

Dearest Emily,
Don't be such a damn fool! You will have a lovely time at the form party, and all the boys will think you are quite

beautiful. If you like, I will cut your hair so that it doesn't look so straight across the edges. All you have to do is smile and be friendly and you will have more boyfriends than anyone.

Here is another photograph. It's rotten and I look so silly, but still I promised, so I must let you have it. I'm glad you like the Toblerone. It was my last bar, but you deserve it because you're so sweet. I hope you are working hard for the exams, because I don't want to be the one who catches you swotting in the lavs at 2:00 A.M. Of course you won't do badly; you are very clever, far cleverer than all that droopy lot in your form. Yes, I'll write in the hols and I'll think of you lots and lots. Sleep well.

P.S. I'm glad you approved of me blowing up that bully Di, she really has got to stop picking on people.

Dearest Virginia,
It's late at night and I'm supposed to be swotting. I'm sitting on the bathroom floor, which is cold, and the room smells of baby powder and smelly feet, and I'm terrified that I'll be caught by Barrel, who's been on the prowl every night. I can't concentrate on this ruddy math. None of it makes any sense. I wish you were here to talk to. I keep wanting to creep into your dorm and wake you up. But I know I wouldn't if I saw you sleeping, because you've got much more important exams coming up, so I couldn't make you tired. Oh, Virginia, I can't bear it for the term to end.

Dearest Emily,
You must stop worrying about the holidays and about not seeing me. Lots of new and exciting things are going to happen to you, and you won't miss me at all. But of course I will write to you, every day. Congrats for the swimming; you did jolly well and, take it from me, if you train hard this term and next term, you could get into the Inter High gala. If you do, you must write and tell me, and I'll come over from England by plane with my children and watch you win the one hundred yards. I must end now as the bell's about to go.

My dearest, dearest Virginia,
It's the holidays in two days, that's all I can think. Everyone in the dorm is madly crossing off the days and pretending they're going to have the most marvelous holidays. But I'd like to break all the clocks and turn the nights back. It is more than I can think about to know that this is your very last year and then you will be gone forever. What will I do?

Dearest, sweetest Emily,
I read your last letter again and again and felt so sad. I shall miss you horribly when I go. I shall be very miz. to leave the school and my friends, even some of the old pengies, but you most of all. But I'm not going yet, and when I do go, I shall not be going far, and I shall come and take you out on going-out Sundays and write every day and send you presents. And then one day not so far off, you'll leave, too, and if I'm in England, you can come and live with me. And perhaps I shall have a bald husband and a brat or two. But I don't think so, not too soon. And we can have long conversations over coffee late at night or walk down lanes with cobbles and blackberries—and plan how our lives shall be. We shall have splendid lives and do wonderful things. And go all over Europe on boats together and have thousands of boyfriends, but still love each other better than all of them—until we marry, of course! And now, my girl, you must stop having these gloomy thoughts because it's *ages* before I'll be gone. But still, you must allow yourself a best friend—what about Penny? Everybody needs a best friend at boarding school and you just don't trust yourself to spend any time with one person, do you? You think you'll mess it up. Well, you won't. You are becoming very admired, you know! People think you're courageous and don't give a damn! What higher praise? So keep your eye open for a friend, and don't be so silly; of *course* I don't think it would be disloyal. I want you to have a best friend when I have gone. Oceans of love and a kiss on every wave!

Dearest, dearest Virginia,
This is the last letter of the term. Thank you for yours, which was very wonderful and encouraging to me—so encouraging

you always are, and I have never known it before. But thank you. I shall never, never while I am at this school, care for anyone as I have and do and always shall for you. I shall never, never make another friend. I shall be faithful to you forever. And about that there is nothing you can do. Have a lovely holiday. I shall be waiting for your letters, if you are not too busy with all your admirers!

For the first time, Emily had a requited love. Now the whole school, the whole world, had shrunk to the circle of one pale face. Emily felt raw and frightened: she only felt the sunshine if she could see Virginia walking in the distance, only join in the singing if Virginia was in the chapel—only smell, feel, breathe, if she used Virginia's presence to do it by. She was lost to herself.

Virginia watched her and grew alarmed. For a person so gentle and compassionate, she also had a secret strength. She was a person who would snap the neck of a bird without a second's squeamishness to prevent it suffering.

She was extraordinary in that she clearly felt that every act she made or saw required of her an examination. She was committed to understanding her life and motives, and those of the people close to her. Then she would try to draw out the positive element in what she saw and nurture it. She did this with the same concern that another teenager might bestow on her personal appearance. But there was no indulgence in her introversion. For Virginia, to be good, to be kind, was a piece of work, a creative challenge.

Now Virginia was becoming concerned about Emily. She asked her to come to the prefects' study for tea. When Emily came in, she saw the tea arranged around a bowl of pansies. Virginia looked up and smiled. "Do you know what I want to talk to you about, Em?"

Emily felt she could see right into Virginia, see the words forming in her mind as clearly as her own thoughts came and went. She said quietly, "Maybe."

Virginia came and sat on the floor close to her; she began to pour lemonade into glasses and Emily watched—as though it were the most important thing in the world—the bubbles rose and burst in the glass as the froth swirled and spat at the lip.

"Emily, last term, you needed no one; you were a free spirit, and now . . ."

"Now I need you."

"That's what I mean—and it hurts you."

"I'm more used to being on my own, that's all. And now I'm not, but I somehow feel more lonely. Are you trying to get rid of me or something?" she snapped.

"Don't be silly, but I think that maybe you're getting too dependent, clingy, on me. And that will only make you miserable."

"Because you're going?"

"No, because if you need someone else to give you happiness, they can also take it away."

Emily considered this, "Hm, that's right, I suppose."

"When I was thirteen, I used to think it was romantic and gorgeous to be sad. You're not really like that, I know, but perhaps a little. And did you know, after that, I went through a thing when I really wanted to be a nun, to perfect myself, to give myself to others, like they tell you all the time you should be trying to do."

"Do you still want to be a nun?"

Virginia laughed. "No, not now; it's something a lot of girls at convents feel at a certain age. Three of us went around thinking we were purer than snow and all wrapped up in God, and then, suddenly, it was gone."

"You would have been a beautiful nun."

"No," Virginia said, almost sharply for her. "I wouldn't have been, because, you see, Emily, I'm not beautiful at all. Any beauty you see in me you have given me. I decided not to be a nun because I saw that what nuns believe would be wrong for me. If you believe what the Catholics believe, you become helpless, like a stuck pin on a huge machine. If God decides everything, then only He can change it."

"Em," she said urgently, "it's up to us, each one of us, to change, to make things better. But we have to change ourselves, too, first. I've got a cousin who is always going on about what he wants to do for the Africans, and how appalling things are for them—but he's the most selfish bugger, and he never actually does a darn thing about it. While my dear ma spends hours each day down at the township and at the hospital actually nursing and talking to the mothers about how to feed their babies properly; she goes into their shacks and sits down and does it with them. That's what I mean."

"Do you think I should change myself?" Emily asked, startled.

"Yes, a little. We all have to change all the time, don't we? You know, Immac once said about you—you don't know this, but she used to discuss everyone with the prefects. She said that you could soon begin to influence—for the worst in her view—the people around you. Now this frightened her, though she adored strength, because she couldn't get her mitts on your strength. And that's the best bit of you, Em. You are strong; you've made yourself that way. And you're clever. You could do anything in the world, as long as you believed it of yourself. You're stubborn enough. My ma says women have to be very stubborn or else they'll achieve nothing. That's why it would be so bad for you to rely too much on me, or another person. I think you might be one of those people who do something noble, really grand, one day."

Emily looked at her. She was almost tearful.

Virginia said quickly, lightly, "Emily, your eyes are disappearing again!" Emily looked back at her and forced a grin.

"Do you know what an angry person you are? Underneath, I think you're nearly always angry." Virginia's face was very solemn.

"Well, I do have a violent temper." Emily said fiercely.

"Oh, I know! People are a bit frightened of you." She laughed and smoothed Emily's arm, saying, "You're angry now, aren't you?"

"Yes, I'm angry about things I can't change."

"If you're angry, it's because you're unhappy and you're blaming someone for it. What do you want to change?"

"Oh, everything. I want to be able to do as I please, spend my time as I please, be with you as much as I want. I feel so cramped here; there's no air. I sometimes feel I'm on a hook."

"You are. But it's your hook. You can *make* yourself free. You once told me you were free in your mind; well you're nearly *all* mind. These little schoolish restrictions won't last; they don't matter. You have to be free inside, really; then you'll be happy."

"What does happiness matter?" She was almost surly.

"Oh, it does matter. Terribly. If you're happy you can be good or, rather, *do* good. Unhappy people are dangerous. I believe in goodness. And if we are good for God and He doesn't exist—it won't hurt us. Father Comber said that. I learned a lot about goodness from him when I was trying to be holy! He's good, but he's weak, really. God, I sound just like old Immac! And she wasn't good. Come on, you're not eating the cakes."

Emily took one and said simply, "Don't be worried about me, Virginia. I'll always be strong underneath. It's just that I've never known anyone like you—good, clever—like that. It's rather knocked me over. I won't try to hang on to you, that's what bothers you, isn't it?

"Don't be daft. I just don't want you to be hurt, or to feel lost when I go. We are very good friends; we will always, always be. And look, I have a present for you, an end-of-term present." She took out of her pocket a little parcel wrapped in crushed tissue and handed it to Emily, who opened it slowly. Inside was a plain, smooth silver chain.

Emily said, "Is this for me?"

Virginia nodded. And when Emily lifted her hands and let it circle her neck, she felt filled with Virginia's magic. She wore it around her neck as actresses wear the personalities they don; as kings are made magnificent by the crowns on their heads. Wearing it, she could face the holidays, bear the absence, and move back into herself without being frightened by the emptiness she would now feel there.

Over the course of the year, Emily was able to see that the convent atmosphere inspired other such passionate friendships. Normally they developed between girls of the same age, who could look into each other's eyes across dormitories or chapel and walk arm in arm up and down the hockey field, shelling the secrets of their hearts. Sometimes, after years, a friendship like this would come to a violent end.

Under Immaculata such relationships had existed, but took on an illicit air. Without her the school was ablaze with warmth and tenderness and tears. A girl walking into an empty classroom to find two others in deep discussion would mumble, "Sorry," as though she had intruded upon nakedness, and withdraw immediately. The sending of notes put the post office to shame in the efficiency of their dispatch. Presents and mementos changed hands, and so, occasionally, did razor blades, until Sister Benedict was asked to ban the ritual of cutting the skin and mingling the blood of two friends bent on eternal fidelity.

Emily had been a little contemptuous of these dependencies at first. Even after forming a similar intensity herself, she did not consider it to be at all the same thing. The fact that Virginia was more than four years her senior supported this view.

For the remainder of the year, before Virginia left, their relationship developed, as Emily did herself, at an accelerated pace, like a speeded-up dream. Until the time of her meeting with Rena, Emily had no ideal of how a woman should be. And she was aware now of how very quickly she was becoming one. When she had looked at her mother, her reaction was one of dread. Only with Rena did she find a woman worthy of emulation. This reached its conclusion with Virginia, who became the woman Emily aspired to be.

Virginia left at the end of the year. The last day of the last term was a sad occasion, and during the end-of-term assembly, while Sister Benedict talked of those who were leaving, what they had achieved, before wishing them a happy, fruitful future, there were very few girls who did not feel the lump of their own departure in their throats. During the singing of the last hymn in chapel at night—"Round me falls the night;/Saviour, be my light./Through the hours of darkness shrouded,/Let me see Thy face unclouded./Let Thy glory shine,/In this heart of mine"— most would succumb to tears and would find the sight of the packed, stacked trunks as mournful as the siren of a departing ship.

Emily, who had not experienced an end of year before, stood silent, tearless, apart from it all, consumed by her own grief. She took a walk with Virginia out to the tree at the end of the hockey pitch, where they sat on a log and could find nothing to say. Emily was trying to repress an anger in herself at the injustice of the situation. But she also knew this to be selfish. Finally, Virginia, who had been holding Emily's hand, a little the way a nurse would, placed it back with Emily's other one.

"I have to go now, Em; my father's coming a bit earlier because he has an appointment."

Emily then hated Virginia's father with all her might; the hatred was all the more extreme because here was a father who would collect his daughter, not send her on the train.

Emily got up and ran, ran like a wild thing, away, away, across to the other side of the hockey pitch, where the morning sun was just beginning to make steep shadows beneath the trees. She did not stop until she had reached the shade. Then she turned, expecting to find that Virginia had gone. But she stood there still. Emily could not believe it. When she did believe it, she began to run back, in a dead-straight line, to that steady, immovable figure.

My dearest Emily,
After I took you back to school, I found your mac behind the door, and seeing it hanging there, I felt terribly sad. I wanted to write straightaway, but I'm afraid my eyes would not stay open another minute. So, with the rain battering on the roof and an empty feeling in my heart, I went to sleep and had nightmares about you!

It was horrible leaving you last night, and arriving home, I felt sadder and sadder. I only hope you felt better after a few hours, because to feel miserable at school is really AWFUL. About now you will be having lessons, math perhaps, and that silly young teacher will be rambling on about squares and triangles. Ma thought you looked most intelligent, which you are, so I'm awaiting the exam results—honors, please!

I am afraid I didn't thank you properly for the wonderful birthday present you gave me. The scent is delicious, and I'm going to use it for a film we are going to see today and on the first night of the ship. The hankies are the sweetest I have ever seen, and when I'm miz., I'll hold one of the hankies and I'll feel better straightaway, and as I'm getting miz. more often now I'll be clutching them all the time.

You are so much more grown up now. I'm so proud of you, and of how brave you were when I told you the exact day we were sailing. And, you know, I do not want to go at all now. I shall miss everyone and this house and all the people at school that I like. And, oh, how I shall miss this beautiful, beautiful Rhodesia and the Falls, and the sun and all our sweet servants who have looked after me since I was so little. And my uncle's farm, with the maize and the tobacco and the beautiful baobab trees and the dam with the fan palms. But I'm the one who says we must be HAPPY and here I am almost about to howl! Sorry.

And you will be happy, won't you? Though I shall miss you so, so much I can't bear to think about it. But I'll come back. I must. I couldn't live anywhere else for long. I'll come back and be a nurse in one of the mission hospitals, and then I'll start one of my own, a really super one for the black children, to stop all those babies dying—with enough beds and nice sheets, at a place where they don't travel so far to get there. And you will help me, won't you? You can be in charge, and then it will be run superbly. There, now I feel better; now I know it is not just now that matters, but tomorrow, later, other days that we must be preparing ourselves for.

So you must get a First Class Matric, my girl! Work hard, play games well, and then you'll be a prefect! When I come to Old Girls' Day in a few years' time, you'll serve me with watery tea and fattening cakes.

I must go and wash my hair; it is absolutely filthy, and yours was so clean and shiny yesterday, I felt ashamed of my awful straw. I'll write again tomorrow.

With all my love and kisses,
Virginia

Virginia left Rhodesia and went to Oxford to train as a nurse. But to Emily, it was as if she had not gone at all. She retained a picture of Virginia so clear, so distilled, that it was almost as tangible as a presence, and so she could bear the separation.

Whatever Emily did, she was aware of Virginia's gaze on her; she referred to her judgment, quite unconscious that Virginia's personality was different from her own.

Emily would now stop instead of merely reacting to situations; she would take time to consider. She ceased forever to have a totally pure, primitive response to everything around her; her observation, once so cruel and precise, was no longer directed exclusively at the twisted aspects around her. No longer threatened, she began to seek happiness.

Later, as a prefect, she fought any cruelty and unfairness in the convent system and rallied all the other prefects to encourage the head mistress to take on more non-Catholics. She had refused to be converted to Catholicism, and had never been confirmed, and yet there she was—a prefect, a respected member of the establishment. She had proved by her own example that it was possible not to conform, not to be bullied, and still succeed.

And then, in the last year at school, she began to feel again the little scratching fingers of desire. It was not a new passion; it came from her twelfth year. And now, as Virginia married and settled in England, so Emily tracked back slowly to her first holiday at the le Roux farm. She began again, no longer just at odd moments, but increasingly, to explore the possibilities of Patrick. She dug up the dream; she gave it new colors. She found him lacking in nothing. He remained as clear as a mirrored image in her heart, unchanged by the years or by experience. Just the Patrick she once knew and loved, who had spoken so easily with that rich, swaying lilt to his voice. He had told her to wait for him; to grow for him, and then to seek him out.

Now she was ready.

PART THREE

Twice or thrice had I loved thee,
Before I knew thy face.
DONNE

EMILY CAME OUT OF THE CONVENT SCREAMING FOR LIFE. She came home on a blistering afternoon to find the normally dolorous household in a state of excitement and bustle. Her mother had put on a new face: it was round and pretty, and her hair, which was longer and more softly curled, no longer accentuated the dangerous slopes of her cheekbones. She wore a bright dress, where the cotton bloomed with rosebuds. Lilian was in the kitchen; the floor was taken up by large tea chests full of packing paper, the table precarious with towers of crockery. Her father, who had collected her from the station, was demanding a cup of tea, but no one could find a teacup; it seemed some idiot servant had packed the whole lot. A cup was finally found, but not before Emily felt a familiar weariness returning. She looked about her in dismay.

"Where are we going next?" she asked. For this packing, these moves, they took place every year or so. And always there was a lot of bickering and accusing of the servants for a bit of lost silver, for the odd broken cup or plate.

"Oh, this is different, Emily," her mother crowed. "This time we are going home."

Home? Did she mean to the river? No—Jesus God—she didn't.

"Do you mean England?"

"Yes, of course. Home. And don't look so startled. We didn't tell you because we wanted it to be a surprise."

"It's not my home. My home is here."

"Don't start any of that, Emily. You're an English girl. England is your home. You should be proud." Emily looked at her father, who was drinking his tea urgently.

"Your father has been transferred to the Colonial Office in London. And so we are going home at last."

"Well, I'm not, I'm not going."

Bernard Jones snorted into his tea: some of it went up his nose and burned there. "Oh bloody hell, you hear that? She's not going!"

He was red in the face. He was angry because he wasn't sure that he wanted to go himself, not really. But damned if he was going to put up with her saying it.

"Go and change," Lilian said, finding the sight of the convent garb offensive.

When Emily came back in shorts and a shirt, Bernard Jones was still there. He did not fancy going back to the office; the new chap was there, acting as if he knew it all. Seeing his papers all stacked, his reports put to one side, well, it was depressing. He had another cup of tea. And wondered if this move had any connection with the fact that he had recently had another combustion with old Hampton.

Emily began to enclose the plates she was packing in old copies of the *Mafeking Mail* and the less crushable pages of *Panorama*. The possibility of going to England seemed remote as the sun slammed through the kitchen window, as Mpande trekked in and out with the heavy crates, and her mother of all things, was humming.

"When's all this happening?" she asked vaguely.

"Well," her father said sheepishly, "as a matter of fact, we are going before you—your mother and I—to find a house, settle in, before you come. You'll be spending a couple of months at the le Roux."

Well, here was a reprieve, but she must be careful. "That's nice," she said, adopting her best tone. "Perhaps I could just come back here afterward?"

"No, you could not," her mother snapped. "You're only seventeen. What are you thinking of? What do you think you could *do* here?" She didn't know what anyone could possibly do here.

"I was thinking of going to agricultural college. There's one—"

Now here was something for Bernard to laugh about! "Agricultural college? Are you daft? Girls don't go to agricultural college. What on earth for? Don't be so stupid."

"Well, I must do something. It's what I wanted to do." Oh, Lord, what a weariness to be home.

"Oh, indeed you must do something," Lilian shot in. "All girls need something to fall back on, like typing or nursing, in case the husband dies or something." Lilian Jones could neither nurse nor type. She had only a bed to fall back on; she knew the dangers.

"There are good secretarial colleges in London," Bernard said. "There's not much else you can do."

She was furious.

Nothing irritated him more than other people getting angry. "Don't get so worked up," Lilian said absently, catching sight of her daughter's face. "You will have to settle down when you get to England, Emily, English girls do not carry on. Nor is there anyone to clear up after them. No servants. Oh, no! You clean your own shoes. English girls cook and wash up and clean."

Emily began to think with pleasure about the le Roux. "When am I going to the farm?"

"In a few days, at the weekend." Lilian was sailing away on decisions, heading for home and safe harbor. "Your hair's awful! We shall have to get it cut. And your nails are so long. What's that on them? For heaven's sake, do you see that, Bernard, silver nail varnish! Go and get it off straightaway. It's disgusting. Girls in England don't wear makeup."

Emily stared at her mother: who was this person come to life so vehemently? And all because she's going home? Lilian was radiant with change, and a little alarming.

Bernard was worried about the change, too. He couldn't make up his mind which was easier to bear: the chronic silence or the inflated optimism. Now she was making demands again—where they should live; how they should live. She was puffed up with her own importance and had begun to be snooty to everyone—like someone who has won the pools and cannot afford to be friendly any longer.

Bernard had heard what people said after a trip home. How dull it was, no parties, no servants, no gaiety, just like India after the Raj. Dreary, boring. He'd never understood why everyone had said they should get out of India. The Indians, the wogs, they'd had nothing to complain of under colonial rule; it was a good life for everyone.

He dreaded the future. The continent falling into wrack and ruin without the British backbone and the making-the-idle-devils-work. He liked the place. He did not want to go. She was making him. She could not bear it another minute. And people over the years had said that the place did not suit her, that she was not well, that she looked peculiar. Wasn't there some story about a bit of insanity in the family somewhere? Well, never mind about that. Anyone could begin to crack up under these conditions. There was a time once, in the bush, one night when all the natives had been leaping and dancing drunkenly around the fire, that he had felt a strange feeling of disorientation . . . but he didn't believe in insanity. Not in people he knew. And he supposed she was better now, seemed damn cheerful. Hadn't seen her like this for years: bustling and organizing, packing and planning. She didn't even take a nap in the afternoon anymore. Couldn't complain, could he?

Before Emily went to the farm and her parents to Cape Town to catch the ship, there was a row, one last confrontation.

Emily was sitting in the back of the car. They had a few minutes before she caught the train. She said, calmly but carefully, "I really would rather not come to England. Can't I stay here? I've thought about it. I could learn to type very quickly in Bulawayo or Salisbury, get a job, support myself. I know some people there."

"No, just bloody no and shut up about it now, do you hear?" her father said.

Emily restrained herself. Her mother had gone poker-faced, her lips a pale, drawn ribbon. She was tired of her daughter, who was trying to spoil things.

"You're to do as you're told, Emily," she snapped. She sat up eagerly, "Isn't that the train now?" She began to think of what clothes to pack for the boat. She wished she had more evening dresses, but would have to make do. "Now, look here," she said, realizing that the train had not come in, "stop sulking; take that look off your face."

"But this is my home. I couldn't live anywhere else."

"Your home is where we are, Emily." This from her mother.

Something was going on inside Bernard, and Emily was too busy marveling at her mother to pick it up. He swung around in his seat and yelled at her furiously, "You are going where *I'm* going. And *I'm* going to England."

"Well, good luck to you then."

His eyes began to flicker and his voice to stutter. He looked the perfect imitation of a lunatic.

"What the bloody hell? And after all I've done, all that she can fucking say . . ." He smashed her across the face with the side of his hand. Her nose began to bleed profusely, like something spilled.

She opened the door of the car and got out. She pulled a tissue from her pocket and wedged it into her nose. She got her suitcase and walked toward the train that was galloping in. An old Afrikaner woman on the train looked at her as she pushed past and noticing the blood all down her front, said, "Ag, shame, and it's such terrible stuff to get out."

In a little while the train pulled out. Her father and mother sat silently in the car. They had not moved. Lilian was bitter against her husband, not on her daughter's behalf, but on her own.

"Lord, how lovely, you can stay three whole months." Jean was leading Emily to the dormitory, to her old bed by the screen door.

"Oh, missy, what a pleasant thing to see your face again," said Isabella, one of the Damara ladies, "Would you take a piece of cake? You're thin now, too thin; take a piece of cake."

"But round in the right places," Henri said, digging Emily in the ribs. She ate the cake and one of the dogs flicked up the crumbs with an expert tongue.

"But that's easy," Jean said, "I can teach you to type. I'm going to stay here till February, then my new job starts in Joburg. They showed me the office—oh, it's so lovely, high on the tenth floor: my own office, my own boss. I'm going to be a personal assistant. There won't be so much typing then, I'm sure; more contact, you know. Hey, you can come and see me, Em! First I'll be staying with Joy, then I'll find a little place all of my own."

"And I want to learn to drive, too, Jean, I can a bit already."

"Oh, Danny Boy can help you there," Henri said with pride. "He's driven since he was nine. And you should see David now. My God, he's marvelous with the boys, can get anything out of them!"

Emily felt nervous at the prospect of seeing David again.

"Now, where's Rena? I must see her right this minute," Emily said.

"She's in the store, waiting for you."

"I can't wait to see her. It's been such ages."

"Well, you shouldn't have gone so far away." Henri beamed. "Hell, we were glad when your pa asked if we could have you."

"So am I. I never want to go."

"Well, stay then, man, stay. You can learn everything you need to right here." Henri gave a chuckle. And she remembered his body after the swimming in the reservoir and the smell of tobacco in his hair.

It was dark, her first night there. The bats were shrieking in the roof; the crickets made a continuous chatter. She lay in bed, her arms flung above her head, stiff with excitement. Patrick, Patrick, where are you? When will I see you? How will it be? Will you remember? But of course you'll remember. It's impossible that you'd have forgotten. Quite impossible. Oh, but will you like me? Will you think I'm a looker?

She learned to drive very quickly in order to find him. Danny Boy taught her in Rena's old van. The gears groaned in protest, but soon she had everything in control and roared up and down the drive, terrorizing the chickens and the piccanins.

They were having dinner and she managed to ask casually where Patrick's farm was.

Rena looked at her over the bowl of pumpkin, "I shouldn't go there, you know. I know you had a crush on him when you were little, but he's—Oh, Jean, *must* you put all that butter in? It's so fattening, do you want to end up looking like me?"

Henri splayed his hands down contentedly on the table and leaned back to announce, "So, who'll come shooting with me tonight? We need a nice supply of venison."

And so the talk continued, and people began to eat more quickly. And Emily was saved.

David walked over to Emily as the table was emptying. "Are you coming, Emily? They tell me you used to shoot pretty good once. Haven't forgotten, have you?" He was shy and a little flushed, very eager for her approval; for the past few days she had barely noticed him. She looked hard at him before replying; his face had sweetened and the lines were less sharp, more human. He still had the rash, but it was not so bad.

"Ya, I still shoot. Do you ever see Willie now, David?"

She was always so sharp with her questions, used them like a fork, to jab at the tender places.

"Hell, no, he's gone to the dogs, man."

"And Lottie?"

"Well, she comes to visit us here sometimes. She's better for being away."

"And you, too."

So she approved; he smiled for the first time. "And me, too."

It was a long conversation for him.

"You've changed, David." How softly she said that! Did she remember as he remembered—each little gesture of that day?

"You also."

"Yes? In what way?"

"Well, it's funny—in some ways not at all. But you had a face then like a wolf."

"Oh, thanks, thanks a lot."

"Heck, I'm sorry." His face bunched up with misery. He so wanted her to like him. She was prettier now, but her face was still like that: sharp, watching, weighing up.

"Ag, forget it," she said. "Get the guns, I'll see what I do remember." And she felt ugly again, like a wolf, and suddenly a whole wave of uncertainty flooded her. She went to get a sweater. David watched her go. She walked like a boy, was unaware of her hips, but very aware of herself, of his eyes on her exposed back.

She had chosen the time carefully; it would take her less than an hour to drive there. She walked to the van, hoping no one would see her. She had on her tightest shorts and a pale pink blouse. She was damp with nervousness. It was the day.

Driving down the dirt track past the plantation she nearly ran into a young springbuck; the brakes slammed down, the car skidded and came to a stop. She let her head fall onto the steering wheel, and almost burst into tears.

No, it's ridiculous. I must go back. (But he said, but he *said*.)

It's six years later. It's crazy. I must forget the whole thing.

No, I'll go. I can pretend I got lost.

I'll just sit here a little longer.

He said, he *did* say. He promised.

A little shiver of wind ruffled the damp hair at the back of her neck. I'll have to go now or it'll be too late. He'll go back to the lands after lunch. Switch on ignition, balance clutch, off with the brake, here I go.

She had dreamed all those years how it would be: walking up to his house with a long cool veranda and a green water tank, acacia trees all around it, red-hot pokers against the walls. Looking up at the veranda, through the netting, to see a white rocking chair, a soft swing sofa, a hat on a chair, a pipe—no, not a pipe, a packet of Rothmans.

She used to think of finding him sitting by a window in the early morning, and she would enter the room wearing a pale dress and would touch him and say, "Here I am." He would turn and smile and move to where she could sit beside him. On other days, she would imagine it would be raining when she came and the ground plastered down like wet hair. Or in bright sunlight, as he sat smoking beneath a tree.

He is richer than I thought. That's a new Chevrolet. And the house is big, with new buildings added to the right. The garden is beautiful, like an English garden in a painting; you could almost see hollyhocks and foxgloves with their backs to the walls. So green it's almost spooky in this heat. There must have been a child here once, because there's a swing, and the ground beneath has been scraped into a hollow. Come on now, ring the bell, ring it. No one's coming. Oh, thank heavens! Now I could go; I've been; now I could leave. Someone's coming!

He looks sleepy; the black hair glossy as a blackbird; the skin of his throat smooth and dark.

He was exhausted: he had spent the morning, since dawn, rounding up a herd. He opened the screen door and leaned against the side of it. He rubbed his hand across his forehead.

"Yes?"

It couldn't be that he was impatient? She couldn't say anything; it was no good, she couldn't think of the words; there was this scythe, and each word that surfaced was sliced under. She looked at him desperately.

"I'm sorry? I've got a terrible memory for names," he said. She was standing there as if she expected him to know her.

She could tell: he had forgotten, completely—he hadn't a clew. She wanted to run a mile for the shame of it. Then her heart hit rock bottom—and cleared. Now she could use her convent training.

"I'm sorry to disturb you. We did in fact meet, it was years ago [the bastard, the bastard] at the le Roux. I'm staying with them at the moment; they suggested I drop in as I was passing your way."

"Oh, yes, of course I remember. . . ." He hadn't a clew.

"Actually"—she laughed, and oh, amazement, it didn't sound too false—"it was rather funny; you gave me a tickey then and told me to ring you when I was sixteen. . . ."

He laughed with her. It was a little remark he had used quite often. When she scowled, he thought he did perhaps remember her, vaguely, something about the eyes.

"It must have been years ago." That should sound flattering to a young girl.

"It was almost exactly five years ago. I was twelve."

"What a memory!"

"Well, here I am. I've come." She was as cool and calm as a pool into which a man could only plunge and drown.

He smiled; he thought her magnificent: her back straight, her head erect and defiant; she wasn't going to let him get away with a thing. His eyes began to splutter with mirth.

"In that case, come in. I've been expecting you."

"Thank you." She walked into the cool. There was no rocking chair on the veranda, but there was a desk, papers, cigarettes. He led her into the drawing room.

She sat down on the edge of a deep, blue sofa. It was faded on one arm. He noticed her caution as she sat.

"Why didn't you come before?" he asked gently. "Why wait all this time?"

"Because I wasn't ready." A little sullen.

"And you're ready now?"

"Yes, I'm ready now, I'm seventeen."

"Ah, a great age."

"Don't be condescending. It can be a great age."

"Yes, I can see that." He studied her quite openly; he imagined the shape of her body, but could not tell quite how the skin would feel. She waited, then said coolly, as she imagined a sophisticate might do, "Well, will I do?"

He looked again at the small, bright body, the button straining against its anchorage.

"Oh, yes, you will do." Then he laughed and it came from deep inside him and felt real, wonderfully, sparklingly real.

She said, "You didn't remember."

He felt a little apprehensive; something you feel when the lightning crackles too close to a tree.

"It was a joke, a game. . . ."

She set him straight. "No, you are fooling yourself."

His eyes darkened; he was no longer quite so amused.

"What do you mean?"

"I mean that at the time, when you said it to me, you meant it. It was a true wish."

"Yes, I suppose so." She was right there, but it was hardly

relevant. Then, thinking a little, he was impressed by how direct her logic was.

"You're pretty unusual," he said softly, and he leaned forward and did up her top button; her breasts looked pale and neat. "But you know, anything might have happened since then, it's a dangerous game you play." He could see out of the corner of his eye the little rosewood box which held his wife's cottons; the bottom drawer was open, watching.

"But nothing did happen. And it's not a game. You are here and I am here."

"That's all that matters?"

She nodded. He picked up her hand and looked at it carefully; she had once bitten her nails.

"Will it make you angry again if I tell you I can't remember your name."

"My name is Emily."

"Emily what?"

"Emily Jones."

"Good. I am all yours, Emily Jones. What can I offer you? Lunch? Tea? Coffee?"

"A beer."

"A beer." He tried not to smile. She was as straight as an arrow.

"I think I should warn you, Emily, I'm a broken reed."

"Are you?" She thought the better of him for it.

His smile was disarming; his teeth small and white with a tiny chip missing on one of the top ones. "You seem so old for your age. I was appalling at seventeen."

"Girls are better."

"Certainly, I'd agree with that."

She followed him to the kitchen, trying carefully not to get too close. She sat on one of the old stools and looked at the remnants of his lunch: cold beef, some tomatoes, onions, and brown bread. She immediately wanted to take care of him.

"Who does your lunch?" Her mother would have said, "Do you have a decent cook?"

"Well, the cook, Winston, just leaves me a plate of something. I don't expect them here when I'm alone."

Seeing her perched bravely on the stool, he began to feel protective. After all, the girl was very young for all her bravado. She must be someone's daughter; he had better be careful.

"I wonder why you chose me?" he asked sweetly. "I'm so old; there must be better game."

"You're thirty," she said firmly. "That's about right." She was thinking of the gauche young men she'd met at parties, and how she'd set them up against his memory and found them lacking. He was rubbing the bread between his fingers and making little pellets, which he then flicked off the table.

"I suppose you must have gone to that convent that the le Roux girls went to?"

"Yes."

"Girls from convents, they're the worst, of course."

"In what way?" He was put off by the bluntness.

"You think they're fast?" she put in quickly.

"Don't know, could be . . ." He could not make out whether she was offended.

She looked thoughtful and serious. "Would you like it if I were fast?"

He roared with laughter, "I like you just as you are."

Thirty minutes went up in smoke. He should be getting back to work but did not want to. She could certainly take care of herself, no flies on her, but he began to wonder about himself. He changed the subject again.

"Oh *that* Jones! Yes, of course I know. Some good reports on cattle and disease. Have you known the le Roux long?"

"Yes, but I haven't seen much of them really, except at school."

"Ah, yes." (He remembered Joy all right, she'd once seen him off.)

"You'll have to get back," she said, looking at her watch, "and so must I."

"Will you come back?"

"Yes, if you like."

"Tomorrow?"

"Yes."

"Come at the same time then; I want to show you a place near here that I like."

"Where is it?"

"Oh, just down the road." They were standing facing each other, very close together. He turned her with his hand, "It's an old Bushman cave; it feels like a church inside, only better." She looked up at him as if expecting something.

"Aren't you going to kiss me?"

He smiled and cupped her face and kissed her softly on the mouth. She was a little disappointed, a little relieved.

"You *are* unusual." He smiled. "See how well you make me behave?"

She loved him. Oh, how she loved him!

They were standing on the veranda, close to the door. Now there was an awkwardness because they did not quite know how to take their leave of each other.

"Well, till tomorrow," he said, toying with the idea of kissing her again. But he did not trust himself to bring it off so coolly.

She walked to the van, climbed in it, and drove away.

Ten minutes later she was crying. She went on driving, finding it difficult to see through the bug-smeared window with her soaked eyes. Slowly, she stopped; she shook herself, she gathered the shattered fragments of her dream and shuffled them together in a new pattern. She was here, so was he, they were together. And it was happening. There was no question but that he would love her. Even though he had forgotten.

He watched her drive away, almost exasperated. He had an odd feeling that he might have got something wrong, that if he had been able to handle the situation differently from the outset, the continuation might have been easier. Then he grinned and walked happily inside. He was exhilarated by the thought that she had re-membered and come, to find *him*. She had waited all those years, for him, just for him. And then turned up, bold as brass. It was incredible and most flattering. She was superb. He had thought for a moment how dangerous to live in the romantic imagination, now it passed through his head again but he dismissed it—such courage was a little beyond him.

He walked back into his house and felt dissatisfied with his whole life; it seemed suddenly a sham and a painful one at that. He had married Owen's eldest daughter, but it had not won him the farm as he had intended. He felt just like a hired laborer, dependent on the goodwill of his mistress. Which was just what her canny father had wanted and carefully organized. He had not worked all these years for such a meager reward. The place would be nothing without him.

Of course, the trouble was that his wife knew somehow that he had been thinking of selling. That business at Sharpeville; it had shocked the hell out of everyone. There had been an exodus from South Africa, and those left had felt the cold, dark wind blowing at their backs. It was like the Mau Mau, only closer—it was that terrifying, that raw. It left the same legacy as the Mau Mau: it disturbed their dreams and made them look nervously at their servants. Could they also, after all these years, betray us, too? Could old Sampson open the back door in the night and let the knives in? Could he hand over my baby son and watch my wife's stomach being sliced open? Could he batter my head with rocks and roar with laughter? Jesus, it was beyond imagining. But he wanted to think about it, he did not want to bury his head in the sand. Things were changing, the Africans beginning to organize: protest marches, strikes, the lot. People said that the Nats. could sort the blacks out all right and that should keep the whole of the south safe. But it was the fear that bothered Patrick. The fear settled into hatred, hatred and entrenchment; no going back. Yes, he had thought of leaving, everyone did. He was no dedicated pioneer, no settler. He liked to eat and run. But his wife held him, kept him on the chafing lead of his determination to get the land, to own it. She would never sell, never. Home to her was where her father lay buried. A horde of savages could kill her but not budge her. She was worse than a bloody Afrikaner.

And now there was Emily, Emily Jones. Along she had come when he was most lonely. Perhaps she could comfort him; perhaps she could really love him, but love was not one of his priorities.

When she came the next day, she stood and waited behind the

screen door, so that, approaching her, he saw her as if through a veil. It was as much as he could do not to tell her to go away.

"I wasn't sure you'd be here," she said.

"I came back a bit early; I didn't want you to come and not find me. Here, come and have some lunch."

This time she noticed the kitchen; there were bunches of herbs hanging above a marble-top table; there was a row of different-size water jugs against the wall and a dresser with old, blue-and-white china plates. The floor was cold stone and very clean; the table was scrubbed white and the sink was spotless.

"It's a lovely kitchen, you must have a good cook." She went and looked at the shiny copper skillets and caught her reflection in one; she made a face.

He looked a little flustered, guilty even, but led her to a chair by the table. There were little embroidered cushions to sit on, but she was blind to these feminine traces. She was intent on his hands as he sliced the bread into thick chunks. She felt very shy suddenly. He passed her a plate and said, "Here, help yourself; the lamb's good. Winston puts some African spice on it, don't know what it is." She felt she might expire.

Patrick came and knelt by her; he took her hands, which were cold, "You all right?"

She nodded.

"I'm not going to eat you," he said, kissing her. It was the gentleness that took her breath away. She began to shiver. He got up and led her into the drawing room. She went over to the window and stood looking out at the light.

Standing behind her, he put his hands on her waist. She began to shake violently. It was little to do with physical touch; it was an aching to be rid of the self, to be absorbed into another. She moved sharply away from him.

"You weren't brought up by the Jesuits, were you?" He gave a little laugh and she began to relax. She turned to face him. His hands wound round her back and knotted there; her arms rose involuntarily.

He thought he might rip her. She was clenched fast around him, but her arms lay flat by her sides. Her mouth was salty and you would think each touch was unexpected. Christ, was she seventeen? No, she must be, she even seemed more. But so stiff; her responses so raw. She was a virgin. It shocked him, stopped him. "You didn't say, I mean, I didn't know . . ."

She turned her face to look at him, stunned: didn't he know? Didn't he know that she had been created solely for him?

"You really *were* waiting for me?" He couldn't believe it; he was overwhelmed. She was like the first woman on earth, like Eve before the apple. "I love you, Patrick, I love you."

Jean, standing there with her hands on her hips, demanded, "Come on, Em, don't mess around, you must tell me. You've been gone for hours. And I don't believe it about the typing because I went into the study a few times. Go on, tell me. . . ."

"I've just been driving about."

"It's you and David, isn't it?"

Emily looked blank. "No, why do you say that?" She was even offended that she should be connected with any person but him.

"Just the way he looks at you, the way he stays up after dinner, instead of scuttling off to study like he did before you came." Her voice was curt.

Emily went through the loophole, "Oh, what does he study?"

"You know perfectly well, don't change the subject."

"As a matter of fact, I don't."

"He's doing a postal matric. I've been helping him with it."

"No, I didn't know that. But there's nothing, Jean, honestly. I hardly see him."

"Well, he's nuts about you."

"How do you know?"

"By looking. Clearly you don't look."

Emily looked out across the neat row of beds in the room; she could see him as he lay with his arms folded beneath his head. What are you doing now, Patrick? Are you sitting by that desk? Are you smoking a cigarette? Are you thinking of me? Four hours. I'm alive, at last I've come to life.

"Hm? I'm sorry, what did you say, Jean?"

"Perhaps you're worried about something?"

Here was a way of smudging the scent. "Yes, I am a bit. I don't want to go to stinking old England."

"Well, I suppose you have to." Jean was so phlegmatic it was infuriating, "You're not likely to persuade your parents."

"No, and I keep driving around trying to think of a way out of it. I thought maybe if I just went off and got myself a job."

"That won't work. Pa has agreed, in any case, to pack you off as soon as he's given the date."

"You're not being very helpful," Emily snapped, suddenly aware that she'd avoided thinking about leaving.

"Sorry, keep your hair on. Anyway, you might like it. I've always wanted to go to England for a bit. And if you don't like it, earn some money and come back."

"It's only six thousand miles!"

"That's right, nothing is it?" They both laughed.

Jean said she would go and find David to suggest they go through some English grammar that night. Emily called to her as she made for the door.

"Do you remember that man who came when last I was here—Patrick, I think his name was. Does he ever come here now?"

"Not much, not since he married, anyway. . . ."

Jean walked away. The door slammed shut, with Emily stock-still on the wrong side of it.

The next day was like a white endless path with a dead thing upon it.

He was sitting on the veranda; he got up when he heard the van approach, went slowly to switch on a light. A circle of yellow pooled on the floor beneath it. He was afraid, as though what lurked in the darkness was more powerful than he. The door slammed behind him. He stood on the red steps and looked out. He had that Catholic ability to know everything that was to happen slightly in advance of its occurrence.

The moon was high; half of it had been eaten away. The sky was as wide and cool as the reaches of pale dead grass below it. Emily stood by the van, her head high, her teeth clenched: a perfect convent girl, sanctified by suffering. She waited as he walked over the gravel; it crackled like fire.

"Emily, why didn't you come yesterday?" He was in despair suddenly. She looked at him, wondering, why did I come? Why am I here at all?

"What happened?" he asked. But he knew.

She folded her arms across her breasts, "Why didn't you tell me?"

"I thought you might go."

"I would have respected you for telling me."

"So you don't now?"

"Now I don't know."

"You're shivering. Come inside." She stood there still. If he showed any indecision, any weakness, he would be lost.

"Come," he said firmly, turning to walk. She did not come.

"Come," he ordered.

She came, walking behind him very quietly on the gravel. Then she ran and hurled herself against his back, pounding it with her fists, pummeling the broad stretch across his shoulder blades. He turned sharply and crushed her hands together, pulling them down hard so that her body was bowed. Looking at her raised, livid face, there was no question that she wanted to kill him. He released her and turned again. He understood her now: She was able to live out the violence in her heart. He could not.

The coffee tasted burned, but they drank it. All noise was external: insects were battering against the windows, the crickets were in a fury.

"You said nothing else mattered, just that we were here, together."

Her teeth ground together, so that the lines of her face took on the sharp edges of a coin.

"Is there a child?"

He braced himself, he had thought she must know everything.

"Yes, one, a boy."

"Just the one?"

It was so green and slimy, the emotion she felt. She turned away from him. He surprised himself; he got up from behind his coffee and went to kneel by her chair. He was aware now that he did not want to lose her. She had come, so there was a chance that he could hold her. He turned her face toward his and looked at her, speaking earnestly.

"I think I love you."

"You think?"

"Yes, I think." She recognized it as being one of the first straight remarks he had made.

She smiled and touched his cheek. He thought he had won her.

Now he was no longer afraid he could afford to be a little less careful.

"It hasn't ever been, you know, a good marriage. I was pulled about by the two of them, her and her sister." He didn't like the way this presented him, so he spoke more emphatically. "I encourage her to spend most of her time with her sister, that's where she is now, that's where she mostly is."

Emily wanted to know if they still slept together. "And what about the child?"

"Oh, he's a good enough kid. But he is still so small, really." She sensed the sadness.

"But I couldn't malign her, not really, you haven't seen her, she is so . . ." He reached for her. "I'm sorry, I won't talk about them. . . ."

"No," she said sharply. "No; I asked. If you ask you must expect to know."

He liked this toughness; he liked the strength of the broad brow and the way her hands always remained perfectly still however agitated her voice became.

"Don't think that I want lies, Patrick." At this moment a lie would have been quite welcome.

"I don't know what I'd have done, if you hadn't come back," he said. "I've been thinking about you all day."

"I only came to say good-bye." Her face was cool and remote, the eyes composed; she turned to look directly at him. He was wearing a gray sweater; there was a strand of pulled wool and she longed to correct it. He got up to walk to the sink, where he poured water into a glass. She felt exultant; his back was eloquent with disappointment.

"So much for your unbounding loyalty," he said bitterly and spilled some of the water on the floor.

She was touched by this clumsiness, by his loneliness. The radio was playing a Christmas carol; it was the beginning of December, and it made her feel maudlin. That he should be alone: his wife could not possibly love him. He stood looking down at the water, his brow rumpled. She went up to him and rested her face against the gray sweater; it smelled faintly of mothballs.

He jerked her back by the shoulders and hissed, "What the bloody hell d'you think you're playing at?" He let her go quickly.

"I'm sorry." She covered her face with her hands; she felt lost, a child alone in a dark room trying to outwit the shadows.

He pulled her close to him and rocked her. Her voice, ragged and forlorn, whispered, "I love you, Patrick, I love you."

The hours between her visits to him were like roads so long and empty they might never end. He had said, "Come tomorrow to the dam; it's beyond the farm and easier to get to if you follow the road rather than the track, then take the turning to the right."

She parked beneath some thorn trees and walked past a few old Afrikaner oxen with long curly horns—archaic beasts, ponderous and magnificent, but a little awkward without a plough in their wake. She walked farther and found him sitting close to the bank of the dam; he was tossing pebbles across the water's surface. She saw that he was naked. His back was long and lean as a Masai warrior's; his thighs taut and gleaming with no pinch of fat. She sat down beside him and drew up her knees.

"Did no one ever teach you to kiss when you say hello?" he asked lightly, turning her face. He plastered it with his two wet hands and gave her a loud convincing kiss. He thought how shy she was for all her natural sensuality. He watched as a hornet landed on her wrist and balanced there in its elegant black. It flew off and began to burrow into an apple core that he had tossed there earlier.

"I hope you swim well, I like to go right across."

"But it's miles," she said, straining her eyes at the curtain of harsh yellow light reflected by the water.

"Two miles. It's nothing. There are some quite decent trees on the other side, even a jacaranda that someone must have brought here." His forehead creased and he thought a bit, then said, "There's also a tangled little garden where the dam leads off into a small creek; the most extraordinary exotic flowers there—all gone to weeds. Years ago, I suppose, some old lady must have planted it, dreaming of England."

She got up and took her swimming costume out of the towel. He picked it up and threw it away into the bushes, "No one comes here, we're on the other side from the house. Nobody will see you." He grinned wickedly, "And I've seen you already." He ran and dived straight into the water. She began to pull her clothes off, and seeing him swimming strongly and swiftly away, she called out, "Oh, wait for me, don't go so fast."

"Jesus, with your hair wet you could be twelve!" In retaliation, she grabbed his hair and pushed his head under the water; up he came spouting water like a whale. He slid his hands under her arms and her legs floated to the surface. "You can barely stand, can you? Let me carry you."

"Oh, it's beautiful, so lovely. I used to swim naked when I was little, in the pool in the garden at night, with Julian. . . ." She was smiling, but at the name her smile slipped.

"Who's Julian?"

"Oh, someone, you know, just a boy, a friend."

She had almost admitted it. She had almost said, "Julian didn't exist, I made him up because I was so lonely." She saw now how lonely she had been. But he had lost interest. He was fondling her breasts under the water.

"Look, I can support you with one hand." He laughed and she laughed, too, shrugging off the sadness. She began to swim out far into the water, slowly, rhythmically, the water lapping her chin. In the middle of the dam she felt safe. There were trees all around it, mopani trees and pale, dizzy willows with their branches upside down.

He swam powerfully. He looked relentless coming toward her, never stopping for breath. She watched him in admiration, with no trace of envy—she who could only manage a slow breaststroke for long distances. He swam right past her, then turned and called, "Come on, we're over halfway." She followed in the bubbling current that his body made.

On the other side, he stretched out on the ground and she did the same. The sun was a little lower in the sky, but still very hot.

"It's the best time of day. I often swim here." He thought how unlike his wife's her body was. It was more like a boy's; it was neatly divided into those areas which were suntanned and the pale shape that her costume covered. Her breasts were very hard, the color of vanilla ice cream, and the nipples were pale pink and small.

"What's wrong?" She trailed her finger along his chin.

"Nothing's wrong."

"What are you thinking about?"

This was going to be tricky; he sat up and scratched his head. "You know, we ought to be more careful."

"What of?"

"Babies." Then he laughed. She turned away in confusion.

"We can't go on like this. I presume you don't want to get pregnant?"

Oh, no, she did not want that, not that, but she didn't want him to say it—it smacked of rejection, it brought to mind the question of wife.

"I've always thought I wouldn't be able to have them," she said stiffly.

"But you don't know that?" That would be too easy, to just endlessly swim into her with no thought.

"No, I don't. I just feel it." She put her hand over her mouth, beginning to feel distressed. She did not know what to do. After a minute, she got up and walked off into the trees. She leaned against one and pulled off bits of the bark, it was sticky; she rubbed her hands in the earth and crouched there, almost huddled.

His arm came around her back and lifted her.

"It's okay. I'll fix it."

She did not dare ask how, but was grateful.

The next day, when she was trying to sneak out to see him, Jean ran after her and grabbed her arm.

"Hey, you can't go anywhere this afternoon. And I don't believe you, you should see your face, there's guilt written all over it. You *are* up to something."

"Look, I've got to go."

"Why?"

"I thought I'd go swimming."

"Where? In the dam?"

"Yes, of course."

"Well, where did you swim yesterday that left you all sorrowful?"

"Was I?"

"Yes. Now stop mucking about and tell me."

"I can't, Jean." It was almost a wail of protest. Emily's eyes filled with tears and Jean was too kind to pursue it.

"You're not doing anything you shouldn't?"

"No. No, of course I'm not."

"Okay, then. But listen, you really can't go anywhere this afternoon. Don't you remember, Ma asked Mrs. Brand to come in and measure you up for some dresses. She's got some gorgeous stuff from that Indian store—muslins and thin silky cloth . . . come on, she'll be here any minute."

"Oh, Lord, I'd forgotten!"

"Never mind. Come along. Hey, look, there's David. Do, for God's sake, take a bit of notice of him."

"Hello, David."

"Hello. Where're you two going?"

"Ag, just to get measured for some dresses. D'you want to come?" Jean loved to tease him.

"No, I want a beer. What are the dresses for?"

"Christmas party. There's one next week at the Petersons' and there'll be lots more."

"Look, Jean, I'm not really sure I want to go," Emily said nervously.

"But you have to, doesn't she, David? You can't not go. Everyone goes, for miles and miles around. It's terrific. Lots of nice blokes."

David scowled. "I'm not sure I want to go, either."

"You went last year." But he felt that he was so ugly; everything embarrassed him. Sometimes when he looked at Emily, some evenings, she looked as though something was on fire inside her. He wanted to catch a spark of it to ignite his own cold center. When he approached her, she was kind, but she was absent from them now, as if she had moved into a different season.

She knew it, too: she was trapped now, by her emotions and the terrible demands they were making on her to give up her idea of a free, independent life; her long solitary dreams—and all for this odd, changeable man who still had not said that he loved her.

She woke when a few stars were still in the sky and a single drum was tapping out a slow, sleepy melody in the distant kraal. She knew that Patrick would be cross because she had not come the previous afternoon as promised.

She wanted to creep in and kiss him awake, but the door was locked. When he came to open it, his face was crumpled by sleep, and there was a round dent where he had slept on his watch. His eyes screwed up as he said, "What are you doing here?" Then, more moderately, for her face had fallen, "The servants will be here any minute." And she had hardly slept; had kept waking up through the night, so that she would not oversleep and miss him. She wanted to go.

"Oh, I'm sorry, you're so sensitive. I've just woken up, that's all. Come on, come to bed." But it was spoiled.

"Why didn't you come yesterday?"

She was looking down, sitting on the very edge of the bed. He opened the curtains and a lovely wheaten color flooded the room. The big bed was covered by a single white sheet with a mosquito net suspended above it. There was a dressing table with little silver-topped bottles on it and a silver hairbrush. There was a photograph of an elderly man on a horse, and one of a small boy. Somewhere there must be a wedding photograph. Under the pillow there was perhaps a nightdress made of silk and lace. And she wanted to see all those things—to look, to know. It was agony not to know, only to suspect. And then, in a moment, she could not bear to be in the room. She headed for the door in panic. Then stopped as a voice from behind it called out.

"You up, baas?" It was Winston, bright and breezy, having just ridden his bicycle from the village. He had gone down to the chickens and collected some fresh eggs and a chicken for killing.

"I don't want any breakfast today, Winston."

"But, baas, I have fresh eggs, from the chicken you like best, the big black lady."

"Just coffee, Winston."

"As the baas wishes." He pursed his mouth and thought that his madam would not be like that, would not refuse, not when the eggs were there.

Patrick locked the door. "You're looking like a scared rabbit, Emily, calm down." There was something so exposed about her face, she hid nothing.

"But how will I get out of the house with Winston here?" She found her new propensity for tears utterly annoying.

But he settled her down on the fur rug and put his arms around her. "Come on, Em, it'll be all right." He was slightly impatient—but he concealed it. He noticed with pleasure that she was wearing the pink blouse with the accessible buttons that she had worn the first time they'd met.

"No, I want to go, not here, not now, Patrick. . . ."

"You can't come in here naked underneath and expect to escape. Here, if you like, I'll pretend to rape you, shall I? Or shall I tie you up to the bed legs?"

She covered her face with her hands. He was never confused or frightened or felt as she did. He took her hands away and kissed her. But she was fighting him. "Hey, hey, what's up, Em?"

"Not here, not here, Patrick, please."

"It's not a church, you know!"

"But you're married and it's your bedroom! Oh, Patrick . . ."

He looked at the other side of the bed. "Well, you've known that from the start, almost. You're sounding like the nuns really did bring you up."

He led her gently to the bed; he wanted to put her in it. She lay there stiffly. He thought, poor thing, poor little thing. Thank God she's gone quiet. Her crying brought to mind the time when he had had his wife's sister in this bed. He forgot it; he lay back calmly. He'd always needed lots of women, it was the colonial instinct. It was the African wealth instinct, to be able to buy as many wives as you could afford; to have them as symbols of your own prestige and virility.

"Now come, Em, take a deep breath."

With a sharp movement, she pulled his head down and kissed him all over his face.

"Oh, I love you, Patrick, I love you."

His silence was like the quiet steady drip of acid; it settled on her heart, it feasted there.

Two days later, Emily sat on his veranda waiting for him to return. It was the time of sundowners. Emily had spent much of the day discussing two Germans who had been found that day: they could not speak because their tongues were so swollen; they were almost blind and had lost their wits. They had ignored the desert advice and had pulled off the road, only to get stuck in the deep, loose sand. They had been looking for the Lost City—that mythical place buried beneath the red sands. Thinking of them, Emily remembered how she had once driven with Henri and Danny Boy to a large empty pan in the center of the Kalahari. As she had looked out across the vast, uninhabited plain, a woman wearing a black veil and a man in a bush hat came walking slowly toward them. The couple had passed—not lifting their faces, not calling out, just walking rhythmically. Had it been a mirage? One of those fleeting dreams that come to lonely people in lonely places? No one could decide, though Henri had seen them, too. She wished she could decide now. She was uneasy.

It was getting very cold, it would be one of those deep, solid nights. Why didn't he come? She had only dared come herself because it was Winston's afternoon off. She walked up and down the stoep, rubbing her hands, almost wringing them. She was drawn to the inside of the house, as one is drawn to a frightening shadow in a dark room. She was plagued by memories of the colonel's bedroom: his sheets, the smell of him. She opened the door to go inside and jumped to hear a sound coming from the marula trees at the side of the house. She thought of lions and mambas and felt afflicted for the first time by the solitude and the dark.

He came driving up the gravel as he had done all those years ago. He slammed the door of the Jeep; she stood very quiet in the gloaming as he walked toward the house, as the screen door clattered to. He saw her and ran—swinging her around and around in a great hug. His smile was warm and buoyant. "Emily!" he seemed to sing it.

"Have you been here long, waiting for me?" He liked the idea, for a woman to do nothing but wait for him.

"Oh, I thought you'd never come!"

"Were you thinking of me?" It wasn't conceit; he had to be sure, had to hear it said. She smelled the drink on him.

"Mostly, but I was also thinking about those Germans." He was disappointed, but she did not notice. "Do you think there is a Lost City, Patrick? That's what they were after, wasn't it?"

"I think there is one somewhere." He sat down and was beginning to undo the laces of his boots. She went and knelt down at his feet and pulled them off for him. This was very nice; he liked this. She let his hands wander through her hair.

"Your hair's getting long."

Emily thought that her mother would cut it off the minute she clapped eyes on her; she did this increasingly as Emily got older and prettier.

He lay back and looked at her, "You look very nice today," he said sweetly. "The green dress suits you, makes you look like an elf."

"Perhaps there's gold in the Lost City," she said dreamily, turning to rest her face against his legs. He lit a cigarette and blew a halo up at the ceiling.

"Not bloody likely. You're too romantic, Em." He put his hands on her shoulders suddenly, "Hey, I know what: why don't I take you for a holiday? To the Kruger National Park or something."

"I couldn't go."

"We could sleep in a hut—it's good there . . ."

"You know I couldn't."

"Well, if you don't want to."

She turned and clung to his knees, looking up at him fiercely, "Oh, I do, I do, but you know I can't."

"Oh, shit!" He wanted another beer.

"That's what you've got to expect if you take up with minors," she said bitterly.

"Ah, Em, don't get like that now. Come and sit on my lap." She came, slowly. "You know how I'd like to sleep with you all night, to wake up in the morning with you and just stay in bed all day."

The images racked her by their impossibility. And the wife— when was she coming back, bearing their trophy: the son? She dared to ask.

"Oh, I don't know." His good humor was leaking out of him. "Maybe never." That was unfair and a lie. She'd be back. But he did not want her back; his feelings for her were raw and confused. They had had a row before she left; he had wanted to apologize, but had not. It had left a coldness. He did not miss her at all now. He wanted this one, this wild one who just sat on the stoep waiting for him.

"I have to go, Patrick, I'm late already."

"No, stay, please stay."

"I can't, Patrick. They're very suspicious already." She got off his knees. He did not touch her because of his frustration.

"I'll come back later, if I can, I promise."

"Don't bother, it's probably too difficult."

"I'll go then." She walked clumsily, but he thought her gestures quite beautiful.

She whispered, "You don't love me." It was barely audible, but he caught it full on the heart.

"I've just never said it, you see, not to anyone, really. Oh, Emily, Emily, please, I'm sorry. . . ."

It was to his credit that he picked up her despair and was brave enough to bear it. And to take her hand, kiss it, and say, "But I adore you, I worship you."

She did not want to be worshiped. He did not really know what it meant: love. He got by on charm; and his charm was never directed exclusively; it was for everyone, like the beauty of an actress.

"But I *think* I love you," he said again, "I think I do."

"No," she said, eyes clear with conviction—and, oh, how he loved that look! "No, you wouldn't dare."

He got up and walked to where she stood looking out across the gravel drive; her back was very straight. It was cold now. She gritted her teeth to stop them chattering.

"Come tomorrow and stay with me, please? I can't bear all this going."

"I'll come tomorrow." She turned to go.

"Kiss me first."

She did not want to. She turned and kissed him quietly on the mouth.

"Wait, Em, I'll drive behind you. It's very late and dark."

She saw his headlights following her as she drove expertly down the rutted road, swerving away from the potholes. The eyes of wild animals made stars in the grass. There was a smell in the wind, an indescribable smell—home. She was torn suddenly by the thought of leaving and how painfully she would miss it. But she lifted her eyes and he was still there, following. She felt safe as a woman wearing a ring. He left her at the gate, turned quickly and roared off. He felt desolate.

She stood a while in the dark before going in, to compose herself. Henri looked very angry; Rena had been trying to calm him down. They were all sitting on the veranda drinking coffee and talking about things they no longer had any interest in because she had arrived. David was looking most unhappy, and Jean and Danny Boy were pretending to play draughts.

"Where the hell have you been?" She'd never seen Henri angry with anyone but a servant.

"We were very worried," Rena put in softly.

She rubbed the tears away angrily and said, "I'm sorry, I know it's very late." The truth had to be told now.

"I met that man, that friend of yours, Mr. Gallway, on the road. He asked me if I'd like to see his farm and have a drink."

"Was his wife there?" Henri asked sharply, knowing perfectly well she was not.

"No, she's in Cape Town or something."

"Well, as long as you're all right," Rena said quickly. "Come on, come and have some supper. We left some in the kitchen." She put her arm around Emily to protect her from any further questions.

"No, wait a minute," Henri said, and both women stopped. "Have you been with him before?" Henri looked at her shrewdly.

"No," she said, but everyone knew she was lying; and the strange absences, the melancholy—it all fell into place, and they looked at her differently. Henri couldn't bear to think of her with that womanizer. He drank his coffee noisily; now it was too late to think of going shooting.

"Damn you, that's my last king," Jean said, feeling suddenly far more worried than she had been before. David disappeared.

In the kitchen, Rena placed a plate full of venison, carrots, beans, and potatoes in front of Emily, who felt she was going to be sick.

"I'm not really very hungry."

"Well, just eat what you want, or nothing if you don't want." Rena sat down beside her.

"You're in love with him," she said gently, "just like you were when you were a little girl." Emily did not answer; she ate the carrots mournfully.

Rena took Emily's wrist between her fingers. "Oh, Em, I can't tell you not to be, but it will end in tears. You know that, don't you?"

Emily nodded; she knew that all right.

"Has he been kind to you?"

She nodded.

"Well, go carefully, don't get in too deep. His marriage isn't too successful, I don't think. She's so self-contained; she's a good person, but I know he's lonely. He used to come over a bit when she first started to go to her sister's. He missed his little boy—but he'd never let you know it. But Em, believe me, marriages have a kind of glue, and sometimes the pain's the glue. You mustn't expect it to end—the marriage, I mean. I don't think it will. Patrick has invested too much there."

"I don't expect it to end."

"What do you expect, then?"

"Only for it to last as long as it will."

"Em, I feel very worried. Your people have entrusted you to us; we're responsible. I don't want it to go too far." But she knew it had already. "I should forbid you to see him again."

"You don't because you know I'd still go." Emily looked at Rena tenderly and took her hand. "You've done the responsible thing by telling me the dangers; now it's my pigeon."

"You will be careful?"

"Yes, I will, I promise. And he, too, he is being careful." She felt very clumsy, but desperately wanted to reassure Rena. She was almost adult, but not quite. It was mortifying.

There was a little shuffle in the garden outside. Emily got up, opened the door, and peered out into the dark. Someone was running away. The door slammed behind her as she pursued the figure out beyond the camelthorn trees to the bush. The wind was high, clouds were smothering the stars. She caught him by the arm, "What the hell are you running away for, David?" She was standing very close to him and he looked like a frightened boy running for cover.

"Hey, come on, what is it?" His eyes were very large. The moon was precociously bobbing behind the clouds so she only saw him briefly.

"Oh, David, you break my heart." She turned from him in distress, seeing in his face the reflection of herself—and she thought she'd changed, how she'd thought she'd changed! She remembered Virginia, and the memory filled her with courage. "Ag, David, why are you so sad? Why are we all so sad?"

He didn't answer. He knew why he was sad and now he knew why she was sad, too.

"Tell me, please talk to me." But how could he tell her? He had waited with such longing for her to come; he had dreamed of how she would look; where they would go together; what they would say. He had made a glass case for all the birds' eggs he had found and marked each one with its name. And most of all, he had had these long conversations with her; there was so much he knew he could tell her that he had never revealed before. She had been on the farm for six weeks and barely a word had been said.

"He's a bastard, you know that." She was startled by the vehemence.

"Who?"

"That man you've got off with."

"Why d'you say that?"

"You should just see him at the parties—he goes always for the prettiest girls. He has them all dangling off his fingers."

Now she had become one of those little mice he used to trap; now she was a butterfly without its wings; a dragonfly with a pin through its heart. She turned and walked back to the house; it was very difficult to breathe.

"Emily," he called out desperately after her. She walked on.

He flung himself down into the sand and lay there. Thunder rolled over on the right. The wind began to rise; soon it would rain. He thought of the newly planted crops and how the maize had formed itself into little green beaks. He did not give a damn. He could have trampled the whole lot to pieces.

Patrick had spread out a rug in the shade. They were lying on it together, side by side, holding hands. Today he was sullen, and she felt he did not like her; he seemed just to have a compulsion to bury himself in her and stay there as long as possible.

"What is it, Patrick? Tell me, what's wrong?"

He wondered why things seemed to affect him so much these days; he was on edge, like an animal sensing the abattoir.

"It's Stalin, you know, that boy I told you about. I've been having trouble with him again. He's going to pot. Keeps hitting the bottle, their stuff, not ours, and it makes him mad. It's dagga, too, I suppose. But he tries to beat up all the younger ones, though he hasn't the strength or the energy. He's a boss boy; he looks after the soya fields. But I couldn't stand it today—he'd kicked one of them in the head, while the poor bastard was sleeping under a tree. Of course he shouldn't have been sleeping, but he didn't deserve a boot in the brain, either. When I got there, they were all yelling like a troop of baboons. And blood all over Lucky's scalp. So I gave Stalin the sack. Said I'd had enough."

Patrick sat up, his body violent, the muscles in his neck and back knotted and dark. He turned on her as though he included her in the complaint. "But it's this place, it's the bloody country, you know, that I've had enough of. We should all get out and leave them to it. Sometimes I feel like kicking people in the head myself. You get so twisted in this place—everything's back to front, everything's crazy. We're all crazy—what the hell are we doing here? Wasting our time, waiting for the bloodbath?"

"You must give him his job back, Patrick. You must tell him to stop drinking."

He shrugged and looked out across the gray water, "Yes, I told him I'd give him one more chance. He's made it up with Lucky. But I suppose it'll all just happen all over again." He turned to her and said, "You've got to put it behind you, you have to—or leave the ruddy country."

He got up and dived straight into the water; it splashed onto her baking skin, and she thought, I'm leaving the ruddy country, I'm leaving in a few weeks. And I love it so. All the sadness that had been accumulating day by day as the date grew nearer came to a head. She lay on the blanket and wept. Patrick was swimming far out across the dam, he was swimming with the urgency of someone leaving something behind. All his concentration was in his arms and his legs flaying the water. She would be gone soon; he felt each day fall off the edge. His wife had written to say that she did not know when they would be back. Cape Town was so beautiful; the people so English and kind, and the beaches were all golden.

When he came back from his swim, she had disappeared. He walked into the trees and saw her sitting on a tree trunk.

"They know," she said, looking at him remotely.

"Who knows what?" He felt better after the swim, and talking to her helped, it always did: she was logical; she had a way of saying the right thing, making him feel he'd done the right thing.

"About us. They know about us."

"Did you tell them?"

"No, they guessed. I was so late."

"Well, Rena will understand."

"Yes. But I feel bad. They look at me strangely, especially Henri, as if I'd deceived them, as if they're disappointed."

"Well, it's probably better if they do know."

"Why?" she asked sharply. "Why is it better?"

He was thinking that it would make things simpler; she could come more often.

"I don't like what you're thinking, Patrick."

He laughed. "You can read me like a book. You know me very well."

"You're not a book, you're a comic, you're that easy to read."

"It's too late for me to change my life; I can't undo anything," he said humbly.

"No, you can't." She turned. "And I'm going away."

He took her in his arms and rocked her. "How strange that I should find you in a place like this."

"Have there been others—since you've been married?"

"No. No one."

"But they say you're a flirt; you get off with girls at parties?"

"Do they? Do they say that now?" He laughed mockingly.

"Yes, they do. And now you've had time to think of an excuse."

"I was lonely, that's all. I don't have a wife to speak of."

"Don't speak of her, then."

"No, sorry."

"Will you go to the party at the hotel, Patrick, on Christmas Eve?"

"Are you going?"

"Yes, I'm going."

"Then I'll go."

"But what will we do?"

"No one will take any notice of us. There'll be stacks of people there. The parties at the Grand are always wild; everyone gets drunk and then falls into bed because they're too pissed to drive all the way home."

"You've been before?"

"Of course."

"On your own?"

"Usually."

"I see. Okay, Patrick, I'll see you there. Now I must get back."

Driving to the hotel for the Christmas Eve dance, Emily had to sit very close to David in the car. Rena and Henri sat in the front and Jean, Danny Boy, David, and Emily were squashed into the back of the Cadillac.

"For God's sake, Danny Boy, you're sitting right on my skirt."

"I've got to sit somewhere—and what the hell have you got under it anyway?"

"Why you two couldn't have gone in the van I don't know."

"Stop fussing, Jean, some people travel a hundred miles wearing their best dress."

"Hey, Em." Henri turned round and grinned at her still face. "Who are you going to get off with tonight? Let's see now, there's that nice van Rensburg boy, or the Swift boy; he works in Barclay's Bank, good prospects there."

"Henri, be quiet," Rena said firmly. "Let the girl be."

"David looks very handsome," Jean said, to try and take the look of strain from his face. "Who lent you that silk tie?"

"It was mine," Henri said. "I bought it to have dinner in the Carlton in Joburg once, but it looks better on David."

"I wish Joy were here," Henri added. "She always sings, and then people aren't so nervous."

"Who's nervous?" Emily asked sharply.

In the hotel, people were standing about at the bar; the women wearing homemade dresses and the men in dinner jackets. They drank whiskey or gin in long glasses with thick cubes of ice. The talk was what it always was: the trouble with the natives, the stupidity of their servants. If this flagged, a little malicious gossip might liven up the atmosphere for a short while, but they would grow dejected afterward and reach for another drink with the same urgency as the black people of the surrounding compounds.

Emily felt as though she were floating above the crowd; she could hardly hear what they said. The young men had bright, open faces; the girls were confident and clean-looking; they giggled among themselves. Emily kept to the outside of the group. David had disappeared, probably into the large garden at the back of the hotel.

Patrick came late. Emily had been staring desperately at the balloons, the colored trailing paper, the silver balls and decorations. He came into the room just as the band stopped playing. He flicked his eyes around the room. They stopped briefly at Emily. She felt hot and her skin was prickly. He bowed in Emily's direction; she did not smile. Patrick looked across at the bar, back to Emily, then back at the bar as if to say, "I'm going to the bar to create a diversion." She wished that he had thrown caution to the wind, walked up to her and kissed her.

It was over an hour later; the music was loud. People were jiving recklessly; the girls whirling to show long beaches of golden thigh. Everyone was hot and happy, determined to enjoy themselves. She could see David watching her from some dark corner and felt irritated by him. Patrick was still at the bar, laughing loudly with a group of men; he barely glanced at her.

It was well past midnight. Emily was dancing slowly around the room with a quiet blond farmer. She saw Patrick dancing with an Afrikaans girl; she had a short blond ponytail and enormous blue eyes in a long, pale face. There was an orange balloon between him and his partner, pressed between their stomachs—he thought this hilarious—both he and the girl were shrieking with laughter. His face was red now; he looked Irish suddenly—drunk, debauched. No one else was dancing, just Patrick and the girl, in the middle of the room.

He had not spoken to Emily all evening. Now she could bear it no longer. She was making for the garden. It was freezing after the heat of the room. A waterfall fell into a pool with pink water lilies; snapdragons grew in long beds along the grass. The doves were asleep in the trees. She sat very straight in a dark corner, trying to control herself. She failed. And just sat there, stooped, sobbing.

It was David who came. He had seen her leave the room and followed her. "Um, here, have this. . . ." And he thrust a none-too-clean Kleenex at her.

She took it and pulled herself together with a mighty effort.

"There are more fish in the sea," he said gently.

"Is that all you have to say?"

He knew he had made a mess of it again, but could not see how to right it. Finally he managed to blurt, "Don't stay out here, Em, it's so cold."

"What do you want, David? Why are you waiting?"

"I can't just leave you here, like this, all alone."

It was his misery that righted her, pulling her out of the dark hole of herself. She turned to look at him.

"David, I've learned to be alone; it takes years of practice, as you know."

"Emily, you're shaking all over," he said quietly.

"Come back with me," she said, and took his hand.

The lights in the room were dim; there was a blue haze of cigarette smoke, made eerie by the yellow lighting. It was three o'clock in the morning. There were only a few couples still dancing. And Patrick. Still with the blond girl; she was smiling dreamily, with Patrick coiled around her like a python.

The next day was Christmas Day. When she woke she felt exactly as she had as a small child, waking on Christmas morning only to remember that she had mumps. She felt ill. And sullied, as though she would never be clean again. No one mentioned it at all.

Two days later, when the misery was beginning to dry out a little, she passed the sitting room and heard Rena say, "No, it's not a good idea. I think it's best just to leave it now. She's been terribly hurt: you've no right to mess around with people so unkindly."

And Patrick, ashamed, could be heard to mumble, "Look, I know, and I am sorry. I had an odd idea that I was being unfair to her—starting it at all, I mean. I thought that maybe I should just let her find some nice young man there."

"That was hardly the way to do it."

"I know, I know, it was stupid. But Rena, I don't want to end it so badly, not like this. I want to speak to her."

"It's no good. There's no point; she'll be gone soon. Much better that she can forget about you before she goes. Don't start the thing off again. She's not as strong as she'd like us to believe."

Emily walked into the room and stood by Rena, who laced her arm through Emily's.

"What did you want to say to me, Patrick?"

"I came to apologize, that's all." He was defensive now and did not feel charming anymore. She waited.

"Now look, I've said I'm sorry. I was just smashed. It was nothing." He needed women so much; he needed the approval of them all or that old, lost feeling returned.

Rena left the room after whispering, "Make sure he's gone before Henri gets back."

"Have you anything else to say to me, Patrick?" She meant it to sound pompous, but it ended up a little feeble. She made herself angry. But now Rena had gone, and this weakened her. They were in the front room and the dark-yellow sunlight ate into the mahogany furniture. Some red-hot pokers were fading in a thin glass vase. He came up and put his arms about her; she watched him coldly.

"Come on, Em, let me explain."

"There's nothing to explain. I saw how it was."

"Well, what did you expect? Did you want everyone to know?"

Oh, liar, cheat that he was! She stared him out.

"I wouldn't have cared."

"Your parents might."

"They've left the country—as you know."

"Okay, but I was protecting you as well."

"Balls!"

"Okay. So I was just stupid, then."

"I want the real reason."

"What real reason?"

"The one why you did it, really."

"Don't know what you mean." Now he was intimidated.

"Well think, then." She was suddenly way ahead of him, years in credit.

"What were you trying to tell me?"

"I wasn't trying to tell you anything."

"I think you were. I think you were trying to tell me that you didn't belong to me, that you could do as you bloody well liked."

He looked at her, was about to deny it, but did not.

"Well, you can be possessive."

"So you say."

"I like to be my own man."

"I like to be my own woman."

He laughed. "You're only a girl."

She thought this a coward's way of pulling a punch. She moved farther ahead of him. "Well, Patrick, you've said your bit and I've said mine. Let's call it quits."

"You don't mean that, do you, Em?" His eyes had gone black with softness.

"I always mean what I say."

"No," he said firmly, and she breathed again. "No, I'm not going to let it finish like this. It's ridiculous."

"What do you suggest, then?"

"That you forgive me—please—I promise it won't happen again."

He had a sure touch. He began to rejuggle his motives to his advantage, "I suppose you're right; I did think you were perhaps trying to own me."

She was willing to believe it was her fault. He approached her again and kissed her on the chin. "I'm sorry, I was a sod."

"You must go, Henri's pretty mad with you." She forced herself away from him.

"Okay, but will you come later? Please?"

"I don't know. Maybe."

"Promise you'll come."

"No."

She didn't go that night; she went the night after and resented the loss. And when she came, he was so tender. He had bought a long string of beads for her, kaffir beads, he said apologetically, but they were unusual, with small smooth bits of ostrich shell, like those Bushmen women wore, among the blue beads. He said he thought them so pretty he had wanted her to have them. She would not find any like that in England.

"A good-bye present?"

"Of course not. Don't keep thinking of that. Let's think about now."

But she couldn't.

They were sitting on the veranda. He was smoking. The light was dwindling fast and bats were reeling in the sky. She went and knelt at his feet and slowly drew off the dusty boots.

"How will you manage without me to take off your boots?" she said with a trace of mockery.

He did not reassure her. "I'll just have to do it myself," he said.

One night there was a storm. They stood together by the window and heard the rain slashing the roof, saw the water gathering in pools beneath the trees.

"Oh, it's so beautiful!" she cried out.

He did not notice her tears, but felt sorry for her because he wondered whether he would be able to live away from Africa now; he did not think so, not anymore. He had come out as a certain kind of human and had been turned into another. He had been improved by the country, stabilized by it; he could almost stay forever—if only things would continue the same, with no threat.

Patrick had gone back to the blanket on the floor and was smoking a cigarette. The small red butt glowed in the dark. He lay back with his head on his arm and felt concerned about Emily. But he did not approach her; she stood alone by the window, and tears were pouring unchecked down her cheeks. She was biting her lip till it bled: I want to stay here forever. I want to grow into this place, grow old and be put in the ground like the Africans and come up as a tree. I want to be dug deep into it till my bones rot and turn to powder. Her unhappiness was so profound that it began to frighten her. She moved back from the window. "I must go now."

"No you will not. Wait till the rain dies down, and for heaven's sake, close that window. Come back to the blanket."

"No, I'll go; I'll be fine."

"What is this? You must do as I tell you or you won't be my darling."

"But I'm not your darling." She forced a laugh. "Darling" was not a word he used seriously.

"Anyway, you could be struck by lightning."

"All right, I'll wait a little."

Once he had her firmly against his side, with his arm bearing down hard on her ribs, he fell asleep. It had been such a hard, hot day; his best horse was ill and he must get up later to look at her.

She lay and listened as the rain weaved in and out of the trees and was sucked down into the red earth. She fell asleep clutching his hand.

It was dawn. She opened the front door and saw a land soft with life: the water had all seeped away save for a few deep puddles. The ground was smooth and dustless, the trees clean-green. She took it all in, tried to embed every detail in her memory. She walked to the van, which looked polished; before getting into it, she stopped to look back at the window, behind which he lay asleep on the floor. She felt guilty then, that he should have to sleep on the floor for her sake, who could not face the bed upstairs. She had a fierce desire to see him once more. But her courage slipped away.

It was their last night. Patrick was talking a lot; it helped him not to think. And he did not want to think at all tonight. He had his frailties, too.

"Perhaps if you're a black man, you think of nothing but food and sex, sex and food. If they got like us—wanting money and land —then I suppose they wouldn't want so much sex."

"You sound as if they make you nervous," she said quietly.

"Me? C'mon, what do you think?" He stretched out his legs. "Let's get the worst over with," he said.

"What?"

"When are you going tomorrow? What time?"

"Early in the morning."

"Have you packed?"

"Yes, straight after dinner. Before I came." These were easy questions, she could sail through them.

But then, unbidden, his melancholy pricked the surface of his thought. "Will you come back?"

"Yes, I'll come back, but not here." She wondered about this, about whether she would come back and watch him through the trees, walking arm in arm with a pale wife, bouncing a little boy up and down.

"I'd like you to come back."

She wanted to say that if she came back, it would have to be for different reasons.

"I just don't want to go, that's all." And then she had a wild idea, an idea positively dazzling. She ran to him and buried her face in his neck, "Oh, let me stay here with you, let me stay."

He moved a little, startled, his hands lifted as if to ward off something. "But, Em, how can you? What about my wife? And Dylan?"

For a moment she was shocked, as though he had thrown cold water over her. But then she knew: he is afraid of me. She put it behind her; she was still mad and reckless.

"But, Patrick, what do they mean? What do they *mean?*"

He was quiet and deadly, "Em, I cannot give them up. I can't leave here and just ride off into the veld with you at my side. Even if I wished it . . ." He knew suddenly that she was a woman who would walk to the ends of the earth for him, kill for him. He could not reject such adoration. He needed it so badly. But he also knew he could not have it.

"Em, sometimes we can't have what we want." She could have strangled those words, and the throat that so piously uttered them.

"Oh, you're wrong, wrong—we can always have what we want.

We can make anything happen, anything, if we want it. I can prove it. We can prove it. Say yes, say *yes*."

He was tempted.

She gathered up his hands and gripped them hard, "Patrick, be brave. We are meant for one another, I know it. We could be so happy here. I'd do everything with you." His old loneliness came and tapped him on the shoulder. Now he could actually visualize, as she had many times, his wife staying in Cape Town; a divorce. He could see himself riding to the lands with her laughing beside him; he could imagine the nights and how she would love him. He faltered, she pleaded.

"It's only once," she insisted. "It won't come ever again." Pride was for people who didn't know about passion, pride was for fools.

"But, Em . . ."

"Oh, God!" Her courage collapsed. She cried out and ran into the herb garden, where she began to pull the rosemary to pieces— but the roots were so deep and tough she could not shift them.

The things she was now suspecting were terrifying. He loved his wife, he must.

"Oh, Em, you get yourself so sad, so twisted."

She looked up; he gasped.

Her eyes narrowed, she was breathing heavily. She suddenly grabbed his arm and pulled him down to earth and began violently to kiss him, to make love to him. He was exhilarated and over-whelmed. But then he felt daunted; it seemed an affront, a rape, it was so abandoned that it left him shivering. She got up, she looked at him as though she would strike him. She walked off into the bush and did not return until it was very dark.

He was asleep. He did not want to wake and say good-bye; he had hoped to avoid that. She knelt on the floor and watched him.

She left. She had hazarded everything and lost. A great defeat is much like a victory. He would not forget her, she swore it, he would not, not ever. He would be watching each day, looking out across the veld to see if she would drive up again.

Patrick woke and was shocked to find her gone. He had an irrational desire to follow her, to get to her before she left. He remembered her fierce, fearless face. He thought of the depth and intensity of her feelings—there weren't many, perhaps one in a thousand, who could actually muster such passion. He felt cheap and unworthy. It would take many weeks to rid himself of the intense loathing he felt for himself. After that, something inside him would keep insisting that it was not over—that one day she would come marching up again and say, "I am here, I have come back for you."

PART FOUR

. . . This soul hath been
Alone on a wide wide sea:
So lonely 'twas, that God himself
Scarce seemed there to be.
COLERIDGE

ONE NIGHT, LATE INTO WINTER, EMILY WALKED OUT OF the house and looked up at the sky. There were no stars, no golden spires of moonlight. Gone were the night smells of manure and smoke and sour beer from the kraal. No drum throbbed in the distance, no lion gave its sharp roar. There was not even the memory of witchcraft on the air.

The night closed in around her like a cold, clammy hand. Remnants of snow made dirty patches on wet grass. The coldness to her southern skin had a bitter tang—it crept through to the bones and the marrow froze over. She shuddered. The garden was small; there was room for one holly tree and a young pear tree that had given up the ghost. All was dormant, as though life were in hibernation, as though this were a time only of sleep and death.

She pulled herself upright and blew out her breath in little gusts. She shut up her heart, as one shuts up a house when leaving it forever. The greatest love affair of her life was over; her love affair not just with Patrick but with Africa, with that chunk of Africa that she had made her own.

The world she faced now was one of rooms with closed doors and netted windows; the sky a distant patch between brick buildings and grime-laden trees. Here there was no nobility of view, no stretching of the eye to its outer limits. From a lean place, clean as a carcass, she had come to suburban streets crammed with identical houses, cement paths, parks with rusted grass. The houses did not huddle warmly to the earth, spread over a good length; they rose high and stiff with no space between. The air had no vigor.

"Perhaps we could have a fire? The fireplace looks as though it would draw. I could get some logs," she suggested to her mother, as they sat on secondhand chairs of no particular age or distinction in the sitting room.

"If you had to clean this house every day, you wouldn't even think of fires. What about the smoke and the grate to clean and . . ." Lilian looked as though even the suggestion had been too much for her.

"Of course. I'm sorry," Emily said gently, watching her mother tug at the edge of a thin carpet. Having done this, she made for the ornaments on top of the fireplace. She began to straighten and tidy them, so that in the end the little china jugs and ornaments stood ranged like soldiers. At the end of this formation was the wooden elephant, the trophy Bernard had presented to her once. Seeing it, Emily was crushed by homesickness. She wondered at her mother, who seemed to feel no loss, who, like her father, had set Africa aside with the same indifference that they put away their summer clothes.

But Lilian, in her own way, was shattered. Emily could see that. Her moods were now quite beyond her control; she became sullen and speechless for days on end, or would take to attacking Emily for some minute untidiness, some slight wastage of food. She began to talk in a quick, disjointed way; her conversations had no thread to keep them together; she began on one subject and veered unaccountably into another. She was so racked by anxiety she could not keep still; she rushed from one room to another as if searching for something.

One Monday morning, when Bernard had eaten his poached egg and driven to the station, Emily, who was due to leave for the bus stop, said to her mother, "I'll stay with you today and help you clean the house."

Lilian looked up, she had not eaten breakfast, her lipstick was intact and it signaled dark red. Then she frowned irritably, "You have to go to college."

"No, I can go in the afternoon, there are only the speed tests now. I should get my diploma next week." She talked flatly, as though she were discussing someone else's life.

Lilian wondered if it would be wasting money if Emily did not go.

"Come on, let's get it over with," Emily said brightly, and Lilian rose and then sat and then rose again.

It took virtually the whole day to clean the house as Lilian insisted it be cleaned. Lilian now felt reduced to the status of a servant in her own house, and it was a home far more arduous to clean than any colonial household. She carried out her tasks as though her life depended on them, as though the beginning of each week must be redeemed somehow by exhaustion.

At five o'clock, when it was done, she and Emily sat in the kitchen looking out across a winter garden. It was beginning to get dark outside, and lights went on in the houses on either side of them. The house was very cold and they sat huddled at a table covered with red Formica. Lilian was rubbing with one finger on the shiny surface of the table. Her finger began to cause a squeaking sound as she pushed more vigorously. The little table began to rock and the sound became a shriek. Lilian stopped, her head dropped, she whispered as if to no one, "I am so depressed."

Emily left her chair and went and knelt by her mother. She took the dry hands with the nails now short and unpolished. "I know, I know, we must do something. Perhaps you could get a job?"

"A job?" Lilian looked perplexed.

"Well, you're so lonely, there's no one here all day to talk to. Soon I'll be gone, too. You need something to take you out of the house."

"But I wasn't brought up to work."

"That doesn't matter. Lots of women start later."

"I couldn't. There's too much to do at home. He'd be angry if his shirts weren't done and the food wasn't right."

"You do too much in the house. It isn't necessary."

"It wouldn't be my money," Lilian said vaguely, as though confused.

"Yes it would. If you earned it, it would be yours. If only, if only you had some money of your own. It would give you a life of your own. You wouldn't have to ask, you wouldn't be so humiliated." Her cheeks were pink and her eyes wet; she felt her mother's humiliation as her own.

"I suppose so." Lilian began to massage her fingers. She was thinking now of new dresses, a smart coat for winter. She was thinking of herself as she used to be. She put her rough hands away from her.

The previous carefulness of the Jones's way of life had now descended into a neurotic worry about money. Without the low tax and cheap life-style of their old existence, a meanness had descended on their lives. Some of it was necessary; the rest could be traced to Bernard. With money he felt safe; without it he would have been pathetic. Even when he had had money, he had never had the gift of spending it gladly or generously. His most common complaint to Lilian was "How can you possibly have spent so much?"

Emily, at the age of departure from her parents, found that her mind was no longer so hard that it could take one imprint only. She was learning to make allowances. Lilian grew daily more pathetic. Bernard, riding the train to and from a job that barely touched the perimeter of his intelligence, now emerged as a man of prejudice and not much else. He bellowed to the television set about the bloody Socialists or the moronic unions, while Lilian looked on disdainfully from her chair across the way and withdrew the last of her audience. He screamed at the stupidity of women drivers on the road and Lilian ceased to hear him. He would look at her sharply sometimes and see that she had gone.

Emily, at twenty, lived in one room. The window looked out across the rear view of a street of houses. She could see the bathrooms and kitchens: bottles of washing-up liquid and Harpic, washing spun out across ceilings, indoor plants drooping in pots, and far down in a courtyard—a grapevine flourishing against a gray wall, bubbling out sour grapes which would never ripen. Her room contained one small bed, a gas fire that fed on shillings, a double-ring stove next to a sink hidden by a green curtain.

A man from a film studio where she worked as a secretary for a week took her to dinner. She ate a great deal, and it amused him, as though her hunger were a welcome unsophistication.

"You're the kind of girl who would eat an apple in a crowded train compartment and not give a damn about the crunching!" He laughed also, to himself, at her choice of food. She was like someone who had not been taken out to dinner often. She was unaware of her naïveté until it was transmitted to her by the bemused and slightly patronizing expression of his eyes. She dropped her spoon.

"Oh, don't, don't stop eating, I like to see you eat, you look as though you hadn't eaten for weeks."

She was humiliated and sat erect, avoiding his face, looking across the other tables.

"I'm sorry; that was clumsy. I've offended you." He reached out and took her hand. "Tell me about the place you come from, South Africa, isn't it?"

She would not tell him. Instead, she said, "What makes you so arrogant?"

He was put out, then gave a shaky laugh. "Do you know what impressed me about you the first day you were at the office?"

She did not care what impressed him.

"You were typing that script, the Ibsen one, and you were looking up a word in the dictionary. I said—do you remember?—I said: 'Nothing is spelled wrong in that.' But you said: 'I know, but I don't know what this word means.' Often after that I saw you looking up words; then you wrote them down, with their meanings beside them. Not many secretaries would do that—or give a damn what a word means, what a whole ruddy play means. I thought it showed promise."

"Promise of what?"

"I don't know—wisdom perhaps."

He began to stroke her fingers; she returned them to the coffee cup. He began to tell her she had wonderful eyes, though he had barely glanced at them. Without any real experience, her instinct spread the whole procedure of the coming night before her. She decided not to stay and observe it.

She would walk at night down streets, her hands stuffed into her pockets, her eyes staring straight ahead and seeing very little. She would walk for miles and then take a different route back so that she did not need to pass the same shops and houses. She was restless: the greasy streets frightened her, but she felt a need to conquer the fear they generated. She thought the people on the streets were like zombies. The seasons slipped into one another with no great upheaval, and the elements seemed to come from far away: the wind was secondhand, the rain diluted and weary.

She knew she was being followed, but only turned once. The man did not stop when she turned. She could only distinguish a tallness, a gray-coated shape. She began to tremble and walked faster. The echo of his footsteps clanged on the railway bridge.

Her feet clattered up the stairs and she began to jerk the key into her lock. It would not go in; it fell; she snatched it up. A hand took the key from hers and applied it smoothly to the lock, which turned. She spun around in rage.

"Just leave me alone, will you?" she snapped.

"I'm sorry I startled you." His voice was soft, slurry; he articulated each word slowly. She slammed the door in his face and rushed up the stairs, quivering and damp. The dingy room was a haven of silence.

The following night he was waiting outside when she came out. She jumped back inside. An hour later, she did not notice him as she left the building. He only caught up with her on the corner as she was crossing the road. Then she was livid; she turned on him, "Look, what's the matter with you? Can't you bloody well leave me alone?"

"Don't be unfriendly." He smiled, showing strong, even white teeth set in a square, well-contoured face. "Let me at least buy you a drink as a penance for frightening you yesterday."

He followed as she continued to walk. When he asked again, some perverse impulse made her accept his offer of a drink.

His face in the shaft of light above the row of glasses revealed his skin to be the color of an apricot—Bushman color. His hair was thick and black and looked as though it had some kind of light oil on it; his eyes were made more narrow by the heavy lines of his eyebrows.

"So, what have you been following me for?" She was drinking her mother's drink: gin. She liked it; she drank it too fast. As a child she had drunk it, by mistake, because the water in the fridge was always kept in Gordon's bottles. She'd liked the taste then, too; had drunk a great deal of it. (Mpande had been blamed; an equivalent sum had been sliced off his salary.)

He was staring at her intently and he found her face intriguing.

"You can't be English." He meant it as a compliment; he did not like English girls.

"I thought we were discussing why you were following me," she said sharply, feeling the gin comfort the nerves in her stomach.

"I have given you part of the reason," he said coolly.

"And the rest?"

"Also, you looked guilty." He stared her out.

"Guilty. Guilty of what?"

"Well—" and he grinned—"you looked like someone running away from something."

"That's ridiculous!"

"Probably, but you were running away from something. And you looked strange."

"And that's why you followed me?"

"Yes, that's why."

"What do you do?" She asked it with indifference.

"I'm a medical student."

She was disappointed and became sarcastic. "I thought you might be a slave trader, snatching women off streets to sell in a market somewhere. Where do you come from, anyway?"

"Turkey." It sounded cruel. "Come to my place and I'll show you how to drink vodka," he said, pushing the empty glasses away.

She went with him, courting danger. She considered changing her mind on the stairs leading to his flat, but indecision led her through the door into a large room with bare floorboards; red rugs with black fringes were tossed in front of the fireplace and irregularly around the one chair in the room. She looked up at high Victorian ceilings and felt redeemed by the space.

"You like the room." It was a statement only. "Now you are better, you feel happier." She looked at him, surprised to find that he spoke only on an emotional level. He cut up some red apples and put them on a blue plate. He handed her a glass.

"Sit on the floor," he said.

"Do you have any ice?"

"Not with ice." He handed her the plate of apples; she took a quarter, it snapped in two between her teeth and left a sharp acid taste that mingled perfectly with the tight, clean taste of the vodka. He sat on a large wooden chair like a throne.

"Women always sit on the floor where I come from. You will be more comfortable if you cross your legs."

"What else are they expected to do in Turkey?"

"They do as they're told."

"How nice for you."

"It's nice for them; there is no conflict; women are better without conflict. I couldn't marry an English girl; they have a knack of complicating the simplicity, even the stupidity, of their lives." He smiled haughtily, "I couldn't marry an English girl—never."

"I don't suppose she'd like it much either."

"You should not feel insulted; what is demeaning in one country is not necessarily seen the same way in another."

"It's always demeaning for one person to be on a different level from another."

"Is that so?" His eyes had curved upward; he smiled sadly. "What a shame, and I had such hopes that you might be suitable."

"Suitable?" She frowned, but he did not enlarge on the remark.

"I want to go now," she said suddenly.

"No, you don't. I know what you want." He set his glass down carefully on the window ledge. She tried to ease past him; but an arm, with abrupt speed, reached out and held her.

"With some women you can recognize it instantly, what they want; what they are trying to escape. You can tell it by the way they walk in the street; it's as if they waved a flag." His voice was caressing and deeply offensive. His hands landed large, hard, on her hips.

"I can give you everything you desire," he whispered.

His mouth bit brutally at hers; he toppled her expertly to the floor.

"No, wait, wait just a moment, please. . . ."

He shifted his weight for a second, "You're not going to be one of those?" He smiled, confident of himself, his position, the room, the night. She was up and scrambling for the door; falling down the stairs, running.

After that she was more careful. She now began to seek out, without being aware of it, a familiarity. A voice with a soft edge, a body that strode across a road a little like Patrick might have done; a head that in the distance seemed to turn as his did. She would follow such shapes down the streets, sometimes certain that it was he. When she looked closely, she was stunned by the realization that she could not remember his body now; that the years had misted the profile of his face. As she could not bring him back—she tried completely to shut him out. For now, forgetting him had become more terrible than not having him.

She began to feel the need to change her room for one on the other side of the park. Here she decided to relinquish all adventures, and cloistered herself away. She became involved with no one. She made a retreat from the world as complete as that of the convent. But she did so with a purpose that was not negative; that seemed totally to understand her own special requirements. She had embarked on a journey.

And then, for the first time in her life, she began seriously to read. She started at the beginning. Slowly, she made her way through the Greeks and the Romans and then on to the English classics. Here she stopped—as she had with Homer and Euripides

—breathless with excitement: finding the intellectual flight as transporting as sexuality. It was, for her, to become the same thing.

Instead of dreaming, she read; instead of walking, she curled into bed and visited people and places beyond the reach of the richest experience. She consumed books instead of food—reading novels during the snatches of the day and poetry at night. From English novels she traveled to French and German translations. Her appetite became so unappeasable that she joined libraries, and seeing the rows and rows of books, she felt released again into a wild, free country where her imagination could roam unchecked. Literature held her as no learning had held her. And now, without the comfort of a printed page, she felt deprived and flat. What she had always drawn off from stark imagination, she now drew off from books.

And when life seemed most settled, most unlikely to change—like a wheel turning on the same habits, with defenses as familiar as the stains on the carpet—it was, in fact, just then that it came to alter radically. Years had passed and seemed as if they must pass forever in the exact same way: time marking time, with nothing to say where it had gone except that she was still reading the nineteenth century.

She was sitting at a desk, at another temporary job, at another office, and was reading *The Times*. Normally she did not bother with the births and deaths column; there was no one she knew intimately enough. But close to the top of the column, a name caught her eye, "To Virginia Boston, née Blackwood, a son, lived three hours . . ." She threw down the paper and ran to the cloakroom and hid there, banging her head repeatedly against the white wall.

An hour later, she walked out of her office, caught a train and was walking down a street of large brick houses. They had small, neat gardens in the front, and looking through the large windows, she caught sight of a willow tree or a hedge. Sometimes a side gate revealed a patch of grass, a swing, a cat dreaming on a dustbin. The trees were soft and billowed in the breeze, their leaves chips of copper in the sun. Maple leaves were sharply edged like mopani leaves; their dark red leaves kept falling, settling in a pile on the pavement below. The sun was warm; she felt it keenly against her face. She turned into a narrow avenue lined with tall plane trees. She began to run. She began to run as fast as she could to Virginia, to the past, to the last person in the world who had known her as she had once been.

She rang the bell and waited. Then walked back down the steps, looking up at the house. It was set back from the road; there were blue petunias in pots and snapdragons crowding in untidy beds. The house was quiet and calm. It seemed, because it was Virginia's house, to have taken on her attributes. No one answered the door. The silence of the street and the house united and excluded Emily. No dog barked, no cat stretched or stared. It was eleven o'clock.

Emily sat down on the last step. She had rung the bell again and heard it echo down a corridor. The door opened and she turned. It opened very quietly and only a fraction. Whoever was behind it did not trust her face to the sunlight. Emily stood up and took a step forward.

"Yes?" The voice was muffled, as though caught behind a scarf. It was Virginia. But so quiet, so lost. Emily ran up the last three steps, but the tall figure by the door seemed startled by the speed and took a step backward into the house. But then she came back, opened the door a little more, peered out shortsightedly, then pushed the door wide open. She whispered disbelievingly, "Emily?" and then louder, joyfully, and then again, "Emily?"—a wail, like someone falling.

Virginia began to cry, then pulled back, "What a way to greet you, what a way." To see her as she was Emily felt a cut in the center of her stomach. The soft golden curls were flat, the hair pressed around her face, which was thin and gray-looking. Her eyes had purple circles beneath them like bruises, and she had the exhausted look that people have when they've been too exposed to the sun.

She turned her face away. "I look terrible, I know."

"No you don't, just tired."

"But how did you know to come? Oh, you are a miracle." She began to cry again and lifted the corner of her dressing gown to rub her eyes. Emily went and put her arms around her, and they stood a moment that way until Emily said, "I saw the newspaper this morning."

"Yes, yes." Virginia moved away and walked to the center of the room, where she stood helplessly. "I couldn't bear to put it in before, it should have gone in last week." She snatched up the newspaper; she put it back on the chintz sofa without looking at it. "I keep reading it, again and again, those three words. . . ."

"Don't, please don't."

Virginia shook herself; it was so characteristic of her and so brave.

But then she began crying; she cried for a very long time while Emily sat with her and held her hand. Then Virginia sat quite still. "I'll go and wash my face now." She had pulled herself up straight.

When she came back, Emily had made some tea and they sat in the kitchen and drank it. Virginia's face had taken on an icon quality again; her misty eyes, with their dangerous full gaze, had receded now, she was no longer the girl with the face of the poet; the strength and the reserve had been ravaged into something more beautiful.

Emily touched Virginia's arm lightly, "I thought I'd never see you again."

"Did you try to? Since you came?"

"No."

"Why not? Had you forgotten me?"

"No, I hadn't forgotten, though I wanted to, I wanted to forget everything, everything I'd ever known, even the happy things."

"You've been unhappy. Oh, I know so well, Em, so well. It's terrible at first, isn't it? I hated it here, hated it so. I thought I'd never get used to it: the villages that ran into one another, one after the other, with no clear space in between. And not enough sky. And so cold. My father suffered, too, perhaps worse. He felt adrift. He couldn't bear it; he couldn't write. He said he knew how those Russian writers felt when they had to leave Russia. He was very bad for a year or more. Of course Ma just got busy as she always does. But we two were so miserable that we couldn't even speak to each other. Then I began to do nursing and that helped. I felt at home again in a hospital, part of a big, warm complex."

"Another family," Emily said bitterly, remembering how jealous she had always been of Virginia's family. And now there was a husband. She looked back at Virginia and saw that the dark strain in her face had lifted; she had been talking easily, as though it were a relief to think of other things.

"Yes, you're right, another family, another institution like the convent. But I felt needed again, and soon I wasn't so unhappy. But you, Emily, what have you been doing? What did you *do* all those years?"

"I was living. No, I was existing—that's all." She was thinking that there were spaces where no light came in, so there was nothing to see or to remember.

Virginia looked sad; she had moved out of herself a little. Her face became sweeter. "Oh, Em, you've been wretched, I can tell. Why didn't you try to find me?"

"I didn't know your married name."

"That's no excuse. You could have found out. The nuns knew."

"Yes, I suppose—but once you were married you seemed gone somehow."

"But that's silly." She looked at Emily, "I'm just the same, Emily. I've got lots of friends here. When I'd been at the hospital a bit, I started to meet a lot of people from home, doctors and nurses; they had South African friends and we all got together. I still miss it; I often pretend that I'm still there. I remember the little black girl that I used to play with in my back garden."

Emily had screwed up her forehead, and seeing it, Virginia looked at her affectionately. "I always thought you'd have huge lines on your forehead, you've been frowning like that since I first met you."

Emily said, straightening her forehead, "Yes, I remember playing with the kids from the kraal when we were very little. Nobody minded so much then. We had a girl who worked with her baby on her back, and then later the two of us used to play on the kitchen floor together. But after a certain age, it changes. I remember I wasn't allowed to play with her. Then there was no one to play with. Then there was nothing at all between us— except our difference. And it grew all the time. How strange it was, the way we were then." She turned to Virginia and whispered, "Was it all a dream? What we had, was it a dream?"

She closed her eyes and saw moths and butterflies sipping at dark green water, a lush swamp that was alive, that breathed in and out and never stopped moving.

"It does seem like a dream, Em. Sometimes when I wake up early in the morning, I think I will see Sister Aggy walking up and down the corridor with the crucifix flapping against her starched chest and the bell ringing. 'Pray for us now and at the hour of our death, Amen.' Sometimes I think in plainsong. Sometimes, when I hear a boy soprano singing like a bird with a crystal throat, I think of how Sister Christiana used to say that our voices would be clear as glass because of the air, the altitude. We should sing like the Africans." She began to sing softly, "As it was in the beginning, is now and ever shall be, world without end, amen." They were both silent, in another place. Then Virginia said sharply, "Em, you fell through the dream, at last, didn't you?"

"Yes." How bleakly she said it.

"I never thought you would. But what did you see?"

"Nothing. I saw nothing. There was nothing on the other side."

They were sitting together in the nursery. The floor was highly polished, with a fat sheepskin rug curled up by a white crib. The sun fell on a black-and-white rocking horse with a red mane; it looked like an old horse that someone had carefully repainted; the mane and saddle were both new. Virginia was arranging a big bunch of white daisies that Emily had picked. She said, "I wonder if many people realize how comforting flowers are." She placed them on the white table beside the crib; as she touched the petals, her face went stiff. Then she made an effort; she forced herself to look down into the empty crib. She turned to Emily. "I couldn't come in here before. The door was always closed."

Emily said very quietly, "You are the most extraordinary, most wonderful person I'll ever know."

The next day, they were walking through the woods. It had rained the night before; Virginia wore Wellington boots and an old gray raincoat tied up at the middle.

"It feels as if it's still raining."

"It's just the water falling from the leaves."

When they reached the lake, Virginia sat down on a log and looked out across the water. A heron flapped down out of the sky and disappeared among the rushes. The sun was shining as if through smoke. There was no one in sight. The leaves were laid deep and red beneath the chestnut trees and the air had a sharpness like sulphur.

"You can't say it's not beautiful here, Em."

"Yes, it is beautiful." Oh, but what she needed was a huge blue sky with the sun booming down on scorpions and praying mantises, ants, and brown skins. "But it's different, it's sad," she said.

"Yes, well, I suppose it is. England does seem a melancholy place. It's melancholy and masculine and often dour. But now I've come to love it for all that." Virginia seemed almost surprised to hear herself say it.

"When I first came," Emily said thoughtfully, "I didn't see anything at all, I noticed nothing. Then one day I took a train and went to the sea. I thought it would have great waves and breakers. But it was dull and gray as a flat piece of cloth, and the sky was the same. I was so disappointed."

"It is quite different, when I think of the Cape sea and the colors there. But it's because here there's so little sun. When you live close to the sun you see everything in white and gold, and you feel the life; you can feel the happiness through the warmth."

"I suppose the Africans at home, that's where their laughter comes from—the sun. How could they have borne it without the sun? And they laugh so much. And we laugh so little!"

Virginia suddenly bent across and looked intently at Emily.

"Em, listen, there is so much that I want to tell you. So much

I've learned since I've been here that I'd never have known about if I'd stayed at home. At first I wouldn't believe it, I couldn't, because it had been going on under my nose, and I suppose that I—all of us—didn't want to know. It's only by getting away that you can really see, or afford to see, what's been going on."

"What do you mean—going on?"

"When you live in South Africa, you're blinded; you only see what you want to see. You knit a few sweaters for the poor black kids, and your conscience is clear. You never make comparisons between them and us. Oh, Em, I have changed so much and I've learned so much, too."

"So have I," Emily said dully.

"Ah, but what you don't know yet is that you will again, and again. You've been lonely and sad, but it will pass."

"I used to feel that it would never pass. I was so lonely that I forgot about other people."

"Well," Virginia said briskly, pulling herself gingerly up off the log and feeling her back return to its old position after months of being curved out of shape, "well, we will just have to do something about that. You'll have to start doing things that give you a bit of confidence in yourself."

"I never had any of that." Emily laughed.

"Well, you certainly gave a different impression, and you must do it again," Virginia said, kicking up the damp leaves as she strode along. I think that when people change their aspect to the sun, they suffer a disorientation. Lots of Africans feel that: they go through a physical upheaval that is like a chart of what's going on inside. One woman said to me that her soul had moved and she would not find it again. In the end she had to go back to Africa."

As Emily got to know Virginia's husband, Mike, and their friends over the next few months, she became part of a group of people who met regularly to discuss South African politics—to go to antiapartheid meetings, to collect money for political prisoners, to take part in protest marches and walks. She met people who had been persecuted or exiled. In all of them she found the dichotomy between love of the place and hatred of its policies.

And in herself she began to feel a curious mixture of emotions. In one way she had been set free: these people, their suffering, had set her free, had saved her from her self-obsession. They had showed her a way back into the world. And through it all she watched as Virginia enveloped people in her kindness, cared for them, consoled and encouraged them.

She found herself increasingly in a charged emotional state. Everything that she was learning left her feeling frightened and confused. Afterward, when she went over it again, she felt raw, as if all her nerves had moved to one place. At the beginning she had had to justify things, as if by so doing she justified her own ignorance. She had once felt: it can't be as bad as all that, it must be exaggerated and distorted. But then she began to see the straight logic in the apartheid policies: if one embarked on that particular doctrine, then what followed was inevitable.

Emily gave up her temporary jobs. She began to work with Virginia: sending off letters and petitions to Labour Party politicians, to charitable and African liberation organizations. She helped organize tours by prominent South African spokesmen for the African National Congress and other banned political bodies. When she ran out of money, she took a job to tide her over.

She now lived at the top of a Victorian house that was very close to Virginia's, but in a more run-down part of the borough. The flat belonged to a South African journalist called Reuben who was working in France for six months. The arched windows of the flat looked down over a small park, and she could see the tossing heads of the chestnut trees and the sparse foliage of flowering fruit trees. She used to walk in the park in the evenings. The rain had got at the chrysanthemums; the petals had withered at their edges and it was too cold for the buds to develop. She watched the children collect conkers and rub them against their pockets. The street cleaner swept the leaves into damp piles; the wind was changing, it was nearly winter.

Emily's reading began to change. The novels and poetry were being replaced by history and politics, by every book she could get her hands on that dealt with social conditions for blacks in South Africa. She then moved on to psychology. Now all of her time was spent nurturing her new compulsion; she could forget her isolation and the real loneliness of her life.

One day Virginia came around; she seemed a bit quiet and sad; her face was tired again.

"Have you been sleeping properly, Virginia?" Emily asked sternly.

"Yes, I'm fine." But she sounded a little cold, and Emily said: "You're not cross with me, are you?"

"No, of course not, it's just that I miss you, I suppose. You don't come around so often now. And if I come around here, there's usually some half-baked idealist talking to you. We never seem to have any time to talk like we used to."

Emily went up to her. "Oh, I'm sorry. I've been so busy that I've neglected you. You were right, Virginia, so much has changed now." She sat down in a chair opposite Virginia, "Do you want some tea or anything?" Virginia shook her head and Emily went on, talking excitedly, "I feel as if I should be having growing pains or something. My head seems so full. I read and read."

Emily was sitting on the floor and she drew up her knees.

"Virginia, last night I dreamed that I was home again. I dreamed I was walking far out into the bush, and coming toward me was a whole lot of people, walking quietly, and I was going to join them, I didn't know what for. But I was so happy, Virginia. I knew that those people and I were going to do something, go somewhere, and that it couldn't fail."

"You're happy now, aren't you? You like being part of us."

"Mm, it's like a family, I suppose, a community. When I follow up those recruits who are crossing the border into Botswana, to go on for training, then I feel marvelous. I feel that something's really happening. That women will follow, that more and more will go and learn how to fight, and that inside the country itself those things are happening, too. That they can't be stopped. Before, I used to just think: no, no, if they know all that, they'll just kill us, once they have guns, it'll be the end of us."

"Well, that's the risk. One never gets rid of the idea of the apocalypse. It's always there."

Emily went quiet. She lay back on the carpet with her hands under her head and stared hard at the ceiling. She suddenly had the most acute sensation of joy. She thought ecstatically, I'll go back, that's what I'll do, I'll go back. She sat up; she couldn't keep from telling it.

She gripped Virginia's arm, "Virginia," she said quietly, "I'm going home."

"Ah, I thought you might." She smiled, "But why now?"

"Because now I'm ready. It's the right time, I don't doubt it at all."

"All right, then, you have my blessing, even though I'll miss you like anything."

After a silence, Virginia said, "It's odd, but maybe it is the right time. Reuben, the man who owns the flat you've been staying in—well, he's coming back next week, so you'd have to move out of there anyway."

"Well, that's perfect." She wanted to sing and dance, she wanted to put an announcement in the paper. "I'm on my way, Virginia, at last I can go home."

Reuben was sitting with his back to the light that was sweeping through the Georgian windows in Virginia's sitting room, shaking gold particles of dust onto the brown carpet. It was October, but warm as a summer's day. One of the trees outside the window still had an abundance of ripe yellow leaves, so that the tree seemed to be laden with peaches. The other trees were almost empty; now that the leaves had decided to go, there was no stopping them. They chased one another through the wind and stuck to the road and the pavement. Reuben turned to Virginia: he felt excited by the weather; it heralded change; it gave him energy.

"I like the autumn best, don't you?"

Virginia murmured something that he did not catch.

"So," he said briskly, "what poor down-and-out, or exile, has been living in my flat?" He had always teased her about her resurrecting of strays. Mike and he had sometimes had to intervene when the thing got out of hand, or when a limp young man became too dependent or too demanding of her. He did it better than her husband, who had a terrible temper and was likely to unpick all the good she had done with her quiet voice and her practical encouragement.

"Oh, I think I'll just let you see for yourself," she said, with a mysterious smile. "In the meantime, I'll make you some coffee."

Reuben Potgieter was thirty-nine, a journalist, the son of an Afrikaner and a Huguenot. Reuben's family had been involved, emotionally only, on the fringe of the political landmarks in South Africa's history of resistance. But they had never got too close; they were supporters, not activists, and had suffered no persecution. But once Reuben had begun to follow his career as a journalist, on the *Sunday Times* and then the *Rand Daily Mail*, he had become involved in antigovernment activities. He was now a named person, but had avoided so far the restrictions of a ban. He knew that his movements were watched and that he could forfeit his right to return if he was not careful.

Now he was back in England—after spells in France and Holland—to write a series of articles for a Sunday paper. After that he intended to go home. But now, sitting in Virginia's sitting room, he was suddenly aware of how much he was going to miss England, and the simplicity of his life, living with the latch off his tongue. He had been away from his home for almost two years, how could he bear to go back to all that? He decided what he would miss most was the conversations that he had had in drawing rooms like Virginia's. His South African friends were not given to introspection of any kind, public or private.

Virginia was talking about Emily, and in so doing, her face lost its weariness.

"You know, when I first saw her I didn't recognize her at all. Of course, it was over ten years since we'd last seen each other, but I'd always had the feeling that she's one person I'd recognize anywhere. I think it must have been because she looked so different, so un-Emilyish. Her cheekbones looked so high and she had these dark hollows, almost like bruises, in her cheeks. She was very thin.

"Did she know you didn't recognize her? That could have been quite a shock for her, too, if you were once so close."

"I'm not sure. I didn't admit it, of course. It was only after I'd seen a familiar little twist of her shoulders, something she's always done, only then did I know it was her. And, as for me"—she grinned—"I was such a wreck then, too. It was all very strange."

"Ginnie," he asked softly. "Why do you keep playing that music?" She had kept on repeating the same tape. It was Handel.

"Oh, I just love it, I suppose. I don't know, perhaps it reminds me of a time, being so at peace once."

He was firm. "Play some Brahms, the Fourth Symphony."

She watched, smiling, as he seemed to expand with pleasure as the music rose. Then he said, "Okay, now I've heard that bit, go on, tell me more about Emily. It's nice to know who's been in the flat; they always leave some vibrations behind them."

"Not to mention that colored gentleman who left behind ten crates of empty beer bottles!" She suddenly felt happy, to have him back, to remember things with him. Her happiness was not so difficult to reach these days; the worst tyranny of the depression after the baby's death was over.

"Well, I think Emily's really the strangest person I've ever known. Whenever I talk to her, I dream. We talk about the past a lot, I suppose. Last night, Mike said I began to cry in my sleep. I remember that dream: she was sitting crouched, near a dark pit in the ground, and she was digging at the earth with a stick. Her back was to me, and when I called and she turned her face, it was all covered with white stuff, like a mask. She looked at me the way she does: absolutely still; her eyes hardly flicker; they are beautiful eyes, but sometimes not quite real, like glass."

"You sound frightened of her."

"Oh, no, not Emily, I love her. She's like a sister to me."

"Where was she living before?"

Virginia put down her coffee cup emphatically. "Oh, my God,

you should've seen the place! I couldn't believe it. The wallpaper was all torn off the walls. But she'd just left it like that. There was a narrow bed in the middle of the room, and books—books everywhere. Nothing else. I wanted to get out of there straight-away. She stayed with us a few days before I asked you if she could use your flat. She couldn't take a joke then—she couldn't take anything. Mike said something to her once about what really went on between us in that convent. He was being silly—he can be clumsy. She stared at him for a long time, but said nothing. She used to resent him terribly."

"And he her, by the sound of it."

"Yes, that, too. She'd just ignore him. But now, they seem to be getting on much better."

"And she's all right now?"

"Oh, yes, I can't really believe the speed with which she's changed. She'd been living a totally isolated life for years and years, with no commitment to any human being, except her mother, whom she only saw occasionally."

"Has she got a father?"

"She doesn't talk about him."

"Any boyfriends?"

"No. When I met her, there seems to have been nothing—except her books. She was quite passionate about them; they all had to come with her—it was as if all her love had gone into them."

"And now she's channeling all that intensity into politics?" He poured himself more coffee, interested by the story.

"I'll have some of that, thanks," Virginia said, holding out her cup.

"Yes, sometimes I get the feeling she could become quite fanatical."

"She sounds as if she was looking for a commitment and found one."

"She said something like: it's made her forget herself, it's made her free again. She's always had a great thing about freedom."

"And now that she's swallowed up again, she feels free?"

"Exactly."

"Well, she can be made use of, then."

"Oh, don't, Reuben. It sounds so cruel!"

Reuben stood up. "Well, I must meet her. When am I coming around to dinner?"

"Well, you'll have to be very nice to her; she'll be shy after living in your flat."

"And when am I not nice?" he asked archly.

"You know what I mean." She frowned at him. "I've just got this nasty feeling that she may be your type."

He looked at her hard, and said, "How would you know? You never met my ex-wife, did you?"

"No."

It was at this point that Virginia realized she had not really looked properly at Reuben. She noticed slight changes: there was the faintest bloom of a tan on the upper part of his face, but his brown eyes were tired and his hair needed a cut. She realized also how good he was at making people talk without revealing much of himself.

"No, I didn't meet her. Mike did, didn't he?"

"Yes, and he warned me against her at the time." He was looking out of the window now, and his back was less reassuring. There was something isolated about him, even lonely. She'd never realized it before; his life had seemed so glamorous.

"But you wouldn't be warned?" she asked quietly.

"No. She seemed to need looking after, I suppose, she'd had a bad time."

"That's just what I meant—don't you start taking responsibility for Emily!"

"Well, that's terrific, coming from you, Ginnie!" He pulled one of her curls.

She began to move restlessly in her chair. Then she looked straight at him, as if she were challenging him. "Reuben, you know, I think I'm really turning into a nasty person. I'm getting so sick of all the things I do in my life. I can only admit it to you, because you've a nice cynicism about what we all think we're doing with our fund-raising and our revolutionary plans. But, it is all real, isn't it?" Now she was uncertain. "It's all starting to happen, isn't it?"

"Yes, it is. But"—he smiled—"I thought you were sick of it all."

"Yes, I am. I used to accuse Mike of losing interest, now I realize it was me! She rubbed her hands crossly down her skirt. "Oh, I don't know. I think I'm just so tired of all the wretchedness we keep hearing about, the suffering. I mean, how much misery can one *bear*?"

"Maybe it's just yours you can't bear." He took care not to look at her.

She spun up off her chair, disposing of his last comment. "It's the bleeding South Africans themselves, they're so blind, they're becoming so paranoid."

"Americans are like that, too," he observed, "but for different reasons, different guilts."

She shook herself and let her hands plonk down on her lap. "Oh, I just feel a bit burdened by it at the moment, that's all."

"Perhaps it's just your age," he said kindly, coming to sit beside her. "Women are marvelous at thirty, but they tend to want to start tearing up their lives a bit, wondering what they'll be left with at forty."

She smiled at him gratefully. He had a great ability to comfort women; it was because he admired and respected them; he found them more civilized than men.

His eyes turned penetrating, and he added, "Things all right with Mike?"

"Oh, yes, he's been very good, very patient. It's just so hard to shake it off, you know. I can't quite seem to. I can't talk about it, either." Her eyes were quivering, and though they were tearless, they seemed to be pressed back to their limits, to prevent tears forming. She walked quickly to the window and looked at the bedraggled petunias in the window box. She said forlornly, "I don't know whether to stop watering them or to go on caring for them. The frost will get them anyway."

He came and stood beside her and said sympathetically, "You know what your trouble is? You spend your time listening to everyone else's problems, and you've got no one to tell your own." She ran a hand across her eyebrow; she was almost in tears again. "Come on," he said. "Let's give those flowers a drink. I'll open the window for you."

When she'd watered the limp petunias and dusty leaves, she felt better.

He said, "Why not take a holiday somewhere, just you and Mike. Go somewhere for a bit."

"Yes, maybe," she said vaguely. "But I don't know if now's the right time. We were very close at first, but now we don't seem able to help each other very much."

He put an arm around her and walked with her toward the hall. "We men are frightened of these things, you know, we try to keep our distance from the babies and the sadness. But Mike will get better. He was very helpful to me once, when Diana ran off with that sculptor; he even succeeded in making me laugh about it—said it was like her running off with the milkman, because she saw more of him than she did of me!"

She turned to smile at him, "Well, it couldn't have been for any other reason," she said sweetly.

"Don't you go underestimating yourself, Ginnie," he said firmly. "You've done very well."

She clutched her hands together, "Yes, but I do so want to be happy again. I *like* to be happy, and I sometimes feel I have to go deep down before I can come up again and be happy."

"Well, remember you're not alone. You've got a good marriage, and we all love you. You probably don't realize how many people do love you, Ginnie; you're like a saint to most of your friends."

"Oh, now I do feel awful," she said, "showering you with all that stuff—I am sorry."

"It was my pleasure," he said, and kissed her.

The door closed and she looked at it for a time, then went back to her desk, looked at the pile of papers, then abandoned them and went into the kitchen to make an extravagant pudding for supper—something with chocolate cream, and nuts. For the first time since leaving the hospital, she felt suddenly very hungry.

When Reuben first met Emily, he was relieved that he had some way of breaking into conversation with her. He felt that she was nervous and not sure how to thank him for the use of his flat. So he solved it by saying, "I found this silver chain under the bed. Is it yours?"

Emily took it as Virginia said, "God, have you still got that?" She turned to Reuben, "I gave it to her when she was twelve!"

"Of course I have!" Emily said fiercely. She put the chain into her pocket, and he watched her, feeling a small suspense.

He remembered walking close to her when he first entered the room, and how, from that minute, a physical energy had sprung up between them. He had turned to look back at her, nearly knocking over a small table as he did so. Her eyes were wide open, watching him. She had felt a shock, as if from cold or heat. He had wanted to get back to her, to make sure she was, in fact, who he thought she was. But she had moved away; she had set aside her instinct as she moved over purposefully to talk to a colored man from the Cape. He was an expert on explosives.

But she found she could not concentrate or settle to the subject and went to help Virginia in the kitchen. She cooked once or twice a week for ten or more people, mostly South Africans in trouble of one sort or another. Emily was tearing the lettuce into pieces while Virginia chopped a cucumber. She said, "I'm amazed at how much they care, how much they're prepared to suffer and have suffered already. All of them."

Virginia looked thoughtful. Her hands were surrounded by curls of carrot peelings, the spiky ends of radishes, the green-leather skin of an avocado. She had had her hair cut very short and her curls had gone, leaving wisps and little waves of fair hair around her face. Her knife began to slice the cucumber again as she said, "I think it has almost reached the stage when a revolution can take off—when their lives have become so intolerable to them that they're prepared to sacrifice anything to be free."

"When they're prepared to be martyrs?"

"If you like."

"And when most people reach that stage—then it goes off?"

"Ya, except that in most revolutions, you'll find that just before it happens, the people in power begin to make concessions, begin to appear a little liberal. And that's precisely the point when everything goes up."

Emily arranged all the different salads into large glass bowls and sprinkled olives on top.

Virginia lifted a huge stack of china plates and staggered slightly.

"Hey, put those down," Emily ordered. "I'll carry them—go on, put them down, Virginia!" Virginia did what she was told.

Virginia's face, which was always pale, took on a hard, white sheen. She went and sat down at the table, took up a bunch of parsley, and with her head bowed, she began to chop at it fiercely. She was frightened, something was rearing up in her and threatened to overcome her.

Emily went and sat beside her. "Virginia, what is it? Tell me. Something happened, then; what was it?" There was no sound but the dull tapping of the knife against the wooden board. "Please tell me, Virginia." The knife fell flat with a thud.

Emily covered the hand that held the knife. It was a little time before Virginia lifted her head, before she had mustered her control and was able to speak.

"There was a nurse at the hospital, after the birth, she did . . . I mean, it was the right thing to do in the circumstances, but you see, I wouldn't, I couldn't . . . ."

"Couldn't what?" Emily held the hand fast. She had ceased even to hear the noise from the other room.

Virginia's words fell out in a heap, "You see, she said to me, would I like to did I think it would help for me to for her to bring me the baby to look at after the baby was dead to look at to hold the dead baby it was important it would save a great deal of . . . if I could hold it accept it dead."

"Is that true?" Emily was appalled.

"Yes, it's true; it makes you face the truth, understand that what has been growing inside you all that time has left, is dead, is finished, must be faced, must be looked at, like corpses must be faced by the bereaved. Or, or—" and her eyes flew up—"or you don't believe it, or you walk into a room and think, he lies in his cot. You even think you hear him cry."

She was shaking now, she was weeping. "But I didn't do it, I said no, don't bring it, don't make me hold it." She fell forward onto the table and buried her face in her arms.

"Oh, Virginia, Virginia."

Mike walked into the kitchen with a smile on his face, and, seeing his wife collapsed, her body heaving with sobs, he turned on Emily and said angrily, "What've you done? You've frightened her! You've made her cry." Emily went stiff. Virginia began to shake her head, to push at him as he tried to touch her.

Emily said quietly, "She isn't frightened. It's you who are frightened. She's just sad."

His face flushed and he pushed past her. He went and stood behind Virginia with his hands planted firmly on her shoulders; it was too harsh a movement and she moved away from it. He said in a whisper, barely looking at Emily, "She's got to forget, she's got to get over it. You're not helping."

"She is helping," Virginia gasped. "But you, you just want to forget it, you pretend it hasn't happened." He was silent, angry, about to leave the room. Emily took his arm. "Don't go, please, Mike. She's just very sad and she needs you. Take her upstairs. I'll see to this lot. Go on. I'll manage."

He looked very unhappy, "I'm sorry, Emily, really I am. I've been so worried about her, that's all. I didn't mean what I said." He began to gather Virginia up as though she were a child; she gave the impression of having no bones in her body.

Emily was putting the plates on a tray, trying desperately to calm down. Reuben came in. He took one look at her. "What's happened? Where's Ginnie? What's wrong?"

She wanted to cry; she wanted to say, he thinks it's all my fault, he hates me—but she bit her lips for a second and said, "She got upset. It's all right now. Mike's taken her upstairs. Can you tell them that she's not well or something, while I just get the food finished?"

"Right, I'll tell them and then I'll come back and help you. We'll feed them and get them out as soon as possible. Ginnie would be most upset if they all went home hungry." He looked at her hard. "Are you sure you're all right? And can you manage?"

"Of course I can," she almost snapped.

But when he'd left she felt sick with herself, with the thought that perhaps she had wanted to force something on Virginia, something which she was not strong enough yet to bear.

Reuben put her in the Victorian button-back chair in his flat. He said, "Now you sit down and I shall bring you a large glass of brandy." It was strange for her to be back there. The flat looked quite different; Reuben had brought in all the plants from the courtyard, and the table by the window was covered with trailing plants and delicate Japanese trees and ferns. The desk, where she had sat and read until late at night, was now piled high with typed papers and newspaper cuttings. There were photographs in silver frames on the mantel shelf, which had previously been bare. Photographs of an elderly couple, the woman slim, wearing black, the man with the same gentle expression that Reuben often wore; but the face in the photograph was broader, less sensitive, the nose strong and large, whereas Reuben's face was less solid, less Dutch.

Emily was studying him closely from the safety of her chair, behind the balloon of the brandy glass. What she had taken at first to be a gravity, even a sternness, in his face, now seemed to her to suggest that he had suffered in a way other men had not; that he had undergone not only political persecution (she knew a little of this from Virginia), but also a private and intimate hell. It gave him an appearance of maturity and strength that she found appealing.

"It was very bare when I lived here," she said, turning to pull at the fronds of the fern with a restlessness that she might have applied to her hair. He looked at the clutter of plants and sat down in a chair close to hers, then moved it a little closer. He wanted to touch her, but she sat upright in the scarlet chair, with her hands cupped around the brandy bowl, her feet close together.

"You're not still worrying about what Mike said, are you?"

"A bit; he seemed so angry."

"He said he felt very bad about it afterward."

"Yes, I think he did, but he meant it all the same. He doesn't trust me, and he *is* frightened."

"Yes, that's true. But I think he feels he's rather lost Ginnie, and he wants to blame you rather than himself."

"Did you tell him that?"

He wrinkled his nose, "Sort of, but it wasn't really the right time. I think it's hard for him to understand the hell that Ginnie's been through. She was terribly shocked that there had to be a postmortem on the baby."

Emily's face turned white with emotion. "But I'd never do anything to hurt her. I've never known her so frail and sad—she was always so happy." He saw straightaway how much she needed reassurance. He wanted to comfort her and wished he could just take her in his arms, but decided it was safer to use her methods for the time being.

"Yes," he said, "she is a happy person, but I think maybe that's something she's always tried to cultivate as a front. And we have to consider Mike in this—he hates to share her, and now, when he needs her most, she seems to be turning to you."

"I realize I have to be careful," she said in a low voice. "I don't want to get between them, if that's what you are implying." She drank the brandy down in a gulp.

He reached over and touched her hand briefly, "No, of course I'm not, but the fact is, you have, a bit. But, if I got it right, it seems as if you stepped back tonight, which was absolutely the right thing to do. How was she, by the way, when you went to say good-night?"

Emily looked hard at the emptiness of her glass, "She was very quiet."

"Then I think she'll be all right now." He smiled. "I don't

mean, by the way, that you should keep away from her, just that you should try to shift her dependence back to Mike."

"Yes, I agree, really I do. I had the strangest sensation, sitting there in the kitchen with her earlier on." And then she stopped. She was taken by surprise by the suddenness of the intimacy that had developed between them in the room.

"Go on," he said, leaning forward.

"Well," Emily said, "it was the way she was holding the knife—as if she wanted to use it, you know, it was odd, on herself." She checked herself again, and he poured more brandy into her glass and said again, "Please, go on." And as he asked, he saw how important it was to him that she should trust him.

"Well, it wouldn't be interesting to you," she said defensively.

"Yes it would, go on, try me."

She frowned hard. "Well, when I was small, I remember being very aware of the knives in the kitchen. I remember one, it had a dark brown wooden handle, and the blade got thinner and thinner—it had been sharpened so much that it was thin enough to bend right back. I used to watch it." Her voice sank to a whisper. "I wanted to use it. I wanted to kill." He saw that she was talking to herself; she did not even see him.

He smiled. "And you think that's appalling, don't you?"

She looked up at him. She said quietly, "When you understand it, it isn't so appalling."

"No, when you take responsibility for things, there's a freedom in that."

"I've always *so* wanted to be free," she said, with her head flung back, her mouth open, so that the word itself seemed to transform her.

"And can you be free?" he asked gently.

"Oh, yes, yes. Some part of me I've always kept free."

"Your heart, I imagine," he said, and smiled, but he felt sad for her.

She did not speak for some minutes, and he felt that she was holding back her tears. But then, when she looked up at him, her face was clear, without a trace of the melancholy he had just seen there.

"We've always talked so much about dreams, Virginia and I." He held her hand; she looked down.

"Heavens," she said, and stretched, "I must go, I'm so tired."

"Or you could stay," he said.

She looked across at him, hesitated, looked down, and then said softly, "Yes, I'll stay," then added quickly, "for a little while." But when she smiled, it was with such warmth that he now took courage and did what he had restrained himself from doing all evening, and kissed her.

Virginia was better and brighter now, and she was moving away from all her lame ducks; and as fast as she let them go, Emily was there to scoop them up. But then, at a certain point, she needed to retreat altogether.

"I like to be with them, Reuben, I suppose it feels warm and safe, like when people say 'we'—but I'm not, can't ever be a 'we'. I feel as if I'll always and only be a 'me'—it sounds so selfish, though."

"It sounds defensive."

"I like it, I like to be alone."

"You keep trying to create a desert around you," he said.

She looked alarmed; she began hammering the onion she was chopping into the table.

"What d'you mean?"

"You won't give yourself to me, you won't close in the space around you."

"Don't be obscure, what are you complaining about?"

"I'm not complaining."

She looked at him sideways.

"I'm saying you won't really let me get close to you. We're happy and together for a few days, and then you do a Garbo—you disappear."

She was hurt, thinking that he mocked her. "But I need to." The onions made her eyes swell.

"Well, I understand that, and I wouldn't mind, except that it feels that you're always alone, all the time, whatever we do."

"It's you," she said softly, scooping up the transparent cubes of onion into the saucepan. "You don't tell me the truth. You hide from me; we hide from each other. And when I feel alone, I go."

Her hair was long now, not hacked off around her face, as Virginia had once described it. He was struck by a great fear of losing her; that at any moment she might disappear for good. He went and stood behind her and locked his arms around her waist.

"I've hurt your feelings," he said sadly.

"No." She brushed her hair back so that it flicked in his face.

He went back to his chair at the kitchen table and looked hard at the bowl of anemones. "What did you mean, about not telling the truth?"

This was important to her. She put away the chicken with a sharp push and sat down, looking at him.

"You told me, at the beginning, that you'd only been in prison for a week or so. But someone let slip the other day that you'd been in for *months,* and that you'd been in solitary confinement."

"Yes," he said, pressing the ends of his fingers together. "So what?"

"Only that you deliberately misled me—why?"

He smiled at her, "Ag, Em, it's a natural instinct in people who've been under surveillance for a long time, then detained and interrogated; it's natural to trust no one, not to reveal the political facts of one's life."

"But it meant you didn't trust me!"

"Come on, Emily, everyone becomes like that; it's a way of life—caution and paranoia."

"But you've known me for weeks!" She was breaking up matches and pushing them into little piles.

"Well, later on, then something else happened, then I wanted to keep you clean of it, for it not to get in the way."

"But that can't be right," she said sadly. "You have to live intimately with me; you have to share it all with me. I can't just be given the kind, sweet Reuben, the professional journalist. I want to know you, and what happened there. I need to know."

He couldn't understand her intensity; he had put it all away and wanted the dust to settle. "But why?" he asked aggressively.

She reached over and held his hand. "Because you're incomplete without it. I sense it all the time, and I feel excluded."

He said wearily, "People want to know what other people suffer, as if they enjoy it. In cases of illness or grief, they don't like to ask, but political suffering, well, there are people who take a vicarious interest in all the cops-and-robbers stuff. They imagine it exciting, glamorous somehow, they don't see how it's the tedium that kills: the people who are under house arrest, who can't work, who sit and pull themselves to pieces, having given up a normal life, and often feeling—for what?"

"Are you trying to say my interest is like theirs?" she asked stiffly.

"No, I'm not saying that."

"You don't sound too sure."

Then she gripped his hand hard. "Well, I'm not like that. It's you I want to know all about, it's you I want to understand properly. What you've been through, what you thought even before I knew you, it's important to me."

He grinned, "Like some women want to know the details of past lovers?"

"Yes, a bit like that."

She returned to the chicken and brought the conversation sharply back to politics. "You seem to be questioning things a lot these days, Reuben. You keep saying you're not sure whites have any role to play anymore."

"Ya, that's right." He was almost curt, he didn't want to talk about it, but he could see by the tightness of her body that she wouldn't leave it alone.

Her eyes were glinting fiercely and he loved her desperately, seeing the passion there and wanting it. But he watched it go to other things as she insisted, "No, we must go on, fighting with them, we must, not for them, but for *us*."

He got up from the table with impatience and walked over to the window overlooking a balcony. "So what's your personal reason? And mine? So that we can feel, when it's all over, that we've earned a place in the country?"

"If it came to that, being white would be enough to damn us."

"So why, Emily?"

"Why you? Why go back?"

"Because I must. I'm a son of the country. I have to do whatever I can. Some people can pretend it isn't happening, others can't. That's all."

"But if you don't think it can be a white struggle now, what's the point?"

"The point is, I want to *live* there. I was born there. To be a South African, for me, means that you must take upon you what the situation demands, according to your conscience. I can't turn my back on it. My place is there, and nowhere else. And once there, I can only behave one way."

"But if you do that, they'll just put you in prison."

"Of course. But for me, Em, there's no ecstasy in suffering, not like with some, not like with you. I want to be free! I want to walk where I like, see who I like. And be with you."

"What d'you mean, not like with me?" she asked in a low voice, feeling him reach close to a nerve.

He ran his fingers through his hair, "You seem to think that you need to suffer, that you deserve to suffer. If you went back, you'd be up to your neck in no time. It would give you an old security, a security of suffering that you couldn't find in normal life. Like your family, like the convent."

He saw that her cheeks were flushed, and he knew that if he approached her she would back away. He spoke very gently, "But I won't let you."

"Won't let me?"

"No. I'll just tell you how it was, Emily, I'll make you live it through me. And hope that you won't need to do it yourself. You must be pulled away from this need to sacrifice yourself. Because there are far, far better things for you to do with your life than be incarcerated in a South African jail."

She was struggling with the ideas that he'd thrown at her.

"Like what?" she asked.

He came and sat down close beside her, taking her hand in both of his. "Look, I have a plan for you, Emily, that you just might be able to accept—something to dedicate yourself to without being hurled into the life of an activist. I don't know quite how to say this, I'm not even sure that I understand it properly myself, but I think we have to look into your reasons for wanting to go back very carefully."

"You're saying they're suspect."

"I'm saying none of our reasons are altruistic. Mine are selfish, too. But since you asked me, I'm going to tell you just what happened to me out there." He looked at her tenderly. "But I tell you, not to make you suffer, but just to see if you'll find some parallels."

She smiled, "You want me to change my mind."

"Maybe. Or maybe just shift your approach!"

He turned in his chair to be able to reach her quickly and easily. "Do you know what happens to people's faces in prison, Emily?" The roundness of his own face seemed to go; his bones stood out in his face. He talked very deliberately, using his hands for emphasis.

"My mother came to see me when I was in prison. When she saw me she said I looked like something out of Belsen. But I wasn't starved, it was after we'd given up the hunger strike. We gave it up because, one by one, we'd begun to crack under the strain. People get very worried when they can't shit; they become delirious when their bodies change, when they no longer look like themselves. They begin to imagine things. I soon discovered that in a situation like that, like in concentration camps—in any situation where all hope is taken away—there seem to be only three ways out: to go mad, to become self-destructive, or to become violent to the people around you."

He looked at her and it was as if there was a trial of strength between them. He saw in her set face himself as a small boy, when he'd forced himself to walk out beyond the fence of his father's farm in the pitch-blackness—to test his strength, to pull himself above his fear and conquer it. She now exercised the same ability to look the beast in the face. Finally she said, "Perhaps I am trying to be self-destructive."

He looked at her in concern, "I wasn't aware that I was drawing a diagram. But you do seem to live your life as if you're in a situation of threat. But I didn't mean—"

"No, it's okay," she cut in quickly. "You're right."

She sat with her head down for some time, deep in thought, and he did not disturb her. He was conscious now of having forced her down her own dark maze. But he had hoped that being with her might in some way bind them together, so that they might emerge at a new place in the end, where it was possible to look up and see light. She was struggling with herself: the things that she had begun to understand intellectually now hit her with emotional force. She left the room, too upset to speak.

When he came in to find her, she was curled up in bed, lying on her side with her knees drawn up. He got in beside her and curled around her back. She began to cry, then turned and buried her face in his chest. They lay like that a long time, not speaking.

When she woke up, she gathered him into her arms and hugged him hard. "What will I do when you've gone and I don't have you to keep me sensible?" she said.

"Oh, you'll manage."

She smiled. "Yes, I will." She looked over at him as he sat with a pillow propped sideways against the wall. She moved over and nestled against him. Then, she took all her courage and said, "Can't I come with you?" She made it sound casual, but he knew it was a big commitment from her, who had tried all along to preserve an impermanence in their relationship.

"I never thought I'd hear you say that. I presumed that you'd want to go back alone."

She began to worry that she'd said the wrong thing.

"I daren't take you with me; Em, just to be with me would involve you in all sorts of trouble. But I have been thinking about it, and I have a plan. It would mean us not being together immediately, perhaps not even able to see each other for some time. You see, what I thought you should really do is to go back home —to Botswana."

He thought she was going to cry. Then he thought she was going to jump up and down, because her whole body was alight with excitement. She pulled at his arm and said, "Reuben, I'd love that more than the whole world! And of course it's right, it's the only, only place for me to go."

It was after midnight, and the snow falling softly past the window smothered all sounds and gave the light from the streetlamps a pale blueness. Now that she was to leave England, she felt a sudden sharp affection for it; for the people out there in their isolation, those island people—still tough, still decent, when it came down to it: when the right thing was required, they'd still do it: at the final fence, they'd pull themselves up sharply and behave like gentlemen. It was the in-between that they bungled.

The snow nibbled into the windowsills; it curled into the nooks and crannies; it poked between the cracks and spat upon the windowpanes. She sat up in bed and pulled her knees up to her breasts. Reuben was still writing at the desk and the glow from the green glass shade of the lamp revealed him in all the frailty of a person who is being watched without his knowledge. The light exposed the looseness of his skin, no longer clamped tight around his bones. His glasses slipped and fell forward a little; the dome of his head was vulnerable. He rubbed a hand wearily across his face.

She got out of bed and pulled his navy-blue dressing gown around her. She walked toward him, watching the skin around his eyes fall into crevices as he smiled. Looking at him looking at her with such tenderness, she felt tearful with love.

She was resting her chin on his shoulder and looking at the notes he had been writing. "Are there really more Zulus in South Africa than whites?"

He nodded wearily.

"Come on," she said firmly, beginning to pull him off his chair, "let's go to bed."

With a smiling, quizzical expression on his face he followed her. Watching as her flat feet splayed confidently on the brown pelt of the carpet, as her hips swung rhythmically, he had an extraordinary impression of her somehow carrying a bundle or a jug on her head.

Reuben had been in Cambridge for two days. When he'd left, both he and she had presumed that she would return as usual to what she referred to as the "cupboard"—the small, white-walled room above a bakery in the High Street. But she had not done so.

The key turned in the lock and she heard his step on the wooden passage that led to his bedroom. She imagined him throwing his coat onto the bed covered with its plump nest of feathers, and seeing the bowl of early daffodils in the Victorian glass vase.

When he went into the sitting room, she had her back to him, looking at the fire. She was wearing a long, pale blue skirt with a deep band of black at its hem; it was spread out behind her like a train. She sat quite still, a black sweater outlining the hard, strong lines of small shoulders, the narrowing fall of her back. He wanted to say something remarkable, something that would sum up his feelings as he looked at her—in front of the fire, there, in his flat. But he stood just watching her, not speaking at all.

Then she turned. She scrambled up from the floor—awkward, eager, and ran to him. Normally, it took her so long to get used to his presence after he had been away. And here she was, in his flat, waiting for him, running to him. As if she had discovered suddenly where she belonged.

"I've been here ever since you left," she said, shy, looking down.

"Well, I'm so glad. Emily, I can't tell you how glad I am that you're here!"

He couldn't sleep, though he was exhausted. He kept thinking how strange it was. Just before he had left, and again now, their passion was running over. Normally it happened at the start of an affair, but not with her. With her it had been the other way around, and for him, it was like approaching a different woman. Now she was making her first proper physical commitment to him, as though all the other lovemaking had been merely a rehearsal.

He watched her as she slept through a cold gray light. Her

cheek was round as a saucer, it had fallen asleep on her hand and her head flopped languidly in the deep pillow. She suddenly seemed the dearest thing in the world and the thought of leaving her was too painful even to contemplate.

It was the first day that it had felt like spring. The sun swam through the window; it curled up across their bed, and he watched as she edged over so that she could feel it on her skin. She stirred and reached across for his hand, then slept again. He had given up the idea of sleep. He sat and pulled himself up so that his back rested against the wall. He decided that it was the day to buy a ticket, two tickets, but in different directions.

When she woke, she seemed to have similar thoughts. "When you go back," she whispered, "will they ever let you out again?"

"I doubt it."

"So what will happen?" He could sense how her apprehension was heightened by fear.

"I don't want to think about that," he said shortly. "When the time comes, I'll just go."

And he began to wonder about her, about whether he wasn't still just an idea to her: an idea filled with her need for excitement and her old longing for Africa.

Over the weeks they spent together, Emily questioned and dissected all the political facts of his life, as if this, and this alone, gave her the outline of him that she wanted. It created for her a man who could, like the imaginary boy of her childhood, be a heroic brother who made the grand gestures that she still did not dare to make herself. It was as much of him that she had the strength to absorb.

Reuben had decided that she must be pitched into life, but a life she could manage, and in a place that would comfort her. He wanted to protect her from herself and from the politics that would provide her with the violence she craved but could only stunt her. He knew that if it worked, or if it did not, he could still lose her; but it was a gamble essential to take. Because he loved her. Even if it was more for the woman he believed she would become than for the one she was now. It was her potential that he had recognized and fallen in love with. And somewhere she knew this also.

But he wanted to know if he had simply been a dream to her or whether, in fact, he had helped to pull her from the dark. So he asked her, "Have you been happy with me?"

"Oh, yes, happier than ever. And I could just stay like this. But we must both go back. I know that. It's what I want."

"But you're frightened, too, aren't you?"

"Yes. I'm excited, but afraid. I don't know how it will be."

He was gentle. "There's nothing there, Em. You look down from the plane and there's a splattering of mud huts stuck on the bush. You walk a few miles out of Gaborone and you're in the wilderness. There's nothing there."

Her eyes danced and her face looked elfish. "Then it's exactly as I remember; it's exactly what I want!"

"And it's a black state, too, remember."

He smiled at her elated face. "It's no use trying to caution you, is it?"

"No," she said. "I feel so excited right now, I could just scream." Then she looked at him softly and said, "But it's so precious, too." Her voice fell. "It feels like a door being opened into sunshine after a long dark tunnel."

He said, "Life is suddenly more precious to you than your precious past—your miserable, bitter past. And yes, you must take it, with both hands, take it." He felt suddenly afraid. And she felt it, too, for she whispered in a panic, "Don't go. Come with me, why can't you?"

He shook his head carefully, "No, you know I can't. I have a different journey; we must both go our own way for a bit." He watched as her eyes quickened with pain, then took her face in both hands, "You do understand, don't you, if I'm there with you, it wouldn't work for you. You have to do it alone."

And it was in late February, when winter seemed at last weary of its bleak vision, that Emily was able to put away the childish affliction that had led her so often to a damaged aspect of life.

She found that when she ceased to seek out these things, they no longer had the urgent existence she had once given them.

When Reuben left, it did not crush her. It was no longer a desertion, merely a parting. She could survive in peace. She packed away her thick dresses and shoes, she stacked her books—and with a light heart, two suitcases, and a ticket to Botswana, prepared to take leave of her past.

PART FIVE

I have spread my dreams under your feet;
Tread softly, because you tread on my dreams.
W. B. YEATS

WHEN EMILY WENT TO SAY GOOD-BYE TO HER MOTHER, she found her curled up in an armchair that seemed suddenly too large for her. She was huddled; her back seemed to have grown a hump. It was impossible to say, "I've come to say good-bye."

But before Emily had even sat down, her mother said, as though Bernard were not present, "He's gone off with another woman."

Bernard smiled with exasperation.

Lilian insisted, "He's not here, my husband's not here."

Bernard walked out of the room; he was sick to death of this: first she had lost her wedding ring; then she had hidden all the money from her bag; then she had moved out of his bed. And all she would ever say was that her husband had gone.

Emily went over and sat beside her mother; she wanted to take her hand, but it was clasped together with the other one in her lap.

"What do you mean, he isn't here?"

"He isn't, he's gone."

"Where to?"

"Away."

Emily rubbed her mother's arm; she spoke soothingly, "Well, he'll come back, don't worry."

"No. He isn't—my—husband." Her voice almost stuttered, as

if the words were hard to come by. "He isn't—a husband—or a father. He—won't—come—back." Now she was distressed.

"You mean, that that man who was just in the room was not your husband?"

"No." Lilian was quite emphatic; her eyes looked vicious.

"Who is he, then?"

"He just—looks after me." Then she looked puzzled. "My husband wouldn't; he's gone, gone with another woman." Now her speech was fluent, she sounded exactly as she usually did.

"Is he kind to you?"

"This one is."

"And will your husband come back again?"

"No."

Emily was struck by a strange thought. She asked, "Do you want him to come back?"

"No."

When they were going upstairs, Lilian suddenly caught sight of her face in the hall mirror. Her hands flew up to her hair and began clawing at it. She looked quite distraught. She looked at her face as if she had not seen it for a long time.

"Is that *me*? God—God—me?" She was frantic; she began to rush up the stairs. Emily caught up with her at the top and put an arm around her; she led her toward her bedroom.

"Your hair's just a bit messed up, Mummy, let me do it for you. Come on. Let's put some makeup on you." She smiled encouragingly at her mother. "I've never seen you without makeup on."

Emily stood behind her mother, who was sitting in front of the big, old dressing table, looking now quite blankly at her reflection. She smoothed on some foundation in a vague way, while Emily tried to comb some life into the dull hair that sat close to Lilian's skull like a cap; her curls had gone. Emily gave up, the hair was too greasy, but she said brightly, "There, that's better. Put on some lipstick now. Here, you do it."

Lilian took the bright red stick and raised it; she then began to apply it, heavily, to her eyebrow. Emily wanted to run from the room.

She forced herself to rub the lipstick off the eyebrow and then applied the lipstick cartridge to her mother's mouth.

"Stiffen your mouth, yes, that's better. There." She stood back in relief.

Lilian smiled at herself in the mirror. "Yes, that's better." Now she recognized herself again. She turned on the stool. "Now, tell me what you're going to do, you said something—about—what was it about? You haven't been—some time."

Emily was reassured by the relatively smooth flow of these words and the face, calm now, pretty and relaxed, looking much as Lilian had always looked. She sat on the bed and said, "You tell me about yourself first, how have you been?"

Lilian smiled so much that Emily felt concerned that she might break into laughter. "Oh, fine, fine," she said. "The same as always." Then, "Nothing happens here."

Her voice was trailing away, and Emily rushed to catch up with it. "He's retired now, Daddy I mean, he's retired, so he can be here with you all day now?"

Lilian was irritated, "No, I told you, he's gone."

"But you're not alone, anyway."

"No, not alone." She sounded vague; she plucked at her hair. "You—did you? Were you—going—somewhere, can't really—seem to—remember."

"Yes, to Botswana. I came today to tell you when I'm going." Emily's breathing was sharp now; she watched her mother's face to catch any shadow of reaction. There was none.

Then, "That's nice, you always—liked it."

"Yes, I always liked it. You didn't, did you?"

She shook her head violently. "Hated it, dirty bush—flies, horrible—horrible people—savages."

She swirled around on the little stool with its pink frill and almost shouted at Emily, "You must go, must get away from here." She pushed at her, "Go, go, don't—come—back—ever. It's all finished. Get away." She pushed at Emily again, her face twisted with resentment.

Emily felt as though she were swallowing glass. She mentally took herself to one side and asked herself what had she wanted: her mother's blessing? Her mother's grief? Then Lilian began to mumble again, the same words but without the bitterness; there was almost panic in her voice as she repeated, "Go, go," with her hands fluttering, her head swaying, so that, to Emily watching her, it was as if she really begged, "Stay, stay." Then the impression was gone, so quickly that Emily felt she had imagined it. Her mother leaned forward, "Go, go," she whispered, her face bird-like, "Don't come back, not ever." Now it was a conspiracy, the two of them against the world. And she smiled, she smiled as though she knew what she was saying.

Emily's father was sitting in the garden under the holly tree, with a small table in front of him. He was reading the *Daily Telegraph*. It was cold, but the sun was shining and he was wearing an old pair of khaki shorts. Emily watched him from the kitchen window.

A young girl came walking in from the garden next door; she had long blond hair and was carrying some books under her arm. Bernard looked up and smiled at her. She sat down on the chair next to him, spoke a moment, then opened one of the books. She handed it to him and pointed at the page. He adjusted his glasses, read silently for a minute. She looked at him expectantly, then flipped up her hair and tied it back with a band. Bernard then appeared to be explaining something to her. The girl leaned over the table; their heads were close together, looking at the book.

She was a medical student and she lived next door. Bernard had always secretly wanted to be a doctor; now he was living vicariously through the girl. She liked his interest and encouragement, but knew that his motives were mainly selfish. Lately, she was also beginning to resent his intrusion in her work and life; he seemed to want to take it over—take her over. But she had no one else. Her own father was an ignorant man, intimidated by his daughter's abilities. She needed someone to talk to about what she was doing, so she came and sat with Bernard and they would talk for hours about medicine, about lectures she went to, books she was reading.

The girl had felt guilty at the beginning that Lilian was never included in these discussions, that Lilian should feel left out. But Bernard was right when he said that Lilian couldn't understand such things, it was above her head; she had never been an intelligent woman. And now? Well, now she seemed almost to be going ga-ga, to use Bernard's new phrase for her. Soon, the girl, too, had begun to forget the silent woman in the chair; soon she regarded Lilian in the same way that Bernard did. It was a collusion. But the girl was not to blame. She was lonely. As soon as she got the chance, she would be gone. Bernard knew it. He dreaded it. Without knowing it, he tried to hold her back, to keep her a young girl. He insisted that she work, work, work—that the only way she would ever succeed was by total industry. She bowed to his demands because of an undeveloped strain in her. She began to go her own way, in secret, but cautiously, like a child afraid of being caught in her independence. But still, she was waiting; she would be gone. In the meantime, she was fond enough of him. And she, too, had learned how to manipulate him; in a strange way she had come to control both Lilian and Bernard when she was in their house.

Emily watched the two of them under the holly tree—the girl chewing a pencil as Bernard spoke, his glasses pushed back, his face warmer, softer, than it ever lived in his daughter's mind. She could feel glad for him now that he had found at least a little tenderness; she understood how she had always denied him this herself, through fear, through distrust of his motives. The girl looked toward the window—she saw Emily, but looked quickly away.

Emily waited until the girl had gone; and when Bernard had turned to his paper she went out into the garden to speak to him.

She said, "I've come to say good-bye."

He looked up, an almost timid look in his eyes; he said loudly, "You off, then?" He pushed his paper aside. "How did you find your mother?"

"Not too good, it's sudden, isn't it, this?"

He cut in quickly, "Yes. Confused, she's confused, doesn't seem to know who I am—ha-ha—thinks I'm some chap looking after her."

"Have you looked into it, seen a doctor?"

Now he was nervous, he didn't know what she might say next. "Hm, something's up with the old brain cells. That's what they say."

She shifted her tone. "It must be hard for you."

"No." Nothing was hard for him.

"To manage, I mean."

"Oh, I manage all right."

He looked thinner, strained. She wished he could admit to vulnerability, but if he recognized it, it might finish him. The lack of it made him difficult to approach. She tried again.

"Looking after her, it must take so much of your time. You can't get enough time for yourself."

He grunted. "I've nothing to do. No life here, never cared for hobbies, never been a pub man. Doesn't bother me—looking after her—doesn't bother me. What else would I do?" He gave the old ha-ha laugh, but it seemed against himself.

Emily felt tired; she said, "Well, I'd better be going now. I'm flying on Wednesday, you know."

"Yes, hope it all goes well. Can't imagine . . . but never mind about that . . . it's your life. We've never interfered, not that you'd let us. Wouldn't want to. Off you go, then." He stood up, embarrassed by the proximity of emotion. He folded the newspaper noisily.

She stood there.

"Well, good-bye, then." She kissed his cheek—the high color of the old days had faded; there was a little network of veins on his nose.

"Good-bye." His voice rattled a little; he righted it. He moved off, calling back, "You've said good-bye to your mother?"

"Yes, I've said good-bye."

"Well, I'd better see she's all right, then." He added, "You can see yourself off, I imagine?"

He moved toward her as if to kiss her; she moved back. It was such an old instinct; when she realized what she had done, he had gone.

She watched him stride back into the house; the kitchen door banged shut behind him. She stood a little while looking after him, half in relief, half in regret. Then she walked around to the front of the red brick house, got into Virginia's car, and drove off.

A mile down the road she had to stop because she was crying so much that she could not see.

Emily was sitting in Virginia's kitchen, drinking tea. Her eyes were dry, but they were still swollen. Virginia was sitting at the other end of the table, holding the saucer of her cup; she did not look at Emily, carefully averting her eyes because the silence between them was full of Emily's emotion.

"I know, I know," Emily whispered, "I must give her up; she keeps pulling me back into the shadows. To go on living to try and capture her, please her—it's hopeless, it pulls me toward—what? I don't know—what?" Her face was pierced with misery.

"Death," Virginia said softly. "But she's gone. She was never really there, and now she's gone, for good. You must let her go, Em."

Virginia thought a moment. "Perhaps you can forgive your mother now because she seems almost dead? Perhaps you'll only feel truly free when she is dead, when there's nothing more she can ask of you?"

Emily was stunned by the truth of this insight. "That's true; the absolute truth. I never realized it." Then her face brightened. "And in a sense, she has let me go herself; she sort of pushed me out." She jumped up and went to the window and looked out. Then she turned back to look at Virginia. "I'm going home, Virginia, at last I can go home."

Virginia took her hand. "But you're not alone now, Em, remember that. You're not going back to the bleak isolation of your childhood. You have Reuben. You have me. You can trust us both to love you."

Emily said brightly, "You know, Virginia, I could just have

stayed here, lived a little life, been a wife, packed away my old dreams and dresses. And stayed. But he's gone. He's gone back. So it's different. And I'm glad; I'm lucky it's different!"

"But a little worried, too, I think."

"Yes, a little."

"It'll be all right. I know it will."

Emily's face flushed with pain and her eyes filled with tears. "But now, I have to leave you as well. I have to always be leaving. I hate it so. I thought I would die when I left Africa, and now I'm leaving here, leaving so much again."

"But you'll come back. I'll go there. I'll bring my babies to see you."

"Oh, yes, you will. You must do that." Emily was almost crying again. Virginia said nothing; they looked at the grain of the table; they held each other's hands like sisters.

Then presently, Emily got up. "Here are the car keys. I won't come back and say good-bye tomorrow. I couldn't bear it." And then suddenly she wanted to tell Virginia what she'd always felt about her, and she said, "Virginia, I owe you everything. I feel as though I owe you my life."

She darted out of the door and ran down the steps and into the street without looking back. She walked quickly down the street, seeing the brown buds crack into life on the black branches of the plane trees, the yellow heads of crocus press through the wet earth and open like beaks. There was a strong, rich smell, like fruitcake, manure, like a black man's beer. She began to walk faster. She began to run.

Every morning, when Emily woke, it was like the first time again: home, home. She woke within the sweet earthy smell of a rondavel; a circular scoop out of one of the mud walls let in a clear moon of morning light. Her brown arm reached out and felt the wall— cool and smooth.

She took out Reuben's letter and read it for the fifth time:

You must wait for me. Out there in the bush, you must think of me, and then I will be there for you, as you are here for me in this awful little flat where I expect always to be interrupted one night. But, Emily, it is so exhilarating to be here, on the brink of something. Even cut off from it by this ban, I still feel it; it's happening. We won't have to wait too much longer.

Someone said that the country will last as long as the gold and diamonds, but they're wrong; the country will only last as long as the workers will bring up the gold and diamonds. But I feel that you are safe there, that it is a place of refuge for you again, but in a far different way. Your letters are lovely, full of simple things. And I'll come and live there with you. It won't be too long. And in the meantime, Mary and Lukas will take care of you. I hope you have enough to eat. Who would have thought, a few years ago, that Africa would be so decimated by poverty and famine, even the rich south. This country's bargaining power is becoming a question of whether they will or won't give food. But you'll be all right. So grow your mealies and beans and potatoes and prepare for a hard time. Keep a place for me. Wait for me. I love you better than all the world.

When she walked outside, the light was already sharper. Some women were carrying seeds in sacks down to the fields to plant. The African women had their babies strapped to their backs in blankets, while one white woman had hers slung and strapped across her stomach. There was a drone of conversation and little ricochets of laughter among them as they followed the path, single file, down to the mealie fields, where the mealies would be planted in straight lines and shaded with branches cut from the bush.

Emily pushed the hair back from her face; there was a strong, hot wind. An old collie dog lying in the sun jerked in his sleep; far away by the dam, the herd of cows milled about in their boredom, bumping one another along and tugging out snatches of grass near the banks.

All night she had heard the wind clattering along the tin roofs of the mud houses around her rondavel. Now, a child was yelling; there was always a child yelling. Flies made a black crust on a discarded husk of corn. She looked around her as though to reassure herself that she was in fact there. She smiled up at the sky, breathless with love for it all.

Emily walked over to Mary's house. In the kitchen Mary was sitting at one end of the table, drinking tea. Her face, sharply defined by tiredness, looked more like a wooden mask than ever. It was a very striking face, with the definitive lines of a carved African mask. Her skin was darkly tanned; she had a long, wide mouth. Her hair, flecked with gray, was parted severely down the middle and was pulled back into a bun. It was a face that could almost be off-putting because of its primitive force, but when she smiled, you had to smile with her.

"Where's Lukas?" Emily asked, then looked at her watch. "Oh, he must be at the clinic."

"Thelma had her baby this morning, at four o'clock, of course," Mary said. "Want a cup of tea? It's very weak, I'm afraid, John says he's running out, can't get his hands on any more."

Emily went to fetch an enamel beaker. "The baby okay?"

"Delicious," Mary said, almost smacking her lips. "It made me quite broody."

"Thinking about babies," Emily said, "did you hear what that man from Uganda said the other day?" She stirred the sugar noisily in her tin cup.

"No, what?"

"Well, he said a lot of the tribes are getting like the Bushmen women. They get sterile in times of severe drought, sometimes for years. In the famine areas, women are simply not conceiving."

"It's quite incredible, isn't it," Mary said, "how the body adjusts to the mind, to the bloody climate, to the threat of death."

"I suppose so," Emily said uncertainly. "I suppose they'll be all right again when they get enough to eat?"

"I imagine so, but sometimes, it doesn't work out. I remember when Lukas and I were farming in the bushveld, we had women there who'd come from up north and had lived through years and years of near-starvation when they were children. When the time came for them to have babies, their hips were too narrow; their bones had not formed properly, so they couldn't give birth. That's when Lukas first started doing Cesareans, there was no other way. It was like the old movies, almost, a slug of brandy and hope they pass out soon. It was only later that we managed to get hold of some gas and decent equipment."

"Lukas wasn't a doctor then?"

"Hell, no, Lukas isn't a doctor now, if it comes to that. He's never had any proper medical training—just a quick course in Salisbury once. When you're out in the bush, you've just got to get on with it. We learned how to cope with the usual things—typhoid, malaria, bilharzia. Africans are trained, in about a month, to be able to diagnose and handle all the usual illnesses they're likely to come across."

"How much do we get here, in the way of drugs? Lukas is so careful with everything."

Mary leaned back on her stool. "Not nearly enough. We could probably keep our own lot in good shape, but it's all the refugees who keep flocking here. We are beginning to have to turn people away. Still"—she grinned—"now that you're here, you'll pick it all up very quickly. We all do shifts with Lukas, and if there's a lot of people, we drop other things to do it. If only there was more money. We'll run out of bloody aspirin one of these days!"

"Do you get any aid?"

"A bit, and in emergencies we start yelling and can drum up quite a bit from the Red Cross and organizations in England. But the problem's too large. Finished your tea?"

"We'd better go, then?"

"Ya."

"Who's doing lunch today?"

"Ruth and Elizabeth."

Lukas was slapping the arm of a small girl before giving her an injection. She was lying on a stretcher with a hole cut into its center and a bucket underneath. Her stomach, which looked as though it was stuck to her backbone, convulsed for a moment and she jerked her head sideways, showing her teeth. There was a strong stench. The girl lay back; she was shaking and damp.

"How are you feeling?" Mary asked the girl in Setswana, placing a large, flat hand on the damp forehead. Then she turned to Lukas, "Will she be okay?"

"Of course," Lukas replied, as he always did.

He was a tall man, with deep creases on the back of his neck, sparse gray hair that must have been blond once, pale blue eyes set far back in his skull. There was something ferocious in his determination.

"Right, you two," he said in a voice that was unmistakably English after a lifetime in Africa. "Mary, can you do the clinic with Emily? Make her do things now, she's been watching for a week. There are some Sowetans outside in bad shape, been shot up in the bush by guerrillas. Need stitching and bandaging. Can we put a couple of them up for a day or two? Two are in bad shape."

"How many in all?"

Lukas was taking an old man's temperature in another bed; he talked to him quietly a moment, then answered Mary's question. "Two men, four women, and five kids. They're okay, the kids, just terrified. Only one woman hurt badly and one of the men."

Emily said, "I'll ask Mrs. Mboene to take the kids in the crèche so the women can rest."

"Fine." He walked off to the next bed and began peeling off a bandage. There were only six beds in the little room; the other beds were filled with children suffering from malnutrition.

While Emily checked the children, Lukas said, "We'll have to move them soon."

Mary protested, "Oh, Lukas, why can't we build another room? We always have to move them out too soon."

"No," he said sharply. "You know we can't." He added impatiently, "We must recognize our own limits."

Mary looked downcast for a moment, then she knocked his arm apologetically. "Yes, yes, I know, my dear."

Emily went out to the new arrivals; she managed to get the women to take the children to the crèche. Then one of the women unpacked a small baby off her back and handed it to Emily.

"We find this one. Find it in the bush next to dead mother."

"Do you know what happened?" Emily said, looking at the little bundle in alarm.

"No. Just bodies all over the show."

"How many?"

"Three women, some young girls. Children all dead. But this baby, the gun go through the woman, leave the baby alone." She grinned. "Lucky as the devil, this one. But not mine," she added firmly.

Emily looked down at the little thing wrapped up in a strip of red blanket, but otherwise naked. The infant fixed her with a stare, terrifying and helpless. She sat down and began efficiently to check that there was no injury; the small black body was perfect, unscathed but pitifully thin. It was a girl; there was a tiny string of unusual beads around her neck, made from clay with a few cheap imitation pearls thrown in for good measure; but the effect on the delicate neck, against the soft brown skin was quite beautiful. The big woman said, "You have babies?"

"No," Emily said firmly.

"Okay. You have this one."

Emily laughed at her.

"Plenty good baby, no crying, sleeps good. You got a husband, lady?"

"No." Emily smiled at the wonderful bustling quality of the woman, with her wide white teeth and round shiny face.

"Then you need baby!" She roared with laughter. "You go walking across the border"—she meant into the Republic—"with that black baby, they kill you in one minute. You stay here, you fine." She laughed, having settled the whole matter.

Emily stood up and was about to be firm, not to allow herself to be manipulated. But the wretched child had nestled against her and fallen asleep. "I'd better just hang on to her for a bit," she said sheepishly, adjusting the baby's position so she could carry her more comfortably.

"Now you ladies come with me. You can have a little water for washing, but you must throw it where I show you; it goes on the plants. I'll give you each a bowl." The large woman undid the bundle on her head and produced a chipped enamel bowl of her own, as did the others. "Okay, good," Emily said. "After you've finished, you come to the kitchen and help. We all work here."

"Ai, ai." They all laughed and jostled together as though she were offering them a new game.

"Here, I show you." The woman who'd handed Emily the baby took it back. "This baby she feeds with this one." She indicated a young mother with her own baby asleep on her back. "She has plenty of milk." The young girl looked shy; she dropped her eyes. She was wearing just a traditional strip of cloth bound about her with a shawl to keep her baby in place. "But baby full now, she wants to sleep." She bound the baby quickly and expertly onto Emily's back, so that the round bottom of the child was scooped into the red blanket and the head lolled against Emily's back. The woman laughed. "You look good; you be good mother for this one. You put something down your back later, so she don't wet on you." She laughed again and nudged Emily affectionately.

"She can stay there for the time being," Emily said, and walked on toward the washhouse, hoping that the soap had not run out again because these women certainly needed it. The baby was small and warm on her back; the position was very comfortable, the baby light.

In the washroom, the women stripped off and, talking loudly together, began to wash. The washroom was just one large brick building with rusted strips of corrugated iron for a roof. There were three square basins with taps. One had hot water, but it was erratic; the water always came out brown and then gradually turned beige. The only bath in the village was in Mary and Lukas's house. It was a brick house, built in the colonial days, with wide verandas all around and a long gravel driveway, set off by flower beds. Mary always insisted that any of the facilities in the house could be used by anyone, but in fact the Africans preferred to wash themselves, their babies, and their clothes, in the washroom, all together, preferably with as many of them in there as could fit at the same time.

Emily turned to the big woman who appeared to do all the talking. "What is your name? I'm called Emily."

"Ah," she said brightly and sang out the name in three syllables, "Em-il-ee. Very good. My name is Lala."

"Lala?"

"Yes, I sing pretty good." She roared with laughter and the others laughed with her, although not all of them understood English.

"And your friends, what are their names?"

Lala rattled off a string of impossible names, then said obligingly, "We all have our 'other' names—you call this one what the mission called her, Lucy, because her name means brightness, and this—" she pointed to the young mother—"this one is Mattie." Mattie lowered her head, but then went on to lather her big, full breasts and the long length of her neck.

Emily said, "I feel ashamed that I don't speak your language, but I'm going to learn."

Lala nudged her again, "Is no trouble, we are the same under the names."

Emily called over and introduced the new women to two women who had recently come from the Republic and who were still awkward with Europeans. She spoke carefully to them, "Can you help, please? Show them where to hang up any washing, and then, Sannie, when they've finished, can you bring them over to the kitchen, please? I must get back to the clinic." Emily left, the baby banging happily on her back.

Mary looked up from the arm she was cleaning when Emily came in. "My God," she said, "I've heard of instant motherhood, but this is ridiculous! Where did you get the baby?"

"I haven't exactly got it," Emily said snappishly, moving to the table, where she began quickly to roll a bandage, while Mary applied ointment and lint to the the wound on the woman's arm. A needle and some thread were being sterilized. Mary had waited for Emily before attempting to stitch one of the men's legs. Emily passed over the bandage and stood ready with the scissors.

"There's a terrific character who's just come in, called Lala,"

Emily said. "She decided that I should have the baby. The mother's dead. She just handed it over to me."

"Oh, really?" Mary said, lifting her eyebrows.

"Yes, really!" Emily retorted.

The African woman, neatly bandaged, had the washhouse pointed out to her; she looked relieved to be out of the clinic.

Outside, under the shelter of the stoep around the clinic, a large group of Africans sat patiently with babies and children, waiting their turn once the emergencies had been taken care of. They had walked from different parts of the surrounding bush and had been waiting since early morning. Two men walked out into the glare, stitched and bandaged. They walked off looking proud of their wounds and sat down under a tree, waiting to see what else the morning would provide.

The village began to prepare for lunch. Over the years it had slowly merged with what was now basically a refugee camp. There were refugees from Namibia and victims of bombings inside South Africa.

Resources were always stretched, so that people coming into the camp had to abide by certain regulations, the chief one being hygiene. Inspectors from the government checked up on the settlement regularly, to avoid typhoid breaking out, or any of the other hazards of overpopulation. There were regulations about not fouling the water, and on ways of preserving the little water there was. Refugees were only allowed to stay on condition that they lived by the rules, were prepared to work, and caused no friction.

Inspectors also came to ensure that the refugee camp was really what it claimed to be, and not a center for the military training of guerrillas. Occasionally, the South African border police swooped down, but less lately—they had their hands full. Somehow, the settlement managed to absorb a great deal; it was a busy, happy place, under constant strain, like a bag into which too much is stuffed; but it survived on the goodwill of the people, who knew they were lucky to be there, and alive, in the uncertain times.

Now, as they sat under a large old mopani tree eating lunch

in a circle, there was a lot of conversation. The electricity had packed up in Mary's house, so the meal had been cooked outside. Enamel plates, piled with mealie pap and gravy, were being passed around the circle; people ate with a spoon or their fingers.

Ouma, a woman who claimed to be more than a hundred years old, was sharing her plate with a great-grandchild, rolling the mealie pap into hard balls and pressing it into the pungent gravy. Then she handed it to the little boy sitting between her scrawny flanks. He sucked on it and she sat there with her permanent half-smile, like a withered Mona Lisa, her eyes black and shrewd as a snake's.

One of the women from the field came and sat down next to Emily. "Did you finish the field, Elvira?" Emily asked.

Elvira grinned and wiped her hand across her sweating brow. "No, the ground was not properly worked yesterday. We had to do more." She talked very slowly; she was learning to read at the evening classes.

"So who's going to water them in?"

"The new ones will do that, but they must be showed." Emily smiled and looked up at the cloudless sky, blue as enamel.

"We need rain so badly, will we ever get any?"

"The Lord knows."

Emily said good-bye to her and walked back to the clinic with Mary. They did not stop work until just before dark; then people began to disappear back into the bush, trailing or carrying their treated children. Some would wait, in the camp or nearby, to come back for more treatment before making the long trek back to their own villages in the surrounding countryside.

Sometimes, in the evenings, the women would gather in Mary's house to sew. They came from the camp or neighboring farms, even from the capital. There would be an exchange of skills and a lot of laughter and talk of politics. Mary had persuaded Emily to join them.

On this particular night, a number of black teenage girls came in. They lolled against the walls, wanting to pick a fight. They were dressed in very tight jeans and were smoking and whispering among themselves, kicking their high-heeled shoes against the walls. There was no beer that night, nothing going on in the camp, and no dancing. They were bored rotten.

Mary asked one of the girls, in her own language, if she'd like to make herself something. She rustled through a sheaf of well-thumbed patterns and brought out one of a slinky dress with slits up the sides of the skirt. The girl looked at it greedily for a second, then she spat loudly on the floor. With an aggressive toss of her head, she leaned back against the wall, looking bored. Her face, at that moment, to a European was as blank and indifferent as the faces of all Africans of all centuries, everywhere. Some of the African women began to look uncomfortable; one snapped at the girl, who snapped back.

Mary said sharply, "Either you come and join us, you three, or you must all go, right away. You can't make trouble here." She took up her darning of a blanket with determination. The small band of hostile girls looked at Mary, then around the room. Then they left, their faces totally lacking in emotion of any kind.

Lala, who had been watching this with much interest, suddenly roared out, a great grin polishing up her large teeth: "You pretty clever, Mary-Lou. You tell them where to get off, they like it. They gone." The air was cleared, as neatly as if she had swept it with a big broom: everyone returned to her work; conversation began to bubble and rise.

Lala was sitting next to Emily, who turned to her and said, "You're pretty clever yourself, Lala."

"Dead right," Lala said, snapping off a piece of thread. "I had a husband once who give me plenty trouble, plenty trouble that man; he had the devil between his legs. Then one day, I say to him, you stay here and don't drink the money no more, or I forget all my mother teach me about happiness in the bed."

"What happened?" Emily asked, struggling with the smocking on the little dress she was sewing, and trying not to laugh.

"Nothing, bloody rubbish, nothing—so then I pack him off." She turned to look keenly at Emily. "How you get on with that baby now?"

"Fine," Emily said.

Lala smiled sideways.

Earlier, Lala had come and taken the baby from Emily. "She go now for her feeding, and she sleeps next to Mattie's baby. She like that. How about we call her Happy? Because she never cry. Okay with you, Emily? You happy now, too. I bring her back in the morning for you."

Emily had agreed to this arrangement; she'd very quickly grown fond of the baby, who gurgled and chuckled and fastened herself around her fingers. She was to spend some of the day in the baby crèche, when Emily was at the clinic, but could accompany Emily down to the fields like the other babies did. Some of the white women had brought in old nappies and little nighties and dresses for her, and Emily had been bombarded with hints and advice from the African women. She'd become something of a good luck charm, this small survivor from the bush and the war.

Lala said, "You come sit here, Emily, I give you a beautiful hairdo."

Emily felt it would be quite impossible to refuse this big, laughing woman anything, so she went immediately and sat where she was asked to. Mary watched with amusement as Lala began to divide Emily's hair into neat, squared sections; then she plaited the hair in each square into tight pigtails, which she coiled and stopped with a small bead. "Hey, what're you trying to do," Mary said, laughing, "turn her into a black girl?"

Lala said, "Now you a proper mother for Happy." And she beamed.

"Here, take a look at yourself," Mary said, passing a small mirror.

"It really suits you, Emily," a woman from the next farm said. "Shows up your good bones."

"You won't need to bother to comb your hair now," someone else remarked with a grin.

Afterward, when everyone had left Mary's house, Emily walked back to her rondavel under the broad shelter of the marula tree. The sky was full of diamonds and it was humming again. In the bush, just beyond the huts, she could hear the crickets and seemed to feel the presence of African ancestors, protecting and watching over the land. But just beyond that safe circle were the broken and gutted roads, the deserted villages with their burned huts, the fields raided and trampled. She was filled then with a dread of the bush; at night it was always menacing, always on its own side. Soon, like a wave, it would lap closer and closer and perhaps sweep them all away. No one traveled far anymore.

She looked away to all the little fires winking at the entrances of huts. The African life was in full swing now, with laughter and shouting and complaints about the beer, which had run out. A woman was singing a soft rippling song, accompanied by a drum and a hosho rattle. Farther away, a five-stringed lute trickled out an independent melody and a bow blended in with the other melodies, so that they became a haunting intricate whole. Someone was clapping to the rhythm of the drum. A voice joined in the first song and someone hummed softly in another key. At odd moments, one of the women gave a high-pitched howl, an expression of praise and exuberance; it seemed to gather all the harmonies together, acting as a funnel, a conductor in some mysterious sense.

Emily stood quite still and listened; the menace of the night had vanished, or been absorbed, by the delicate beauty of the music. A woman wearing a skin skirt, with a thick belt of white and blue beads, walked past, her broad breasts swinging, her tin bracelets clinking together on her arms. Emily walked into her rondavel and sat down on her low bed. She missed Reuben. The paraffin lamp was flickering as though in a draft; the shadows made black butterflies on the wall. She watched them a second, then extinguished the flame. The music outside was softer now, more melancholic. She recognized a rain song and, listening to it, fell asleep.

She was sitting under her tree, her legs spread out in front of her, her feet brown and bare. She was wearing a faded pink dress with no sleeves and a string of cheap beads around her neck. Her hair was in two long plaits, and she leaned forward, holding her arms out to Happy, who was learning to walk; Happy toppled forward as though drunk and then fell and wailed. Emily scooped her up and held her, rocking her, rubbing the sand off her dress and legs. "Sh," she said softly. "Listen, Happy, listen." The child stopped crying, the tears on her dusty cheeks dried instantly. She cocked her head to one side and listened. "Do you hear, it's a grasshopper, it's singing." Happy began to cry again, then, just as suddenly, she pulled herself up and began to toddle off.

It was a quiet day. Hot and still. The insects had vanished beneath rocks. No one had come to the clinic that day, and this was so unusual that everyone was worried. The Africans looked secretive; they seemed to know something, but would not say. Some of them had the gift of divining when a new group of people were on their way, but now, when asked what was in the air, they would not reply; they walked away as though bored or restless.

One of the young women came up and sat down next to Emily in the shade.

"How is it, Mickey?"

"Not bad. But there are stories. We don't like them."

"What stories?"

"Ask Josie."

"I'm asking you."

The black woman looked at Emily in a particular way; it was the way the country Africans, usually the older ones, looked at a European, with a feeling of forbearance, almost of tolerance. Emily looked at Mickey's feet and thought how old they looked, with the deep cracks in her soles and the skin white and scaly. Mickey began to play with a small stone, making circles in the sand.

"Things happen when bad times are coming," she said dramatically.

"What things?"

"The people from up there," she pointed to the north, "they say that the river birds are falling dead from the skies. And the animals are walking around and around, trying to find their tails. These are bad signs."

Emily spoke calmly, "It's just part of the drought. We see strange things here also."

Mickey shook her head stubbornly. She wore her hair very short; it was dense and woolly, dusty at the edges. She had an old paisley blouse, hanging loose, over a turquoise skirt and wore big brass rings in her ears.

"It is more than the drought," she said. "Always we have drought. We know it. This is other than drought."

"You won't make everyone nervous with these stories, Mickey, please?" Emily pleaded.

"All are nervous. Like before the storm."

Emily smiled. "Yes, I know what you mean."

Happy came crawling back and curled into Emily's lap. Mickey put out her arms and called to the child affectionately; Happy smiled, but she did not move. She looked at Mickey suspiciously and stuffed the end of her dress into her mouth. Mickey got up, shook her skirt of its dust and moved off disconsolately, as if she had been seeking something from Emily that she had not found. She walked back to a circle of people beneath an acacia tree outside the deserted clinic building. Lukas was in there, getting on with a good sort-out. He did not comment on the absence of patients. He had decided that something was up and it was too dangerous for people to move about.

Emily was preoccupied and sensitive. She walked down with Happy on her hip to the fields where the mealies grew high, the ears ripe for picking. No one was there harvesting. Blackjack had crept in among Elvira's neat rows. The beans were ready and sweet potatoes had spread over the dusty red earth. A wind began to blow, full of dust and flies.

Suddenly, without knowing why, Emily began to cry. She buried her face in Happy's small chest and sobbed. Happy's clear white-and-black eyes grew round; she stared hard at Emily, who went on sobbing. She felt very lonely. It was because of Reuben. The long letters, smuggled out so carefully for her, had stopped. She was reduced to feeling a small child again, her mother silent, absent, behind the mosquito net. To comfort herself, she brought out his last letters and began to reread them:

Emily, I wonder how much longer I can bear it without you; the days are so long and dreary since I've been confined to this house; only one or two people are allowed to visit. I've never missed anyone as I now miss you. I feel suddenly the pointlessness of everything. Everything about me is in as much disorder as I feel myself: the government are panicking and losing control—they've ditched all that progressive stuff they tried to fool the world with. Shares are dropping, investments seizing up; all the foreign journalists are being thrown out, and any whispering dissenter or liberal talker is put away.

Last night, at the mine dances, an incredible thing happened. The Zulus were all there, dancing in their traditional garb as always, with the whites clapping and cheering. But all at once, the war dance became reality; their dancing lost its entertainment quality and took on a wild, sinister quality. People became uneasy. At that moment, after a long, chilling yell, the warriors all hurled their spears into the white crowd. People started screaming and running; they were dragged off and beaten up, savaged. Then the police came in and shot all the Zulus.

The thing is, they knew the result: those men were prepared to die, and they died with glory, with a glory that would seem to have gone out of their hearts. But it happened, in Johannesburg, just yesterday, and the repercussions have been awesome. The entire mine community is being interrogated; their methods have exceeded the brutality we all know about. But people are dying rather than admit anything. The whites are quite terrified, and the police have nothing to reassure them with.

Emily, we seem to be getting close to the stage where the hazards of life have outweighed those of war and revolt.

But thinking of all these things just brings me back to you. Often I feel staggeringly alone—as if what I'm going through here is a magnification of my life, really. And all those years rushing around the world as a journalist seem today to have been merely escapes, from myself, from my isolation, and of course in the end—they only increased it. Being exposed to solitary confinement in prison, then this, barely able to leave this house, perhaps it captures in a nutshell all I have been trying to avoid. And here I sit, and you are far away.

But then on other days, I feel that we are together. I feel as close to you as if we were having one of those long conversations about Tolstoy or Jung that we both used to get so excited about. It almost seems that we had the closest connection with our heads, that we couldn't get any closer than that, not even in bed.

And then, his last letter.

Emily, I'm wondering if there's some way that I can get out. I didn't consider it before. But now we sit, idle, we do nothing, we are just waiting for the end. And I want to come to you. I'm going to try and organize it—don't rely on it, it'll be bloody difficult, people are trying to get out all over the place, the country's becoming like a leaking boat, but the exits are all closed, and the airports and ports are a nightmare. But I will try. I sometimes wonder what happened to those recruits that you and Mary hid; do you know if they got to Ghana? I think all that has closed down now. I certainly haven't been able to help anyone.

I loved your last letter: you seem to be so fulfilled there. It all sounds so domestic and simple; a group of people sustaining and helping one another, almost a matriarchal society, with all the qualities that seems to imply. It's so nice that you can talk so easily to Mary and Lukas—though I do feel jealous that it isn't me! And now you are lending books to Josie and so you can talk to her about them. I miss you terribly for that, among all the other missing.

You say that the bush is full of young boys, all on their way north for training. You described so well that little boy with the machine gun, stomping about and firing it into the air. The mind boggles! And then I panic—are you really safe there? Are any of us safe? And I should be there with you. I know now that that's what you wanted of me—to come with you—to stay with you—to give up everything for you. You needed a grand gesture—oh, how long you must have needed a grand gesture to blot out all the past. And I should have made it. I should not have sent you there alone. Well, I shall make it now. I'll come to you, as fast as I can.

When Emily finished reading the letter, she had to stop herself from crying all over again. She looked about her, she forced her mind to concentrate on all the good things. Happy was sitting between her thighs, pushing her plump fingers into the hot sand, making soft singing sounds. But it couldn't console her for the fact that that was his last letter. Every day when she rushed out to see Moremi, as he came swinging on his bicycle with the post, no letter had come from him. Mary kept insisting that Emily just wait and not panic, that letters were always infrequent these days.

But the waiting was terrible. And she found it hard to understand the extent of her pain. Now, holding Happy tightly to her near the mealie fields all brown and ragged in the sun, she wept and wept. Until, finally, she felt better for it. She rubbed her eyes, she kissed Happy and talked sensibly to her, then made her way back to the village again.

The men who had come with Lala from Angola were sitting under a tree in ragged vests and dusty trousers done up with string. It was some time before lunch, but people were sitting around, idle, mischievous, surly with something. There was no sign of Mary. Some women were hanging clothes on the lines behind the huts, some were grinding maize and humming as they banged with the pestles and mortars. The chickens were scratching methodically in the dust. When Emily approached a large group under a tree, there was a little movement and murmur; people shuffled. Emily addressed one of the men whom she knew well, "Kruger, I have been to the fields and nothing has been collected today. What's going on?" Then she turned and smiled at the listless group on the ground, "Why are you people so tired today?" No one would meet her eye; the group consisted primarily of men; some were just soldiers passing through, looking for a free meal; others had no work. Emily picked up a strong whiff of hostility.

"It is women's work, gathering," one man said in a deep voice.

"No," she said quietly, "it is anyone's work, and the women are working already." She adjusted Happy on her hip and saw in the man's eye a look of greed, of sexual appetite, and it frightened and fascinated her; she looked away.

"Then you do it," he said aggressively, leaning back and staring up at her.

"It is for me to cook the lunch today," she said firmly, feeling herself grow hot.

"Perhaps there is no point working," one of the soldiers said, his camouflage uniform torn, revealing a mat black skin, the hair of his chest coiled and dusty. The whites of his eyes were inflamed, the veins standing out.

"We have to eat," she replied stubbornly, "all of us."

"They will be coming soon," another man said gently, almost as an apology. "They will be looking."

"Looking for what?"

"Looking for white people to kill," another said, and he spat loudly.

At that, a babble of excited talk broke out. Emily panicked, because she could not understand the language, the gestures. All she understood was the menace.

"They are saying," the soldier said scornfully, "that they do not wish to be here when the soldiers come, looking to kill; they also will be killed with you. Did you not know there has been killing in the village camps?" He smiled.

Emily stood and stared, clutching the child to her. She saw in the faces around her that look, that waiting for her to do something, to make one false move—which would give them the excuse.

Lala walked up and stood behind her; she had heard the last of the conversation. Her big face was like a thundercloud—when it burst it would douse the lot of them. She drew herself up regally. "You bloody rubbish, Kruger, I always said, you bloody rubbish." The man looked abject immediately; he had turned from a tyrant into a child. She placed her hands on her hips and looked down at him furiously. She made a point of talking to him in English so that Emily could understand. "You think we don't know what you're up to, hey? You think we dumb? You trying to make big trouble. You frighten the men, but not the women."

Other women then walked over and joined the group. The men got slowly to their feet, their position on the ground no longer one of superiority; they were shamed by the standing women.

"Now," Lala said, "we have no more talk about killing. Who's to kill here, you tell me, serpent-face, who? Five white people! The soldiers gonna come all the way here to kill five white people, hey? You shut your mouth now, you hear?" He said nothing. She went on, "You no like it here, there are other places for you; you run back to Angola or Zimbabwe. If you stay here, you change your voice."

Josie came and stood by Lala; she said quietly, "We've all been frightened by the rumors, but we are safe here, all of us." Then she went on to talk reassuringly in her own language, and the aggressiveness went out of the men; they looked a little chastened, but seemed to be enjoying it. Their ancient fear of other Africans, of marauding guerrillas, had sent them into a state of fear. Now the fear was subsiding. Emily was impressed to see how Josie had brought them back, like a mother hen gathering her chicks under her wing. Then Josie turned to Emily, who, for her, had become the provider of new thought, of books, of wonderful ideas; and she handed her brood over to Emily.

"And now what'll we do?" she asked, suddenly at a loss.

"Work," Emily said stoutly. "We must all work and then we won't be afraid. Who will go to the fields?" They began to divide cheerfully into small groups. A string of men and women, some of the men still complaining, went off finally to the fields. By the time they had reached the narrow path, they were singing. The rest of the men set about collecting the bricks and cement for the men's washroom that was about to be built. Emily went to the kitchen to do the lunch with Mary; she felt elated on one level, and yet a feeling of worry persisted.

Mary had already started the lunch; she listened carefully when Emily told her what had happened. She said, "Kruger's a bad lot. I don't think he can stay. He'll really make trouble before he's finished."

Emily's brow furrowed and she said, "Will the war reach us here, Mary? We once seemed so safe; now I don't know."

"Oh, yes, it'll reach us here," Mary said wearily. "On the border, all along the outer rim of the Republic, there are whites who no longer have homes. Their farms have been taken over by black terrorists and their servants slaughtered. Now they, the whites, have become refugees, exiles from their homes and country, landless and desolate. Eventually, some of them will make their way here."

Emily's face became tremulous, "It's just a circle, around and around, the oppressor, the oppressed. Nothing changes."

An Englishwoman had just come in, looking flushed and dusty. She tossed her old hat on the floor, where it let off a puff of dust, then sank into familiar folds.

"Jesus!" she said, rubbing her hand over her sweating forehead, "it's ghastly out there." Her eyes adjusted to the cool gloom of the old kitchen after the blazing sunlight outside. She sat down, and Emily realized that she was more than tired, she was shocked.

"What's up, Kate?" she asked.

Kate pushed back her thick, once-fair hair, which had been bleached by age to a silvery gray. Her face was deeply lined by working so much in the open, and at the top of her shirt, Emily could see her neck, red, as if with a rash.

"I crossed into South Africa today. I still have this crazy idea that Africa is all open, and I can go where I like! I told the guy at the border post that I was delivering some Oxfam supplies. He didn't care, didn't even look." She seemed to feel she had to justify her adventure. "We're so darn isolated here, it drives me crazy; we just don't know what's going on. And so I . . ."

"Did you happen to go in the direction of your farm?" Mary asked quietly. "Just by chance?"

"No, I did not!" Kate said furiously.

"Okay, okay," Mary said mildly. "So what happened?"

"Well, it was just too ghastly, too ghastly," Kate said dramatically.

Emily and Mary both stopped chopping vegetables and looked at her expectantly. Kate had something of the actress in her, and it could be infuriating.

"Well, spit it out," Mary snapped, getting back to the pumpkin and flicking out the tiger-colored pips.

"Something's being going on, very recent I'd say. I saw houses, and farms, with windows smashed and ax holes in the doors; the walls were black and rocks and mortar were strewn all over the place. . . ."

"But, good God, Kate, were there any people?"

"No. Not a soul. It was as if they'd known what was coming and had fled. There were some For Sale signs, but other houses had been left just as they were. But the places had been absolutely *savaged*, that's the only word for it—all the furniture ripped to pieces, burned, shit on the walls—you could feel this appalling kind of atmosphere still, as if, as if, oh, I can't describe it, like something out of Conrad—horror, sort of primitive horror."

"Look, for God's sake, Kate," Mary shouted, "you've got to stop this—you can't go careering about in that bloody car of yours all over the place. It's just plain stupid!" She cut her finger in her annoyance and said the Afrikaans word, "Eie-na!" very loudly, like a yell.

Kate sat down at the table meekly. "I didn't stay long. I was frightened. I thought they might still be hanging about in the bushes, using the houses for shelter. I got out of there very quickly." Then she went on with a frown. "You're right, it is stupid, there's a war on out there, I can never get it into my head; it's spreading so fast." She sat there, looking forlorn, almost in tears.

Emily tried to ease the atmosphere. "Well, let's not get carried away by a little burning." She scooped the potatoes off the stove and put the heavy pan on the table.

She wanted so much to reassure them, and herself; but Kate said sharply, "It's everywhere now."

Emily lost heart, "So it will all be like you saw today, soon, that's all there will be?"

"Maybe, maybe, I don't know. But they can't want to destroy everything, that would be senseless, quite crazy."

"Perhaps that's just what it is," Emily said, lifting her head, "just that—pure madness."

"Oh, but sometimes I get so weary," Kate said. "Pass it over to Freud if you like, Emily, but the fact remains, it's all going to go back to how it was—it'll just go back to a different kind of colonialism."

"Never!" Mary said firmly.

"Oh, yes," Kate insisted, walking to the cupboard and banging down a pile of enamel plates. "All that's happened in the rest of Africa is that there is just a new breed of white masters—Marxist masters, French, Chinese, or whatever. They call them advisers now, or experts, but they're still the new masters. And let me tell you, none of them will be any better for Africa or the Africans than the old colonials were."

Josie and another young woman called Annie came in just then. Annie was the daughter of a Catholic priest in Namibia; they addressed Kate politely, if a trifle distantly, "That's not quite so, Kate. What Africa wants is *money*. That's all she wants. And she gets it." Annie looked at Mary and smiled vivaciously, showing sharp white teeth. "Mary, you're frowning so much, but really, it's not so serious. Listen, if we have to absorb a little indoctrination, that's not so shocking!"

Kate said, "Well, perhaps one should be comforted by your cynicism."

"Of course," Annie said gaily. "What's that old joke: that an African Marxist is simply a man who's got more money out of the Russians than out of the Americans?"

Mary lifted the big iron pot and handed it firmly to Annie, who groaned under its weight while Kate said, with a cockeyed smile, "You'd have made a lousy carrier, Annie; you wouldn't have lasted an hour in the Congo!"

"Bloody right!" Annie said, and staggered out of the kitchen with the pot.

As they sat on the scuffed earth and shooed away the flies, everyone was again back to talking about what was going on in the bush around them. As they looked over their shoulders at the inscrutable thorn trees, with their ragged patches of shade, at the far haze over the blue koppies, the silence there seemed simply to be waiting, for this quiet moment, this peaceful eating in the shade, to come to an end. In the stifling midday heat, Emily was conscious of a chill, of something unseen creeping in on them all.

Just then Lukas came in with two scruffy, exhausted white women and a small girl with two older boys, all of whom looked dazed and frightened.

"Hey, Em," he called, "can you give me a hand here?"

"Come with me, Josie," Emily said, putting down her plate. They went up to the women and Emily smiled; no one smiled back. Emily recognized them instantly for what they were: refugees, ravaged, bitter, with a haunted look that seemed to suggest that their experience lay just behind their eyes and would not leave them in peace. Theirs was not the patient suffering of the Africans she had seen; nor the pitiful desperation of the starving, whose hearts she could see beating behind their gaunt rib cages, who spoke quietly of having eaten the tough veld grass; some of whose children would suffer brain damage as a result of their deprivation.

Lukas said, "They've come from around Zeerust: that area is pretty much a nightmare; the terrorists have taken over and destroyed most of it. One of the children had been bitten by a mamba —that's why they waved me down. They didn't seem to know where they were going; they were just walking, dragging themselves and the children along; but I got the feeling if it hadn't been for the snakebite, they wouldn't have had anything to do with me. They were like people in a trance."

"I couldn't save the boy," Lukas said grimly. "Bloody mambas, they're so quick. I kept the boy away from her, he died of suffocation, really—the venom paralyzes the respiratory muscles—it's too quick."

He rubbed his hand across the back of his neck and Emily said gently, "Lukas, go in and see Mary, you look whacked. We'll look after them."

"Yes, go," Josie said, giving him a push. "Shall we let them wash, or just give them food?"

"Whatever they want," Lukas said. He reassured the women in Afrikaans, then left. They looked frightened when he had gone. Josie also spoke to the women in Afrikaans, but they would not move, would not look at her. Emily repeated the suggestion of a wash in very bad Afrikaans, and they agreed to follow her.

"We're going to have trouble with this lot," Josie said angrily.

"Don't take it personally, Josie," Emily whispered, "they've had a terrible time."

The women washed their children and themselves in a vague, apathetic way. The younger woman, the mother, was clearly in a state of shock, while the older one looked sunken and gray, as if she had suffered a severe illness. They allowed themselves to be led to the group around the tree. Most people had finished eating and gone back to work, but a few Africans still sat in the shade, finishing their meal and chatting. The two women stopped; the Africans ignored them, with no particular interest one way or the other.

"Shall we take them to the kitchen?" Emily said to Josie, who snapped, "What for?"

"Because they don't want to sit down here."

"Well, they'll just have to get used to it," Josie said stubbornly.

"But not today, I don't think," Emily said, picking up the almost empty pot and leading the women back toward Mary's kitchen.

The women and children sat down in the kitchen and seemed a little more relaxed.

"Here, you'll feel a little better when you've eaten," Emily said in English, hoping they would understand most of it. Up to this point they had not uttered one word. They had a distinct aspect of the outback about their faces and rough clothes. Josie began to ladle what was left of the food onto the plates; she handed it around to the children first, who just held their plates stiffly and looked at it. The women looked silently at the food then the older one pushed her plate away sharply.

"They think it's kaffir food," Josie said archly.

The younger woman suddenly took a breath, like someone about to dive into deep water; she turned to her children and ordered firmly, "Eat." They obeyed instantly and began to wolf the food, one of them using her hands instead of the spoon. The woman spoke fiercely to the little girl, who shamefacedly picked up her spoon and put it into the food, then to her mouth. The mother began to eat quietly.

A little later, Josie whispered, "The old one's still not eating." Emily looked across at the formidable woman. She was about fifty, with pigtails bound in coils at the back of her head. She looked like a figure off the Voortrekker monument; all she needed was the shawl and bonnet and a skirt down to her ankles. Her heavy jaw seemed to unfreeze; she got up quickly and began to march out of the room. The young woman called after her, "Ma, Ma," her voice pleading. The older woman stopped, she looked back at her daughter, then continued to walk on. The daughter went very still, resigned; she began to eat again. Then, quite suddenly, her hand fell, it tipped the edge of her plate and sent it spinning; and she broke into loud sobbing. Emily left her until the sobbing had subsided a little; then she brought the children into a small circle around their mother.

The Afrikaner family brought all sorts of new problems to the community. People tried hard to be patient, because the family had suffered atrociously: their farmhouse had been set on fire in the early hours of the morning. Lena Viljoen, her mother, and the children had escaped into the bush, but Lena's husband had tried to shoot it out; he'd been trapped inside the burning house and had not got out. The servants had all been rounded up, and some had had their legs cut off.

The early-evening light outside still held tremors of heat. The children ran between the huts avoiding their mothers. Some soldiers sat under the trees with their knees drawn up, smoking. The men were washing under the tap after the dirty work of laying bricks; they watched the soldiers, who lounged arrogantly on the ground. The soldiers were not allowed to bring their guns into the village or camp, but their uniforms were enough to make them superior. As the working men washed, the water splashing sharply on the flat stone, then running off underneath, they felt angry with the soldiers, who had come from a far place, who made them feel inadequate and inactive. So they stamped their feet and shouted to one another, too loudly, ducking their heads beneath the taps, spitting out the water in streams.

The young women of the village approached the soldiers—as if they had a smell of success, of potency, about them. As a girl sat down close to the nearest soldier, one of the older men called out rudely to her. The girl shrugged it off easily. Her skirt was tight; her hair was high on her head and she wore a plastic comb with orange flowers stuck into it. She jutted out her jaw proudly. But when she spoke to the soldier, she did so coyly, aware of his power. The girls and soldiers sat for a while, not talking, drawing off each other's scents.

In a little while, the girl and one of the soldiers went off into the bush. The girl took his hand; he swaggered beside her, his arms in the short-sleeved shirt full and gleaming. The men at the tap broke into angry language; it was as if they had all been insulted by the girl's behavior. But then, just as quickly, they calmed down, then began slowly to return to their village, where they would settle close to their wives and the fire and begin again the endless conversations about the war, the soldiers, their lives—food, food.

In their house, Mary and Lukas were talking and drinking beer. They had been talking about the Afrikaans women, and Lukas said, "Afrikaners always adapt; they'll fight to the last ditch, but if there's no other choice, they'll adapt. They're creatures of the earth."

"More important, they've got nowhere to go," Mary said, "just like our people here." She smiled, her eyes running up nearer her hairline. "And we'll have to adapt to them, too. Now we'll have to have softer mealie pap in the morning, and we'll have to make our candles out of pig fat instead of buying them!"

Lukas looked hard at his wife and said, "But you look tired, you know. I think you're doing too much. Can't you get someone else to do the poor relief; I don't like to think of you handing out meal and dried milk to that crowd at the gates."

Mary shrugged it off. "Oh, Emily does most of that."

"I've noticed she's been a bit scarce around the clinic lately. I miss the bloody girl! Why doesn't she come these days?"

"I don't think she likes the work much. Funnily enough, she's a bit squeamish in that way, though nothing else seems to make her flinch." Mary looked serious again. She poured some of the can of beer into her glass, put it down, then lifted it to refill his glass. "I'm worried about Emily."

Lukas looked up sharply. "She's not ill, is she?"

"No. It's just, I don't know, she doesn't seem to be managing too well."

"Nonsense, she could run this place single-handed!"

"Oh, I know, I know that." She was impatient. "The darn girl has even started helping Father Tsele with the church."

"But I thought she was an atheist."

"She is, but that doesn't seem to stop her."

Lukas frowned and screwed his nose up at the same time. "So what are you saying, then, girl? Hm? You think she's overdoing it a bit?"

"I just feel uneasy about her, but it's so hard to say why. I mean, there she is organizing and helping everyone; she gets things moving again when they get stuck; she's marvelous, but something's wrong, I know it. She's unhappy."

"Is she?"

Mary pushed back her chair crossly. "Don't be stupid, of course she is!"

"What about?"

"About Reuben."

"Reuben?"

"Yes. I think that as long as his letters kept coming, she felt safe. Now that they've stopped, she seems on edge. It doesn't seem to be just the worry about what may have happened to him, it's more than that, but I don't know what. I can see it in her eyes and the ways she clings to Happy."

"But she's coping?" Lukas said with some determination.

Mary was impatient. "Yes, she is, but sometimes it's almost as if she wants to be an example to us all; to make us believe nothing could frighten or defeat her. Oh, she's much more than coping." Mary's forehead rippled with thought. "She seems to have enormous resources. You know she sorted out all those new refugees who were stealing food from the storehouse, and that family who were chucking their garbage all over the place."

"So what're you worrying about? I heard she did it very well, very tactfully, everyone got the point."

Mary said quietly, "But then, sometimes, I go into her rondavel, and she's just standing there, in the middle, looking sort of lost and alone. She immediately slams on a smile, of course, but she won't tell me."

Lukas was brisk and confident. "Well, I'm sure Reuben is fine. He's not the kind to do anything stupid and he's been at this game a long time now."

Mary looked exasperated. "But what the hell's going on in there? All these awful stories and rumors and whatnot. What the hell is going on?"

"Hey, hang on, don't get angry with me; I'm not doing it!" He squeezed her arm affectionately. "It's impossible to know from here what's going on." He smoothed back his hair. "They're really clamping down on everything. They're becoming very isolated now, gone back to the laager. But two things definitely seem to be happening: they're preparing in earnest for war, for one, and secondly, the blacks are ready for them."

Mary watched her glass fill with froth; it bubbled over. "Oh, God, Lukas, I don't like to think about it."

He took Mary's hand. "Look, our priorities here must be ourselves: this place we're running, and you and I. At least we're together."

"And that brings me back to Emily. I wish Reuben was here." Mary looked worried again.

"She'll be okay. She'll come back to herself for strength, as we all have to."

He got up and stretched. "I'm going out for a bit, Mary. Coming?"

She shook her head. "No, it's just so lovely to have the house empty for once. I'll have an early night. Don't be too long."

He kissed her quickly and went out.

The night outside was warm and soft; he looked up at the sky: the stars were sharp and the black branches of the scrub trees were tangled like coarse wool. He walked in the direction of one of the fires and found Emily. She was sitting surrounded by silent Africans, who were listening to her telling a story, their faces turned up, completely enthralled. Happy was asleep across her knees, wrapped in a blanket.

Lukas sat down, and the circle closed around him again. Emily was talking slowly, rhythmically, letting her voice swell and fall as the words demanded. He listened. "And once, on a very cold night, when the hyenas were howling, a man came knocking at the door, wanting shelter...."

She began to weave a narrative from the half-remembered stories that Johanna had told her: the myths and legends of her own childhood, echoes of books she had read, ideas that sprang into her head without her understanding. She could detail her characters so well that someone might call out, "Ai, he is like old so-and-so, whose house I used to clean," or "She is like the woman who delivered the babies in the village when I was a girl." Among this gathering of different Africans, she had a spellbound audience.

The white people could not seem to listen; they would go off to Mary's house in search of a book, or go to check the children—but the Africans sat stock-still and heard the story out, totally absorbed in the drama of its unfolding. Sometimes they would chip in with "But, no, Emily, that cannot be so, for that man had brown eyes at the beginning," or "How could that woman run like a rabbit when she began the story with a limp?"

Emily herself had learned a secret from this storytelling: she had discovered in the Africans a quality that she wanted. She saw that they had no sense of boredom. Time for them was a wonderful thing—not frightening as it had been to her mother—the more they could have, the more satisfied they were. They had no phobia about the idleness of sitting still, they saw no point in doing a thing too quickly, just to rush on to the next. There was always more time; one should use it leisurely. Life must be lived at its own pace.

The fire burned low, the story began to hasten toward its conclusion. The faces of the people listening were touched with anticipation and then with sadness, because they were nearing the end and a dispelling of the magic. Emily's voice slowed; when she had stopped, they all kept quite still, as if after hearing music, letting the chords trail away. Finally they rose; they stretched; they wished her good-night and dispersed into the darkness toward their huts, while someone stamped out the last of the embers.

Emily, carrying Happy, walked back with Lukas.

He said, with admiration, "How well you do it, Emily, and they all seem to love you so."

She smiled, looked shy and puzzled. "Do they?"

"Oh, yes, they've taken you into their hearts; there's no escape now." He grinned down at her.

When they had reached her rondavel, she seemed reluctant to go in. She said, "Last night, I woke up in the middle of the night; I heard a noise, a soft noise, as if the flap had lifted. I reached out to touch Happy, felt her, then dozed off again. But then I woke again: I was certain that a hand touched my face."

"Are you frightened?" He took her arm. "D'you want to come and sleep over at the house?"

She smiled. "No, I don't. It wasn't frightening; it was like a caress. Perhaps I just dreamed it."

"Perhaps." But he felt worried. "Don't take any chances, though; it might well have been a caress." He looked at her with a frown. "You know what I mean, don't you?"

She smiled, "I'm sure I dreamed it, probably just wishful thinking!"

"Okay, if you're sure you'll be all right."

"I'll sleep like a log. Good night, Lukas."

"Good night."

She stood watching him walk away; she felt lost without him. "Lukas" she called out. He turned.

"No, nothing." She shook her head; the child stirred.

"You're sure?" he said, coming back.

"I'm sure. Just say good-night to Mary."

"I will." He felt a little disappointed, then laughed at himself. She stood a little longer, breathing in the fragrant smell of the bush, of the fire, the wood smoke with its residue of sweat and grease. An owl flew up into the arms of a loquat tree; above her head and as far as the eye could reach were the sweeping solitudes of sky.

The rondavel, when she entered it, was suddenly especially dear. She put Happy carefully to bed. She felt too tired to light the paraffin light and read, so blew out the candle and curled up in bed with her knees close to her breasts. Far away, a lone hyena wailed; she could hear the sneaky shuffle of one of the skin-and-bones dogs of the village. She slept at once.

It was much later. She woke with a start, her heart beating, and sat up, alert. Happy did not stir. Emily thought she could hear swift, light feet on the scraped earth outside, then a sound like a bone cracking, then feet running away. The night was suddenly alive, full of menace, as though a lion were moving in through the trees. Then, from the far end of the village, came a scream. She jumped out of bed, pulling the blanket around her, and ran out into the dark. People were emerging from their huts, it was too dark to see more than their outlines; their voices were sharp, staccato. Lukas and Mary came running up with a lamp that swung a wide arc of light, the wire handle clicking against the glass. Lukas's eyes, with sleep, seemed to have collapsed into their sockets.

"What the hell's going on?" It was Kate, wearing a thick tartan dressing gown and with a heavy shotgun under her arm.

"God in heaven." Mary laughed. "You look like an old—" But just then Lukas whistled, a low, amazed sound.

"The clinic!" he yelled, and began to run.

Smoke and the first long licks of fire began to curl around the window of the clinic building. As they approached it, they could feel the heat, hear a rushing sound like water. People were running up from all directions.

"Get back," Lukas shouted, "get back."

Kate and Mary began to organize people. "Get blankets," Mary yelled, "carpets, sacks, anything heavy." They scattered in the direction of their huts and came back with scraps of old rags and hessian sacks. Their faces shone like copper from the flames, which were now pouring out of the window. The door farther to the right was still intact. Lukas kicked it hard; some of the men came and joined him, and they smashed it in.

"Come on; we can go in; it's not too bad," Lukas said; but most of the men stood back, one looking quite abject with terror.

"Come on, Peter," Lukas said. "We've got to get some of the medicine out."

The men took heart and began swiping at the flames with the sacks, coughing and choking but gradually stopping the flames from spreading. Emily was watching with a few of the women, then went forward with Josie and Elvira as Lukas reappeared and began handing some of the drugs that had escaped the fire. Two stretchers stood charred against the wall.

"How much has gone, Lukas?" Emily asked, turning her face away from the fumes and handing the small cardboard boxes to Josie.

"Just about everything. Most of it was on the side where the fire started. Thank God I keep a supply in the house. There's that stupid First Aid box, which is intact, of course, because it's tin. I picked the thing up like a fool; it was like a ruddy stove!" He ducked back in again and came out almost retching with the smoke. "That's it," he gasped. "The wooden cupboard with all the equipment in it—couldn't get near it. It was blazing beautifully." He stood back and wiped the sweat off his blackened face.

When the fire was out, everyone stood looking in silence at the black, stinking building.

"But who has done this thing?" they all whispered.

Lala had no doubts. "It is Kruger. They were talking of moving on. I will go and see if he is where he should be." She left with a little company of support.

Kate came striding along with a large tray full of steaming coffee; it was weak, but it was received gratefully, and people started to talk volubly as soon as they were drinking. Lala returned with a smirk of satisfaction on her face.

"He has gone, as I said," she announced dramatically, tipping her body back.

"But some of the women also have gone," Josie added. "The boys who took out the cows saw them leave."

"Bloody rubbish, all of them," Lala said with disgust. "One of those women, she says I am a traitor, to join with white people here; she asks if I am cleaning the floors and polishing your shoes."

"Well, I'm sure you told her where to get off," Lukas said with a hint of impatience.

"We will not now know," Elvira said, as if making a judgment, "who it was. They all have gone."

"So let's leave it," Mary said. "But we're going to have to be much more careful."

Josie agreed. "Yes, too much riffraff has been coming in. We have to stop people sneaking in from the bush to steal or beg for food, with nothing to do but make trouble."

"Or they will turn this place into a shanty," another woman said angrily. "People around us are no longer cleaning up their rubbish; they throw it at the back of their shelters; it stinks. It will bring sickness."

"Too many children are coming here who have not had the inoculations; there is an epidemic of measles beyond the river. And now"—Mary looked at Lukas—"our supplies have gone."

"We will get more," Lukas said firmly. "We must not worry about that now."

One of the men admitted something that he'd been trying to keep to himself: he had had a visit from his brother in a kraal not far off. He spoke in a low voice. "There have been murders nearby. No one says why. Sudden killings in the night. And bodies killed most horribly, cut into pieces, then—"

"Okay, okay," Lukas chipped in firmly, "I've also heard those stories, and I won't pretend that they're not true. We're close to the border, that's all. There have been brutal murders; it happens when people are afraid. But now the war is spreading, we must stop people ignoring the safety regulations and trying to put up hovels. We will be all right if we can keep to the regulations."

"Or they will simply close us down—the village, everything." Mary's face in the dawn light was impassive again, and looking at her, people felt reassured.

The sun was coming up, rosy as an apple; the sky was clear and cloudless. As new people came, more exclamations of panic stirred: "And what shall we do now? And there are no medicines if the children get ill. Everything is gone. What will become of us now?" They looked around them helplessly, fastening large eyes on Lukas. But Emily spoke. "Later we'll clear up the clinic and see what needs rebuilding. Then we'll start to put it right."

An elderly man, sitting crouched on the ground, spread his knees in his worn flannels and said, "We and the men who were building the washhouse, we will stop, we will do the hospital first. That is what we will do."

A few weeks later, Emily was sitting in the sun with Happy. In the distance, the earth was piled up in mounds and the mealies stood stiff as spears. She was picking beans and tossing them into a large and battered basket, while Happy cracked open a pod and jangled the beans in her fist.

Emily had left Mary and Lukas working in the clinic, in the part that had been restored; when it was rebuilt, it would be larger than before. More and more people kept coming from the bush with war injuries. Often when they got to the clinic, their wounds were deeply infected and difficult to treat quickly. Emily had been glad to get away from the stinging disinfectants, the needles, the rough bandages seeping pus and blood; the anguished faces of the parents, the endless crying of the children. Now she sat in perfect silence, crouching close to the ground, with her knees bent and the faded green dress pushed up above her knees. She kept on working, her head bent away from the glare, the basket filling with the squat bean pods.

This was a special place for her, a place that filled in her heart the space once filled by the river. She came here to be by herself; she smiled to think of the last time she had come here with Happy, and cried. Now she knew what she had been raging against, and then grieving for, was her aloneness, the thing she had once most prized. With Reuben's silence, which seemed to mean his desertion, she had felt abandoned. Alone, with all the old defenses thrown away.

But then, extraordinarily, she had faced it: she was able to stand back and face the iron truth that dreams are crushed under the boot of reality; people desert or die; do not hear when one is screaming —she stood alone, no human touch could alter that. She was like a lone plant under a blistering sun whom no one would gather or save; she had no choice but to survive. But at that moment, she knew how great was her strength. She had gone through a loop of fire and been forged fine and free: not to escape the world, but to live in it, not through alienation but through kinship with others. And the devastating sense of loss left her completely and forever.

It was late afternoon, but still very hot. Reuben was walking quickly down the little path that led to the fields; he noticed how parched and dusty the ground was; it seemed impossible that crops could grow in such a place. He felt as excited as a boy; his exhaustion had completely left him; he began to run. When he reached the end of the track and saw Emily, he stood there, watching her. The sun seemed to nestle against her, throwing her shadow backward, making a long oval shape. The child, with her legs plumped out in front of her, looked edible, sweet-fleshed as an olive. Emily's hair was done in long plaits bound above her head, the back of her neck had wisps of curling brown hair. From where he stood, she looked thinner, deeply tanned by the sun. She stood up and stretched, putting her hands to the small of her back. She picked up the basket and shook down the beans, then bent and swung Happy up onto her hip. Reuben held his breath. Seeing her there, it was like an illumination, as if he saw her in a dream or a painting. He struggled to put it into words, what he felt, but could not, because it was a moment of pure feeling.

When she turned and saw him, the basket in her hand tipped, the beans fell. She stood quite still, watching him with her eyes screwed up, as if afraid, as if she did not recognize him. He began to walk toward her—as people walk not in dreams but in life. Still she did not move until he had almost reached her; then she smiled, then she ran, holding the child awkwardly against her. When she stopped, she laughed softly and said, "I didn't hear you, you gave me such a fright, you could have been a terrorist!" To hear her laugh like that gave him a feeling of great happiness; her eyes were sharp, close to tears. He grabbed and held her, almost smothering Happy. Then he let her go to look at her again. Happy looked on amiably, winking her two pearly teeth.

"How I've missed you. You look gorgeous, so healthy." He looked at Happy, who was now looking perplexed. "You've been busy!" He shook his head. "No, it's all right! Mary told me just now."

Emily's face puckered. "I'm jealous—she saw you first!"

"Oh, just to tell me where you were. And it's just as well that she warned me about Happy. I've been obsessed with what you might be up to." She took his hand. "I'm a most faithful person, I thought you knew that."

He picked up the basket and wound his arm around her waist,

walking up to a small cluster of scrub trees. They sat down and Happy wobbled off to investigate an old ant heap, looking back at Reuben rather suspiciously.

"I've been so worried about you," she said, noticing how pinched his face looked, the skin stretched tight with strain and fatigue, blue shadows beneath his eyes. "When the letters stopped, I thought they'd got you. . . . I didn't know. . . ." He kissed her.

He lay back on the sand, with his head resting on his hands, looking up into the tree with its long thorns and dry bark. "Yes, I did spend a week in prison, as a matter of fact." He talked lightly.

After a moment she looked down at him, kissed him sharply on the mouth and said, "Well, go on, d'you want me to die of suspense?"

"Oh, there was some article in the *Rand Daily Mail*; they said it was mine—inciting, they called it. This was before they closed the paper. A few days after they'd arrested me, the article and others like it began to circulate in all the leading newspapers. A black organization claimed responsibility, but they decided to keep me in anyway. The government meanwhile was going crazy—shutting down most of the papers, filling up the jails. A couple of us got out late on Wednesday night—what is it today? I feel quite confused. Friday?"

"Yes, Friday." She bent and kissed him again. "It's definitely Friday."

"There was this warder, he was a slightly different type—they're running out of staff and can't get enough of the right type—he was bribable. He'd got his girlfriend into trouble and needed the money."

"But how did you get *here*?"

He sat up and shook the dust off his arms. "Well, basically, we'd arranged for a car to pick us up that night. We were driven to Rustenburg, where one of the blokes left, then John and I went on to Ramutsa and spent the last of the night there on a farm. Some people were supposed to meet us there; we had some information from the politicals in prison, but they didn't turn up, so John pushed off at dawn and I got a lift from a black man; he hid me in the back of his truck. He was delivering equipment to the mine at Morupule. He said not one word to me the whole journey; he knew I was in trouble. Then I had to walk for a couple of hours until a white woman gave me a lift. She also was extremely discreet; we talked of nothing but the weather. She was going to Palapye, but dropped me off just a mile or so from here, and I walked the rest of it." He smiled gently, "And that's it—not very exciting really, is it?"

"But here you are." She looked at him as though it was still hard to believe.

"And here I am." He pulled her to him and felt no withdrawal, nothing but her simple pleasure in his presence.

When they walked back to the village, Lala, who was making her way back to the camp, came up and clapped Emily on her shoulder, "First you had the baby, now the man, so the world has no trouble for you no more!" She laughed loudly.

Emily looked shy. She said, "Lala, this is Reuben. Reuben, this is my good friend Lala; she keeps us all sane here."

Lala beamed with pleasure. She said, dipping her head, "I am pleased to greet you," putting out her hand formally. She looked shrewdly at Reuben's dusty boots. "You look like you need rest," she said. "Here, Emily, you give me Happy; I take her to play." And she strode off with Happy, who let out a wail of protest. Lala swung the child up into the air, looking up at her, talking swiftly, making her chuckle again.

"Come on," Emily said, taking Reuben's hand, "let me show you my rondavel."

"I left my things at Mary's."

"Well, they can stay there. I'm just going to put you to bed." She twined her arm behind his waist and led him firmly toward her rondavel.

He was still there when she woke, sleeping lightly against her side on the rough cotton sheet, covered only by the warmth made by their two bodies. She felt that the afternoon could go on and on. The sunshine dipping through the round window was shuttered by the leaves of the tree outside; it fell in soft ribbons on the hard dung floor. She reached out her hand and touched his cheek.

Outside, the women would be gathering fuel for the night fires; it was Friday, and the village was having a party: a couple had got married in the church that day. Beer was difficult to get now, and expensive, but one of the boys from the camp had a secret source, and he had been around earlier collecting money for it in an apricot jam tin that he kept for the purpose.

Emily could hear children making the sounds that their mothers made while chasing the chickens, who squawked and flew up into the trees to avoid the pot. Farther down, the camp would be doing the same things, but with more frenzy. They lived too close to one another: rows of small fires with cans of bubbling water, strings of ragged washing, mangy dogs, and garbage accumulated for all the vigilance of the women's council. At night, sometimes, this frenzy would spill over into other things, knives would flash out and there would be wounds to deal with at the clinic.

When Emily moved, Reuben woke, his arm coming down heavily across her, pinning her to the sheet. "I shan't let you go" he mumbled, half-asleep still, nuzzling against her upper arm. She turned to look at him, and when their faces were close together, he said, "I love you, I love you." Now, she could accept it, repeat the words back to him, push back the thick brown hair and kiss his forehead.

"Shall I get you a cup of tea?"

"No, not yet, don't run away from me. Just stay a bit and let me hold you."

She curled into his shoulder and lay still.

"What are you thinking about?" she asked, rubbing her mouth against the muscle of his upper arm. He edged his back against the cool wall.

"Nothing, it's just so beautiful to be here with you. Will it always be like this?"

She smiled and kissed him. She felt suddenly dizzy with happiness, quick and tender and warm, and she said, "Reuben, my darling, it will be whatever we make it—we can do anything. But we must know what we want, that's all."

Outside, a boy playing a penny whistle stopped to call out to his friend, his voice high, singsong. Emily could hear Jannie, one of the Afrikaans boys, calling out a reply in Setswana. It went quiet again and she was aware only of Reuben thinking, breathing, of the sunlight becoming faint on the dappled floor. His eyes were closed, he seemed far away, and she was filled with the old desire to shelter him.

She began to swing her legs off the bed, then turned back and kissed him on the mouth.

"I've got to run and get Happy, it's time she was fed."

Reuben slapped her lightly on the rump and said, "Okay, off you go then. I'll come over in a bit." Watching her dress, he remarked quietly, "You're still thin, but it's a nice pared-down look now, there's not that anorexic look that you used to have."

"Oh, thanks!" She turned to scowl back at him, doing up the buttons of the green dress.

"It suits you—to be so brown and svelte," he said approvingly.

"Not according to Lala; she mixes me up some vile-tasting muck that she says will give me good fat hips to catch a husband." She straightened the plaits and pushed a hairpin into one of the thick coils on top of her head, peering quickly into a little mirror on a nail in the wall.

"See you later," she said brightly, and ducked out of the door.

When she had gone, he lay back on the little bed feeling a sharp regret that so much of his life was spent. On the declining side of forty, it seemed peppered with mistakes: a long disastrous marriage followed by years of casual comfort, while all his intensity had been expended on his work. His greatest success seemed to have been his avoidance of any personal commitment. Since Emily, all his huffing and puffing on paper seemed a folly, a sop to vanity, even a cowardice. Now, with her, he would have to prove a different kind of courage, not whether he could bear his own solitude but whether he could dare to live as dangerously deep as she demanded of herself, and therefore of him, too. In the simple rondavel, with the spare elements of her life about him, he felt suddenly confident, determined to get it right. He got up briskly and dressed.

. . .

They were sitting in Mary's kitchen. The electricity had just packed up again, and the large table was illuminated by an old paraffin lamp and a couple of homemade candles near the stove. They had been discussing the drought.

Emily said to Lukas, "We really must get going on that scheme of Davie's to increase the dam."

"There's a river near here, isn't there?" Reuben asked. "What's it like?"

"Very low and overused."

Mary was opening a tin of strawberries. She licked her fingers and said, "Africa's supposed to be moving forward, but in most ways it's going back."

Reuben said quietly, "Africa is what it is. That's all. No one can impose on it for long, no one can really alter it. It will keep going back to what it is."

"And what's going on over the border?" Lukas asked, setting himself back in his chair and sharpening the knife.

Mary brought in the guinea fowl, crisp and dark brown, with little heaps of fried crumbs.

While Lukas was carving the bird, Reuben tried to put his mind back into what was going on in the Republic. As he began to talk quietly about the events of the past months, he was made conscious that a new quality was attached to them because of the calm place he had reached. He had a sudden glorious sense of his freedom, of having escaped from a terrible place. When he spoke again, it was with enthusiasm; suddenly no longer haunted by what he had seen and heard. He found that he was almost making a deliberate choice as to what he told them, concentrating on those things that contained a strong element of comedy, rather than those that were simply tragic.

"When I was in prison, there was a plan to burn down all the railway stations in the country, and in fact some railway lines have been blown up already. But the most ambitious plan"—he grinned broadly—"is the destruction of Jan Smuts and a ritual burning of Pretoria's state buildings! It may sound ludicrous, but I truly wouldn't be surprised if it happened—there's been one hell of a lot of sabotage going on."

"Jesus Christ!" Lukas gave a soft whistle. "Very little of this has reached us here."

"Very little of it has reached anywhere," Reuben said. "That's the point."

Mary looked down into her plate, half nervous, half excited. "It must be frightening," she said, "when what you've worked for all your life begins really to happen."

Reuben circled a strawberry with his spoon. "As someone very wise said, 'Beware of what you want, for you will get it!'"

"But we are all right here," Emily cut in quickly. "We are safe. Whatever happens all around, we are safe, we can keep safe."

Reuben looked at her, at the quiet column of her face—he was struck by how different she looked. It was as though what he had first sensed in her—the possibility of wisdom and maturity—was beginning to be fulfilled. It had replaced the old capacity for suffering; the green eyes looking back at him were filled with confidence.

Mary said soberly, "We don't talk about it much, but just across the border all those graves were dug up. And there are tribal massacres happening a stone's throw from here. How can we escape it?"

But Emily insisted quietly, "We're a community here, most of us are determined to have peace. The camp and the village are quite united in this—they both feel threatened from the outside, they both could be attacked by strange Africans. But we live in a peaceful country. In this one little place, we can transform what is going on around us; we can, if we want it. And we do—look at Lala— and at Davie, planning his dam. Yesterday, I saw Josie getting some of the young girls to paint the walls of the school."

Mary looked a little ashamed and she said, "I'm being negative."

As Reuben looked at Emily, he had suddenly a wider perception, a clear moment of insight—and he ceased to fear for her. He thought of her as he had first seen her, in Virginia's house, and it seemed as if he were looking back on someone else's past, she was so far removed from what she had once been.

A full moon pooled across the brown earth of the village as they walked toward the camp, where the noise and music were vibrating, as though across water. They could distinguish two different drums playing different rhythms, harmonizing perfectly. When they got to the fire, where everyone was assembled, Emily noticed a white man sitting among a group on the ground, drinking beer from a chipped white mug, but somehow doing so with an air that was very precise and correct.

Emily and Reuben approached Josie, who was having a furious argument about religion with an Afrikaans woman. Emily introduced Reuben and then pointed to the man and asked who he was.

"He's just turned up tonight, just before we were to eat. A filthy old man, but proud as a lion! So, in he walks, he talks a bit, we say he can stay, he eats with us; now he is there, as you can see." Josie looked across at him tolerantly, as if he were a child.

Emily and Reuben walked a little closer to him. His jacket was in shocking condition, torn and grimy, shiny with use, the ends of the sleeves flapping like a scarecrow.

"He's a tramp!" Emily whispered.

"Yes, but look at his hands; they're perfectly clean, and the nails are cut," Reuben whispered also, although there was no chance that the old man could hear. "And those whipcord trousers were obviously expensive once."

Emily could see some of the young women looking at him and giggling behind their hands. One of them was wearing an enormous pair of pink sunglasses; she reeked of cheap scent. As one of the young girls snorted with laughter, the old man hurled a ferocious rebuke with his fine cold eyes. All the gigglers went silent instantly. Then he saw Emily and Reuben, and got laboriously to his feet, shunning the hand that was offered him. He approached them rather as if he were the host of a party and they the guests.

"Ah," he said, in a clipped way, "I'm Stanton, pleased to meet you. First whites I've seen around this place. Tell me, what kind of a damned place are you running here?"

Emily said, "It's a refugee camp of sorts, but we don't run it, it's run communally."

"Well, there must be someone in charge."

She smiled at him, "No, not really, but you must have seen Peter in order to have got in."

"The black chap in the hut by the gates?"

"That's right."

Stanton seemed to be thinking; then he snapped, "A refugee camp? Well, I'm not a bloody refugee!" He was outraged by the idea—broken teeth beneath his neat mustache, tatters of hair poking down behind his ears.

"I've seen 'em, of course, trying to lug every blessed possession they've got on the back of trucks. Should have put everything in diamonds and gold years ago."

"Did you?" Reuben asked.

"Lost everything in diamonds," he roared with a choking laugh that almost cut off his breath. "Lost everything! Thought I'd know just where to find 'em, down in dear old Southwest Africa. I've looked everywhere, Nigeria, Ghana, Uganda, been all over the place. They're all in Russia, that's the place, Russia—stuffed with diamonds. Nothing here."

The flames from the fire whooshed up and lit up his face; it was transparent with strain and deprivation, but was turned firmly from self-pity.

"Are you going home?" Emily asked gently.

"Home—my dear young lady, this *is* my home. I came out to the Protectorate in 1920." He glared at her. "It was different then." He looked around, a little dazed, but not disapproving. "Oh, very different."

"Ah, I see, so now you've come home?"

"Yes." He nodded, sharp gray eyes challenging her.

"Well, you must stay with us, stay as long as you like. We could do with a man of your experience."

"And you, miss, what do you do here?"

"I work here," she said. "It's my home, too."

She left him talking to Reuben and went to find Josie, who had already thought of somewhere he could sleep temporarily. Then, Emily stood quietly to one side for a moment, away from the heat and the music, thinking. She thought of the place where she had grown up, the place of her childhood: the lushness of the river, the water lilies blue and pink, flamboyant trees, and coiling creepers. She wanted it again desperately; she wanted to create a little corner of what she had loved when she was a little girl, again—here. She thought of Stanton, his homecoming. She thought of her mother, now like a child, quite unable to take care of herself, and of her father, becoming at last a father by taking care of his wife. She saw how much they had missed by not being able to give themselves to Africa, and how she, too, like her mother in reverse, had been unable to give herself at all to England, had pined there, year after dreary year. Now it was all over.

She went back to Reuben and Stanton and said, "Mr. Stanton, I've a hunch somehow that you're a gardener, that you could perhaps help us build an English garden, a colonial English garden, down by the dam."

He smiled at her with a gracious tilt of his head. "I did have a garden like that, many, many years ago. I believe I could do it again."

She walked with him to show him Kate's room, which he was to use while she was away. After they had walked in silence for a little, she said, "Where have you just come from?"

"I've been all over," he said quietly, "and I've never been harmed. I've always been treated with kindness—the Africans always fed me; they're very courteous people, you know. But if you're asking where my last port of call was, it wasn't too far from here—near Lobatse. I worked there on a big farm, run by two Welsh women and a boy."

Emily stopped and looked at him. "What was their name, the people on the farm?" she asked sharply.

"The wife's name was Gallway, didn't know the sister's name. Owen, I think. Why d'you ask?"

"Oh, nothing."

She was repeating in her mind the name, his name, Patrick's name. She said it softly then, with a strange little quiver at her throat.

Stanton looked gently at Emily, and the light in his eyes was so pure that the battered shell of his face seemed not to exist.

Emily looked sideways at him as he walked vigorously along, clutching his collapsed suitcase, the back of his head bald as a baby's.

"And you say they ran the place alone, the two sisters?"

"Yes, they have a cooperative farm, seems to be working very well, too. There was a husband once, I gather, but neither of them spoke of him."

"So you don't know what happened to him?"

"I do, as a matter of fact. Fellow pushed off years and years ago, according to one of the old servants. To England."

"To England?" she whispered.

"Yes." He looked keenly at her again, feeling the surge of her emotion.

Emily closed her eyes; she seemed to see Patrick again quite clearly: his sideways laugh, his wayward kisses, the temptation of his cruelty. And a sadness rose in her, making her eyes brim with tears. Which the old man saw, and flinched from, as one would from a painful recollection.

"We're here," Emily said steadily. "This is Kate's hut; you and she will get on famously, but she won't be back for some days. By then, if you decide to stay, we'll have something else sorted out for you." She opened the door, and he looked in at the mattress on the floor, at the rough walls, which still smelled a little damp and earthy.

"This will be perfect," he said, "quite perfect. And tomorrow, I'll start planning that garden for you."

Emily and Reuben walked back to her rondavel. Happy was sleeping curled up in a ball like a puppy, with the end of a soft cloth clutched in her hand. Emily covered her up. Reuben came and stood beside her; he put an arm around her and said, "I bet you spoil that kid rotten."

She smiled indulgently down. "Yes, I do."

She sat on the bed and pulled off the old tennis shoes she wore at night. "How strange, how strange about old Stanton," she said dreamily.

"Yes, he's a terrific old boy. We're planning to have a game of chess soon."

She laughed loudly. "What with?"

"Oh, we'll improvise."

"I'll tell you what. There's a man here who carves wonderfully. He could make the pieces."

Then she was quiet, staring straight ahead of her. "Doesn't it all seem far away?" she said softly.

"What?"

"England."

"You almost sound as if you miss it!"

"No, I don't. But I don't hate it as I used to. I understand what happened there now; it's taken me a long time, but I understand it." She stopped, deep in thought.

"Well, go on, tell me, then."

He sat down beside her, and in a little while she was swept up in it again—the intoxication of talking to him, in a way that they'd begun to discover in England before he left. She felt that there could exist between them a perfect intimacy, the intimacy of siblings—of people who have known each other a long, long time. And she felt that only if this was true and she could trust it, would she be able to give herself to him.

It was three in the morning when they stopped talking. They had moved to the step of her rondavel and were looking up at the sky; there were a few icy stars visible, the rest burrowed beneath cloud. The moon was full and mesmerizing. Reuben said, "You've learned so much here, put away so much. Dear Em, you seem almost to have lived out your dream."

He put his arm tenderly around her, but then tightened it. "Let's go to bed."

"Yes," she said, kissing him, wrapping herself around him like a blanket. But just before they went in, she stopped.

"No—wait. Tonight is a magic night and I want to tell you a poem, an old Bushman poem that I first heard as a child."

She spoke quietly, looking up at the moon, then away into the distance of the bush. Her face, when she turned to him, was soft with serenity.

> "When we die, the wind comes
> To wipe us out, the traces of our feet.
> The wind makes dust which covers
> The traces where we had walked."